Praise for bestselling author Leslie Kelly

"The perfect blend of sass and class!"
—*New York Times* and *USA TODAY* bestselling author
Vicki Lewis Thompson

"Leslie Kelly writes with a matchless combination
of sexiness and sassiness that makes
every story a keeper."
—*www.romancejunkies.com*

Praise for talented author Rhonda Nelson

"Readers won't want to miss a word."
—*RT Book Reviews* on *Show & Tell*

"A highly romantic story with two heartwarming
characters and a surprise ending."
—*RT Book Reviews* on *The Loner*

LESLIE KELLY

has written more than two dozen books and novellas for Harlequin Blaze, Harlequin Temptation and HQN Books. She is known for her sparkling dialogue, fun characters and depth of emotion. Her books have been honored with numerous awards, including a National Readers' Choice Award and three nominations for an RWA RITA® Award.

Leslie resides in Maryland with her own romantic hero, Bruce, and their three daughters. Visit her online at www.lesliekelly.com.

A Waldenbooks bestselling author, two-time RITA® Award nominee and *RT Book Reviews* Reviewers' Choice nominee, **RHONDA NELSON** writes hot romantic comedy for the Harlequin Blaze line and other Harlequin imprints. With more than twenty-five published books to her credit and many more coming down the pike, she's thrilled with her career and enjoys dreaming up her characters and manipulating the worlds they live in. In addition to a writing career, she has a husband, two adorable kids, a black Lab and a beautiful bichon frise. She and her family make their chaotic but happy home in a small town in northern Alabama. She loves to hear from her readers, so be sure to check her out at www.ReadRhondaNelson.com.

Leslie Kelly

Her Last Temptation

Rhonda Nelson

Show & Tell

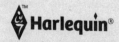

Harlequin®

TORONTO NEW YORK LONDON
AMSTERDAM PARIS SYDNEY HAMBURG
STOCKHOLM ATHENS TOKYO MILAN MADRID
PRAGUE WARSAW BUDAPEST AUCKLAND

Recycling programs
for this product may
not exist in your area.

ISBN-13: 978-0-373-68823-4

HER LAST TEMPTATION & SHOW & TELL

Copyright © 2011 by Harlequin Books S.A.

The publisher acknowledges the copyright holders of the individual works as follows:

HER LAST TEMPTATION
Copyright © 2005 by Leslie Kelly

SHOW & TELL
Copyright © 2003 by Rhonda Nelson

Printed in U.S.A.

CONTENTS

To the Temptresses of the past who inspired me.

To the Temptresses of today who have given me some of the greatest friendships of my life.

HER LAST TEMPTATION
Leslie Kelly

PROLOGUE

IF SOMEBODY STARTED singing that Little Orphan Annie song about the sun coming out tomorrow, Cat Sheehan was gonna hurl. Or run screaming into the street, pulling her hair out and kicking every road construction worker she came across right where it counted. Or maybe just wail to the sky, let the tears she'd never let drip from her eyes fall where they may, and face what she did not want to face.

Her uncertain future. Worse...the negation of her past.

She, her sister and their two best friends were practically alone in their bar, Temptation, shell-shocked by the letter they'd received from the historical society. Their plea to have their building designated a historical landmark—saving it from demolition by the city—had been rejected.

There was no sun. No tomorrow. Sure as hell no Daddy Warbucks. Nobody was coming to save them from the bureaucratic crime that allowed the city to shut them down after twenty-one years just because some newer businesses in higher tax brackets had enough clout to demand an unnecessary road widening.

"It's over," she said, still not believing it herself. "I knew those biddies from the historical society would reject us."

She hadn't really been talking to the others. More to the world in general, if for no other reason than to distribute some of the pain that had landed on her shoulders with a bit more equity.

Seeing everyone else looking at her, Cat busied herself behind the bar, making their signature drink, the Cosmopolitan. Cat and Laine had chosen it as a joke three years ago when they'd taken over the bar from their mom, because Kendall was about as uncosmopolitan as any dusty little Texas town could be.

It was only after she realized she'd forgotten to put any liquid in the shaker—which contained only ice—that she acknowledged how shaken up *she* was. She quickly corrected the situation, going heavy on the vodka.

Then, because everybody seemed to be waiting for her to say something—or else explode—she added quite mildly, she thought— "The city wants a new road, so we're out. Did you really think we'd change anything tonight?"

Passing out the drinks, she eyed the three other women, waiting for the "it'll be okays" to start. Laine appeared on the verge of tearing up; Gracie sighed, looking depressed rather than sad; and Tess seemed more nervous than anything else.

None of them looked the way Cat felt about the loss of this last fight to cling to a way of life her family had held dear for two decades—absolutely furious and utterly heartbroken.

Laine appeared close, however, at least as far as the heartbreak went. The sheen of moisture in her eyes cut deeply into Cat. Her sister never cried. She was the rock—the steady foundation of the family—and the antithesis of Cat. Her older-by-six-years sister was solid, smart and reliable. The calm one. The good one. The angel.

Solid, smart and reliable were three words that had never been used to describe Cat, the younger Sheehan sister. And nobody in his right mind had ever thought of her as good. Her blond hair and green eyes might appear angelic at first glance. But her attitude and never-ending ability to get into trouble had made her seem much more destined for a pitchfork than a halo as a kid.

Her adult life hadn't changed anybody's opinion.

She'd been called the rebel, the bad girl. Her mother had dubbed her the wild child at the age of three when she'd tried climbing headfirst out of her bedroom window to run away from home so she wouldn't have to start preschool. Laine had hauled her back inside by the laces of her Buster Browns that time.

But nothing was going to save Cat from falling now, especially not if Laine started showing emotion over this. Or worse, appearing helpless, as the slight tremble in her lip and the shakiness of the hand holding her martini glass indicated.

"How are we going to explain this to Mom?" Laine asked, sounding bewildered.

Laine at a loss? Unsure what to do? The sky was gonna start falling at any minute. And Cat just couldn't take it, not on top of everything else. So she raised a brow and gave her sibling a challenging look. "Had faith in the system, Laine, dear?"

Bingo. Her sister immediately stiffened. As usual, when Cat went on the offensive, she inspired rapid mood changes, often involving anger. Or sometimes laughter. She'd used the technique all her life and it was a damn good defense mechanism, if she did say so herself. Including now.

Laine's eyes darkened and her jaw tensed as she crumpled the letter in her hand. "Yes, I did. This isn't right. How can they just take away everything we've worked for?"

Cat nearly sighed in relief. A teed-off Laine, she could handle; a bereft one, she couldn't.

Everyone kept talking, but Cat couldn't bring herself to listen. The others all had a sad stake in this, but they weren't going to lose quite as much as she was. Her business, her job, her way of life. Even her home.

Okay, the three tiny rooms over the bar weren't much of a home, but they were *hers*. She loved retreating into her private little world, listening to the late-night whispers and creaks of the aged oak paneling downstairs as the old building settled ever deeper into its foundation. A foundation that had, until the city's road project, seemed incredibly sound.

The trill of birds in the lush walled garden right outside her window woke her every morning. And the tinkle of glasses and muted laughter of their regulars lulled her to sleep on her rare nights off. She loved those sounds. As much as she loved the smell of the lemony polish she used daily to bring back the lustrous shine to the surface of the old pitted bar.

She loved the hiss of a newly tapped keg. Loved the clink of glass on glass when she poured a neat whiskey. Even loved the whirr of the blender when she had to make girlie drinks for the froufrou crowd that occasionally wandered in for happy hour.

Mostly she loved sitting here, alone, late at night when the place was closed, picturing the faces and voices of everyone who had passed through here before her. Her grandparents. Her dad, who'd died so many years ago. She could still see his wide Irish smile as he slowly pulled a draft of Guinness for a customer, explaining that the nectar of Ireland was well worth the wait.

Gone. All the things she loved would be gone. Washed away, like sidewalk etchings in the rain, by city officials who had no idea they were washing Cat's entire world away, as well.

No job. No business. No home. No future.

No identity.

Just who was she going to be when this was all over?

She sipped her drink, depressed and overwhelmed at the thought. She'd gotten so used to her place in the world, stepping in at the bar at such a young age because it was what the family always figured she—the so-so student but A+ party girl—would do. She'd dated poor excuses for men and never been serious about any of them. Worst of all, she'd put away any glimmer of an idea that she could do something different with her life. Like fulfill a long-secret dream to go to college and become a teacher.

She'd shoved all of those things aside, and for what? A business that was going under, a family who had drifted apart, and a life that seemed…empty.

You can change it. Change everything.

She couldn't thrust the unexpected thought out of her mind…maybe she should take this as a sign to move on in a completely unexpected direction, to walk a new path.

She could change. Become somebody new.

The idea grew on her. Since she had no choice, maybe the time had come for her to try something else. To change some things about herself—from her attitude to her hairstyle. Her clothes to her social skills. She could work on her education—slowly—to see if she really would be as good at teaching English to teenagers as she thought she might be.

She could work on her notoriously bad language, her secret addiction to romance novels. Maybe she'd even break herself of her awful habit of getting involved with even-badder-than-herself bad boys, who were ever-so-safe to fall for since they never aroused any ridiculous expectations of happily-ever-after. Just happily-between-the-sheets.

Yeah. No bad boys.

"Who are you kidding?" she mumbled under her breath, doubting she was that frigging strong.

"Did you say something?" Tess asked.

Cat merely smiled, trying to tune back in on the animated conversation the others had been having. "Just talking to myself," she admitted. "Making some plans."

Plans. Yes, she definitely had to make plans. She had time—until the end of the month, at least. Her sister and two closest friends would be right here by her side for every minute of it, riding things out until the very end. They'd be like the string quartet on the *Titanic*, playing their instruments as the ship sank beneath their feet.

She'd use these last weeks to figure out how to become the new Cat Sheehan. Heck, maybe she'd even start going by Catherine. It was something, anyway, along with those other big changes, which she went over again in her mind.

Education. *Check*. Home. *Check*. Attitude. *Check*.

No dangerous men. *Hmm*...

But hey, stranger things had happened. All it would take was willpower. Well, that and the knowledge that no hot-enough-to-melt-a-polar-icecap man with trouble in his eyes and wickedness in his smile had wandered into her world in quite some time.

And one sure as hell wasn't likely to now.

CHAPTER ONE

SIN HAD JUST WALKED into her bar and he was wearing a Grateful Dead T-shirt.

Cat Sheehan paused midsentence, forgetting the conversation she'd been having with one of her customers. Forgetting *everything*. Because, Holy Mother Mary, a man who'd instantly set her heart pounding and her pulse racing was standing a few yards away, completely oblivious to her shocked stare.

He was tall. Very tall. And he had the kind of presence that immediately drew the attention of every person in the place—at least, every *female* person. Their gazes drifted over because of his size. They stayed because of his looks.

A strip of leather kept the man's jet-black hair tied at the back of his neck in a short ponytail. A simple thing, that piece of leather, and she'd certainly seen men with longish hair and ponytails. But on him, well, the look was…rakish. That was the only word she could think of.

Cat liked rakes. Not that she'd ever met one for real, but she liked the ones she'd read about in her pirate romance novels.

A pirate. It fit. From the ponytail to the flash of silver glistening on the lobe of one ear to the aura of danger oozing from his body, this man had the pirate thing going in spades.

His classically handsome face was lean, a faint shadow of stubble adding a layer of ruggedness to his strong jaw. His lips briefly widened into a smile as he greeted someone. For a moment, Cat felt very sure the ground had trembled a bit under the power of his smile. Not to mention the mouth, which looked as if it had been created for the sole purpose of kissing.

His body was a living testament to the beauty of nature—broad at the shoulders, slim at the hips, with long legs covered in tight, faded jeans. His thick arms flexed, muscles bulging under the weight of the sizable guitar case he was carrying, though he hardly seemed to notice. Lifting it higher, he stepped deftly around tables and chairs, skirting the outstretched legs of the few patrons in the place.

He moved gracefully. Catlike.

"Oh, yeah," she murmured. Cat *definitely* liked.

She never took her eyes off him as he approached. Then it sunk in. He was approaching *her,* Cat Sheehan, the woman standing here with her mouth only slightly less wide-open than her eyes.

Blinking, she gave her head a hard shake, then grabbed the nearest cloth she could reach and busied herself by wiping up some spilled beer.

"Hey! What are you doing?"

Cat barely registered the shrill words from somewhere nearby, because suddenly *he* was there. A thick, tanned forearm dropped to the surface of the bar, and she couldn't help staring at his fingers. Long fingers. Artistic-looking. Perfect for a guitar player. Not to mention a lover.

"Wow," the same female voice said, sounding subdued.

Swallowing hard, Cat slowly shifted her gaze, surveying his limb from fingertip to elbow, then the ninety-degree turn up the thick planes of his arm, the tight hem of the black cotton T-shirt. The broad shoulder. The hollow of his throat. The cords of his neck. *Wow, indeed.*

Then, oh, God, the face.

If Helen's face had launched a thousand ships to the sea, surely this man's could inspire *ten* thousand pairs of panties to drop to the floor.

Her legs wobbled, her knees knocking together loud enough to be heard over the sound of the jackhammer outside. But probably *not* loud enough to be heard over the pounding of her heart. Ordering herself to calm down, she slowed her breaths, mentally grabbing for control as she assessed the situation.

She was facing the most incredible man she'd ever seen—the kind of guy women fantasized about meeting for real, instead of on the pages of books or on giant screens in darkened movie theaters. One-hundred-percent pure sin.

Separating them were only the broad mahogany bar and Cat's own resolution to change her ways and steer clear of sexy, dangerous men.

She should have known she didn't have a snowball's chance of keeping that resolution, though, honestly, she'd figured she could last a week. But no. It'd been only three days since they'd received the letter from the historical society and she'd made the stupid promise to herself. Of all the changes in her world since Tuesday— including the shockingly abrupt departure of Laine and Tess for far-flung adventures—she'd thought the ones she'd resolved to make in herself would be the easiest to deal with.

Uh, *not.*

A slow grin tilted the corners of the stranger's lips

up and he leaned closer. As he did so, his dark, intense eyes caught and reflected a reddish glimmer from one of the stained-glass light fixtures overhead.

Devilish. Dangerous. *Off-limits.*

Or so she tried to tell herself. But she suspected it was no use. Unless the guy had a hideous voice, he was altogether perfect. And since conversation wasn't even on the top ten list of the things she'd been picturing doing with this man since the second she'd set eyes on him, she suspected it wouldn't matter if he sounded like Roger Rabbit on speed.

"I think that's her purse you're using to clean up the spilled beer," he said.

Velvet voice. Soft. Husky. As smooth and warm as their very best whiskey—the kind she kept hidden beneath the bar for special customers. She felt every word he spoke on each of the nerve endings in her body.

Doomed. The new, reformed Cat Sheehan was utterly doomed.

Then what he'd said sunk in and Cat looked down at her hand. "Oh, my God, I'm so sorry," she said when she spied what she'd been using as a rag.

It was a small, cloth handbag belonging to a customer seated at the bar. Fortunately, the woman was one of their regulars, a bank teller named Julie. Even more fortunately, Julie was just as drooly-faced over the stranger as Cat, because she seemed to understand Cat's lapse into hot-man-induced dementia.

"It'll wash," Julie mumbled.

The man plucked the damp purse from Cat's limp fingers and handed it to its owner, giving her an intimate smile. "Maybe a drink on the house would help?"

Julie nodded dumbly. Cat was tempted to grab the woman's left hand and flip it over to remind her of the big diamond ring she'd been flashing in here since her engagement to some salesman. But she couldn't blame her. Engaged or not, any woman would look twice…or dozens of times…at a man like this one.

Then he turned his attention back to Cat. His full, unwavering attention. "Hi. I'm your entertainment," he finally said, his voice low and intimate though she'd swear laughter danced behind his eyes.

"You're *very* good," she replied matter-of-factly.

A dimple flashed in one of his lean cheeks. "You haven't seen what I can do yet."

"Wild guess," she mumbled, her mind filling with possibilities of just what he *could* do. She had to give herself credit—only half were X-rated. Well, maybe sixty percent.

"You won't have to wait for long to find out," he said, his tone as suggestive as her words had been.

Oh, boy, did that set her heart flip-flopping in her chest.

Her expression must have given away her thoughts. His brown eyes darkened to near black and he leaned closer, both elbows now resting on the bar. "You sure you're gonna be able to handle it?"

She raised a challenging brow. "You think you're that good? That you can't be *handled*?"

"I've been known to shake the walls when I get going."

Cat grabbed the edge of the bar to steady herself and took a deep breath. She should walk away, ignore the comment, pretend she'd misunderstood.

She did none of the above. Instead, even though she knew she shouldn't step farther into the fire, she threw a spark right back at the solid stick of dynamite watching her with promise in his eyes. "I've been known to rattle a few walls myself."

His cocky grin faded and his jaw tightened a bit. *Tie game.* She'd definitely gotten under his skin, just as he had hers. Then he managed, "So you *play*, too?"

"Not lately," she admitted.

Nope, she hadn't *played* with a man in a very long time. Not since last year, when she'd briefly dated a rodeo cowboy, whose lack of finesse in the saddle had been equaled only by his lack of staying power.

He'd lasted about three-and-a-half minutes. *They'd* lasted about three-and-a-half dates.

"What instrument?" he asked.

The words, "a thick, eight-inch one is my preference," came to mind, but she bit back the reply. This game had gotten a bit *too* reckless for a woman who'd sworn off guys with trouble written all over them. This one was the absolute Yellow Pages of trouble. "Um…"

"I somehow see you as a sax woman."

Her mouth dropped open. She was definitely a sex woman, which she was being reminded of with every passing second. But, lord, he'd skipped right past the subtle innuendo, hadn't he?

"Or maybe clarinet?"

Her brow shot up. "You mean we were talking about *musical* instruments?"

"Of course." He managed to pull off a look of such complete innocence that Cat began to believe she really had misread their conversation. "What else would we have been talking about?"

Feeling heat rise in her face, she opened her mouth, then closed it, wondering how to gracefully back out of this enormous foot-in-mouth moment. She was about to tell him she was a virtuoso on the kazoo when she saw his shoulders shaking with suppressed amusement.

"Dog," she muttered, laughing even as she shook her head in admiration of how well he'd played her.

"Cat," he replied.

"Yes. Cat Sheehan."

He nodded. "I know."

Interesting. He knew who she was. Which left her at a disadvantage. "And you are…?"

He paused, a frown pulling at his brow so briefly she almost missed it. Then he admitted, "Call me Spence."

She'd rather call him guy-destined-to-be-naked-in-her-bed-by-midnight.

Not happening, she reminded herself. *This is supposed to be the new you.*

The new her might be trying to call the shots in the brain. But the old Cat—the hungry one whose entire body was sparking in reaction to this stranger named Spence—had control of everything from the neck down. Especially the, uh, *softest* parts.

Still, even the old, reckless Cat had never done the one-night stand thing. Despite what her sister might imagine, Cat wasn't *that* danger-loving. With a man like this one, however, she was beginning to understand the illicit allure of a bar hookup.

"Hi, Spence. Welcome to Temptation," she finally said.

"I like that."

"What?"

"Temptation."

Ooooh…definitely her kinda guy.

"I also liked the sign over your front door."

She instantly knew which one he meant—the hand-painted sign inviting those outside to *Enter Into Temptation*. She'd thought up the logo three years ago when she and Laine had taken over the bar from their mother, changing the name from Sheehan's Pub to Temptation. "Thanks. Seemed appropriate."

"I just didn't realize it was going to be quite so prophetic," he added, his tone husky.

She got his meaning instantly. He was every bit as tempted as she was. A long, shuddery breath escaped her lips. Unable to do much more than breathe and stand still, she stared at him. Right into those fathomless eyes.

He stared right back, just as intently, neither of them laughing or flirting any longer. They said nothing, yet exchanged a wealth of information. In twenty seconds they covered the basics—yes, they were both interested, and, yes, they were both aware of each other's interest. But it went deeper...they each knew that they could play games or do away with them right now. Because the palpable attraction made something happening between them inevitable.

They all but named the time and place.

Then his lips—God, those lips—parted, and he drew in a long, slow breath of air. His lids lowered slightly, half closing over his eyes, drawing her attention to his long, spiky black lashes. Visceral pleasure accompanied his inhalation, and she realized what he was doing.

Smelling her perfume. Inhaling it. Savoring it. Gaining sensual pleasure from the aroma of her skin.

Dangerous. Oh, he was dangerous. Because he was so damned appealing. A man who appreciated a woman's scent would appreciate so many other delightful things, wouldn't he? Tastes, touches, sensations.

Her pulse raced as the thick, heady silence dragged

on, in spite of the cacophony all around them. At some point, she noted Julie pushing away and getting off her stool, until Cat and Spence were the only two people in this small corner of the bar.

Surrounded by others, but completely alone.

Cat hesitated as a sensation of déjà vu washed over her. How many times had she stood in this room, filled with chattering people—customers, family, friends— and felt that *exact* sensation of being alone, separated? It felt as if the world was moving all around her but she was frozen for one moment in time, looking at her life and wondering if she really was traveling the same path as everyone else. Because she so rarely felt in step with anyone.

Only now, in this timeless instant when she wondered just where she belonged and where she was going, she wasn't completely by herself. This dark-haired stranger was right there with her.

"Cat?" he asked, obviously sensing her confusion.

She blinked rapidly and shook her head, shaking off not only the strange sensation, but also the intensity of the moment. Forcing herself to focus, she shifted her gaze away, toward a customer who'd just taken a seat at the far end of the bar. She stepped over to him, trying to convince herself she had to get back to work when, in truth, she needed a chance to regain her sanity.

"The usual?" she said to the guy in the brown sport coat, a Friday night regular who liked his women easy and his martinis dirty.

He nodded. "If you can…spare the time," he said with a truly amused grin, probably having heard the quiver in her voice.

Behind her, she heard a long, low chuckle. As throaty and sensuous as every word Spence had spoken.

She deserved the reaction. She'd looked away first, losing their silent game of chicken, shocking even herself. Cat didn't remember the last time that had happened to her.

Being disconcerted around a man was something she had seldom experienced. Cat Sheehan had been able to hold her own with men since the tenth grade when she'd started busing tables at the family bar. She'd sassed the old-timers, ducked away from grabby strangers and eventually chosen her first lover from among the Saturday night regulars.

Never before had a man taken the upper hand from her—unless she'd wanted him to. This guy with his jet-black hair and his badass grin and his big, hard guitar had done it with a stare.

Which was why, after she'd served Mr. Sport Coat his martini, she was having such a hard time thinking of a single thing to say to the still-staring musician. How could she even try to explain away that silence as something other than what they both knew damn well it had been?

An invitation. A challenge. A promise. None of which she had any business accepting.

But oh, how tempting it was to consider it.

Good Lord, no wonder she was having a hard time coming up with any kind of response—much less a sassy comeback. Cat felt completely at a loss for words. Continuing the flirtation would be reinforcing her implied acceptance of every wicked thing he'd suggested with his eyes.

Ending it might just kill her.

He finally spared her by steering the conversation into neutral territory. "I do have the right place, don't I? You're expecting the Four G's?"

The Four G's…she instantly remembered the band from Tremont—the next town over—which she'd hired for this weekend's live entertainment. *Of course he's with the band, idiot. Isn't he carrying a guitar case?* She cleared her throat and nodded. "Uh, yes, definitely the right place. I'm… we're…glad to have you here."

Oh, yeah, she'd be glad to have him all right. Upstairs in her apartment. On the swing in the back garden.

Hell, on top of the bar might be nice.

Cat thrust the mental picture out of her head, promising herself she'd lay off the romance novels. And the occasional late-night blue movies on cable. And the erotic fantasies during her middle-of-the-night bubble baths. Because she had obviously become a sex-starved maniac.

She did have to give herself a little bit of a break. After all, it'd been a year since she'd had even bad sex. As for good sex? Whew, she wasn't sure she could remember when that had last happened. Which had to explain why she wanted this guy like a woman on the South Beach Diet wanted a baked potato. With fries on the side.

"Thanks. We were glad to get the call." Spence smiled, a cocky half smile that said he knew what she'd been doing—trying to act nonchalant and not quite succeeding. "Though it looks like a small audience."

"What, are you kidding?" she asked, glancing around the room, where at least twenty people sat at the usually empty tables. "This is a crowd for us, lately. As close to wall-to-wall as we've seen since they tore up the nearest intersection, banned on-street parking, and set up a horrendous detour."

Obviously hearing her disgust, he said, "You sound

like you definitely need some entertainment this
weekend."

Oh, he had no idea how much she needed entertainment. Or maybe he did. His tiny grin told her they were
flirting again. This time—maybe because he'd let her
regain her equilibrium with small talk about the bar—
Cat felt more able to handle it. "I'm a little particular in
how I get my...entertainment."

"Oh? Anything you'd care to share?"

Licking her lips, she did a classic blond hair toss—
which she'd learned around the age of three—and
reached for a martini shaker. She splashed a generous
amount of vodka into it, dirtied it up with a splash of
olive juice, then poured it for the guy at the end of the
bar, knowing by the look in his eye that he was ready
for another.

"I don't think so," she said when she returned her
attention to Spence.

He shook his head. "Too bad. So I guess I'll just have
to do my stuff for everyone else in the room."

"I somehow suspect the women in this place are
going to like seeing you do your stuff," she replied, her
tone dry.

"I somehow suspect I won't care what any *other*
woman thinks."

Cat nibbled her bottom lip, seeing an expression that
somehow resembled tenderness cross his face. As if he
were no longer flirting, but being entirely serious. Which
was ridiculous, considering they'd known each other all
of a half hour.

She shook off the feeling. "They'll be a good audience, since you're here at their request. I asked the
loyal regulars who've been sticking it out through the
road construction to vote on what they wanted for the

last few weekends we're open. Two of the three are strictly country and western, but this weekend Temptation is all about rock and roll, and you guys came highly recommended."

"Lucky me." Straightening, he lifted his guitar case off the floor and looked toward the door, where another guitar-carrying musician was entering. "Guess I'd better go."

He was going to be across the room, but for some silly reason she almost missed him. Maybe it was because she knew in a few minutes he would be the property of every on-the-make woman in the place. "Want me to send over a drink to keep your pipes wet?"

He nodded. "Just water, if you don't mind."

He started to walk away, then paused and looked back. Nodding toward something on the wall behind her, he lowered his voice and said, "By the way...*not me*. And hopefully not *you*."

She was still puzzling over the remark after he'd reached the stage. Then, finally, she realized what he'd been talking about. Swiveling on her heel, she looked up at the sign above the bar. It had been hand-painted by the same artist who'd done the one out front, as well as the murals in the back hallway.

Though Spence's answer had brought up a number of complications, the sign posed a simple question.

Who can resist Temptation?

DYLAN SPENCER HAD FALLEN madly in love twice in his life.

The first time had been at age seven when he'd been introduced to his ultimate destiny: the greatest form of music ever created. He'd been visiting his grandparents' house in New England for the holidays and one of his older cousins had gotten a Van Halen album for Christmas. It had been love at first riff.

The year had been 1985 and the record had been 1984 and Dylan had decided then and there that bass player Michael Anthony had been touched by God.

Dylan had been completely enthralled. His parents—who never listened to anything that didn't feature fat Italian opera singers—had not been. Particularly when they'd caught Dylan entertaining all the neighborhood kids with a rousing, nearly R-rated rendition of "Hot For Teacher."

Thinking they could steer his love for music, and encourage his rather amazing natural musical abilities, they'd signed him up for piano lessons.

He'd been kicked out when he'd broken into Queen's "Bohemian Rhapsody" during an end-of-the-year recital.

By ten he was air guitaring his way through life. By twelve, after five years of relentless begging, he had his own real bass guitar and it had been practically glued to his hands ever since.

Yeah. Rock and roll had been his first experience with instant obsession.

Cat Sheehan had been his second.

Throughout the evening, while he stayed perfectly in sync with his bandmates, putting his all into the music, he kept at least part of his attention on her. The woman who'd taken his breath away from the moment he'd first laid eyes on her.

Cat wasn't hard to keep track of—she definitely stood out. From here, behind the glare of the small spotlights, her long golden hair looked almost silver. Occasionally, she'd smooth it back off her cheek with one graceful lift of her finger, so that it framed her perfect face.

He wasn't close enough to focus on the deep, ocean-green of her eyes. But he definitely watched the graceful movements of her slim body, clad in tight-as-sin jeans and a sleeveless white tank top. Also tight. Also sinful.

Working the bar as if she'd been born behind it, Cat didn't even have to look at the labels of the bottles from which she poured. Her hand never faltered as she made any drink ordered. She moved with a dancer's grace, able to pull a draft of beer off the tap, circle around and set it down in front of a customer in one long, fluid movement a ballerina would envy.

Chatting easily with everyone, she smiled often—that dazzling smile taking his breath away from all the way across the room. At one point, he even thought he heard her throaty laugh over all the other noise in the place. The sound was distinct because of the reaction it caused in him—instant awareness. Instant hunger. Instant heat.

She affected him like the music affected him.

Deeply. Intimately. Physically.

But it wasn't just that. He liked hearing the laugh and seeing the smile because they countered the weariness in her brow and the slight slump of her shoulders, which he'd noticed as soon as they'd started talking earlier. He didn't know what was troubling Cat. But he planned to find out.

"This place is wild," Josh Garrity yelled from the other side of the small stage. The crowd was roaring its approval at the end of their second set. If the walls weren't still shaking from the Aerosmith song they'd just finished, they were from the applause. "You think they'll let us take a real break this time, Spence?"

Dylan nodded as he carefully put his beloved Fender

back into its case and turned off his Voodoo amp. Josh played guitar and sang lead most of the time; Dylan was on bass, doing some of the vocalizations, as well. But it seemed as if all the songs the crowd had been yelling for were Dylan's and his throat was now almost raw. "If they don't, neither one of us is going to have any voice left at all."

Nodding, Josh waved at the audience, which had swelled in size over the past few hours until every table was taken. "Stay, drink, be patient. We'll be back in twenty," he shouted into the microphone, trying to be heard over the applause and whistles.

The audience cheered a bit more, but since the band members were already putting their instruments down, they gradually quieted. The typical mad race for the restrooms and fresh rounds quickly got underway. As did the pickup conversations going on between the hopeful single guys and their prospects.

"The *place* isn't the only thing that's wild," their drummer Jeremy said as he lowered his drumsticks and rose from his stool. "The brunette in the jean miniskirt who was sitting at the table closest to the stage wasn't wearing any underwear." He shook his head. "It was like she *wanted* me to see…everything."

Seeing the shock on Jeremy's face, Dylan hid a jaded grin. Jeremy, Josh's younger brother, was their newest member, a baby-faced nineteen-year-old. Jeremy hadn't yet realized that rock-and-roll groupies didn't always limit their adulation to the famous groups who were household names. Sometimes local bands—like theirs— had their own fan bases. The familiar faces in tonight's crowd certainly bore that out.

That was one of the drawbacks to the business, as far as Dylan was concerned. He played for his own pleasure, his own release. He had never been interested in the fans or the lifestyle or any of the garbage that went along with it. He just liked to head-bang on occasion. Which was probably why he'd never gone any further with his music than to small places like this, in small Texas towns.

"So, you gonna go over and talk to her or just keep staring at her like some lovesick mutt?"

Dylan jerked his attention toward Billy Banks, the final member of their four-man group, who wailed like a madman on the keyboard. Banks was grinning that sardonic grin of his, brown eyes sparkling behind the wire-framed glasses he wore to give himself the appearance of an intellectual rock and roller. He liked to think of himself as the Lennon of their group.

The women seemed to like it, too. Between Banks's brainy persona and deep-rooted mischievous streak, Jeremy's fresh-faced innocence, Josh's breezy surfer style and Dylan's own long-haired rebel thing, they had a regular stream of females ready to keep them company whenever they desired it.

Dylan hadn't desired it. Not in a long time.

But Banks sure had, which wasn't surprising. Ever since they'd met at freshman orientation in college, where they'd been the two youngest people in the room, Billy Banks had proved himself to be two things: woman-crazy and the best, most loyal friend Dylan had ever had.

"Well? You going over? You've been eyeing her all night."

"You're seeing things," Dylan mumbled, choosing to pretend he didn't know what the guy was talking about.

"Oh, come on, man, I thought you were gonna short out the sound system because the mike was getting so wet with your drool every time you looked at that blond bartender."

"Bite me."

Banks smirked. "You oughtta save that line for her."

Shooting Banks—who was as close to him as a brother—a look that threatened bodily injury, Dylan walked to the rear of the stage to amp everything down.

Banks soon crouched beside him to help. "She is totally hot," he said, sounding contrite. Definitely out of character for Banks, who never regretted anything he did.

Dylan hesitated for one second, wondering how much to reveal. Finally, between clenched teeth, he admitted the truth. "She's Cat Sheehan."

Banks jerked so hard he almost fell on his ass. His eyes widened and his jaw dropped. When Dylan confirmed the truth of his words with a nod, Banks emitted a long, low whistle. "*The* Cat woman herself, huh?"

Dylan nodded again, knowing he didn't have to say anything more. Banks knew all about Cat. He was probably the only one who knew the entire truth about Dylan's relationship with the blonde.

The one-sided relationship that had been going on for several years now.

"Did you know she'd be here?"

He shook his head. "I recognized the building when I pulled up outside. Her family used to own the place. But the name's changed. I figured she was long gone."

Banks nodded. "Did she know who you were?"

No. She hadn't. Which still slightly burned him. But he didn't want Banks to know that. So he shrugged in disinterest. "We've barely spoken."

Banks merely smirked, the sorry son of a bitch, knowing Dylan much too well to be fooled by that. Then he looked over Dylan's shoulder, toward the other side of the bar, nodding as he sought out Cat. "So you finally have your shot," he murmured. "Your dream girl has been looking at you all night like she needs a sugar fix and you're a giant Tootsie Roll."

Banks's words brought some intense images to mind and he had to busy his hands winding cable to keep them from shaking. "You're imagining things," he said. "She's barely paid attention to us at all."

Banks let out a bark of laughter that caused several people standing nearby to glance over in curiosity. "Man, you are losing it if you didn't see the way that girl kept her eyes glued to you. Except every time you looked in her direction—then she turned away right quick."

Okay, it was possible. He and Cat had shared a sexy, flirtatious conversation before the rest of the band had shown up. There had been some definite spark, a genuine intensity between them.

A lazy smile widened his lips at the memory. He had never fallen into such instant sync with anyone before. And he'd certainly never been so completely affected by a woman before—at least, not in his adult life. Even now, nearly two hours later, he could still smell the warm, sultry aroma of her perfume and hear her throaty laugh.

"She's yours for the taking," Banks added. "You can finally have what you always wanted."

Dylan was shaking his head even before Banks finished his ridiculous statement. His friend was wrong. Very, very wrong.

Cat might be interested now. Judging by the heat-filled moments they'd shared earlier, he'd say she probably was.

Didn't matter. Because the minute she found out his true identity, the spark would fade, the intensity would disappear and his chances along with it. He knew it. Knew it like he knew his own guitar.

She was interested in Spence, the bass-playing rock and roller with a strut and a sneer and a cocky-as-hell attitude. Which was pretty funny, come to think of it, in a you-poor-sorry-sucker way. Because the man she was attracted to didn't exist. He was a phantom. A facade. A fictional character.

In truth, Dylan Spencer was a complete and utter fraud.

CHAPTER TWO

IF TEMPTATION HAD had more nights like this, they might have had enough money to hire a better attorney for their fight to stay open. Cat couldn't get over the people who'd squeezed in over the past couple of hours, all of them thirsty. And hungry, judging by the way Zeke, their cook, was whipping out everything on their limited menu just as fast as he could.

The Four G's music seemed to have had some kind of Pied Piper effect on the residents of Kendall, many of whom were former patrons who hadn't wanted to deal with the hassles of road construction in recent months. Temptation hadn't been this crowded since the spring, when an erroneous rumor had circulated that they were hosting a wet T-shirt contest.

If it would have saved the bar, Cat would have given it some serious consideration.

"I think I'm going to have to kill Tess when and if she ever comes back."

Cat quickly swung two beers, a Sex on the Beach, and a mojito onto a serving tray and gave Dinah, their part-time waitress, a commiserating smile. "I don't think any of us ever expected to have nights like these during the last few weeks we're open. I'm sure Tess and Laine would both have stuck around if they'd thought we were going to actually be having *crowds*, rather than our usual *quartets*."

Cat firmly believed that. She was still a bit upset with Laine for taking off on some daring, photographic wildfire adventure in California. Secretly, however, she had to concede she was glad Laine was there to help their Aunt Jen, whose house was being threatened by the fires engulfing the state. Besides, Laine had been talking for a long time about how much she wanted one of her photos on the cover of the magazine she worked for, *Century*. This might actually be her shot. So while she was peeved at her, Cat couldn't be too upset.

As for Tess, their other waitress...well, with her, you never knew what to expect. Like the way she'd stumbled into the job at Temptation a few years back. She'd started waitressing to work off a bar tab she couldn't pay and had never left.

Unpredictable. That described Tess. So her deciding to take off last Tuesday night to help distribute some old guy's money was entirely understandable. Unlike Laine, at least Tess had asked Cat first if she minded, and had even offered her some of her newfound riches.

Cat hadn't accepted the money—it was too late for that. But she *had* minded her friend leaving. Not so much because she needed Tess's help—or Laine's, for that matter—but because she'd had this whole sappy image of the four of them crying in each other's arms during the last few weeks the bar was open.

She hadn't told Tess or Laine that. In fact, she'd urged Tess to go. And Laine...well, after their argument, she hadn't been surprised her sister had taken off.

She'd missed them both ever since, much more than she'd ever have expected. Which was silly, really, since she'd always known everybody was destined to leave. Her grandparents, her father. Her remarried mother. Her brilliant sister.

Cat ending up alone had been inevitable. But she'd always thought she'd at least have Temptation.

Dinah clucked her tongue and shook her head, making her poufed platinum blond hair teeter a bit to one side. "I still can't get over the two of them bailing out of here. You sure you don't want me to tell your mama…"

"Don't even think about it," Cat said, already grabbing two bottles of Bud for the guys waving to her from the end of the bar. "She's upset enough about the pub closing. The last thing I need is to have her come down here to help out, because you know her helping out would mean me losing my mind."

Dinah, who'd been one of her mother's closest friends since their high school years, chuckled. "It's just because she worries."

"She worries, I snap. Without Laine here to referee, it'd be a nightmare."

"You think it'll be like this all weekend?" Dinah asked. "Because if so, we might need to call in some backup. Tess did say she was going to be as close as Austin…"

Cat shook her head. "It's okay, I already took care of it. I called an old friend and tapped her to help out tomorrow night."

Dinah, a fifty-something native Texan whose heart was bigger than most people's minivans, sighed in visible relief. "Thank the Lord. I don't think my knees could take another night like this one."

Cat purposely looked at the beer mug she was holding under the tap and kept her voice casual as she asked, "How are *Zeke's* knees holding up?"

Silence. Then Dinah squawked, "You bad girl…as if I know. The man's more skittish than a virgin in a frathouse."

Knowing Dinah had had her eye on Zeke for about two years, ever since Laine and Cat had hired the man to cook for their pub clientele, Cat frowned. "You're running out of time, you know. If you're going to make something happen, you'd better do it while you two are still working together every day."

Dinah rolled her eyes. "Sugar, I could bathe naked in that man's deep fryer and he wouldn't look."

"I dunno...warm oil, a hot kitchen, spicy smells. Sounds pretty sexy to me."

"Me, too," a male voice said. The hair standing on end all over her body told her exactly which male voice.

Crud. She'd gotten so distracted chatting with Dinah about the older woman's romantic possibilities that she'd completely forgotten about her own.

No. He's not a possibility.

She'd been telling herself that for two hours, every throaty, wickedly sexy song the band performed reminding her of just how dangerous getting involved with Spence would be. Even if he had made her almost melt into a puddle when he'd sung one song she hadn't recognized, about making love in the moonlight on a windswept beach to a woman with fire in her eyes. Made her want to take a drive down to the Galveston coast. With him.

But no. It'd never happen. He was a long-haired musician playing tiny bars in Nowhereville, Texas, for heaven's sake. The man probably didn't even *own* a car. Spence was definitely not the steady, reliable type she'd been telling herself she needed to find. Far, far from it!

The flirting was over with. The guy was a hunk and a half, but so were a lot of other guys. And all of them were the type who walked away.

She'd had enough of those, dammit. From here on

out, she was going to be strictly business with this particular one. So she offered him an impersonal smile. "Hey, I was afraid the crowd was never going to let you guys take a break."

"Me, too," he said.

Without being asked, she opened a bottle of icy cold water and slid it to him. He picked it up, giving her a grateful nod, and lifted it to his lips.

Lips. Don't think of the lips. You never notice the lips of the guy at the bank or the post office.

She looked down, her gaze falling on his throat. Her breaths deepened as she watched the way his pulse pounded in his neck and the muscles leading to his shoulders rippled with his every movement. All glisteny with a sheen of sweat. Probably tasted salty.

She added more no-no words to her list. *Neck. Shoulders. Muscles. Glisteny. Salty.*

"Thanks," he said as he lowered the nearly empty bottle. "Those lights are pretty hot. I was half wishing I'd worn less clothes." He cleared his throat. "I mean, lighter clothes. Shorts or something."

Less clothes? No pants? She might as well just give this up right now. Because no matter how hard she tried to keep her mind focused and professional, she kept sliding down this slippery slope of attraction to this man. She couldn't possibly survive another round of sexual roulette with him.

But at least this time, Spence was looking uncomfortable, as well. Funny, the way he'd stammered over the words he'd said, about wearing less clothes. As if he, too, had recognized the naughty implication and had been slightly embarrassed about it.

It was cute, that sheepish look on his face. Not to mention completely unexpected. Embarrassment and this guy went together about as naturally as pork chops and a vegetarian.

"It is awfully hot in here, don't you think?" he finally said, filling the thick silence. How bizarre, this feeling of being in a silent bubble, when all around them voices chattered and glasses tinkled. But, like before, all of that seemed very far away.

"Yeah, well, uh…I guess the crowd of naked bodies makes it feel even hotter," Cat said.

Then she bit her tongue. *Bodies.* Another definite no-no word when Spence was around. If this kept up, she was going to have the vocabulary of a ten-month-old.

"Uh, Cat, did you say what I think you said?"

Sure, she'd said the crowd of bodies…oh, God, she hadn't said *naked*, had she? *Tell me I didn't say naked.*

"Because we're pretty open to playing at unusual venues, but an entirely naked audience, well, that could get a little…sticky." His lips twitched, and she knew he was trying to hold back his laughter.

Cat blushed. Literally felt hot blood rise in her face and flood her cheeks. No guy had *ever* made her blush.

"Slip of the tongue," she muttered, grabbing for any halfway believable excuse she could find. "I mean, you know, the words, they sort of go together. Naked. And bodies. I might just as easily have said *dead* and bodies."

Argh! Just stick a spike through your hand and get it over with, Cat. It'd be less painful than this.

"I think I'd prefer naked ones to dead ones," he murmured.

She kept prattling on, like an out of control car

careening toward a cliff. "You know what I mean, though, right? Some words are kind of a natural fit. Like fried and oysters."

His lips twitched again. "Most people would say fried goes better with chicken…but if you prefer *oysters*…"

"I don't. Prefer oysters, I mean, no matter what their, uh, reputation," she said, wondering why she'd had to immediately latch on the sex food group when there were so many others available. Bacon and eggs. Hot and tamale.

Dead and duck.

"Me, neither. Nasty little things," he said, obviously still talking about the oysters.

Cat nodded in agreement. "Shiny and slippery and wet."

One of his brows shot up. "Shiny…slippery…wet?"

Cat pictured putting her mouth in front of a firing squad for continuing to bring both their minds to places they had no business being. She closed her eyes, unable to manage a single word. She could only shake her head in dismay. When, in the name of heaven, had Cat Sheehan turned into a babbling idiot?

Spence started to laugh—a low, husky laugh that made her tingle, all over. "I'd offer you a shovel, but I don't have one on me. Besides, you're doing a pretty good job digging yourself deeper into this hole all on your own."

"If you'll excuse me, I think I'll go shoot myself now."

"I just told you I don't have a shovel, Cat."

"So you can't bury me?"

"Uh-huh."

She tapped the tip of her index finger on her cheek, thinking about it, even as she gave in and laughed a little with him. "Hmm, so how about backing up ten minutes and starting this whole thing over?"

Spence leaned over the bar, propping his chin on his fist. "Hi. Thanks for the water. What'd you think of the music?"

"You guys really are good," she said, thrilled at the chance to keep the conversation neutral.

"Thanks." He leaned closer, raising his voice as more people crowded close to the bar, waving at Cat to place their orders. "We have a lot of fun doing it."

Getting back to work, she filled a few mugs, poured a few shots, blew off a few jerks, then returned her attention to the bass player in the corner. "I really liked that song you did about the girl with the fire in her eyes and the moonlight on her hair. Who sang it originally? I didn't recognize it."

Spence shrugged, lifted his bottle to his mouth and sipped more water. After sipping, he lowered the bottle and wiped the moisture off his lips with the back of his hand.

Cat just stared, acknowledging the truth: the man was poetry in motion. No small talk in the world was going to make her oblivious to that.

"You didn't recognize it because I wrote it," he said.

Wrote it. Wrote poetry? She blinked a couple of times, trying to backtrack and remember what the heck they'd been talking about before he'd gotten her all distracted with his water-drinking abilities. Then she remembered. "You wrote *that* song? The one about the hot night and the whispers in the dark?"

Wow. She never would have guessed. Not only because the music had been so good, but also because of the unbridled emotion of the words, juxtaposed against

the raw, haunting power of the melody. It had sounded…
hungry. That was the only word she could find to describe it. "I'm impressed. You must have had quite a lot
of inspiration to write such a powerful song."

She hadn't been fishing for information. She *hadn't*.
It was none of her business what inspired him to write
such a sensual, heated ballad. But she still held her
breath, waiting for his response, hoping he wouldn't
say he'd written it for the love of his life. His longtime
girlfriend.

God, please, not his wife!

When his answer came, she couldn't help feeling a
sharp stab of disappointment. Because a faraway look
of longing and hunger accompanied his words. "I wrote
it for a girl I was crazy about a long, long time ago."

HE'D WRITTEN the song for *her*.

Staring at Cat, Dylan focused on those vivid green
eyes of hers—those catlike green eyes. He silently
willed her to read the truth that screamed loudly in his
brain but didn't cross his lips. *It was you. It was always
you.*

The girl in the song, with moonlight shining on her
hair, had been Cat Sheehan bathed in the glow of an
enormous bonfire the night of a homecoming game
many years ago. If he closed his eyes, he could still
see her there, standing completely alone, staring at the
flames. She'd been lost in thought, seeming separate and
distinct from the rowdy teenagers all around her.

It was so easy even now to remember the way her eyes
had glittered and her skin had taken on the golden sheen
of the fire. Her hair had positively come alive, as brilliant and dazzling as the flames that leaped and crackled
against the star-filled night sky. And even from several

feet away, he'd seen the way her lips had moved, as if she were whispering something for her ears alone.

He'd wanted to be the one she whispered to.

Wondering why she looked so sad, so serious and so lonely, he'd even moved closer. He'd been driven to understand why she stood there by herself, as if a curtain had descended between her and everyone else. Everyone except him.

Then someone had taken her arm and she'd rejoined the living, laughter on her lips, as always.

And, as always, she hadn't even noticed him standing there in the shadows. Apparently, she'd *never* really noticed him. Certainly not enough to make an impression. Because judging by tonight, Cat had absolutely no idea that they'd been classmates at Kendall High a mere nine years ago.

It wasn't her fault. Cat had never shunned him; he'd just been too intimidated to *make* her notice him. Not intimidated by her...but by the intensity of his own feelings, which had simply overwhelmed him, particularly after the night of the bonfire.

Because that had been the night he'd realized there was so much more depth to the beautiful, vivacious Cat than she ever let the world see. The night he'd realized the two of them had something very deep and intrinsic in common.

Their solitude.

Things had changed, though. Because now, she definitely noticed him. For the past ten minutes, during her adorable, fumbling conversation—which was so unlike the self-assured Cat he remembered—she'd been staring at him with intensity, interest and pure, physical want.

He knew the look. Tonight, he almost certainly mirrored it.

Then again, if she'd ever really looked at him, she would have seen that look on his face throughout the entire year they'd gone to school together.

Not meeting his eyes as she rubbed the surface of the bar with a damp rag, Cat said, "You have a lot of talent."

"Thanks. Music's my passion."

"Your *only* passion?"

"Not only. There's also video games."

One of her delicate brows lifted. "Rock and roll and video games. So are you just a mature-looking fifteen-year-old?"

"Smart-ass." He didn't elaborate on the video game thing, thinking she probably wasn't ready to hear that he didn't merely *play* them. He created and developed them. Very successfully.

"Goes with the territory," she said with a shrug.

"Being a smart-ass?"

She looked past him, nodded at someone, then got busy making a couple of scotch and sodas. "Yeah. Can't take things too seriously when perfect strangers are talking to you like they're your best friend night after night. Telling you their troubles. It'd be too damned depressing, especially for someone like me."

He hadn't thought of it that way. Then, curious, he asked, "Someone like you?"

Cat shrugged, suddenly looking uncomfortable. "I mean, well, anyone who gets riled up a bit too easily, like I used to do."

Riled up easily? Oh, yeah, Cat Sheehan had had a reputation for that. He didn't know if the Kendall High football team had ever gotten over being told they were a bunch of spiteful, fatheaded kindergartners with big egos and little dicks.

She'd done it during a pep rally.

Over a loudspeaker.

In front of the whole school.

Cat had gotten suspended. She'd also earned the never-ending devotion of all the freshmen who'd been used as walking punching bags by some of the bullying members of the football team.

"So you still get riled up too easily?" he asked.

She shook her head. "Not me. Miss Reasonable, Miss Calm, Cool and Collected, that's me these days. I can handle anything."

She tried to meet his eye, tried to maintain a sincere expression, but didn't quite manage it. Dylan couldn't help it. He started to laugh.

She shot him a dirty look, then dissolved into helpless laughter, too. "Okay, so maybe you are getting to know me. And the answer is yes, I probably do take things too personally and get myself in trouble on occasion. But I have handled things pretty well all on my own for a long time now. Despite what anyone in my family might say. And I'm determined to stay out of trouble, in spite of some of the things I'd really like to do."

He wanted to ask if she'd told off any dumb jocks lately but didn't want to tip his hand too soon. "For instance?"

Her smile faded, that tension returning to her slim body. "I fantasize about driving one of those bulldozers outside right onto the lawn of the courthouse and leaving a big Porta-John on the front steps. It'd have a big Welcome Home sign for the city officials who voted me out of business."

Cat's words gave him the opening he'd been waiting for…a chance to try to find out why she appeared so tense. "So, are you really closing the bar?"

Her mouth tightened. "End of the month. Demolition ball swings in July. Gotta make way for progress…how could we ever live without four lanes?"

"That blows."

She nodded, blinking rapidly, and Dylan recognized her anguish. He now understood the slump in Cat's shoulders, the unhappiness that had likely caused those dark circles under her beautiful eyes.

Cat was hurting.

Sure, she was playing tough girl—hadn't she always? But the pain beneath the surface would be obvious to a blind man.

"Is there anything I can do?" He figured there wasn't, but needed to ask, anyway.

"Just keep rocking the walls down this weekend so we can go out firmly in the black…and so I'll have a little money to live on while I figure out what I want to be when I grow up."

"I can't picture you being unsure of yourself for long, Cat Sheehan," he murmured, hearing the intensity in his voice.

She apparently heard it, too. Her eyes narrowed in skepticism. "You think you know me already, huh?"

Oh, yeah. He knew her. He'd known her for years. He'd watched her with simple devotion when he'd been a young, geeky kid to whom she'd never have given a second look. And he'd seen her in his dreams in the years that had followed.

"Yeah. I think I do know you."

But not as well as he planned to.

LATE THAT NIGHT, as Dylan helped the rest of the guys load their equipment and instruments into Josh's van, he tried to ignore Banks's curious stares. Banks had been watching him, a knowing grin on his face, every time Dylan had wandered over to the bar to talk to Cat when they were on break. During their final set, he'd thought his friend was going to explode with curiosity. Only the fact that the crowd had been so responsive—not letting them wrap up the night until they'd played an hour longer than scheduled—had distracted the guy.

But now they were alone. Josh and Jeremy had gone back inside for the last of Jeremy's drums. Banks made full use of the opportunity. "So, what happened? You going back in there for a late-night *rendezvous*?"

"Big words, Banks. Still working on being the smart one?"

"I don't think anyone's going to figure out I've got a 130 IQ just because I know how to pronounce the word *rendezvous*."

"One-thirty, hmm? I'm so sorry."

It was an old bone of contention and a constant source of baiting. Because Dylan's was just a smidge higher.

His friend smirked. "Warning, warning, comparing IQs…your geek-o-meter is in the red zone."

"F. You." But Dylan was smiling as he said it. He finished storing the microphones and amps, then helped Banks load up his keyboard.

"So, seriously, man, what are you going to do about the Cat woman?"

"Don't call her that."

"Right, 'cause, uh, she was much younger when you went nuts over her? So, it's Cat girl, huh?"

"Do you ever shut up?"

"You roomed with me in college, so you already know the answer to that question. Now stop stalling. Did she recognize you? Did she realize you were the same nerdy little nobody who used to practically wet your Dockers whenever she came around back in high school?"

Banks. Couldn't live with him. Couldn't kill him and throw his body off the Chrysler Building.

"She didn't remember me."

Banks had the courtesy not to laugh. In fact, he frowned a bit. "Well, you can't be too surprised, can you? I found your high school yearbook one time in college. You look *nothing* like you did back then."

High school. Seemed like a lifetime ago.

He'd only attended public school for one year—his senior year—and he'd been only fifteen years old the day he'd started. A skinny kid who'd been accepted into a dozen colleges before he'd even started shaving.

He'd wanted to be normal. Just…normal. Instead of the whiz kid who'd skipped a few grades in the exclusive private schools his parents insisted he attend. His one outlet—which had driven his parents nuts—was his nonstop devotion to his music. Even though his mom and dad had ranted about how he was burning his brain cells, betraying his intelligence and making a mockery of his brilliant musical gifts, he'd never stopped working out his teen angst with his stereo or his guitar.

Until that year. When he'd finally gotten them to agree to let him finish out school with regular kids for a change, in a public high school.

Their agreement had come at a cost. A high one.

His music. For the entire school year.

That'd been the price—he could spend his senior year at Kendall High if he agreed to let his father lock away his guitar and his entire CD collection.

God, it'd been hard. Particularly when he'd started school and realized a fifteen-year-old senior wasn't going to fit in very well anywhere. He'd missed his music terribly. So badly he thought about giving up—about going back to his old school less than a week into the new year.

Then he'd seen her—Cat Sheehan, the high school sophomore who'd fired his imagination and awoken every angsty teenage hormone in his body. She'd been the most beautiful girl he'd ever seen and her smile had literally made the breath leave his lungs.

So he'd stuck it out, somehow making it work, if only so he could catch glimpses of her throughout the day. Could feel his heart skip a beat when she smiled that smile. Could share, if only from a distance, in her delightfully wicked personality.

And after the night of the bonfire, he'd made it his personal mission to find out why there seemed to be another side to Cat that no one else in the world ever saw.

He never had. But maybe now, he'd have another chance.

Eventually, he'd found a way to fit in at Kendall High. He'd built his own group of friends. He'd done the brain thing—chess club, honor roll, debate team. He'd made his parents proud, devoting the entire year to more "appropriate" pursuits.

And he'd kept his promise, staying away from his guitar. But that hadn't stopped him from writing songs in his head. Songs about the blond angel who barely even knew he existed.

"I mean, it's not like you two had any classes together or anything, right?" Banks asked, still apparently thinking he needed to make Dylan feel better. "You were the same age, but you were a couple of years ahead of her."

"Right."

"So it's not like she knew you and then forgot about you."

"You don't have to try to cheer me up," Dylan said, surprised to realize it was the truth. "Like you said, I don't look anything like I did then."

Definitely not. Then he'd been a skinny runt, a geek and a freak. Nowhere near the realm of Cat Sheehan and her crowd.

Her crowd…well, actually, she hadn't had one. She'd fit in everywhere. Not a stuck-up cheerleader, not a druggie, not a jock, not a brain. She'd just been this nice, smart, funny girl who happened to look like a goddess. One who had a caustic wit and a strong sense of justice that could either get her out of trouble or—probably more often—deeper into it.

She'd been the girl everyone wanted to be like. The girl who'd told off the football squad. Who'd organized a blood drive when one of their classmates had been in a serious car accident. And who, on one occasion, had come to the vocal defense of a nerdy kid who'd made the enormous mistake of sitting at the jocks' table at lunchtime.

That'd been him.

She'd swooped in right before he'd gotten himself pounded. Taking him by the arm, she'd smiled brightly, saying, "You promised you'd sit with me, cutie." Then she'd pulled him up and tugged him away, the determination in her eye and the firm set of her lips daring anyone to try to stop her. Beelining to another corner of the cafeteria—a *safer* corner—she'd pushed him into a seat and plopped down next to him, staying for a good three minutes, to keep up appearances.

He hadn't been able to get a word out of his sawdust-dry mouth. But that'd been okay. She'd chatted nonstop about inane things—teachers, grades, the unfairness of the dress code.

Personally, Dylan had blessed the dress code. Because if her skirts had been any shorter, he'd have been unable to function at all in school.

Once the beefy crowd had left, she'd stood, saying, "Stay away from the fatheads, kid. Just remember, you'll be buying and selling them a hundred times over in ten years." Then, with a wink, she'd snagged his apple off his lunch tray and sauntered away. Leaving him sitting there, gaping, staring after her.

He'd loved her from that moment on, even knowing he'd probably never see her again after he graduated from high school. And he hadn't.

Until tonight.

"So are you going back in there to make something happen?"

"Why the hell are you so interested in my love life?" Dylan asked with a frown. "Weren't there a half-dozen women slipping you their phone numbers tonight?"

Banks shrugged. "A dozen, at least." Then his eyes narrowed. "Which was nothing compared to the ones trying to slip *you* their phone numbers. By the way, thanks for the spillover."

Dylan just shrugged, saved from replying when Josh and Jeremy returned from inside. They quickly finished loading the gear, then closed up the van.

"See ya tomorrow night," Josh said as he got into the driver's seat.

Dylan nodded, then glanced at Jeremy, who was climbing onto the enormous motorcycle he'd bought a few months back. Since Dylan cringed every time he saw Jeremy on the thing, he could only imagine what his parents thought. "Don't kill yourself, kid," he called as the younger man rode away.

"Now, go back in there and make your move," Banks said as he unlocked his car."

Dylan shook his head. He wasn't ready yet. Wasn't ready to deal with the repercussions of what would happen when Cat found out the truth. "It's late. I'll talk to her tomorrow."

Face it, you want to enjoy it a little longer.

He did. He wanted just this weekend—tomorrow and Sunday night—of being the dark, dangerous stranger Cat Sheehan had been so attracted to. Then he'd tell her the truth. And go back to being the invisible guy.

But not now. Now it was time to go home and process everything.

Unfortunately, Banks, the bastard, had something else in mind. "By the way, Spence, are you missing something?"

Dylan raised a wary brow.

Banks's expression screamed mischief. Dylan had seen the look enough in college to know his friend was up to something. Something he wasn't going to like. Like the time he'd taken Dylan's clothes out of the bathroom while he was showering in their coed dorm, stranding him there.

Of course, Banks's plan had backfired. Wrapped in a towel and dripping with righteous anger—not to mention water—Dylan had gotten the attention of a *lot* of girls as he'd stalked down the hall toward his room. Including one Banks had been after throughout their junior year. Whenever his friend got too obnoxious, Dylan mentioned the name Karen Dennison and it shut him right up.

"What did you do?" he asked, not sure he wanted to know.

"You forgetting you need something to get in your car?"

Patting the pocket of his ratty jean jacket, which was slung over his arm, he winced when he did not hear a familiar jingle. No keys. "You sack of…"

"She'll be happy to let you in to look for them, I bet. She's just all alone in the dark," Banks said with a wave of his hand. Then he got into his own car, revved up the engine so he couldn't hear the names Dylan was calling him, and took off.

Leaving Dylan stranded, with no way home and no keys. Not unless he entered into Temptation and found them.

CHAPTER THREE

EXHAUSTED AND CONFUSED about the amazing man who'd walked into her life tonight, Cat was about to flip the lock on the front door when she saw a large form appear right outside. The unexpectedness of it brought a startled gasp to her lips—until she recognized the face.

"Spence?" she said, opening the door.

"I forgot something," he explained, looking uncomfortable.

Hmm…had he *really* forgotten something? Or was this a ruse to get her alone. More important—did she care?

Cat stepped back and ushered him in. "You just made it. Ten more minutes and I'd have been upstairs, sound asleep."

Looking curious, Spence stepped inside. "Upstairs?"

She shouldn't have given him that information. Shouldn't have let this gorgeous stranger—to whom she was altogether too attracted—know she lived right upstairs. Slept right upstairs. Had a big, comfortable bed, right upstairs.

She told herself all that, then nodded and spilled her guts, anyway. "Yes, I have an apartment right above Temptation. Live there all by my lonesome."

God, she might as well have invited him up, it

probably would have sounded more honest and less pathetic.

"Convenient," was all he said as he stepped aside so she could push the door shut behind him.

The click of the door shut out the rest of the world, leaving them entirely alone. Completely, intoxicatingly alone.

The lights were all off in the main seating area of Temptation. One fixture, covered with smoked red glass, remained lit over the bar. It cast interesting pools of crimson throughout the room, its color whispering of sin and wickedness.

One additional dim light, which she usually left lit for security, provided a bit more illumination from the back hallway. Enough to reveal the skeletal legs of the chairs rising from the tables where Cat had put them up to sweep. But it wasn't strong enough to banish the shadows in the corners, on the stage or beside the jukebox. Nor to illuminate Spence's face well enough for her to gauge his mood. His intentions.

The pub at night was moody, secretive, sensuous… which matched *her* mood. The wood paneling caught bits of light, even as it creaked in late-night restlessness. Overhead, a fan spun lazily, its whir rustling the front blinds a bit. Their click was the only sound in an otherwise silent room.

That silence was thick, palpable, and Cat would bet Spence could hear the pounding of her heart if he listened for it.

All her internal alarms were ringing at the danger. Not that she feared physical danger from Spence. No, she simply feared she could very easily make a mistake she'd regret in the morning.

"Did you really forget something?" she finally asked,

wondering if he heard the huskiness in her tone, the thickness caused by her suddenly dry mouth.

"Yeah."

She crossed her arms and tilted her head back in challenge. Leaning her hip against an empty table, she peered at him in the darkness, more convinced than ever that he hadn't forgotten a damn thing. Except, maybe, to make a move. "What'd you forget?"

He stepped closer. Close enough so his jeans brushed against hers. Their arms met, too, the contact unexpected because she hadn't seen it coming in the dim light. Cat flinched, caught off guard by the heart-stopping sensuality of such a simple touch. She'd been touched much more intimately by men before. But even the most evocative ones hadn't been able to inspire the heat she was feeling now.

"You think I intentionally left my keys so I'd have to come back and get them?"

"Keys, huh?"

"Why else would I have come back?" His tone dared her to tell the truth—to admit the heated images filling her mind.

Cat shifted, brushing her bare arm against his again. This time he was the one who hissed—softly, almost inaudibly—but she heard it. So, he, too, was feeling the energy snapping between them, so potent and heady.

The tension built. She was barely touching his forearm, the hard angle of his wrist, but she reacted as if she were caressing the most sensitive parts of his body. The hairs on her arm stood on end and the nerve endings there tingled. She couldn't even imagine what it would be like to touch him all over.

"Maybe you came back for a good-night kiss," she said, dying for it to be true.

A kiss. Surely one little kiss wasn't going to stop the world and ruin all her good intentions.

And you really think a kiss is going to be enough?

No. Probably not. But she wanted it, anyway. Right at this moment, she wanted it more than she wanted to save the bar.

He laughed softly. "What makes you think I'm the kind of guy who kisses on the first day?"

Because I want you to be? Instead, she replied, "There's something between us."

"Yes."

"You're attracted to me."

"Yes."

Cat licked her lips. "So what are you gonna do about it?"

He said nothing for a long, heady moment. Then he leaned even closer, close enough so she felt his warm breath against her cheek. Smelled the aroma of warm cologne and warmer man.

"Kissing's very personal," he whispered.

She wobbled. Because his whisper had been right by her temple, so close she felt the brush of his lips. She tingled there. Everywhere.

"Very intimate."

This time, his words were accompanied by the soft, slight brush of his hand sliding up her arm. His palm just barely connected with her skin as he slid it from wrist to elbow, then higher, until his fingertips rested as light as a butterfly on her bare shoulder.

And suddenly she realized that he was seducing her. Not with anything as blatant as a kiss, but with these incredibly sensuous whispers, the almost-there touches that had her silently screaming for more. "Spence…"

"Shh," he said, coming closer, so his leg was almost between hers. Their thighs converged, sending a spiral of warm longing straight between hers. His long, smooth hair brushed against her cheek, his fingers still rested on her shoulders. His dark eyes glittered in the half light and she sensed the beating of his heart across the scant inch that separated her chest from his.

Every one of her senses roared to life, clamoring for more. Much more. She'd never been so aroused in her life. Never.

She was too weak to lift her arms around his neck. Too besotted to tilt her head back for his kiss. Too overwhelmed by the sensations battering her from every side to do much more than stand there and experience the intense awareness, the sound of his breath, the anticipation of his touch in the darkness.

"Please…"

Before she could say another word, he lowered his head and pressed one hot, erotic, open-mouthed kiss to the hollow of her throat. Cat's legs buckled. She grabbed for the nearest table, not sure she was going to be able to remain upright. "Oh, my God," she choked out.

Spence continued to delicately sample her skin as if tasting something delicious. "You know," he said softly, pulling only a breath away, "sometimes when you know something is going to be incredible, waiting for it makes it that much better."

He touched his lips to that hollow again, sliding them up the column of her throat in one smooth, delicate caress. And oh, Lord, he was right. Knowing how incredible—how explosive—their kiss would be when their mouths met, Cat practically groaned.

But just as he reached her chin—just as he built the anticipation of his lips on hers until she was as tense as a taut wire—he straightened and pulled away. And then he did the unthinkable. He stepped back, offered her one small, intimate smile, then turned around.

Cat could only watch, jaw hanging open, while he jumped up onto the stage and grabbed for something sitting on one of the chairs there. A clink told her it was his keys. It was a miracle she could hear them, considering her breathing was louder than a freight train.

"Good night, Cat," he said as he stepped off the stage.

Watching in shock, she couldn't manage a single word. Not until after he walked by her, right out the door. He pulled it shut behind him and disappeared into the night.

For several long moments, she remained silent. When her vocal cords did start working again, the only word she could manage was one she was supposed to have stricken from her vocabulary. And it sure wasn't ladylike.

"I NEED THE SLUTTIEST pair of shoes you've got."

Cat's jaw dropped open and she gaped at Gracie, who stood at her door Saturday morning. Way too early Saturday morning.

"What time is it?"

"Ten."

Cat groaned and staggered back, clearing the way for her usually quiet friend to barrel in. Gracie owned Between The Covers, the bookshop next door, and had apparently forgotten the cardinal rule: no banging on Cat's door at 10 a.m. on a Saturday when she'd been closing down the bar until three that morning.

It was a wonder she'd even heard Gracie's pounding, because she still felt half asleep. Not only because of the short duration of her night, but also because of the rather, uh, *interesting* dreams she'd had about a certain hot guitar player who'd aroused her nearly to the point of orgasm before walking out the night before.

He'd been naked in most of them. Naked and holding a jar of peanut butter.

"Cat, did you hear what I said? I need to borrow some shoes. The sluttiest ones in your closet."

Cat raised a hand to her chest. "Slut shoes? Moi?"

Gracie lifted one brow, just watching, until Cat grudgingly said, "Okay, slut shoes, *vous*?"

"Yes, me." Her tone said she wasn't kidding. Without another word, Gracie marched down the short hallway between Cat's living room and kitchen, heading toward the back of the small apartment. Once inside Cat's bedroom, she practically dove into the closet.

Cat followed. "You're serious?" she asked, leaning against the doorjamb, watching her friend dig frantically through her stockpile of footwear.

"Very. I want something high, strappy. Shoes that say I'm wicked and willing and sexy as can be."

Wow. This was so not Gracie. Not just the shoes, but the whole nervous, energetic frenzy. Gracie was the calm one of their foursome. The quiet, graceful one with her soft brown hair and lovely blue eyes. Not the one she'd expect to be on all fours in Cat's closet, flinging shoes over her shoulder one after another.

"Hate to remind you, but my feet are bigger than yours."

"Half a size. I'll stuff the toe."

With a chuckle, Cat knelt down to help look. There was a lot to look through. Cat had sort of a little thing for shoes. Actually, sort of a big thing for them. Imelda Marcos-size. Which anyone could tell with one look at the mountain of footwear in varying shades covering the entire floor of her closet.

"What color?" she asked, trying to narrow down the search.

"Black." Gracie brushed a strand of hair off her face, and squared her shoulders, looking resolute. "I'm going to my ten-year reunion tonight and I want the kind of shoes that make men drool and women think catty, mean things about other women."

Gracie didn't have a catty, mean bone in her body, so Cat immediately took her request more seriously. "Okay, forget this stuff, we need to go up a level. And oh, sister, are you in luck, because I have got just what you need!"

Cat rose to her feet—staggered, really, since her bones hadn't yet achieved her brain's level of wakefulness. Standing on tiptoe, she reached up to the top shelf of her closet, where another dozen or so shoe boxes were stacked in neat rows. This was where she stashed the good stuff. The ones on the floor were the throwaways. Up here were the jewels in her collection.

She zoned in on the third stack, where the black shoes began, organized by heel height. It didn't take long to find the box she was looking for. "I fell in love with these on the Jimmy Choo Web site and ordered them last year."

Gracie's eyes widened. "Jimmy Choo?"

Cat nodded. "Yep. I think I owe someone a kidney, but it was so worth it because they're to die for. And they're a teensy bit small on me, so they might fit you just perfectly."

Of course, they could have been three sizes too small and Cat would have done a Cinderella's stepsister thing and worn them, anyway. If it came down to a choice between toes and Jimmy Choos, the shoes would win every time.

She wondered if Spence liked women in spiked heels. And nothing else.

No. No more fantasies about the guy. After he'd walked out on her last night, she wasn't sure she'd ever let him back into her real life *or* her fantasy one.

Shrugging off the image, Cat watched Gracie nibble her lip in anticipation. Before taking off the lid, she cautioned, "You can't tell Laine about these, okay? She wouldn't understand that I considered it totally worthwhile to live on peanut butter sandwiches for a month so I could afford these."

Mmm. Peanut butter. That brought Spence right back to the forefront of her mind. Again. Dammit, he had no business being so desirable, not after the way he'd aroused her to insanity, then left her hanging there. She might never speak to him again, much less get personal with a jar of peanut butter.

Unless he kissed her throat again. Then she was a goner.

Gracie nodded. "Deal."

Cat removed the top and peeled back the paper, watching for Gracie's reaction.

Silent awe. They shared it for a few moments, gazing at the glory of the shoes, as would any other red-blooded American female. The other half of the population didn't get and never would get the shoe thing, but women of all ages, shapes and sizes would pause to pay homage to these things of beauty.

Then Gracie whispered, "Those are perfect!"

"Haute couture slut shoes," Cat said with pride.

"I owe you."

Cat shrugged. "Just don't knock on my door at 10 a.m. tomorrow to tell me how it went."

Gracie's pretty blue eyes suddenly shifted away, and Cat wondered exactly what the woman was up to. But she didn't pry. Everybody had secrets—including Cat.

Besides, considering Gracie's bookstore was going to be every bit as out of business as Temptation, she figured the woman was entitled to her own private let-it-all-out party.

"I hear the place was packed last night," Gracie said. "Must have been some band you booked."

Cat looked away. "Uh-huh. He was something else."

"He? A one-man band?'"

Cursing her dumb, sleepy, one-track brain, Cat said, "Oh, no, sorry, I meant they. They were something else."

Gracie wasn't buying it. "Who's the 'he'?"

Cat couldn't even try to come up with a cover story. "He's a drop-dead gorgeous bass player named Spence who is exactly the kind of guy Laine and my mother would have heart attacks over if I ever brought him around for dinner."

Nodding, Gracie put the lid back onto the shoe box, then gave Cat a tiny half smile.

"Then I'd say it's a good thing Laine and your mother are far, far away."

DYLAN DECIDED BEFORE leaving his house in Tremont Saturday afternoon that come hell or high water, before the night was out, he'd have kissed Cat Sheehan. *Really* kissed her.

One kiss. He'd deliver the kiss he'd all but promised both of them last night. The one worth waiting nine years for.

Then, and only then, would he be able to tell her the truth: who he was, how she knew him. He'd come clean about where he lived, what he really did. All of it.

Except, perhaps for the song. He wasn't quite ready

to share that, or his memories of the bonfire. But everything else was getting laid out on the table.

Too bad *he* wasn't.

"Knock it off," he told himself, knowing he'd better not let his mind go down that road. Not if he wanted to be comfortable in his jeans for the rest of the night.

He forced himself to focus on his confession. Honesty was the key. He'd tell her everything, right down to that moment in the cafeteria when her pretty white teeth had bitten into his apple and taken a chunk out of his heart.

Okay, strike that, too. He'd mention the apple part, but not necessarily his heart. Because he certainly wasn't the same nerdy fifteen-year-old kid he'd been then. He now knew his teenage infatuation with Cat had been merely that…infatuation. First love, when love had seemed to be the only explanation because of the goofy smile that always came to his lips whenever he saw her walk by. Or the way time had seemed to stand still whenever he'd heard her laugh. Not to mention the way he'd made himself believe he was the only person who saw the serious, lonely side of the most popular girl in school.

Then it had felt like love. *Now* he recognized it as a raging case of hormones. Those immature feelings had nothing to do with adult emotions, and it would be silly to bring them up. He'd embarrass them both, particularly when the keen interest and heat faded from Cat's eyes as she realized he *wasn't* the dangerous, reckless guy she'd always seemed to date back in high school.

Not even close.

He was still a brain, still quiet, and still kept to himself when he wasn't on stage. As for dangerous? Well, he was about as ruthless and tough as a guppy. The only part of the wild side he walked on with regularity these days was when he appeared with the Four G's.

And considering what the name of their band stood for, that *wasn't* very wild at all.

Dylan arrived in downtown Kendall a little early Saturday, hoping for some alone time with Cat before the bar crowd drifted in. Actually, he arrived a *lot* early. It was only five and they weren't due to play until eight. "Too early," he told himself. "She'll think you're a stalker."

He sat in his car in the parking garage a block away from the bar. He'd parked here instead of in the small lot behind her building for one reason: because he didn't want Cat to know he drove an expensive, boring, imported sedan. Just like he didn't want her to know he lived in a moderately pricey neighborhood in Tremont, in a large, modern three-bedroom house, whose only claim to being hip was the incredible sound system he'd had built into it during construction.

She wouldn't understand any of it. Cat wouldn't be able to associate the car, the house—and certainly not his job as a software designer and consultant—with the laid-back band member she'd been coming on to last night.

Coming on to. Yeah. She had been. They both knew it. Like they both knew he could have taken things a hell of a lot further last night if his conscience hadn't kicked in and demanded he leave.

Which was why he knew he had to take his shot and kiss her, just once, before telling her the truth. Because if he knew Cat—and he did—she would *not* be coming on to a guy she thought was a boring software geek who had his oil changed every three thousand miles and invested in tech stocks.

Besides, it wasn't as if he'd be taking anything she didn't want to give, judging by the way they'd danced around the sizzling awareness last night. Only a fool wouldn't act on that awareness at least once before it disappeared forever.

Hoisting his guitar case over his shoulder, he hoofed it to Temptation, walking through the front door to find the place pretty much deserted. Though it was just after five on a Saturday, not one pub diner sat at any of the tables munching on a greasy burger. No hard-core, all-day weekend drinkers were staring up at the television, where a ball game was going on.

The only person around was Cat.

Who was lying flat on her back on top of the bar.

He grinned, unable to help it, and quietly approached her. Wondering what she was doing, he stood in the shadows several feet away, just watching. With a sigh he could hear from here, Cat lifted a pencil, took aim and threw it straight up. Following the pencil's ascent with his gaze, he saw it join several others sticking into the ceiling over the bar.

Somebody had obviously been bored today.

"I think it took Mulder about three seasons of *The X-Files* to get that many pencils on the ceiling of his office."

She didn't even look over. "Took me about three hours."

"You know, a fly swatter would probably be more effective."

She chuckled. "If I were going after Texas houseflies, I'd be using a shotgun, not pencils."

He walked to the bar, putting his guitar case on the floor beside it. Sliding onto a stool, he smiled down at her. "Bad day?"

She rolled her eyes. "You're the second person who's walked in since we opened at one. And the first one was a construction guy asking to use the bathroom."

He frowned. "You didn't shoot him, did you?"

Cat finally looked over, her eyes twinkling in sudden merriment. "Not even with a pencil." Then she looked up at the ceiling again. "It's not his fault. He just works for the bureaucrats—he doesn't make the lousy decisions."

He gave an exaggerated sigh. "Whew. Because I still don't have a shovel handy."

A tiny grin tugged at her lips. "You'd help me bury the body?"

He leaned closer over the bar, looking down at her beautiful face. "Oh, absolutely."

Their eyes met, their stares holding for a long, thick moment. Cat's grin faded and so did Dylan's.

That awareness was back. Made more intense by her provocative position—flat on her back. And his position—above her. They were both remembering the last time they'd seen each other, right here, during their relatively innocent exchange that had been so incredibly intimate.

Cat was the one who looked away first, though the color in her cheeks made a lie of her casual tone. "Well, thanks anyway, but I haven't murdered anyone yet."

Dylan followed her lead, ignoring the sexual attraction dancing so strongly between them. She obviously wanted to pretend last night hadn't happened. That was fine with him.

For now.

Straightening a bit on his stool, he asked, "You have fought this road issue as far as you can, I assume?"

She nodded. "Yeah. There's nothing more to do. The

city has named the date and time of demolition. We have to be out of here by June 30 at the very latest."

He shook his head. "I'm really sorry, Cat."

She picked up another pencil from a pile next to her jean-clad hip. "I'm handling it." This time when she threw it, Dylan was much closer. Close enough to see the way her tight, sleeveless red shirt pulled even tighter across her body as she flexed her arm. And a tempting, creamy strip of skin across her belly where her shirt pulled free of the waistband of her white jeans.

She didn't even seem aware of how each graceful movement accentuated the soft curve of her shoulder, the vulnerable, pale skin of her neck. Nor how she was affecting him. Which, for a woman as sensually aware as Cat, indicated the depth of her bad mood.

He glanced away, trying to keep his breathing slow and steady. Swallowing hard, he forced his attention back to their conversation. "So what are you going to do after you close?"

She shrugged. "Not sure yet."

"I assume the city's giving you a fair price for the building? The law requires them to give you market value and downtown properties sell for a good amount."

Cat looked over again, raising a curious brow. Dylan realized he'd sounded a little more like a lawyer than a laid-back musician. He gave her a self-deprecating look. "I watch *Law & Order.*"

"Well, that's good to know, in case I do murder the next construction worker who comes in looking for a bathroom." Grinning, she abruptly sat up on the bar and swiveled around so her legs dangled off the front of it. She was close. So close her hip almost touched his arm. And the awareness factor shot up a notch.

He tightened his fingers into a fist on his lap and

forced a casual tone. "You never answered my question about the sale."

"The city is paying a good amount for the land, but since my mother and uncle still own the building, the bulk of it will go to them."

Ouch. He hadn't figured on that. He'd assumed Cat owned the place and would be financially stable after the shutdown. Stable enough to stick around town for a while.

"I'm hopeful, though," she admitted softly, "that I'll have enough to help me go to school part-time." She looked as if she regretted it the minute the words left her mouth.

"School? You want to go back to college?"

"Basically *start* college. I think I lasted one-and-a-half semesters at the community college before I dropped out. But I'm ready for it now."

"What do you want to do?"

She looked away. "You'll laugh."

"No," he replied, meaning it, "I won't."

Lifting her hand to her mouth and almost covering her lips, she mumbled, "I'd like to teach high school."

Dylan coughed a bit as the air in his throat turned a little grainy. Talk of high school cut way too close to comfort.

"You're laughing," she snapped.

"No, I'm absolutely *not* laughing. I think that's fantastic and you'd be a great teacher. Being able to deal with people from all walks of life, to listen and advise and befriend anybody who pulls up a stool at your bar is a remarkable bonus for someone who wants to teach teen-agers."

She didn't look entirely convinced, but finally, she shrugged. "Well, who knows. Right now all I've done is call for an application. I haven't even visited the university campus."

"You should. You definitely should."

She again lowered her head, shielding her expressive face with her long hair, appearing uncomfortable at having started the conversation. "We'll see. There's so much to do in the meantime, and without anybody else around, it's not going to be easy."

"So why *aren't* they here helping with all this going-out-of-business stuff?"

"There's a good question. God, all my life I've been waiting for my family to treat me like a responsible adult who can do more than pour beer. Be careful what you wish for, right? Because now they're all gone and I'm handling everything by myself."

She let out a tiny laugh—definitely forced—which made Dylan reassess her mood. Cat being alone in the bar when he'd arrived hadn't merely been about a lack of customers. It had somehow symbolized much more. As if she were totally alone in her life. And more than a little unhappy about it.

Which got him thinking about those occasional lonely moments he'd witnessed in high school. The other Cat only he had seen.

Judging by the way she crossed her arms and looked away, she didn't want to continue that conversation, so Dylan looked up at the ceiling. "You gonna leave them hanging there?"

She shrugged. "The wrecking ball can handle a few pencils, I think." Then she added, "This looks pathetic, I know, but I've always wanted to do it. I used to imagine lying on top of the bar when I was a kid. I figured I might as well do it while I have the chance. Nobody was around to see."

Since she was now sitting above him, instead of lying below him, Dylan had to look up again to answer. He tried to focus only on her face, but it was tough with her curvy body so close to his. Her breasts were at eye level and it was all he could do to keep his stare firmly above them. "Anything else you've always wanted to do in here?"

She looked around the room, studying the groupings of tables, the small stage, the jukebox. Then, with a small nod, she admitted, "Yeah. A few things."

The secretive smile playing about her lips made him very curious about what kinds of things. When she didn't elaborate, he prodded, "One of them have anything to do with that stage?"

She nibbled her lip and nodded. "Uh huh. And different colored spotlights."

The wicked glint in her eye told him she wasn't necessarily thinking of performing on that stage, but he still had to ask, "Are you a closet singer?"

"A shower singer," she admitted. "A tone-deaf shower singer. Even worse than Tess."

"Tess?"

A tiny frown appeared on Cat's brow. "She's one of our waitresses. She had to leave town unexpectedly."

Sensing the subject was a sore one, he didn't ask for details. "So what do you see yourself doing on the stage?"

Her eyes flared and her lips parted as she drew in a slow, deep breath. The intensity shot up, as he imagined Cat, naked, highlighted in the colored spotlights she'd mentioned. Having hot, erotic sex on the stage, bathed in all that light.

"I'm not sure I'm ready to share that particular fantasy."

Dylan shook his head and managed a rueful grin. "To be honest with you, I'm not sure I'm ready to hear it."

"Chicken?"

"Self-preservationist. I have to go up there and perform in a couple of hours. And it won't be easy if I'm imagining you the way I'm picturing you right now."

His husky words dared her to go further in this sexy game of supposition—to ask him what he was picturing. But Cat didn't take the bait this time. Just as well. If she confirmed his most heated imaginings, Dylan didn't think he'd be able to stop at the one simple kiss he planned to have from her in a very short while.

Reaching into a bowl on the bar, he grabbed a fistful of peanuts and tossed a few into his mouth. A stall for time, but it worked. Because eventually his pulse stopped racing and his groin obeyed his brain's command to go back into standby mode instead of running things, as it wanted to.

"So," he asked, "what else do you plan to do before you shut the doors for the last time? Tap dancing on the tables?"

She snickered. "Tap dancing? If my mother had tried to put me in a pair of tap shoes as a kid, I would have used them to kick down the nearest door and escape."

Sounded like something the wild young Cat would have done. Sounded like something the *adult* Cat would do now.

"But I might just have to dance on top of this bar one of these nights," she added, stroking the smooth wood surface with the palm of one hand. "To something slow and smoky."

Smoky. A word most people wouldn't think of in connection with music, but one which made perfect sense to Dylan. It was sensual, perfectly apt for this woman who continued to caress the wood with lingering strokes of her long, delicate fingers.

Unable to resist, he smoothed his own hand over the mahogany, feeling what she was feeling. Experiencing the same touch Cat so obviously savored.

It was smooth. Warm. Slick. Strong and solid. And probably held a great many memories for the young woman sitting there, touching the surface of something that meant so much to her. Something she was being forced to give away.

His gut twisted. Cat revealed so much, without even saying a word. The way she tenderly rubbed the tips of her fingers over a scratch here, a gouge there, revealed the depth of her emotions.

It had to be like losing a part of herself.

God, he wished there were something he could do to help her through it. Then he realized there was. Because until he'd walked through the door, she'd been completely and utterly alone.

And now she wasn't.

"So," he finally said, "is there anything else you have to get out of your system before you move?"

She cocked her head, thinking about it. "Well, I fully intend to sunbathe naked in the garden out back at least once before they kick me out."

The air in his mouth suddenly tasted thick and dusty. Dylan couldn't help coughing a bit at the mental image of Cat lying naked in the sunlight, glorious, pagan and seductive.

"Sorry, did I shock you?" she asked, not sounding a bit sorry. "You don't look like the type to be easily shocked."

No, the wild, up-for-anything rock and roller she saw when she looked at him wouldn't be easily shocked.

And he wasn't. The images cascading in his brain weren't shocking. They were...intoxicating.

"I'm not shocked," he said softly, letting her see the heat in his eyes. "Just picturing...the possibilities."

This time, Cat was the one who appeared a little breathless. Her lips parted and she nervously licked at them, eliciting another nearly silent groan of reaction from him. Dylan covered the sound by clearing his throat.

"Oh," she said.

"Feel free to let me know when you're going to be checking off all the items on your to-do list," he said, not quite achieving the light tone he'd been going for. "I'd be happy to keep watch."

"You mean you'd be happy to watch."

"What if I gave my Scout's honor not to even sneak a peek?"

A grin tugged at her mouth. "Then I think I'd be terribly disappointed."

"You flirting with me again?"

Raising a hand to her chest, she said, in feigned innocence, "Flirting? Me? When have I ever flirted with you?"

"Uh, I think last night when you were working the bar there was some definite flirting."

"No, last night when I was working the bar there was some definite foot-in-mouth disease going around."

"I liked that about you."

"That I came across as a stammering idiot?"

No. That *he'd* made her react like a stammering idiot. But he wasn't about to admit that. "It was cute."

"Puppies are cute." She sounded disgruntled. "I prefer to be a sleek, mysterious feline."

"Hence the name."

"Speaking of names, you going to tell me the rest of yours?" she asked.

He could. Here was the golden opportunity to jog Cat's memory and see what happened. He almost did it, wanting to see something—a spark of recognition, anything—on Cat's face. Only one thing stopped him.

He still hadn't gotten his kiss.

"Spence is enough."

She shrugged. "Suit yourself." Then, swinging her legs back and forth over the edge of the bar, she asked, "So why'd you show up here so early tonight, Spence?"

She sounded friendly, almost glad that he had. Not suspicious at all. Which made him suddenly feel uncomfortable for not being honest with her. He really needed to come clean. But the only words he could manage were, "No particular reason. I can leave if I'm keeping you away from any pressing...pencil-tossing."

She shook her head, sending that long cascade of golden hair bouncing over her shoulders. A sudden rush of longing flashed through him, making his hands tingle at the thought of burying them in all her glorious hair. And he refocused on his goal: one kiss. One kiss before he lost his chance with her forever.

"So, do you want me to go?" he asked, his voice low but intense.

"No," she replied, suddenly sounding much less jaunty and much more serious. "I think I want you to stay."

CHAPTER FOUR

CAT HAD BEEN TRYING since the previous night to convince herself that a long-haired, dark-eyed musician was not someone she could allow on her radar, much less into her life. She'd been hammering the point home in her brain with every toss of a pencil into the ceiling, building up strength to be cool, aloof and reserved when he showed up that night.

Not bloody likely.

Because he'd gone and shown up early, looking all sexy, scruffy, dangerous and hot, and her good intentions had gone right out the window, along with her common sense.

Now things had gotten worse. Because now, when she was truly alone with him, she had to concede it wasn't mere sexual attraction she felt for the man. She liked him. Liked spending time with him. Liked the husky timbre of his voice and the way his eyes crinkled when he smiled.

Mostly, she liked the way he looked at her: as if he could see past every facade she'd erected, into the deep, innermost woman known to no one else in the world.

His intensity charged her up like nothing else. More than his sex appeal, more than his incredible looks, or his great sense of humor, it was the certainty that he knew exactly what made Cat Sheehan tick that she found nearly irresistible.

So, for the next hour or so, she didn't even try to resist. It wasn't *too* dangerous—after all, though they were alone, somebody could walk into Temptation at any moment. She couldn't get into too much trouble.

Yeah, right. She was the one walking into Temptation. Because if he so much as lifted a finger to touch her cheek, she'd almost surely be diving into his lap.

The realization should have been enough to make her get off the bar, walk behind it and busy herself doing nonsense work. Anything to give him the message that she was not interested.

It didn't. Instead, she set aside thoughts of where she'd be living next month, of the changes she was supposed to make, the swearing off of guys with no future and danger in their every movement. And she allowed herself to enjoy his company.

Probably would have been safer to just leap on him, kiss the taste out of his mouth and give in to the attraction. Because the whole liking thing seemed infinitely more dangerous.

Still, how could she *not* like him? He had a wicked sense of humor, kept up with her in the one-liners and had been incredibly understanding when she'd gone on a long ramble about the loss of her family legacy.

He wasn't too chatty, but his carefully chosen words both amused and intrigued her. Especially because every time she tried to learn more about the man, he managed to change the subject.

Curiosity. It was Cat's downfall. Hers was now killing her.

She wanted to know him better. Who he really was. Where he was from. What made him tick. What his amazing mouth tasted like.

"So," he said, interrupting her heated musings, "since

you're not exactly packing them in, why don't you take a break. Let me wait on you for a change? I make a damn good margarita."

Cat's jaw dropped. "You want to wait on *me*?"

Nodding, Spence rose from his stool and walked around behind the bar. "When's the last time you sat out there and let someone make you a drink?"

Uh, never, that she could recall. By the time she was old enough to drink, she was already working at the pub, and was running it—with Laine's help—a year later. "I'm not sure I've ever sat on the receiving side of the bar," she admitted, looking down from her perch. Realizing it was one more thing she could do that she'd never done before, she hopped down and slid onto the stool Spence had just vacated.

Tapping her finger with mock impatience, she said, "What's a person gotta do to get some service around here?"

"What'll it be?"

With a saucy tilt of her head, Cat said, "Maybe I want a Slippery Nipple."

His eyes flashed, but his jaw didn't drop in shock. Instead, he leaned an elbow on the bar, and leaned over it. "Well then, maybe you should take off your shirt and I'll see what I can do."

Hers was the jaw that dropped. "It's a *drink*. Irish cream and butterscotch schnapps."

Raising a brow in complete innocence, he said, "Well, how could I *possibly* have known that?"

The tiny grin he couldn't hide made Cat shake her head in rueful amusement. He'd turned the tables on her. "You got me."

"You started it."

Yeah, she had, to her dismay. Because, wow, the echo

of this man's voice telling her to take off her shirt was going to be ringing in her head all night.

"Most people don't know what it is," she said, hoping he wouldn't notice the weakness of her voice. "Women are usually too embarrassed to order it from male bartenders. And guys don't drink it."

"I dunno," he said. "Sounded kind of interesting to me. Warm. Sweet. Creamy." His voice was a little thick as he continued. "Might be something I'd like to try late some night."

Cat's body immediately reacted to the suggestive words and tone. Not to mention the way his gaze shifted so he could cast a lazy, appreciative look down the front of her body.

Drawing in a slow, steady breath, she shifted in her seat again, the stool hard and uncomfortable against her suddenly very tender bottom half. Her nipples grew taut and tight, achy, as she pictured Spence having his drink…sucking and licking it right off her breasts. Just as he'd intended her to.

"Now, do you really want a Slippery Nipple?" His tone was pure velvet. Pure seduction. "Because I'd be happy to take care of that for you."

Oh, God, yes!

If her breasts could speak, that's exactly what they'd have screamed. Because she was dying for him to kiss her, stroke her, run his tongue in lazy circles around her nipple before taking it into his mouth and sucking. Hard, fast. Deep.

A tiny sigh escaped her lips and she closed her eyes briefly. When she opened them again, she realized Spence had straightened up, giving her some space.

The sensible Cat—the one who knew somebody could walk through the door at any moment, and that if she continued with this sensual game, she might do something really dangerous—answered. "Margarita will be fine."

He nodded. "Frozen or on the rocks?"

"Rocks," she ordered, unable to do much more than stare as Spence got to work squeezing limes and grabbing for their best tequila. Triple Sec. Then he proved he really knew what he was doing and reached for the Cointreau.

"Salt?"

A margarita without salt? Horrors. "Of course."

Finishing her drink, he slid it across the broad surface of the bar, looking pleased with himself. When she brought the drink to her lips and sipped it, she knew why. "This is good."

"Damn good," he said.

No false modesty here. She liked that about him, too. And she wondered what else he might be damn good at.

She sipped again, using the tart iciness of her drink to cool off the heat of her thoughts. Because other than his bartending and musical skills, she had no business wondering what else Spence was good at. No business at all.

"So no guy has ever made you a drink?"

"Most people are scared to serve a bartender," she admitted. "I guess it would kinda be like somebody cooking for a chef."

"You're *that* good?"

Cat wasn't falsely modest, either. "Yeah." Then, with a wry laugh, she admitted, "And, of course, most of the guys I've dated wouldn't know how to *spell* margarita, much less make one."

"No Einsteins in your little black book, hmm?"

"Uh, no."

"Why not?"

Why not indeed? She almost told him the truth. She was the one who usually threw up barriers with smarter, everyday nice guys who occasionally came into her world. Laine had once said it was because Cat had self-esteem issues—not about her looks, but about her personality and brains. As if thinking of herself as the black sheep of the Sheehan family had made her think she wasn't qualified to seek out a nice, respectable guy.

Cat didn't know much about psychology, but she sometimes wondered if Laine was on to something. Because Cat did have a history of sabotaging any relationship with a decent man that looked as if it could actually go anywhere. It seemed safer to stick with the bad boys because there was no danger of getting her heart trampled on when they walked out the door. If she started out expecting them to go, she couldn't be devastated when they did.

Wrong. Don't think like that.

Just because practically everybody had left in the past—through death, retirement, remarriage or wildfire adventures—didn't mean everyone would in her future. One way or another, she was going to convince herself it was possible to find someone to share her life. Someone normal and safe who'd actually want to stick around.

Someone totally unlike the incredible guy she'd been flirting with since last night.

She sighed heavily, then stiffened her shoulders in resolve. Dammit, she was going to change if it killed her. And she had to admit it, watching the way Spence moved with such casual, male grace—knowing she would never *really* see what he could do—it just might.

"No time for any little black book these days," she finally said. "I've been focused totally on the business for the past few years."

"And now?" he asked.

Now? What now? Well, wasn't that the question of the hour? Of the year, really. What was she going to do now?

"Let's talk about you for a while. Why don't you tell me about her?" Cat asked, surprising even herself when she voiced the question.

"Who?"

The woman you loved. The one you still think about, judging by the way you sing her song.

Instead, she explained, "The woman who inspired the song you wrote. The one with the fire in her eyes."

Spence said nothing for a moment, simply looking at her intently. Cat forced her stare to remain steady, as if she was merely curious, making idle conversation. Instead of prying deeply into this man's heart—his romantic past.

She had no business asking, she had less business knowing.

But she couldn't help it.

"She was someone I knew a long time ago," he admitted.

"She broke your heart?"

He laughed softly. "She never knew it was hers to break." With a shrug, he added, "She hardly even noticed me."

Unrequited love? Didn't seem possible—not with this man. What woman could have him in her life and not notice him? Not be overwhelmed by all that confidence, that sexy, seething attractiveness? "She must have been an idiot."

His eyes twinkled. "No. She was just…out of my league."

Oh, now she got it. He'd fallen for some snotty rich bitch who'd thought a down-and-out musician was beneath her.

Isn't that what you've been trying to tell yourself?

No. No, it wasn't. Spence wasn't beneath her. Ha. If anything, she *wanted* him beneath her. On top of her. Anywhere she could have him.

Don't go there, Cat.

No, her need to keep some kind of barriers between her and the hunky musician had nothing to do with class or status, and everything to do with her need to change direction in her life.

He was just the wrong guy at the wrong time.

Lifting her glass, she finished her drink in two deep sips, smacking her lips together when she was done. Spence watched her intently.

"What?"

"You liked it."

"I liked it."

He leaned across the bar, resting on his elbow. "So I guess I'm gonna get a pretty big…tip."

The way he said the word *tip* made her think he had something other than money in mind. When he caught the base of her margarita glass between two fingers and pulled it out of the way so he could lean closer, she began to figure out what it was.

"If you wanted a taste, you could have made your own," she said breathily.

"I don't want my own drink, Cat," he murmured. "But I definitely want a taste."

"A kiss for a tip?"

"Uh-huh. One kiss."

Oh, God, one kiss. That was like saying one potato chip or one M&M. Some things were just meant to be done in multiples.

She should tell him to shove off. Should send him out the door and order him not to come back until showtime.

Instead, she scowled and answered with the first words that came to her lips. "If you kiss my throat and then walk away from me again, you're going to be wearing what's left of this drink."

He laughed softly. "I have no intention of wearing your drink. And no intention of walking away until I get my kiss."

Her heart raced as Spence touched her cheek with the tip of his index finger and tilted her head up. He didn't try to grab her, didn't force her toward him, but the touch of his finger on her face was magnetic. She leaned closer. Closer. Until their lips were a whisper apart.

Then, suddenly, there was nothing between them at all.

A kiss, it's just a kiss, she tried to remind herself.

But it was no use. Because the moment Spence's warm, tender mouth met hers, she was lost. Lost in his taste, in the warmth of the breaths they shared. In the slip of his tongue against her bottom lip, which made her whimper with the need for more. He complied, lazily licking at the crease between her lips until she parted them for him and met his tongue with her own.

Soon all thought ceased and sensation took over. Sweet and hot and silky smooth, the kiss went on and on, a mating of lips and tongue as intimate as any embrace Cat had ever experienced, though they touched in no other place.

Whoever said a kiss was just a kiss had never been kissed by this man. Because with Spence, a kiss was flat-out lovemaking. He made hot, tender love to her mouth until she began to quiver, to shake almost with the need for this to go on and on and on.

But it didn't. It couldn't. Nothing perfect could go on forever, and he finally—regretfully—lifted his mouth away from hers. The heat emanating from his eyes warmed her all over again, promising her more. So much more. Later.

Cat couldn't stand it. She wanted more *now*. She leaned forward again, silently begging him to kiss her.

And promptly fell off the damn stool.

DYLAN WATCHED Cat gently touch a fresh bag of ice to her forehead, feeling incredibly guilty for causing her pain. "Any better?" he asked.

"My head or my ego?"

He chuckled, not answering that one.

The two of them were in the tiny kitchen of Cat's apartment, upstairs from the bar. They'd retreated there immediately after her accident. Fortunately, Cat's part-time waitress—Dinah—had arrived for work and was on duty downstairs. Dinah had walked in just in time to see Cat fall off her stool and whack her head on the edge of the bar. So, at least she didn't think Dylan was some kind of abuser.

Good thing, because Cat was sporting both a lump on her forehead and a fat lip. She looked downright disreputable…as if she'd been in a bar fight.

And she still looked every bit as beautiful as she did the day she'd stolen his apple.

"Feeling better?" he asked, watching with concern

while she rubbed the pack of ice back and forth over the small lump, already lightly bruised.

She shook her head.

"Do you need some aspirin or something?"

"I'm not in pain," she admitted grudgingly. "But my humiliation quota has been just about used up."

"It could have happened to anyone."

Sighing, she leaned back and rested her head against one of the upper cabinets. A bit of condensation from the bagged ice slipped down her temple, disappearing into the fine, golden hair just above her ear. Dylan drew in a deep breath, then slowly released it, reminding himself that she was hurting. Picturing slow, seductive droplets of water slowly riding across every curve and indentation of her body was not very gentlemanly.

Neither was watching the way her small pink tongue kept sliding out of her mouth, delicately testing the tenderness of the small lump on her bottom lip.

Clenching his fists and tightening his jaw, Dylan tore his attention away from her face. He did not need to think about Cat's lips—her soft lips, which had kissed him back with such erotic tenderness. Nor about her sweet tongue and delicious mouth, which he'd explored so thoroughly a little while ago.

He didn't know what might have happened if she hadn't fallen. If he'd have dived back in for another kiss—coming right over the top of the bar if need be. Because one thing was for damn sure—one kiss had *not* been enough. Now, having kissed her, he knew the only thing that would satisfy him would be making love to this woman.

"How do you manage to bring out my formerly well-disguised klutz tendencies?" she asked, sounding more amused than annoyed.

Crossing his arms, he leaned one hip against the counter on which Cat was sitting. "The stool was old and wobbly."

"My *legs* were wobbly."

Dylan couldn't help his first reaction—pleasure that his kiss had made her weak in the legs. Or his second—to cast an instant glance toward those long, slim legs. That was when he noticed the flecks of red there, stark and blatant against the white fabric of her jeans. "Uh, hate to tell you this, but it looks like your bloody lip did a little more damage."

Cat followed his stare and groaned. "Dammit, these are brand-new," she muttered.

"You should put something on the stains before they set," he said, figuring she would dab some stain remover on it while she still wore the jeans.

Not that she'd…she wouldn't…

But she did. Before he could say another word, Cat had dropped her bag of ice and hopped off the counter. Kicking her sneakers off her feet, she unsnapped, unzipped, and wriggled out of her jeans while he stood there, watching, wide-eyed and speculative.

As if she'd forgotten he was even in the room, she turned to the sink and put her jeans under some running water. That left him staring at a quite delectable view from behind. Her thick blond hair flowed halfway down her back, bright against her red top. His breathing grew shallow as he focused on her long, bare legs—graceful and slim and soft-looking. Then he allowed himself to glance at the barely covered curves of her bottom, clad only in a teeny pair of white nylon panties that barely qualified as underwear.

Could have been worse, he supposed as he tried to control a shudder of pure, undiluted want. She could have been a thong woman. Though, only in his immediate circumstances would that have been a bad thing.

Then he noticed a swirl of color peeking up from the hem of her panties. Cat had a tattoo. A sexy-as-hell, breath-stealing tattoo. Blues and greens created delicate patterns on the small, vulnerable part of her back, right above her delectable cheeks, and he realized he was looking at a butterfly's wings unfurled in a delicate spiral. The cacophony of delicate color and vulnerable skin begged to be explored. With his mouth.

"Is it cold water for blood, or hot?" Cat asked, looking over her shoulder just in time to catch him staring at her ass. Her face pinkened and she slowly turned around.

That's when things went from bad to worse.

A saint would have looked, and Dylan was no saint. He allowed himself about three seconds of wicked visual indulgence, during which he noticed every detail. The jut of her hip. The wide swath of pale, perfect skin between the bottom hem of her shirt and the top of her nearly-there panties. The thinness of the nylon. The tiny bit of elastic scraping just above a shadow of curls visible through the fabric.

Dylan's pulse skipped a few beats. Then, using every bit of strength he had, he forced his eyes to shut, his imagination to shut *down*, and his libido to shut *off.*

When he opened his eyes again, he expected to see an empty room—expected Cat to have darted out for clothes.

She hadn't moved an inch. She simply watched him, silently, a hint of challenge evident by the slight quirk of her lips.

He groaned, low in his throat, and gave her a warning look. "Cat…"

"I don't usually whip off my clothes in front of strangers," she said, taking a step away from the sink toward the middle of the room. Toward him.

"We're not strangers," he pointed out, taking a step of his own. One step toward insanity.

"But really, I've got bikinis that are smaller." She sounded a little defensive. Not to mention breathless.

He risked another step. "Uh-huh." Raking one hot glance from her face down to her toes, he bit out, "Probably not quite as sheer, though."

Cat's eyes widened. Even from here, a few feet away, he could hear the rasp of her choppy breaths, could see the color rise in her cheeks and a sparkle of excitement glitter in her eyes. "So," she whispered, "I suppose I should go get some other clothes."

They each took one more step. Now he was less than a foot away from her. Less than twelve inches. Easily within arm's reach of all the delightful places on her body that he longed to touch. He kept his hands at his sides through sheer force of will. "You don't have to on my account."

One of her fine blond eyebrows lifted. "A gentleman might have turned his back."

Tilting his head to the side, he responded, "Whatever made you think I was a gentleman?"

His hand reached out before his brain sent the message not to, and within an instant he was touching her hip, then tugging her forward. Trailing his fingertips along the edge of the elastic, he caressed that soft, intimate skin between her stomach and heaven, until Cat literally gasped and quivered beneath his hand.

"Spence…

"Obviously you don't have bikini bottoms smaller

than these. Because I can definitely see below your tan line."

She glanced down and made a funny little hissing sound. Probably because of the intensely seductive way his dark hand looked against the smooth flesh well below her belly.

Closing her eyes, Cat dropped her head back and arched toward him, just the tiniest bit, inviting more. More heat. More intensity. More danger.

More of his hand.

He slipped one fingertip below the panties and slid it into her curls, closing his own eyes and echoing her moan of pleasure. She was incredibly soft, incredibly welcoming, and he tangled another finger in that warm thatch. Unable to resist, he leaned down to taste the vulnerable skin on her jaw, then her chin and her throat, touching her ever so lightly all the while. Dipping close, but not going too far to turn back.

As much as he wanted to, he didn't kiss her. He couldn't... not with her tender-looking lip. And not without torturing himself even more.

"Please touch me," she said on a shaky moan.

"I am touching you," he whispered against the corner of her mouth. The uninjured corner.

"Touch me *here*," she ordered. She took him by surprise then, arching into his hand, until his fingers connected with hot, wet womanly flesh.

"Oh, yes," she cried, blocking out the sound of his own hopeless grunt of pleasure.

God, she felt amazing. Slick and silky smooth. Warm and wet and welcoming.

"Yes, yes," she muttered. Reaching up, she tangled her hands in his hair and tugged his mouth to hers, taking the kiss he hadn't given her.

He was careful, licking delicately around her sore, then letting his tongue tangle with hers in a deep, hungry mating.

She continued to move, to arch, to quiver, inviting him even farther. Dylan couldn't resist. He slowly slid one finger into her hot, tight channel, savoring her cries of pleasure almost as much as he savored the tightness of her skin against his own.

He touched her deep inside, then withdrew, only to ease in again, setting a slow, steady rhythm of lovemaking with his hand. The flicks of his thumb on her clit and his tongue in her mouth soon matched the thrusts of his finger, until there was nothing but sensation. For both of them.

The pleasure intensified…for him as well as her, until Dylan was as hungry for her release as Cat. His own would have to wait. Though he was hard enough to burst out of his jeans, there was no way things could get that far. Not yet. So for now, he focused on her, determined to make her come in a powerful explosion of ecstasy. And to watch her do it.

Cat's moans grew louder, finally turning into orgasmic cries of release. Dylan couldn't contain a masculine smile of accomplishment, because seeing Cat go all the way was almost as good as climaxing himself.

Almost.

She shook and shuddered, sagging against him while he sampled the soft skin of her jaw and her neck. He continued to make lazy circles with his fingers, enjoying the drenching feel of her, knowing she was still aroused, in spite of her orgasm.

"I wanna taste your tattoo," he whispered against her earlobe, forcing the words out of his tight throat. "I want to turn you around and strip off these silly things you call underwear and get down on my knees to kiss and lick every inch of it."

She gasped and jerked against him. "Oh, God."

And then she came again. Just like that.

He'd barely had time to wrap his mind around it—around her incredibly passionate responses, when he heard someone yelling from outside her apartment.

"Cat," a voice called, "you okay? It's getting kinda crazy down there." The words were accompanied by a sharp rap on the front door.

Cat's eyes flew open, and Dylan immediately looked across her tiny living room to the door. "Is it locked?" he asked, regretfully pulling away from her and rearranging her panties.

Nodding her head, she cleared her throat. "I'm fine, Dinah. Give me five more minutes, okay? Then I'll be back down."

He watched her hold her breath as they both listened for—and finally heard—the waitress's footsteps walking away toward the stairs.

"Close one," he said with a tiny smile.

"Close? It was a little more than close for me," she replied, sounding a bit stunned.

"You complaining?"

"Do I look crazy?" she asked, cocking her head to one side.

He grinned. "Good. Because I have to admit, I got a hell of a charge out of it, too."

Cat straightened, smoothing her shirt, then running a hand through her hair. Drawing in a few deep breaths, as if trying to clear her head or calm herself down, she finally said, "It was incredible. But...unexpected."

"Definitely. So when can we expect to do it again?"

His words surprised a laugh out of her, but it quickly

faded. "Spence…I…wow, what do I say to someone who just did *that* to me, but hasn't even seen me naked?"

"We can fix that." He reached for her shirt.

She leaned back and wrapped her arms around her waist. "No, we can't. Look, this was unbelievable, but it shouldn't have happened."

Didn't she think he knew that? Hell, all he'd come around looking for was a kiss. Not a sexual encounter just this side of sinful. Or maybe *that* side of it. "I know."

"And it can't happen again."

For a second, he thought he'd misheard. Because after what they'd shared a moment ago, he couldn't imagine she was any less anxious than he to find out what they could make each other feel without any clothes at all. In a bed. All night long.

"You wanna run that by me again?"

"I'm not in the market for a lover, Spence," she said. "My life is changing and I'm trying to change with it." The resolute stiffness of her jaw told him she meant business.

"You going into a convent after you close Temptation?"

A sound that was half laugh, half groan escaped her lips. "If I did, I'd have to buy stock in a vibrator company."

A sexy vision shot right through his brain.

"But no," she continued before he could interrupt, "I'm not giving up sex completely. I'm trying to…change my focus. My direction. My choices."

He wasn't sure what she was getting at, but he could tell by the stiff way she held her body that she meant what she said. Cat wasn't in the market for a relationship, even a purely sexual one. She was putting up barriers and, judging by the mournful look in her eyes, they were as difficult for her as they were for him. But she obviously trusted him to respect her wishes because she hadn't walked out in search of more clothes.

"All right, Cat," he murmured, "I understand. I'll give you your space." He stepped back, creating more distance—physically and mentally—between them. "We both need to get downstairs and get to work, anyway."

He'd said what she wanted to hear, but a tiny frown appeared on Cat's brow. Dylan hid a grin, more sure than ever that she didn't *really* want him to back off.

Of course, he'd never *really* intended to.

He'd been sincere…he'd leave now, not push the issue, not force her to act on the attraction so hot between them it could melt glass. Yeah, he'd definitely back off.

But only until he could get her to admit she didn't mean it.

CHAPTER FIVE

By Sunday night, Cat was sure her plans to be responsible, respectable and, well, *good*, were gonna go up in a ball of flames. Flames sparked by a hundred-and-seventy pounds of walking sin named Spence, who'd literally had her in the palm of his hand less than twenty-four hours ago.

And who was, right now, at this moment, making verbal love to about fifty other women.

"Oh, my, would I love to have one hour alone with that man."

Cat didn't have to look up to know the redhead who'd made the comment was staring wide-eyed at the guy playing bass guitar on the small stage in Temptation. Every woman here was thinking the same thing. Of one hour. Or one night. With *him*.

"I'm soooo glad I heard about this," the woman continued. "To think that otherwise, I'd have been at Bible study tonight!"

"I'm sure God'll understand," Cat muttered, not even trying to hide her sarcasm.

Sarcasm obviously wasn't enough to pierce the lust in the redhead's brain. She nodded in pious agreement.

Cat stared around the room at the dozens of other drones looking just as slack-jawed as this one. Word had spread after Friday's and Saturday's performances, and there had actually been a line at the door by 7:00 p.m.

tonight. They were packed, wall to wall, for the first time in months. There were enough women in this place to stock a Mary Kay convention. And she'd lay even money there were a number of females here who'd arrived alone…but didn't want to *leave* alone.

Something deep inside her clenched. If he left with another woman, she was going to get violent. Man, that was hard to admit, even to herself, because it obviously proved she was already hopelessly out of her depth with a guy she'd sworn she couldn't have. Well, couldn't have any more than she'd already *had* him.

"Here's your drink," she said as she swirled a stir stick in the redhead's gin and tonic—heavy on the tonic, because if the woman had too much more alcohol, she'd be diving onto the stage.

To Cat's surprise, as she slid the glass across the sticky surface of the pitted bar, some of the drink sloshed out. That was when she realized her fingers were shaky, as was her whole body. Shaky. Tense. Aware. She'd been all of those things since *he'd* walked through the door forty-eight hours ago.

Man, she needed to get laid. By him.

No. That's the old Cat, she reminded herself. The new one wasn't ruled by her sex drive, her empty pocketbook or her love of adventure. Even if it was nice to occasionally wonder…*what if*? Which she'd been doing a lot after the incredible way he'd made her feel, using only his hand and his mouth. Not to mention his seductive voice whispering erotic things in her ear.

She closed her eyes and sighed at the memory.

What if Dinah hadn't knocked? What if she'd fallen earlier and they'd had more time alone? What if he'd forgotten his keys again last night and come back inside, like he had on Friday? Would she have had the strength to keep her barriers in place?

Probably not.

The fantasies of what could have happened after her barriers crumbled had filled her thoughts all night and all day.

"I need two Sour Apple Martinis and two bottles of Bud," said Vicki, an old friend of Cat's who'd come in to help out tonight. "And maybe a side of band member to go with it."

Cat gave her a look through half-lowered lashes. "Oh?"

Sighing, Vicki said, "I'd love to have a musician sandwich."

"As long as it's a blond musician sandwich," she snapped back, before thinking better of the words.

Vicki's eyes nearly popped out of her head. "Whoa, girl, you got a claim on one of the dark-haired ones?"

Wishing she'd kept her big, fat mouth shut, Cat stepped away from Vicki's curious gaze and busied herself making the drinks. "Never mind," she said as she put them on the waitress's tray.

Vicki merely smirked, having known her long enough to know when Cat was infatuated with a man. "Is it the piano player or the long-haired hunk with the bass guitar?"

"Whadda you think?"

"Bass player," Vicki replied without hesitation. "He's incredibly hot. And he seems familiar for some reason." Staring across the room, she sighed. "Must be the movie-star looks."

After Vicki walked away, Cat quickly got caught up with the other orders, barely hearing the music. When things did slow down for a second, she paused to listen, recognizing an old song. The low note of Spence's bass guitar thrummed in her chest, and the way he growled the words to "Bad To The Bone" made her—and every other woman here—want to find out just how bad he could be.

Very bad. But oh, so incredibly *good.*

She still couldn't get their crazy-wild encounter in her kitchen out of her mind. Whenever she licked her lips she still tasted him there. The way he practically made love to the microphone while singing hot, pulsing, headboard-slamming music sure wasn't helping her forget.

And when the song changed again and Spence invited every woman in the place to light his fire, she was ready to go all teenage-girl-at-her-first-concert on him and start throwing underwear at his feet. Teeny-tiny underwear. Like the ones that had inspired such a powerful reaction in him last night.

"Cat, did you hear me? The phone's ringing!"

Cat finally shook off the warm, lethargic lust and looked at Dinah, who'd obviously been trying to get her attention. Then she turned to the phone, spying the number on the caller ID.

Laine. Calling for her expected "don't screw this up" chat. Cat was in no mood to hear it. Dammit, if her sister was so sure she was going to louse things up, why had she run out on her when Cat had needed her the most? As far as Cat was concerned, Laine had waived all rights to any say in what happened the minute she'd walked out the door without a second thought for the loss of their family's heritage.

She yanked the receiver to her ear. "Temptation."

"Cat?"

"Lainey?" she replied through clenched teeth, knowing the nickname drove her sister nuts.

"Have you called the auction house yet? We need to get some cash for the furniture to pay off the liquor supplier."

Gee, nothing like a little small talk to get the conversation rolling. She couldn't help replying, "Hi, sister dear, how are you? How was your day? I'm sure it's *so* difficult dealing with everything *all on your own* since I left you there without a thought at all for *anybody but myself.*"

"Please don't start, Cat," Laine replied. "You'll be fine. Just follow my list."

Her list. The stupid list. The one that might as well have started with, "Cat, you're useless, so here, I'll save you yet again by telling you every single thing to do."

"What list?" Cat said, wondering if the pounding in her head was caused by the music or by the stress of always playing this role in the Sheehan family. God, sometimes she got so bloody tired of being either the screwup or the bitch.

"The one I taped to the bar that explained step-by-step what you needed to do this week." Laine's impatient sigh was nearly inaudible. Nearly.

Cat rubbed at the corners of her eyes, wondering why it was so hard to tell her sister how she felt. To open up and change the boundaries of their relationship. Laine was warm and smart and wonderful. She would listen, of course she would.

But deep in her heart, Cat knew the truth. Laine might listen. But she wouldn't *hear*. So she responded in Catlike fashion, in words Laine *would* understand. And expect. "Oh, I wondered what that was. Some guy spilled whiskey all over it Friday night. I threw it away."

A pregnant pause followed and Cat almost regretted the lie. Nobody had spilled whiskey on Laine's damn list. Cat had balled it up and thrown it in the trash the day her sister had left. If everybody else felt free to leave her alone to deal with closing down Temptation, then she was gonna do it *her* way.

"I'll e-mail you another copy. And call the auction house first thing tomorrow."

She shook her head. Same old Laine, who'd never believe Cat had called the auction house Thursday. She'd been to the bank. She'd ordered enough stock to get them through the month. She'd contacted movers. She'd called for an application for college, deciding maybe it wasn't so crazy to think she could get a degree and pursue her secret dream of becoming a high school teacher.

Few people knew that dream, which was exactly the way Cat liked it. She didn't want to be laughed at, which, she figured, was exactly the reaction she'd get from most people.

After all, she was nothing like her sister. Laine had been the valedictorian of her senior class.

Cat had been the Girl Most Likely To Meet Hugh Hefner.

"Cat, did you hear me? What have you been doing since I left?"

Oh, nothing much. She'd just handled everything at the bar, looked in the want ads for a job and the apartment guide for a place to live. All on her little lonesome. Imagine that. She'd even had something approaching a sexual interlude with the most attractive man she'd ever known. None of which she could tell her sister.

"I'm busy," she finally said, too tired to continue these dramatic family games.

"Please, Cat. We have to get moving on these things."

As if Laine cared. There was no *we* in Temptation anymore. There was only Cat. "Yeah, sure, *we* do."

Oh, Lord, her voice had broken a bit on the word *we*. She missed her sister. Missed Tess. Missed Gracie, who'd been so distracted all weekend. How, when she was surrounded by so many people, could she still feel so lonely?

She'd never felt more so, not until now, this moment, when she thought—truly thought—about everything she had to do in the coming weeks. Selling her memories piece by piece. Saying goodbye to things that had been so precious to her. Packing up every part of her life and trying to figure out where to go from here.

Alone. Entirely alone.

Then she raised her eyes and looked at the stage. From across the expanse of the room, Spence met her stare. A frown tugged at his brow, and he tilted his head to the side, silently asking her if she was okay. And suddenly, though he'd been a stranger to her two days before, Cat again began to acknowledge those unusual feelings she'd had since the moment they'd met.

That as long as Spence was around, she was never going to feel alone again.

By THE END of the final set Sunday night, Dylan had begun to realize he had a problem. A big one. There was a real flaw with his plan to convince Cat to change her mind about letting something happen between them: after tonight, he wouldn't have any legitimate reason to see her again.

Well, no reason he could tell *her*. In truth, he had

dozens of reasons—like the whole suspecting-he-needed-to-see-her-face-in-order-to-want-to-keep-breathing bit—but that seemed a bit much. Particularly since she still assumed him to be a stranger, which was the other sticky point. He hadn't come clean with her yet…hadn't even told her his full name. He debated on whether to just walk up to the bar during a break, start flirting, and challenge her to remember where they'd met before.

She'd be interested at first, her eyes would sparkle as he dared her to guess, taunting her about their shared past. Then, when she finally figured it out—or when he finally told her—that merry sparkle would fade, to be replaced by the friendly-but-uninterested look she'd always bestowed on him in the old days.

You jackass, you're nothing like you were in the old days.

And he wasn't, certainly not in appearance, and definitely not in attitude or self-confidence. But the same old sensible, introspective brainiac lurked beneath his rocker surface. And he wasn't sure Cat would like that guy, much less want him to put his hand where Dylan's had been the night before.

He closed his eyes and threw his head back, relishing the memory as he backed up Josh's version of a Stones classic. The feel of her drenching his fingers, the taste of her mouth, the coos she'd made as she came, the rich smell of her warm body.

He was getting turned on all over again just remembering it.

"Whoa," someone called.

He glanced over and saw Banks, watching him. "You *got* some."

Dylan shot him a withering glare.

"Or you're thinking about getting some," Banks said, his yell barely audible over the sound of the music.

But somebody obviously heard him, because a few of the women at a table closest to the stage began to whoop and holler. "I'll give you something, baby," one of them screamed.

And she did. Her shirt. With a suddenness that caught him completely off guard, the woman whipped off her top and flung it toward the stage. It came flying at him and landed on his head.

Dylan shook it off, catching it in his hands. Then, because the lights were damn hot and he was damn mad at both the woman and Banks, he used the T-shirt to wipe the sweat off his face and neck. Throwing it into a corner, he kept right on playing.

The women in the crowd went nuts. "Take mine," one yelled.

"Hell," he murmured, watching as several inebriated-looking females stood on their chairs or beside their tables and reached for their waistbands or their buttons.

But before another shirt went flying, a blond figure erupted into his field of vision. Cat leapt up onto the stage, pointing out at the audience. Dylan and his bandmates instinctively brought the music down a notch in volume. "Next woman who removes one piece of her clothes gets thrown out," she yelled. "And possibly arrested."

A few groans greeted Cat's announcement, but she ignored them. She did, however, cast one withering glance at Dylan, her expression fierce and her green eyes snapping with anger.

Jumping back down, she beelined toward the bar, never even looking back. Which was good. Because that meant she didn't see the cocky grin Dylan couldn't keep from his face.

That hadn't been a concerned business owner trying to keep things from getting out of hand in her establishment. That had been a jealous woman who'd been lying through her teeth when she'd claimed she didn't want to be involved with him.

And suddenly, though he still wasn't sure how he was going to make sure he got to stick around, he began to feel better.

When they ended the song—which had been their fifth encore—Banks immediately rose from his keyboard, signaling the definite end of the show to the crowd. He practically danced his way across the stage, his amusement visible in his smile. "You got her, man. She is yours. I thought she was going to go after the brunette who threw the shirt and snatch her bald."

Dylan lowered his guitar. "Shut up, Banks. Don't think I'll forget you caused that incident. And you're as full of it about her as you are about everything else."

Banks, impossible to insult as always, almost bounced on his toes. "Talk about avenging goddess. She must have a total case. I think she threw a beer at someone to get over here before any more women started stripping in your general direction."

"Doesn't matter," Dylan muttered as he turned toward the back of the stage and reached for a bottle of water. He drew deeply from it, needing the fluid on his dry vocal cords. After draining what was left inside, he crumpled the plastic bottle in his hand and two-pointed it into an empty box in the corner. "She says she's too busy shutting this place down to get involved with anyone, so there's no point in even trying. After tonight, I have no more excuses to see her."

Josh and Jeremy walked over, having extricated themselves from the fans who'd crowded around the foot of the stage. Jeremy grabbed Dylan's shoulder. "Man, what did you do to piss off the bartender? She looked like she was gonna rip you a new one."

Josh shook his head, grinning at his brother's naiveté. "Obviously our friend Spence here has been making a little extra time with the Cat woman. It's like a live version of *Revenge of the Nerds*."

Dylan glared at Banks, who had the grace to avert his stare in guilt, the loudmouth.

Jeremy's eyes jaw dropped. "You and the blonde? Man, I've been staring at her for three days, waiting to make my move."

Dylan's eyes narrowed. "Don't even think about it."

The kid put his hands up, palms out. "No sweat, I'm backing off. She probably wouldn't have been interested anyway. She carded me and knows how old I am."

Josh punched his brother in the shoulder. "You tried to buy beer? Dammit, bro, that was part of the deal with us letting you replace Charlie. That you'd play by the rules. All of them."

"Busted," Banks muttered as Jeremy stammered to explain.

God, had he ever been as young as Jeremy? At nineteen, Dylan had been a senior in college. And now, six years later, he felt positively ancient compared to the young drummer. Maybe because his parents and teachers had been treating him like an adult since the age when most kids were just hitting puberty.

By unspoken agreement, the four of them began packing up their gear as the crowd drifted out of the bar, though a few women did try to stick around to offer phone numbers to anyone who would take them.

Cat would have none of that. She practically shooed the stragglers out with her broom, reminding any complainers of the town ordinance against bars staying open past midnight on Sunday.

"One of these days, we're gonna be successful enough to have roadies to do this crap," Jeremy said as he went through the routine of disassembling his drum set.

Dylan doubted it, mainly because he had no interest in going further. But maybe Jeremy would. The kid was more serious about his music than the rest of them ever had been.

The Four G's had been formed in college, when he and Banks had hooked up with Josh and their former drummer, Charlie Moss. They'd had a lot in common—all young college freshmen, Dylan being the youngest. They'd all been studious and smart, they'd all been rock fanatics. Most of all, they'd all been geeks.

Hence their name. The Four G's.

Jeremy still didn't know the full story behind the name. He'd once said he figured it had something to do with their last names, Josh being a Garrity and all. That Banks, Spencer and Moss didn't start with a G hadn't seemed to occur to him. And they hadn't enlightened the teen—because Jeremy probably would have taken offense at the label.

"Well, until those glorious roadie days, every man gets to handle his own *instrument*," Banks said to no one in particular. Then he snickered, amused by his own off-color wit.

Dylan kept his attention on his work, not daring to look in Cat's direction while she wiped down tables with the two waitresses. And he definitely didn't try to talk to her—not while Banks and the other guys were here. The last thing he wanted was one of them stepping in to try to "help" him by telling Cat tonight's incident was nothing to get upset about.

With his luck, they'd make some comment about the girl who'd leapt on him after a performance at a fair in Tremont last month. Or the one who stowed away in his car last winter. Not to mention the one he'd almost had to get a restraining order against. Those incidents were almost enough to make him rethink this whole band thing and just stay quietly in his house, doing the independent software consulting work that was his day job.

Lost in his own thoughts, he hardly even noticed that Banks had disappeared. Casting a quick glance around, he saw his friend at the bar, chatting up the young waitress. And Cat.

"I'll kill him." Hopping off the stage, he strode over to join them. If Banks had told Cat the truth about Dylan's identity, he wasn't going to be responsible for his own actions.

"Hey, man, I was just telling Miss Sheehan how much we appreciate the gig," Banks said, sounding way too innocent for the prank-playing fiend Dylan knew him to be.

"We do appreciate it," Dylan murmured.

"You guys were great," the dark-haired waitress said. Then she peered more closely at Dylan. "Do I know you from somewhere?"

"Spence is famous," Banks said, stepping between them. "Women are always tossing their clothes at him."

Dead friend walking. That was Billy Banks.

Banks looked at Cat and gave her one of those boyish innocent looks that had fooled so many of his competitors back on the political debate team. "It's not his fault,

Miss Sheehan. I made a comment that got that woman riled up earlier. Not Dylan."

Cat's gave him a triumphant look. "*Dylan*, huh?"

She knew his name. Dylan's fingers clenched into fists at his sides as he waited, watching for a spark of recognition, a hint of curiosity, or understanding. Instead, she pursed her lip and asked, "First or last?"

"Huh?"

"Which is your first name and which is your last?"

"Dylan's my first name," he said through a tight jaw and an unexpected thickness in his throat.

Still nothing. No widening of the eyes, no puzzlement on her brow. Certainly no *Aha!* His name meant absolutely nothing to her. Which shouldn't have ticked him off. But it did.

"Seriously," Banks said, still playing some kind of weird matchmaking game, "it wasn't his fault. It was mine."

Cat's shrug was a bit *too* casual. "Not a problem. I just didn't want it to go any further. I plan for Temptation to finish out her run in style. Not with a raid."

"So you're really closing?" Banks asked.

Cat nodded, her jaw tightening. "We have two more weeks. Then it's *sayonara*."

Dylan watched for the pain and sure enough, it flashed in her eyes. Cat was no closer to accepting the reality of this loss now than she had been Friday night. In fact, she looked even more bereft. More tired, world-weary. His flash of anger that he'd been so utterly forgettable dissipated, replaced by a strange ache he couldn't contain.

He didn't like to see her hurting. Didn't like to think of her alone in this place, watching it being torn apart piece by piece as she wondered where she'd go and what she'd do. He'd really like to know where the hell her family was, because he had some things he'd like to say to them about dumping the responsibility for this mess right onto her slim shoulders.

"Speaking of *sayonara*, I'm outta here," Vicki said, grabbing her purse and shoving a handful of cash from her apron pocket into it. "Thanks for the work—great tips tonight!"

"Thank *you*," Cat replied. "We couldn't have managed without you and I really do appreciate it."

Dinah echoed her. "You're a lifesaver, hon. Come on, me 'n' Zeke'll walk you to your car."

The women disappeared into the kitchen to leave through the rear exit. Once they were gone, Banks sat at one of the stools at the bar and stared at Cat. "Well," he said, "I hope you continue to have a lot of help. Looks like there's stuff to be done around here. You could get some real money for some of those antique signs, the mugs, the posters and the old-fashioned jukebox. Not to mention the light fixtures—is that handblown glass?"

Cat glanced around in disinterest. "Yeah." Then she ran a weary hand through her long hair, her fingertips rubbing lightly on her temple, as if easing away an ache. "It's going to be a long couple of weeks with tons to do." Shaking her head, she muttered something under her breath. Something that sounded like "Thanks again, Laine."

"Well, if you need any help, Spence is very handy to have around. And he could use the work. Playing in a bar band doesn't exactly bring home the bacon." Banks managed to keep a straight face as he held a palm up to keep Dylan from interrupting. "Hey, bud, I know you're embarrassed, but everybody's been down on their luck.

It's just too bad you can't live in your car this time since you unloaded it for that crotch rocket."

Dylan's jaw dropped. "What…"

"Jeez," Banks continued, embellishing his outlandish story for Cat's benefit. "He's a wild man on his Harley."

Dylan merely grunted in disbelief.

"Starving musicians, we all do what we can," Banks added, sounding so ridiculous Dylan expected Cat to burst into laughter at any moment. She couldn't possibly believe any of this.

"Shut the hell up, Billy."

His friend ignored him. "I'd give him a place to stay, but I'm crashing with a buddy in Tremont." He gave Dylan an evil grin. "He's got a great house, with a pool…but it's full."

Dylan's house. He was talking about Dylan's house!

"And Josh and Jeremy live with their parents," Banks continued, "so that's no good."

Cat, whose brow had furrowed during Banks's ridiculous lies, turned to Dylan. "You really have no place to go?"

"He's full of crap," Dylan said. "The motorcycle…"

"Isn't running well, I know," Banks said. "You'll be lucky if it doesn't break down on you again tonight."

Motorcycle. As if Dylan would ever sit on Jeremy's deathmobile when it was turned off. Much less ride it on the street! And Banks damn well knew it.

Dylan didn't know what to do first—tell Cat the truth or just beat his *former* best friend to a bloody pulp. Particularly since Cat was now staring hard at him, eyes narrowed and her head tilted as if she were deep in thought. "Is that so?" she asked.

Wondering why her voice had trembled a bit, Dylan immediately retorted. "No, it's not."

Banks shook his head sadly. "He's a proud one, all right."

Clenching his back teeth, Dylan prepared to make his friend eat either his words or Dylan's fist, but when Cat delicately cleared her throat, he paused.

"Well," she said, drawing the word out as she nibbled on the corner of her nicely healed bottom lip, "I hate to admit it, but I *could* use some help around here."

Dylan froze, the heated denial of Banks's story dying on his lips. Meeting her stare, he looked for any hidden meaning, any secret agenda, but saw nothing. Not until a slow flush of color rose in her cheeks as she correctly interpreted what he'd been silently asking: Did she *really* need help? Or had she changed her mind about wanting a lover?

Not even waiting for his reply, Cat suddenly busied herself drying some glasses, turning slightly away so he couldn't figure out what was going on in her pretty head.

"You wanna explain that?"

"I don't want charity," she said, her voice as stiff as her shoulders. Then she added, "And I'm not offering it, either."

"What *are* you offering?" His voice held a challenge.

She put the glass away and finally turned back to look him in the eye. A pregnant pause made him wonder if she was making some big decision, or just being careful with her words. "A job. If you really need one, I *could* use the help."

"Cat…"

"He does," Banks announced, clapping his hand flat

on the surface of the bar. The grin on the guy's face was positively gleeful. Hopping off his stool, Banks added, "I'll let you guys work it out." Then he turned and walked over to the stage, immediately engaging in a lively conversation with Jeremy.

If it had anything to do with the damn Harley parked outside, Dylan was gonna lose it.

But he couldn't think too much about that. Because Cat was still standing behind the bar, a few feet away, suddenly appearing so small and delicate. She looked around the room, shaking her head a bit as if overwhelmed by what she saw.

"Are you okay?" he asked, wondering how serious she was about needing help. She hadn't mentioned it before. Then again, he didn't remember Cat as the type who'd ever ask for help, unless she was truly at the end of her rope.

"I hadn't figured out how I was going to get the fixtures down or get some stuff out of the attic. I guess it hadn't really sunk in until tonight that I have to do all this by myself."

"I do want to help you," Dylan murmured, wondering how to offer to stick around while at the same time disabusing her of the notion that he was an unemployed loser looking for a handout.

She wrapped her arms around her body, rubbing her hands up and down on her skin, as if suddenly cold. "I can't pay you too much, but maybe this could work out for both of us. I know you'd be saving me money. If I have to have the broker do all the work as well as finding the buyers and handling the sales, I won't make nearly as much."

"You don't have to pay me…"

She immediately dropped her arms to her side, her

chin lifting a notch. "Like I said, I'm not looking for charity. If you want a job, I can give you one, short-term." Faint color rose in her cheeks for some reason. When she continued, he began to understand why. "And I can even offer you a place to crash. There's a small storage room in the back, with a cot and bathroom. You can eat whatever you care to fix in the kitchen and I'll pay you what I can."

Stay here. Under the same roof. While she slept up-stairs. If he'd ever had any willpower where Cat Sheehan was concerned, he knew it wouldn't last through the first night.

He wondered if *hers* would.

"Well, what do you think?"

Dylan didn't know what to say. He simply watched her, absorbing her words, but paying even closer atten-tion to her body language. That weariness he'd noticed earlier was back, evident in the tiny furrow on her brow and the slowness of her movements. The slight tremble in her hand as she wiped off the bar told him even more. She was tired, overwhelmed and in over her head.

But there was something else…a faint gleam in her glistening green eyes. A hint of suppressed excitement in the tense position of her body. A sense of expectation in the deep breaths she took in, then slowly released.

Something else was going on, he knew it as sure as he knew the lyrics to every Aerosmith song ever recorded. Cat had more on her mind than offering him a job. But Dylan didn't trust himself to speculate on what.

"He's a con artist, Cat," he said, making one more effort to get things out in the open. "Banks manipulated you into this."

Cat didn't flinch, didn't back down or rescind her offer. Instead, she said, "No, he didn't. I'm not easily manipulated." She leaned across the bar, lowering her voice though no one stood within a dozen feet of them. Licking her lips, she whispered, "I don't want to do this alone, Spence. Will you stay? Please?"

Oh, God. Would he stay? Of course he wanted to, not only so he could spend more time with her, but also because she needed help. Cat truly needed someone to lean on—she was admitting it aloud, for possibly the first time in her life.

And she wanted him to be that someone. At least, the him she *thought* he was—Spence, the broke, unemployed, homeless musician.

If he told her the truth—that he wasn't some down-on-his-luck guitar player—she'd change her mind. He knew it. Cat was too proud to take charity and she'd feel like a fool for ever mentioning it. She'd put up a wall and retreat behind it and he'd be walking out the door.

If he kept his mouth shut, he'd be silently agreeing with all the bullshit Banks had been spewing a few minutes ago.

But he'd be staying.

Dylan didn't want to continue the lie. Now that she knew his name, part of him actually wanted the truth to come out, once and for all. Still, he couldn't risk her refusing his help, couldn't let Cat shoulder the burden her family had seen fit to thrust on her. Most important, he couldn't leave here with so many questions still unanswered between them.

How could he let Cat push him back out of her life before the two of them took a shot at figuring out how he might eventually fit into it?

"Dylan?"

That cinched it. The way his first name sounded on her lips nearly made him shake.

So be it.

He was damned if he told her the truth and damned if he didn't. So if he had to be damned, he was gonna do it right here with the woman he'd wanted for nearly a decade. And let the chips fall where they may.

"Okay, Cat," he murmured, his voice low and unwavering. "I'll stay."

CHAPTER SIX

CAT HAD MADE THE DECISION to seduce Spence about one minute after she'd learned he was unemployed and a drifter.

Soon. Immediately. *Tonight*.

Actually, she'd been toying with the idea from the moment she'd hung up the phone with Laine earlier and had met Spence's stare across the crowded bar. Something had happened—something electrifying and emotional and completely unexpected. She wasn't sure why, but she hadn't been able to shake the feeling that this *thing* building between them had been destined to happen. In that moment, it had risen above the sexual want they'd been dancing around since Friday night and had suddenly become…more. .

Thank heaven she hadn't told anybody else about her new plans for herself and her life, because they'd think her crazy, given this decision. The truth about Spence's situation might have made her run screaming in the opposite direction *if* she'd already succeeded in her transformation from the reckless Cat to the mature, responsible one.

Right. It hadn't happened yet. Because, in all honesty, she'd set out a list of nearly impossible goals. How she'd ever thought she could deal with losing the business, as well as completely overhauling her personal life, she had no idea.

A girl couldn't take on too much at once, right? Saying goodbye to her family heritage was quite enough all by itself, without throwing virtual celibacy into the mix. Sure, she would still do both, only she'd do them one at a time. After the bar closed for good, she could become the new, responsible, non-bad-boy-loving Catherine Sheehan.

Not now. For now she was going to enjoy the hell out of Temptation…and *temptation*. With a man who epitomized the word.

"One last fling," she mumbled as she replaced the last of the clean bar glasses and glanced across the room. The tall, lean man standing there winding up cable was the perfect candidate for a fling. He was laid-back and unencumbered. Probably unreliable, not to mention unpredictable. A guy like Spence was as likely to be gone tomorrow as to still be here. Which meant he'd expect nothing, demand nothing and want nothing in return.

Her heart wouldn't be in danger, as it would have been if there were a chance of something real developing between them. Like if he had a job, a home, roots that tied him to this place, which might mean he could settle down and build a future with a woman.

If he'd been *that* guy, she'd have shoved him out the door, figuring it was better to avoid the chance of heartbreak altogether. But he wasn't that guy, and she could go into this with her eyes wide-open and her heart tightly guarded.

With no chance of getting hurt.

Over the next half hour, Cat finished cleaning up the bar, watching as Spence and his bandmates loaded up their instruments and carried everything out to the parking lot. She noticed the curious, somewhat salacious looks Spence received from the others. To give him credit, he did not acknowledge them in any way or act the least bit cocky about staying when they were all leaving.

Because he wasn't sure *why* he was staying. Not really. He didn't know if she'd asked him to remain here because she needed him. Or because she wanted him.

Both. She did want him, had wanted him desperately since the moment she'd laid eyes on him Friday night. But she also needed help, and he needed a job. It seemed like a perfect solution. She'd have someone to help her close down the bar and get this need for one last wild, reckless fling out of her system. He'd have employment and a place to crash for a couple of weeks.

Then he'd go on his merry way. On to his next town, his next bar. *His next woman?*

Thrusting the thought away, Cat refused to acknowledge the flash of dismay that accompanied it. She had no business worrying about what Spence might do after he left here. Because if she did, that would mean she cared about him.

Impossible. Reverting to the reckless Cat who'd indulge in a passionate affair was all about Temptation and a need for release. Not about genuine emotion and vulnerability. Definitely not about love. She wouldn't allow that, not when she knew damn well he could break her heart when he left. As he inevitably would. After all, didn't everyone?

"G'night, Cat," one of the musicians called. It had been one of the blond ones—the young drummer who'd tried to buy beer. "I'll come back to visit before you close down."

"I'll have the ginger ale all ready for you," Cat replied, grinning as he rolled his eyes.

And soon, so soon she didn't have a chance to prepare mentally—much less physically—she and Spence were alone. Locking the door behind his friends, he slowly turned to face her across the deserted room.

She shivered, just a bit. From nervousness or anticipation, she really couldn't tell. Nor did she care, since they both simply heightened the delicious tension.

"Considering the crowds in here this weekend," he said, filling the silence, "have you thought about relocating?"

Cat shrugged. "It's crossed my mind." Then she ran her hand across the surface of the bar, so smooth and warm—almost living—beneath her touch. "But it wouldn't be the same. What mattered was the place. This particular building."

He nodded, instantly understanding. Then he reached for the light switches beside the front door and flipped them down. The room descended into that red semidarkness, only the overhead, colored glass lamps remaining on.

Holding her breath, Cat waited, wondering if Spence had already realized what was on her mind. When he slowly reached toward the cord for the blinds covering the front windows, she suspected he did. Because with one easy pull of the cord, he shut out the view from the street. Shut out the rest of the world.

"Thanks," she murmured.

He didn't answer. He merely waited for her next move. So she made it. "Have I thanked you for walking through my door Friday night?" Licking her lips, she added, "And have I told you how glad I am that you're staying…with me?"

That seemed to be enough. He gave her one tiny nod of understanding and she waited for him to approach.

Instead, he surprised her by walking over to the old jukebox near the stage. Something of a family heirloom, the jukebox was original to the bar, right down to the music it contained. After her grandparents had died, the rest of the family had decided to leave the records exactly as they were, reflecting that generation's taste in music.

The old standards didn't appeal to their new, younger clientele, so the machine seldom got used. Especially not with the shiny new karaoke machine in the opposite corner. But the jukebox did work, as Spence seemed to know. Glancing over the song list, he inserted several quarters into the slot and pressed a few of the numbered buttons. In the thick silence of the room, he turned around to look at her, the intensity of his expression saying more than words ever could.

The whir of the machinery and the click of the record falling were only slightly more audible than the beating of Cat's heart. When the sultry strains of an old jazz tune emerged from the old, tinny speakers, she closed her eyes, letting the seductive quality of the music fill her head.

She sensed the moment Spence reached her side, though he'd moved with catlike silence across the room. She hadn't had to look to know he was there. Feeling his warmth, she breathed deeply to inhale his male scent. Her whole body arched a bit closer to him, drawn by his warmth. His presence.

When she opened her eyes, she saw him watching her with visible hunger. "Slow and smoky enough?" he whispered.

Immediately knowing what he meant, she nodded. Without another word, she kicked off her sneakers, then reached for his hand. His fingers tightened reflexively around hers for a split second before he helped her onto the step stool she kept for reaching bottles on the top shelf. She stepped up, then up again, until, with his help, she ascended onto the bar.

Within a heartbeat, he joined her there. "Dance with me?"

Feeling the thrum of the music—not to mention a bone-deep, sensually inspired lethargy—Cat nodded and stepped into his arms. And was utterly lost. Lost to everything else but this time and this place and this man.

Their bodies fit together as if they had been made for one another, the soft curves of hers mating perfectly with the hard breadth of his. She'd been incredibly intimate with Spence in some ways, but had never been held this closely by him. The contact was both electric and erotic. She felt it from head to toe.

"Careful now," he said softly, beginning to sway to the music, still holding her tight.

"You won't let me fall," she replied, meaning much more than physically falling off the bar.

Bathed in the reddish glow of the overhead light, his eyes glittered as he replied, "No, Cat, I won't let you fall."

Then they were silent. Cat tucked her head against his neck, resting it on his shoulder. Her lips brushed his skin and she couldn't resist sampling his salty taste with one gentle swipe of her tongue. He reacted with a hiss, nothing more.

Inhaling his earthy, spicy scent, she completely relaxed and gave herself over to the music, instinctively following his every move. She should have known he would be able to dance, since he moved, breathed and thought in rhythm.

What she couldn't have imagined was that slow dancing with Spence would be like making love. Sweet, hungry, erotic love.

"I like this music," he murmured.

"It's not exactly AC/DC."

He laughed softly. "It'll do."

Yeah. It would do.

With one hand curled over her hip, he used the other to lazily stroke the small of her back. His fingers dipped low, sliding beneath the waistband of her jeans. When he began tracing small circles there, Cat knew he was picturing her tattoo, following the swirling pattern with his touch. The wicked images he'd spoken about in her apartment the previous evening made her shiver with anticipation.

"You're not cold are you?"

She shook her head, saying nothing, not having the energy to form words in her brain, much less speak them. She had only the energy to keep moving her feet, to keep shifting her thighs against his, to keep feeling the incredible delight of her breasts rubbing against his mile-wide chest.

The record ended but they didn't stop moving. Soon enough there was another whir, another click and the strains of another song banishing the silence. This one was just as slow, just as smoky.

So was her whisper. "Kiss me, Spence."

He complied, dipping down to catch her mouth with his, parting his lips and allowing their tongues to meet and dance, as well. He tasted delicious—hot and sweet—and Cat tilted her head, kissing him back with lazy, lethargic lust.

Without giving it any thought, Cat reached for the waist of his jeans and tugged his T-shirt free. She slid it up, her palms gliding over his taut skin every inch of the way. He was warm and firm, his body a little slick from his performance on stage, and the heat of the night. Not to mention their dance.

Cat couldn't resist running her hands over his chest, scraping the tips of her nails lightly across his flat nipples, rubbing at the flexing sinews of muscle on his shoulder. The man's body was to die for—hard and ripped and hot all over.

Reaching for the bottom of her shirt, Spence equaled things out a bit, pulling it off her with the same deliberation Cat had used. His fingertips danced across every bit of her skin as it was revealed.

"Mmm," she moaned, unable to manage anything else except the deep, throaty sound of pleasure at the warmth of his touch.

Echoing it, he reached around and deftly unfastened her bra, pushing each strap off her shoulders. Cat shrugged and the flimsy fabric fell to join their shirts, then she pressed against him again so they could dance topless.

The feel of his chest rubbing at the tips of her breasts through their clothes had been incredibly pleasurable.

This was mind-blowing.

"You're beautiful," he murmured. Raising a hand, he cupped her breast, tweaking her nipple with delicate flicks of his fingers until Cat was ready to beg for more. Like his mouth.

He seemed to read her mind. "I want to taste you."

Answering with her body, she leaned back and offered herself to him. He nibbled his way down her neck, pausing to lick the tiny hollow beneath her collarbone. She whimpered as he moved lower, until he was kissing the top curve of her breast. And when he slid his tongue farther to delicately lick at her hard and sensitive nipple, she cried out incoherently.

"You taste as good as you look," he mumbled before closing his mouth entirely over the tip of her breast and sucking deep.

Thankfully, Spence still had an arm around her waist because Cat's legs began to shake. "I've got you," he whispered.

Somewhere far away, there was brief silence, then another click and another song began. This one with a stronger, more driving beat that seemed to echo the rising tempo, the heat building ever higher between them.

Lowering her to the top of the bar, Spence knelt in front of her, still doing crazy, heavenly things with his mouth and his magical hands. Leaving her reclining there, he hopped down to the floor and stood before her. He leaned down, continuing his hungry exploration of her breasts, her midriff and her stomach.

When he reached for the snap of her jeans, Cat moaned again. "I want you so much."

"Ditto."

"I don't know if I can even walk long enough to go upstairs to my place," she whispered, unable to bear the thought of even a brief interruption.

He took hold of her hips and tugged her toward him, until she was sitting on the edge of the bar, her legs dangling over the sides. "We're not going anywhere," he said. "I can't wait one more minute for this. I've wanted you for too long."

Even more inflamed by the raw power of his desire—as if he'd hungered for her for years instead of mere days—Cat arched back. Lifting her hips, she watched as he unfastened her jeans and tugged them down.

"Cat, I've dreamed of this, of having you," he murmured as he looked his fill at her. "You're more beautiful than I ever imagined."

Bathed in the soft light, and in the heat of his eyes, Cat *felt* beautiful. Powerful. Irresistible. Like a pagan creature of sensation and shadow.

Unable to contain it, she gave a soft, sultry laugh full of invitation. "Then *have* me, Dylan," she whispered, knowing she wanted the taste of his real name in her mouth as she made love with him.

Groaning, he lowered his head to her body, licking a path from the tip of her breast, down her midriff, to her belly. After circling her navel with his tongue, he moved lower until his lips were scraping the edge of her curls.

She couldn't contain a moan, or stop her hips from thrusting up a tiny bit in wanton invitation. "Oh, yes."

When he went even lower, delicately licking at her most throbbing, sensitive spot, she almost flew out of her mind. He tasted, gently nibbled, then carefully sucked her until she became nearly incoherent, begging him not to stop and to give her even more.

"Open for me, baby," he growled, dipping lower to lick even more thoroughly.

Then she really did go out of her mind, exploding with pleasure as he devoured her. He was relentless, taking her even higher, not letting her descend from the heights of her orgasm. Spence continued toying with her, tasting her, sliding his fingers over her swollen flesh and taunting her with the promise of what was to come.

"Please," she begged, desperate for more. For deeper contact. "I want to feel you inside me."

Cat shimmied off the bar, her hands on his shoulders, trusting him to hold her. And he did, letting her slide down his body in one long, intimate caress. Facing each other, they both panted and stared for a long, heady moment, knowing the best was yet to come.

Another unexpected moment of silence descended. Then a whir, a click and another song. Faster. With a stronger bass note and a louder drumbeat.

"You choreographed this perfectly," she said.

He tangled his hands in her hair and drew her close. "Just wait until you see what I can do to some Metallica."

Then he caught her mouth in a mind-blowing kiss, deep, hungry and carnal. They were gasping when it ended. Gasping and reaching blindly for one another. She grabbed his zipper as he thrust a hand into his pocket. Cat shoved his jeans down one second after he retrieved a condom.

"Boy Scout," she said when she saw it.

"No. But I *do* believe in being prepared."

She held her breath, watching with both curiosity and avarice as he pushed his briefs and jeans all the way off. And when she saw him—*really* saw him, so big and hard and ready—she moaned and started to shake.

Glorious. And all hers. At least for tonight.

Sheathing himself, Spence bent and effortlessly lifted her into his arms. She clung to him, her arms around his shoulders, her legs around his waist. His guttural growl told her he was just as affected by the brush of her wet skin against his erection. Pressing openmouthed kisses against his jaw, Cat began to whisper hungry, pleading things in his ear.

"Anything worth having is worth waiting for, Cat," he said, his voice thick and tight as he rubbed against her, teasing her with the promise of his entry but not giving her what she craved.

Whimpering, she tightened her legs around his lean hips and tilted farther, trying to take what he wasn't giving. He laughed softly, kissing her again.

"*Please*, Dylan," she cried against his lips.

"Ah, Cat, I love the way you say my name," he said on a long sigh. Then, cupping the curves of her bottom in his hands, he moved her, lowered her and finally thrust up into her.

Cat dropped her head back and savored the deepness, the tightness, the joining. Sex had never been like this—never. She'd never felt as filled or as cherished or as ravenous as she did with Spence. And her moans probably told him so.

As he began to move, slowly easing out of her body only to drive back in, Cat leaned back against the edge of the bar. Still holding her by the hips, he dropped forward and covered her nipple with his mouth, sucking deeply, and an explosion of warmth and delight surged through her body.

"Cat?" He drew her up again, pulling her tightly against him as he continued his sensual strokes deep inside her.

"Mmm?" was all she could manage.

Pressing a sweet kiss of pure emotion to her lips, he whispered, "This was worth the wait."

OVER THE NEXT FEW DAYS, Dylan did everything he could to help Cat, liking that she really *did* need his help. Despite being certain she'd wanted him to stay for more sensual reasons, she'd also been honest about the amount of work she was facing. There was a lot to do, and frankly, he didn't know how she would have managed it on her own. But he had no doubt she'd have tried.

Thankfully, being a freelance software designer, he didn't have to make a lot of arrangements to walk away from his private life for a while. He had no boss to report to, no family nearby who'd question his absence. No projects that couldn't wait.

And Banks was taking care of his house. The shithead.

His friend had come by Monday at lunchtime, bringing Dylan some clothes and stuff. Meeting him in the parking lot, he'd been about to thank him for doing it. At least, until he saw what his clothes were packed in: the rattiest duffel bag Dylan had ever seen. "If my clothes are infested with crawling creatures, I am going to make you eat them one by one," he'd bitten out.

Banks had laughed, unflappable as always. "It's clean. I actually got it from Jeremy and Josh's basement and I ran it through your washer this morning. Come on, admit it. It definitely suits the wild, reckless rock and roller." Pointing toward Jeremy's Harley, still parked in the corner of the lot, he'd added, "As does that." Then he handed Dylan the keys.

Dylan had rolled his eyes. "What's it gonna cost you for getting Jeremy to leave his baby here?"

Banks's grin had been evil. "It's not costing *me* anything. But you owe the kid one weekend in your house for a party."

He'd nearly groaned. A bunch of teenagers tearing up his house…all so he could claim to own the death-on-wheels vehicle sitting outside Cat's business, which he wouldn't ride in a million years? This was getting ridiculous.

Then he'd thought about the previous night and acknowledged the truth. It was *so* worth it.

Before he'd been able to say anything more, Banks

had reached over to the passenger seat of his car. "Here," he'd said, tugging something heavy across his lap while Dylan shouldered the scruffy bag. "I brought you this, too."

When he saw his old banged-up guitar case, Dylan had raised a questioning brow.

"You can't exactly serenade her with your Fender. Need a little more than a bass line for some of the sappy songs you wrote about her back when you were young and hairless."

Dylan could only shake his head. "Serenade?"

Banks nodded, then said, in all seriousness, "I know you're mad as hell at me, but you deserved your shot. Now you have it." He handed the guitar case out the window, adding, "Make something happen, my friend, because there's no doubt in my mind you're gonna love her until the day you die."

Shocked by his normally wise-cracking buddy's serious words, Dylan had taken the guitar and watched as Banks roared out of the parking lot. He'd stood there for a long time, thinking about Banks's crazy claim.

Yeah, he'd loved Cat as a kid and he craved her now. But loving her for the rest of his life? Was is really possible?

And, if so, what was he going to do about it…particularly when Cat learned the truth about who he really was?

He hadn't had much time to dwell on it because Cat had been true to her word and put him right to work. When he wasn't scouring the attic and storage room for treasures or junk—or some things Cat insisted were both—he was packing boxes or hauling trash. Negotiating with a greedy used-furniture broker, he'd made sure the guy agreed to buy what he wanted piece by piece, instead of paying one set price for everything, as he'd originally demanded. That would mean a lot more money for Cat when the sale went through at the end of the month.

She'd been very appreciative. And Lordy, did the woman know how to show it. In more positions than he'd imagined possible.

Inspired by her, er, gratitude, Dylan had begun to research antique lamps on the Internet. That, too, had paid off. He'd found a unique lighting company which specialized in old-fashioned colored glass, and had contacted them about the fixtures over the bar. He'd even found an electrician who specialized in delicate work to remove them once Temptation closed its doors for good. The money from those fixtures alone would keep Cat in the black for a while after she closed down.

She appreciated that, too. Appreciated it so much he really wasn't sure he was gonna be able to walk away on Thursday morning.

Which was saying a lot, considering every other night had been just as miraculous.

Making love with Cat was so perfect, such a part of him now, that it felt more natural to be touching her than not. Wherever they were—in her bed, in the bar, in her living room, in the downstairs kitchen—didn't matter. He hungered for her and she was equally as ravenous.

He'd taken special delight in making another of her fantasies come true Tuesday night. Bringing down some blankets from her apartment, he'd led Cat to the stage and loved her there, with the small spotlights splaying pools of color and light all over their bodies.

It had been incredibly erotic. Made more so by his certainty that what was happening between the two of them was so much more than he could ever have anticipated.

They *both* felt the intense connection, he didn't doubt that. He'd become adept at reading her moods, and she knew exactly what he was feeling. Spending practically every waking—and definitely every sleeping—minute together, they'd gotten to know each other like longtime lovers.

They laughed a lot. They loved a lot. They talked a lot. About everything except the past. Not to mention the future. But he sure had been thinking about them both, wondering how long he could let this go on before he came clean with her.

And what would happen when he did.

CHAPTER SEVEN

LATE THURSDAY AFTERNOON, Dylan returned to Temptation after making a trip to a moving supply company. He'd gone to pick up some boxes for Cat to use for packing up her apartment. He found her behind the bar, a smile on her face, hanging up the phone. No one else was around.

"Hey," she said, watching him walk in. Scrunching her brow, she looked doubtfully at the big pile of flattened boxes he dropped onto the table closest to the door. "You do realize I only own a small dresser full of clothes and a mismatched, incomplete set of dishes, don't you?"

Walking over, he raised a challenging brow. "These are for your shoes."

She nibbled her bottom lip. "You peeked into my closet, huh?"

"I've seen less footwear at Payless."

She tossed her head, sending those blond tresses bouncing. "Everyone deserves one decadent indulgence."

You're mine flashed through his head, but he didn't say it.

"Well," he replied instead as he leaned across the bar and ran his fingers through a long, silky lock of her hair. "I'll approve of your vice if you wear those knee-high black patent leather boots for me some night."

"Oooh, you saw those, hmm?" She licked her lips. "They were part of a Halloween costume…but I kept them. Just in case."

"Just in case you wanted to drive a man insane with lust?"

"Well, yeah."

Without being asked, she reached down into the fridge and got him a cold bottle of beer, pushing it toward him. Dylan took it gratefully. He didn't drink much, but when he wasn't performing, he liked an icy beer at the end of the day. She already remembered his brand.

"I must say my shoe wardrobe does seem to come in handy for seduction," she said.

"Oh?" He tensed at the thought of Cat seducing anyone else.

Nodding, she explained, "My friend Gracie who owns the bookstore next door borrowed a pair of my sexiest shoes last Saturday night."

Gracie's seduction. Not Cat's. Thank heaven.

Dylan had heard about Gracie, as much as he'd heard about Cat's friend Tess and her sister Laine, but he hadn't met any of them yet. Unless… "Gracie—she's not the one with the prosthetic leg, is she?" he asked, thinking about the flamboyantly attractive young woman he'd seen coming out of the bookstore yesterday.

Cat shook her head. "That's Trina, her assistant, who is a riot. She was in here a while ago having a big blowout with this guy who spends his days writing in Gracie's store. Then they made up. Big-time. I thought I was gonna have to turn the hose on them." Grinning at the memory, she added, "If you'd met Gracie, you'd remember her—she's got the prettiest eyes you've ever seen."

Dylan doubted that. Seemed to him he was looking at the prettiest eyes he'd ever seen.

"Anyway, she wore the shoes to her ten-year Kendall High reunion the other night."

"Ten years, huh?" Good thing Gracie wasn't one year younger. That would have put her in *his* graduating class—and her memory might be a little better than Cat's.

"Yep. And the shoes apparently brought out the very naughty Gracie who almost never comes out to play."

He winced as she wagged her eyebrows suggestively. "Don't tell me she had one of those reunion hookups. I thought they only happened in chick flicks. Or horror movies."

"And in romance novels," she replied airily. "But yeah, she really did. She came in for lunch on Monday and told me all about her wicked evening in my wickedly hot shoes. It was very exciting, right down to a case of mistaken identity." Emitting a tiny wolf whistle, she added, "And when I met the guy earlier today, I totally got it. He came in looking for her and had a beer. Whoa, mama."

Dylan narrowed his eyes, though he knew she was teasing him. "Oh?"

"Hunk-a-licious." Then, taking mercy on him, she admitted, "Only, he's no rock and roller. Has this upper-crust Boston voice. And he probably likes elevator music or something."

"Horrors," he replied dryly. Then, still amused by her cute effort to make him jealous, he added, "Because I know how you like to move to more *sultry* music."

Her expression grew a little dreamy. "Oh, yes. I like moving and dancing and *living* in rhythm with the sultry stuff."

Perfect. Because so did Dylan.

Thinking about what she'd said about her conversation with her friend, he fished around for some more information. "So, uh, you and Gracie were sharing some big secrets, huh?"

Her eyes twinkled and she didn't answer the question she knew damn well he was asking: whether she'd been talking about *him*. "We always share secrets," she replied with a prim nod.

Twining his fingers into her hair and cupping her head, he tugged her forward and leaned over the bar, meeting her halfway. As their lips came close enough to share a breath, he whispered, "So did you tell her I made you come while you were mixing a couple of mai tais right here behind the bar Monday night?"

She shuddered a little, her lips parting in a tiny gasp of memory. "God, you were so bad to do that to me. I can't imagine what the couple at table four thought about how long it took you to hook up the cable you were *supposedly* working on back here. Or how long it took me to make their drinks."

"I don't imagine they realized I was kissing your bare thighs under your skirt, or that I had my hand on your—"

"Shh," she said, putting her fingers over his lips with a helpless giggle. "Now I know why you told me you wanted to see me in a skirt instead of jeans some night. And that cable story...sheesh, I'm so gullible."

Giving her a wolfish look, he said, "Yeah. You are. As for the couple drinking the mai tais? Well, any guy pansy enough to actually order one in public probably had no *idea* what I was doing to you under there."

"Pansy, huh? Guess that means you won't be ordering a Slippery Nipple anytime soon?"

"No, but I sure as hell plan to serve one."

Unable to resist any longer, he pressed his lips to hers, falling into the same sweet, hot, delightful place he always went when he kissed Cat Sheehan. She tasted like cherries and laughter and sex and sunshine, all rolled into one.

When they pulled apart, she admitted, "By the way, I don't share all my secrets." Half lowering her lashes over her eyes, she added, "Especially not the ones I want to happen again."

He leaned even closer, practically lying on his stomach so he could see all of her. "You wearing a skirt today?"

She stepped back so he could see her sexy, tight jean miniskirt that revealed those endlessly long legs. "And nothing else," she said, pure wickedness in her voice.

At that, Dylan went right over the bar, crawling toward her with deliberation.

"What are you…"

"You awaken the beast, you deal with the consequences," he growled.

She began to giggle as he hopped down beside her. Reaching toward his jeans, she squeezed him lightly, gasping as she realized he was already hard for her. "Well," she said regretfully, "the beast is gonna have to stay in his cage for a while unless he wants to get caught rampaging by any customers who might wander in."

Shaking his head and laughing, he swooped down to kiss her, quick and hard. "I'm the beast," he said once he pulled away.

"No, you're the rebel."

Rebel? "Uh, not exactly."

She reached up and rubbed the tip of her index finger across his bottom lip, until he nibbled at it. "You are.

From the top of your head to the tip of your boots and every delicious inch in between." Shuddering a little, she leaned against him and cupped his cheek in her hand, tangling her fingers in his hair. "And you drive me crazy. From your eyes to your voice, to the tight way you wear your impossibly soft and threadbare jeans, to the sexy hoop in your ear, you make me absolutely wild."

He wondered if now was a good time to tell her the earring was the magnet kind and his ear wasn't pierced.

Probably not.

Especially because her words bothered him. The intensity in her voice, the hunger in her eyes…they were for Spence. She was no longer talking to Dylan, the man she'd gotten to know all week. She was talking to the homeless rocker she'd taken in Sunday night.

It was ridiculous to be jealous of himself, yet that's exactly what he was feeling.

Before he could do anything about it—and he honestly didn't know what that might have been—the front door swung open. Two women entered, looking around the empty room. Waving them toward one of the dozen vacant tables, Cat stepped back, creating a more sedate distance between them. Her cheeks pinkened and Dylan almost laughed, the blush so unexpected on the face of a woman so sensual and provocative.

"I should go make sure Zeke's still here to cook anything," she murmured. "I've been having him leave around two all week, then come back in at five."

Looked around the empty tavern, he frowned. "Not much of a crowd at all since Sunday night, huh?"

She shook her head. "There were a few people in around noon, like there have been every day this week. The business people still drift in Monday through

Friday for lunch since they're downtown, anyway, and don't have to deal with the detour hassles. Nobody else bothers."

A sad, faraway look darkened her expression as the reality of her situation returned full force to her mind. For a little while, he'd succeeded in lightening her mood, making her laugh, making her forget. But the truth of why he was really working here and the uncertainty of her future had returned.

Dylan knew enough about Cat to understand why the closing of Temptation would hurt her. He just hoped his presence in her life was making it easier. And would, perhaps, give her something to look forward to once this was all over. "You okay?"

Inhaling and then releasing a deep breath, she nodded and offered him a tentative smile. "Yeah, I am. Not fabulous, but okay, which is exactly what I was telling my sister right before you walked in."

"Laine?"

Cat nodded. "She called from California. It seems the wildfire threatening my aunt's house is out. Laine offered to come back here."

Laine coming back…that could be a good thing for Cat. But it sure would eliminate her need for *him*. He didn't move a muscle as he waited for her to continue.

"I told her not to," Cat murmured.

His heart started beating again. "Oh?"

"Yeah." She glanced around the room, her expression tender as she studied all the empty tables and the single occupied one. The stage, the jukebox. The windows and the overhead lights. "Don't get me wrong," she finally said, "this totally sucks. But I'm getting used to the idea. I'm…dealing. Even seeing beyond this month and making some plans."

God, he prayed those plans would somehow include him.

"That's thanks to you, Dylan," she said, placing her hand flat on his chest. She stared up at him, emotion shining clearly in her green eyes. "You've given me strength to face all of this without feeling so...abandoned. Once I had your strength behind me, I began realizing I will survive this."

He covered her hand with his own, wondering if she could feel the way his heart was pounding in his chest. Because there had been feeling in her words. And the way she was looking at him now...well, he could live on it for weeks.

"I'm glad you asked me to stay," he admitted.

One of the women at the table cleared her throat, and Cat pulled her hand away. "I'll be right over," she called.

"Guess I'd better get back to work," he said. But before he left to carry the boxes upstairs, he asked, "So, did you happen to tell Laine about having a little help?"

She shook her head. "I want to keep it...close. Private."

"Intimate," he murmured.

"Exactly."

He understood that. Because he was feeling the same way—wanting the rest of the world to just leave them alone for a while. At least long enough for them to figure out where they were going and how they were going to get there.

"All I told Laine was that I'm okay, and that I don't need her back here until the twenty-seventh."

Tilting his head in confusion, Dylan said, "But your last day in business is Sunday the twenty-sixth."

"Yes, it's our last *official* day. But if Temptation's going out, she's going out with a bang, not a whimper. That Monday is going to be an all-day party for everyone who ever cared about this place. Family. Friends. Regulars." Winking, she added, "Musicians."

"I'll be here," he replied tenderly.

"I know you will." Her voice was just as soft. "In fact, I wouldn't want to have it without you."

DESPITE GOING THROUGH one of the most difficult periods of her life, Cat was feeling better than she had in a long, long time. It was so strange. She was still depressed about losing Temptation, yet, if asked, she'd have had to answer that she'd never been happier in her personal life. Because of Spence.

It's a fling. She kept having to remind herself of that, though, honestly, she didn't know if what was happening between them had any sort of name.

Enchantment?

Maybe.

All she knew was that he constantly made her laugh and made her hot and made her feel protected and definitely not alone.

She'd quickly become accustomed to sleeping beside him in her bed, sometimes waking up deep in the night, just looking at him lying there. Perfect and handsome and amazing, even when asleep.

Sometimes during the day, she'd catch him humming under his breath and more than once she'd considered asking him to sing for her. Only for her. But she hadn't… it seemed almost *too* personal. Too intimate.

And she didn't want to hear him sing her a song that he'd written for another woman.

Though she kept telling herself she didn't have much

more time—that as soon as Temptation was gone, Spence likely would be, too—she couldn't help wondering if there were any chance for them beyond this month. Beyond forever sounded good, too.

Cat forced the hopeful image out of her brain and looked up as the door opened early Friday afternoon. To her surprise, Dinah entered the bar. The waitress was early—she'd been coming in at five all week, though, honestly, tonight was probably the only night Cat would need the help. Since they had a live country-and-western band coming in to perform, she expected a crowd of people to actually show up ready to drink and party, unlike every other night this week when a handful of people had shown up ready to die or take a nap.

"Hey, what's up?" she asked the older woman. "Zeke's already gone if you're, you know, on the prowl."

Dinah rolled her eyes. "I've given up on Zeke. The man's blind as a bat if he can't see what a good thing he's got right in front of him."

"He's shy."

Startled by the male voice, Cat whirled around and saw Spence approaching from the back hallway. He'd been working all morning, taking down some old photos and posters, and trying to figure out if there were any way to salvage the beautiful mural Cat had had painted on the wall last year. The same artist who'd done the Temptation signs had created an elaborate piece of artwork that literally embodied the spirit of Temptation.

The Garden of Eden. Complete with fig leaves.

Dinah snorted. "Shy? Ha."

"I mean it," Spence said, sliding up onto one of the stools and reaching for the bottle of water Cat had already pulled out for him. "He asked me yesterday when exactly it became okay for a man to let a woman ask him out on a date."

Color rose in Dinah's cheeks. "I most certainly have not asked him on a date."

"Lemme guess," Cat said, tapping her cheek with the tip of her finger, "you asked him to have sex?" Dinah swatted at her with her handbag and Cat stepped easily out of the way, laughing at the woman's outraged expression. "I'm kidding. I know you're not completely desperate."

Spence sipped from his water bottle. "I think what Zeke was asking was whether it would be okay for him to say yes." Dinah still didn't say anything, so he added, "Just in case someone…anyone…ever *did* ask him out on a date."

The woman's jaw dropped and she patted her hair, looking pleased. "Meaning me?"

"I think so," he said.

Dinah grabbed Spence's face and smacked a loud kiss on his lips. Cat almost laughed as his face reddened the tiniest bit. For someone so sexy and self-assured, the man was sometimes easily disconcerted.

"That was worth coming in here early," Dinah said as she came around behind the bar and tucked her purse away on the bottom shelf.

"Why *did* you come in early?" Cat asked.

"You tell me," Dinah said with a sly look. "I got orders to cover this afternoon."

"Orders?" Frowning in confusion, she glanced at Spence and saw his self-satisfied expression. "Did you…"

"Yeah," he said, not even letting her finish. "I *asked*. Thanks for coming in, Dinah. She deserved an afternoon off."

"An afternoon off?"

"You have parrot tendencies you haven't told me about yet?" he teased.

"The only bird around here is the peacock who works in the kitchen," Dinah said. "And I'm exactly the woman to ruffle his feathers a little bit."

"No doubt about it, beautiful," Spence said.

Dinah preened, then put both of her hands on Cat's back and pushed her out from behind the bar. Ignoring her sputters and protests, Spence reached for her hand and tugged her toward the front door.

"Wait a minute, I can't just leave!"

"Sure you can. Dinah's got it covered."

Outnumbered and outfoxed, Cat had no choice but to allow Spence to tug her toward the front door and out into the bright afternoon sunshine.

"You don't melt or anything in the daylight, do you?" he asked, watching as she squinted.

"I'm a night owl," she admitted. "And a barfly. But this is actually kind of nice."

"So are toaster ovens," he said, shaking his head in bemusement. "Only they're less hot."

Leading her toward the small parking lot behind Temptation, he headed for Cat's little sedan. She dug her feet into the ground. "How about we take your motorcycle instead?"

He followed her pointed stare, already shaking his head. "No way."

"Oh, come on, I'm not scared."

"You should be," he muttered. Shrugging, he added, "And I don't have an extra helmet."

"So we'll live dangerously."

Her words sparked a strong reaction in him because Spence grabbed her upper arms. "No. I don't even want to think about you getting on one of those things *with* a helmet and I'd spank you if you ever did without one."

Fisting her hand, she put it on her hip and cocked a brow. "Well, darlin', if you're trying to talk me out of it, you're doing a piss-poor job."

He stared, got her meaning, and started to sputter. "Cat…"

"I'm kidding." Under her breath, she added, "Pretty much."

Shaking off his arm, she stepped closer to the Harley, sparkling and bright in the sunshine. "It really is a beauty," she said, running her hand over the padded seat. "Sleek and dangerous."

To her surprise, his frown deepened. Weren't guys usually as proud of their rides as they were of what was in their pants?

"Come on," he said. "Do you wanna drive since we're taking your car?"

Giving him a little pout, she tried one more time. "You're sure we can't take this?"

"It's…it's broken-down, remember?"

Oh, yikes. He was red-faced and she almost bit her tongue, remembering what Banks had said the other night. The bike wasn't running well and Spence obviously didn't have the money to get it repaired.

She was such an idiot. A whiny idiot, playing girlie games when the man obviously had too much pride to admit what the real problem was. Without another word, she slid her arm in his and led him to her car, getting in on the passenger side.

He got in and started the engine, his jaw still tight.

"Look, Spence, I'm sorry," she said, needing him to know she understood. "I totally forgot it was broken-down. After I pay you for working here, you'll have the money to…"

His head swung around, his eyes blazing as he snapped, "You're not paying me a cent."

"But, you're working for me…"

"I'm sleeping with you," he bit out.

"Yes, at night. But during the day…"

"Cat, I am *not* taking your money."

Now it was her turn to stiffen. She wasn't a charity case. "We had a deal. You know I wouldn't have let you do so much if I hadn't planned to pay you for it."

He didn't relent or soften a bit. "That was before you took me into your bed. When I was going to sleep on the cot, it was a job. Now I'm sleeping in your arms. I'm not some damn gigolo who's gonna take money for helping out the woman he's involved with."

She shivered a bit, never having seen the man so utterly furious. He was something to see when he was angry—so big and loud and strong. Yet she wasn't frightened, because she knew he'd never hurt her. She just couldn't help feeling a little intimidated. But she also understood his point of view.

Spence was every bit as proud as she was. And while she wouldn't accept his charity, he wouldn't take her money. Stalemate.

Unless…unless she found another way to compensate him, without him even being aware of it until it was done. Already feeling better, she began wondering which of her customers were mechanics at some of the local garages. Determined to make some calls in the next few days and find someone who could fix Spence's motorcycle, she gave him one small nod of agreement.

"Okay," she said softly, letting him think he'd won this round. "I won't try to pay you again."

"Good."

"But you need to eat more."

Giving her a curious look, he put the car in gear and pulled out of the parking space. "Why?"

"Well," she said, "if all you're getting is room and board, it's not really fair for me to feed you nothing but Zeke's cheeseburgers."

He didn't say anything for a long moment, and she saw his hands tighten reflexively on the steering wheel. Then, in a low, intense voice, he said, "You've definitely been feeding me more than that."

At first, her mind went straight to the naughty possibilities of his comment. But the way he'd said it made her suspect he hadn't been referring to the way he'd been devouring her every night this week in her bed.

And for the rest of the car ride, she couldn't help wondering what he'd meant.

DYLAN HAD NEVER BEEN more angry at himself for allowing this charade to happen than he was when they pulled out of Temptation's parking lot. The motorcycle story was so ridiculous. But so was everything else, wasn't it?

He had a BMW parked in a garage a few blocks away, owned a two-story house in the next town, had a healthy portfolio, a healthier bank account…and was playing the part of a homeless bum. *The things we do for love.*

That word—love—bounced around in his brain as he and Cat drove through the streets of Kendall.

Yeah. He loved her. He couldn't even try to fool himself that this was some dumb crush left over from high school, or that it was just about sex. If he'd never laid eyes on her before last Friday night, he'd still have fallen just as hard.

Cat Sheehan fed his soul—which was exactly what he'd been thinking when she'd laughingly told him to eat more. And he wasn't sure he'd ever feel complete again if she were to walk out of his life.

Which put him in one hell of a position. He didn't want to keep up this ridiculous charade, but he couldn't honestly predict how she'd act when she found out the truth. For all he knew, she'd kick him out the door. Which would be bad enough in terms of his love life. It would be even worse for Cat in terms of her workload.

He'd gotten a lot accomplished this week...but not enough. Not nearly enough. Cat needed him and, frankly, he needed her. And he wasn't willing to risk that by confessing his sins. Not yet. Soon...but not yet.

"So where are we going, anyway?" she asked, breaking the silence in the car.

"It's a surprise."

"Is it the type of surprise that's going to get me back to Temptation by five for the happy hour crowd we might actually get tonight?"

He nodded. "You'll be back in time."

They didn't talk much during the rest of the drive, except when he pulled onto the highway and Cat guessed they were headed for Austin. They were, but she hadn't guessed where.

She began fishing. "We going to the tattoo parlor where I got mine so you can get a matching one?"

Snorting, he shook his head. "Uh, sorry, no needles entering this body unless they contain vaccines against various diseases or pain-numbing agents when I'm at the dentist."

Cocking a brow, she stared at his earlobe. "Ahem."

Without saying a word, Dylan reached up, stuck his finger into the silver loop and tugged. The two-part, magnetic earring gave way, falling to the console between the seats.

"You…you cheater!" she sputtered.

Laughing at the indignation on her face, he said, "You think I'm crazy enough to intentionally have someone poke unnecessary holes in my body? Josh and Jeremy's little sister decided that the long-haired rebel of the group really needed an earring so she gave me this one."

"You're a big phony," she said, beginning to laugh. "This is serious ammunition, you know. Next time some horny bar tramp throws her shirt at you, I might just tell her you're a big fraud with a fake earring."

Fraud. Yeah. That was him. His body tensed, his good humor dissipating. It was easy to forget he was just play-acting for a little while, but the truth always came back with a roar. He was a phony in just about every way, and God only knew what Cat was going to say about it when she found out.

Maybe she'll laugh, like she did about the earring.

Yeah. And maybe it was gonna snow right here in Kendall, Texas, next Christmas.

"Well," Cat said, apparently not noticing his distraction, "I think it's very sexy, pierced or not." She dug around between the seats and came up with both parts of the earring. Without asking, she leaned over and put the thing back on, tenderly brushing the tips of her fingers over his neck, blowing warm breaths on his skin.

When she kissed him there, tracing her tongue over his pulse point, he nearly growled. "I'm gonna drive off the road unless you go back to your side of the car."

She nearly purred. "Oooh, yeah, car sex at a rest stop." Dropping her hand on his leg, she slid it up, getting dangerously close to his suddenly very alert crotch.

"Cat," he said with a groan, "I meant I'm going to *crash*."

Not relenting, she continued to kiss and nibble his neck, her hand moving ever higher until her fingertips were an inch away from very serious trouble and a potential wreck.

He dropped his hand over hers, muttering, "Enough. We have someplace to go."

"So tell me where we're going and I'll stop."

Quickly glancing over, he saw the mischief in Cat's expression and knew she was still very curious about where they were headed. "You'll see when we get there."

"When's that?"

"You're relentless, aren't you?"

Removing her hand to safer territory, she nodded, waiting for him to explain. But he didn't give her even a tiny hint, not until he pulled up to the entrance of the university a short time later.

"Here?" she asked, her eyes nearly popping out of her head. "We're going to the University of Texas?"

That's exactly where they were going. Cat had talked about going back to school, and he'd noticed the application packet she'd received in the mail Monday. But she'd hidden it away, as if embarrassed, and hadn't even begun to work on it. He suspected he knew why—she needed a push, some encouragement, a reason to fill the thing out. A reason to believe she wasn't just grasping at some pipe dream and that she really could do something completely unexpected with her life.

Dylan parked the car in a lot outside the administration

building. Thankfully, since it was summer session, the campus was much less crowded, because he'd heard parking was a nightmare during the rest of the year. "So," he said as he cut the engine, "you think we can pass for a couple of eighteen-year-olds?"

She eyed him up and down, appearing skeptical. "I doubt it. If I ever did register here, I'd stick out like a sore thumb, even if I really was eighteen."

Reaching over, he took her hand in his and squeezed it. "You'd stick out like a gorgeous blonde and every young college dude would be all over you. Don't think that hasn't occurred to me, so you really ought to be rewarding me for my mature lack of jealousy." Giving her a lascivious look, he added, "Sexual favors are always an appropriate reward."

She wasn't teased out of her sudden bad mood. "It's not just my age that'll make me stick out."

"What do you mean?"

Cat kept looking out the window, staring at the buildings, the grounds, the people milling around—obviously students taking summer classes. Her sigh was probably audible to those standing by the tower, which was a landmark on campus. "I belong in a bar slinging drinks and fending off pervs. Not on a college campus." Shaking her head, she lowered her voice. "And certainly not sitting behind a teacher's desk in a high-school classroom."

This doubting woman was *so* not the Cat the rest of the world knew. That woman had boatloads of confidence—with good reason, given her looks, her personality and her wit.

Right now, he suspected, he was sitting with the Cat few people ever saw. The wistful one. The quiet one. The one who doubted her own abilities, her own intelligence. The one who sometimes seemed so alone.

The one he'd first begun to understand by the light of a bonfire so many years ago.

He lifted his hand to her face, running the tips of his fingers across her cheek, then gently taking her chin to make her look at him. She met his stare, her expression serious and her eyes clear. He certainly hadn't expected tears—Cat was not the sort to feel sorry for herself. Neither, however, had expected this absence of emotion.

"Cat, you have so much potential, and you have every right to do whatever you can to make your dreams come true." She opened her mouth to speak, but he touched his index finger to her lips. "I'm not trying to push you into anything, and if you want me to start the car and drive away, I will. But I wish you'd get out and walk around with me, just for a little while, to see how it feels. Then maybe you'll be more interested in filling out the application that came in the mail the other day."

"You noticed that, huh?"

"I noticed. And since you requested it, I have to assume you wanted it. So why not look around and get yourself pumped up about it, instead of hiding it in your underwear drawer?"

She crossed her arms and lifted a brow. "Why, exactly, were you looking in my underwear drawer?"

He rolled his eyes. "Because your washer's on the fritz and I ran out of shorts."

She snickered, her mood finally lightening. "Well, if you want to borrow my panties, you could at least *ask*."

"Forget it," he said with a mock growl as he leaned across the console to nuzzle the side of her neck. "I'd rather go commando. Gotta leave your panties alone, since your supply is running pretty low."

She tilted her head to the side and moaned from

somewhere low in her throat. He followed the sound, kissing his way along her skin.

"If I am," she murmured, "it's only because *someone* keeps ripping them off me."

He chuckled. "That's only because *someone* is so sexy I can't stop myself."

Nibbling his way up her delicate neck, he finally pressed his lips to hers in a warm, wet kiss meant to both arouse her and give her confidence. They only pulled apart when they heard shouts and whooping from outside. Some of the students had apparently noticed.

"Well, now you really fit in on a college campus," he said.

He almost held his breath, waiting for her response. If she asked him to drive away, he'd do so, though not without feeling the slightest bit disappointed in her.

Finally, she nodded. "Okay. Let's go check out the campus."

CHAPTER EIGHT

THE COUNTRY-AND-WESTERN group Cat had hired for the weekend wasn't as popular as Dylan's band had been, but they weren't bad. Not bad at all. They'd certainly had her feet tapping for three nights in a row as she worked the bar, making the drinks as fast as Dinah could place the orders.

She figured the fact that the musicians were middle-aged and paunchy had something to do with the shortage of young, on-the-make women in the audience. Still, they put on a good show, and they entertained the small crowd that did come in each night. She'd sold lots of drinks and earned a lot of tips and made Kendall's line dancers really happy.

To give him credit, Spence hadn't shown any distaste for the whole thing. She'd figured, given his passion for rock and roll, that he wasn't into country. Actually, he didn't mind it. It was the line dancing he hated, which she discovered Sunday night when she tried to nudge him out into the dancing crowd he'd successfully managed to avoid on the previous two nights.

"Go on, give the single women out there a thrill," she said when he moseyed behind the bar to offer her a hand.

As if she'd let him make his famous margarita for any other female. And definitely not a Slippery Nipple...

which she was still counting on him to deliver one of these nights.

"You must be joking."

"You don't like country-and-western music?"

"I like almost any music, except opera. Country-and-western's fine," he said. "Line dancing, however, is for saps and old ladies at wedding receptions."

Grinning, she gestured toward the younger women in the room who were shaking it with gusto. "They're not all old. And they've been eyeing you up all night, sitting there in the corner nursing one beer. Go on, give them a thrill."

His frown deepened. "I'd rather put on a thong and do the mambo than line dance to 'Achy Breaky Heart.'"

"Well, I don't want you giving them *that* much of a thrill."

A grin tickled his lips.

Turning to face a customer waiting to place his order on the other side of the bar, she gave him a wicked look over her shoulder. "What is it with you and women's underwear, anyway?"

She should have known better than to taunt him. Because Spence stepped right up behind her, tucking in close so that the warmest, hardest parts of his front were pressed right against her back and bottom. She hissed, feeling heat rush into her cheeks. But he didn't relent. Instead, he reached around and snaked one arm across her waist, then nuzzled the side of her neck. "How many times do I have to tell you," he said with a hungry growl, "I haven't ripped them off you every single night this week because I want to *wear* them."

Judging by his roar of laughter, the customer—a longtime regular who'd stuck with them through the construction—had overheard. He tilted back his cowboy hat and smacked his hand flat on the surface of the bar. "Oooh, Cat Sheehan, I never thought I'd see the day."

"What day is that, Earl? The day somebody mistook that rug under your hat for real hair?"

He snorted, impossible to offend. "Nope. The day a man got you so wound up you made my Jack and Coke with gin and Sprite."

Glancing down in horror, Cat realized she had, indeed, mixed that unappetizing concoction. Scrunching her eyes shut, she mumbled, "Sorry about that. Next one's on the house."

Earl shrugged, his good humor never fading from his round face. "Not a problem. It's worth every penny to see you looking at someone else the way most of the fellers usually look at *you*."

Cat nibbled her lip, then tried to stare him into silence. "I don't know what you're talking about. Maybe you've had enough, Earl. You better watch it or I'll have to cut you off."

Uncowed, the older man winked at Spence. "She's got the young men all chompin' at the bit and pantin' for her attention, and she never gives any of 'em the time of day." Then, eyes twinkling, he added, "Nice to see your heart ain't froze up solid, little girl."

Cat winced, wishing the floor would open up so she could sink into it. She'd just been accused of being a heartless tease in front of Spence. Could've been worse, she supposed. Being called a tease in front of your lover was probably better than being called a tramp.

"Cheers, y'all," Earl said as he scooped up his new drink, which Cat had just made, and wandered back toward his table, his shit-kicker boots clomping on the wood floor.

"You better watch it, Earl," she called after the laughing man, "or I'll uninvite you from our closing-down party next Monday."

He turned on his heel and wagged his index finger at her. "You're not keeping me away from that shindig, darlin'. I'll come say goodbye to Sheehan's Pub even if I have to crash the party."

Grinning at the man, who'd been a loyal customer way back when her dad had been working behind the bar, Cat nodded and then got back to work, struggling to get caught up with the multitude of drink orders.

The rest of the evening flew by until it was last call and the band started packing up for the night. Rubbing a weary hand over her brow, Cat watched the customers drift out, savoring their good humor and their friendly waves. They were like family, some of them. Like Earl. Another reason saying goodbye to Temptation in another week was going to be brutal.

"You okay?" Spence asked after everyone else was gone and they were alone in the closed tavern. He'd been helping her put up the chairs and sweep the floor. Well, actually, she'd swept and he'd held the dustpan.

"I'm fine. It was a good night."

"Made a lot?"

She shrugged. "Not a fortune. But the feeling was good. You know?"

Thinking about it, he slowly nodded. "Yeah, I think I know what you mean. There's a real camaraderie, isn't there?"

"Exactly." Her chest suddenly felt tight. "I'm going to miss a lot of those people."

He stepped close, taking the broom from her hand and leaning it in a corner. "They'll miss you, too." Tugging her into his arms, he stroked her hair, then her back, trailing his fingers down her spine to cup her bottom.

Cat's melancholy mood immediately disappeared as a new kind of tension—the Spence kind of tension—took its place.

"Cat, do you remember last week when you told me about some of the things you wanted to do before you left this place for good?"

Nodding lethargically, she said, "Yes. Like dancing on the bar." She couldn't keep a dreamy sigh from her lips. "And lying on the stage under all those different spotlights. Have I told you yet how much I liked that?"

"I think the whole street heard how much you liked that Tuesday night," he said with a wolfish chuckle.

"Ha ha. I think you were doing some moaning yourself."

"No question about it. Now, back to your fantasies…."

"Yes?"

He kissed her temple, then the top of her cheekbone, then the top of her ear. She started to sigh, then to moan when he nibbled his way to her earlobe.

"How about we make another one come true?"

DYLAN HAD TRIED TO THINK of a way to make Cat's nude sunbathing fantasy come true, but it'd been impossible. Somebody was always around—or there was the potential of somebody always being around. Whether it was a bar customer, Dinah, Zeke or one of the employees of the bookstore, there was a good chance someone could glance out a window and see whatever was going on in the walled garden out back at any time of the day.

And call him greedy, but he didn't want anyone else

seeing Cat reclining naked in the backyard, soaking up the sun. Just him.

So he'd modified things a bit. Because despite how many people were on the premises during the daylight hours…only he and Cat were here late at night. He'd specifically planned for this night, Sunday, since the bar closed down at midnight instead of 2 a.m.

He only hoped soaking up moonlight would be a good enough substitute.

"Where are we going?" she asked, excitement in her voice as he took her hand and led her through the deserted downstairs.

"You'll see." He'd set things up earlier in the day, knowing she'd be much too busy to wander outside.

Earlier this week, Cat had told him how much she regretted that her hectic schedule denied her many chances to retreat out back alone, as she liked to do. Once he'd explored the garden, he'd understood why. It was a wild and tangled oasis, something he'd never have expected in this busy downtown area. He'd sat outside a couple of times, watching the hummingbirds zipping in and out, drinking from the fragrant blooms of coral honeysuckle. So yes, he could see how she would like hiding away out there to lose herself in thought.

Tonight, she was going to lose herself. But it wasn't going to be in thought. It would be in sensuality.

Walking through the back hallway, past the beautiful erotic mural painted on the wall, he slid an arm around her waist.

"We going to the ladies' room?"

"Uh-uh."

When they got to the back door, he unlocked it and stepped outside into the hot, humid night. Thankfully, a slight breeze had kicked up this evening so the still, sultry air was circulating a bit. Enough to enable him to catch the scent of the sweet-smelling honeysuckle, flowering in profusion on the wildly curling vines.

He paused on the back step, examining the garden by night. The dense shrubs, unpruned, grew in all shapes along the base of the tall, limestone garden walls. The vines and moss completed the illusion that the pale stone wall was actually green and alive. A few tall live oak trees dripping with moss provided shade, shadow and mystery. In one corner stood a small statue of a frolicking Cupid, and nearby, a birdbath, the chips in the stone and the brackish color of the water well-suited to the atmosphere of the place.

The garden, which Cat had told him had been planted and maintained by her grandmother, was like an abandoned paradise, long forgotten about except by a chosen few. A good place to be alone. Which, he supposed, was why Cat liked it so much.

"Oh, my goodness," she said as she spied the reclining lawn chair he'd brought out earlier. Surrounded on all sides by the lush, overgrown vegetation, the chair was covered with a brightly colored beach towel. On a small table nearby stood a pitcher of lemonade and two glasses, plus a CD player and a bottle of suntan lotion. Faint strains of music laid down a low, pulsing beat in the otherwise quiet night.

He cast a quick glance toward the other pitcher—the one he'd brought out just a little while ago when she was locking up. It remained discreetly tucked on the ground behind the chair, to be retrieved very soon.

"I can't believe you did this," she said as she stepped closer to the chair.

"You can't sunbathe naked. Will moonbathing do?"

Instead of answering him, she reached for the

bottom of her shirt, pulling it up and over her head in one smooth, fluid motion. Dylan watched, his mouth suddenly dry. It went drier when she reached around to unfasten her bra, then tossed that to the ground, too.

"Hmm," he said, stroking his chin, "I don't believe the phrase was sunbathing topless. I think there was full nudity involved."

Laughing, Cat kicked off her shoes and unfastened her jeans. He held his breath, watching as she pushed them down. No matter how many times he'd seen her body in the past week, the view always thrilled him. She was perfect—softly curved, creamy-skinned, full-breasted and long-legged. His fantasy woman.

But he suspected she would still be his fantasy woman in thirty years when her body had a few more pounds, a few wrinkles, and maybe, God willing, stretch marks from the babies he wanted to have with her.

Dylan shook the images out of his mind. He knew he was in love with Cat and wanted to marry her, but he couldn't even begin to try to make that happen until he'd come clean with her about everything.

Which he'd do. Soon. But definitely not tonight.

"Are you going to join me?" she asked as she slowly lowered herself onto the recliner and gave him a welcoming look.

"Not yet." Moving closer, he knelt beside her and reached for the bottle of suntan lotion. "Roll over and let me do your back."

Excitement flashed in her eyes, lit so beautifully by the bright moonlight, and she immediately did as he asked. Lying on her stomach, she turned her head to the side to watch him.

He had to pause for a minute to appreciate the sculpted lines of her shoulders, the smoothness of her back and the perfect curves of her ass. After brushing her long hair out of the way, he flipped open the top of the bottle with his thumb.

"Don't want you to get burned," he murmured.

"I think I'm going to go up in flames before this night is over."

He laughed softly. "I'm counting on it."

Squeezing some of the lotion into his palm, he hesitated for the briefest second, building her anticipation. Finally, he lowered his hands to her back. She moaned, low and deep, when he began kneading the silky smooth fluid into her skin. Her eyes drifted closed as he made applying sunscreen more of a massage, easing the tension from her shoulders and the back of her neck.

Soon, the lotion disappeared, soaking into her, but it left a fruity, coconut scent in the air. The smell mixed with the heady aroma of the honeysuckle growing all around them, creating a feast for the senses. Just like everything else about this night was going to do.

Bringing the bottle up again, he squeezed it directly onto Cat, letting the milky white fluid drip onto the base of her spine.

"Ooh," she murmured without opening her eyes.

Dylan reached down and brushed his fingertip through the lotion, letting it glide down her hips. Then he massaged it in, taking special delight in hearing her coos as he kneaded her bottom and the backs of her legs.

When he'd finished, right down to the soles of her feet, he said, "Roll over."

"Oh, absolutely."

He hid a smile, knowing how much she liked to be touched, and exactly *where* she liked to be touched. Her breasts were especially sensitive…but he had something other than tanning lotion in store for them.

Not telling her that, he began to massage her again— the front of her shoulders, then down her sides to her midriff. He ignored her breasts completely, hearing her disappointed hiss. Unable to contain an evil chuckle, he applied more sunscreen, gently rubbing her midriff, her soft belly, then that most vulnerable, tender area below her tan line.

She arched up instinctively, but he didn't give her the touch she craved. Instead he continued stroking her, all the way down her legs to the tips of her toes.

"You're a horrible tease," she mumbled throatily.

"No, actually, I'm a very good tease."

"Yeah. But, uh, Mr. Tease, I think you missed a few spots."

He began to kiss a path back up her legs. "Which spots would those be?"

She squirmed a little, her hips rising helplessly as he brushed his mouth up her thigh, over her hip, then onto her belly. She groaned. "Dylan…."

He ignored her, even when she tangled her fingers in his hair. With an impatient sigh, she grabbed for his shirt, tugging it up and off, not even waiting for his help. Then she reached for his waistband.

He tsked. "Ah, ah, I'm not finished lotioning you up yet."

"No kidding. The most vulnerable, sensitive, pale skin on my body didn't get protected. I could get moon poisoning."

Looking up into her eyes, he saw her cock a brow, daring him to deny it. Which he had absolutely no intention of doing.

He raked a hot gaze across her body, focusing mostly on her breasts, topped with her hard, dusky nipples.

Then he reached for the hidden pitcher—the one behind the birdbath. "This calls for some extra special moisture," he murmured as he removed the lid.

Without warning, he drizzled the butterscotch-smelling concoction across her breasts, swirling it deliberately over her distended nipples, positively drenching her in the stuff. "I think I'm going to like this," he said, wondering if she'd realized yet what he'd doused her with.

Without another word, he bent toward her breast and caught her creamy nipple in his mouth, sucking deeply, letting the flavors of Irish Cream and butterscotch liqueur blend with the delicious taste of Cat.

"Oh, my God," she groaned.

"This is definitely slippery." he said with a chuckle.

"You're wicked."

"You're getting sticky."

He stopped talking for a moment, focusing only on licking and sucking each drop of the creamy drink off every curve of her breast. She began to moan, jerking a little with every strong pull of his mouth, each flick of his tongue.

"I think it made more than your nipples slippery," he said as he tasted his way down her middle. Then, just to make absolutely sure of it, he picked up the pitcher and drizzled a thin line from her belly down into the curls between her legs.

She jerked so hard she almost fell off the chair. "Dylan, you're making me crazy."

"Good." Because she'd been making him crazy for almost a decade. "Whoops. Definitely getting sticky here," he whispered. "I'm going to need to lick every nook and cranny."

"Nook?" she said weakly.

"And cranny."

Lowering his mouth, he followed the gooey line until he reached that sweet spot between her legs. Not even pausing, he licked her thoroughly, drinking up every bit of moisture. Until she came with a cry of delight right against his tongue.

"Oh, yes," she moaned, still shaking and rolling her head back and forth as the pleasure racked her body. "I love the way you do that."

"Then you're gonna adore what I do next." Almost frenzied now to have her—to plunge into her and lose his mind—he grabbed a condom and loosened his jeans, not even taking the time to take them all the way off. Cat opened her eyes to watch, parting her legs invitingly as he sheathed himself.

And Dylan dove right in.

Oh, yes. She was so tight, so wet. Felt so welcoming—like coming back to the place he belonged.

Cat rocked up to meet his thrust, wrapping her legs around his hips and her arms around his neck. "I can't believe you did all this." She kissed his jaw, then his neck. "Thank you."

"You're welcome. So welcome. God, Cat, you feel so good," he said, savoring the sensation of Cat's body wrapped around his own from top to bottom, and *especially* in the middle.

They slowed the pace, rocking into one another, exchanging slow, deep, wet kisses and slower, tender touches. Until finally, with a guttural cry to the full moon overhead, Dylan took them both hurtling over the edge.

CAT FILLED OUT the application to the university Monday and got it in the mail Tuesday. Spence didn't comment, though he knew what she was doing. When he'd heard her groaning as she tried to remember some of the courses she'd taken in high school, he'd given her shoulder a squeeze of encouragement, but hadn't said anything. It was as if he knew she needed to do this completely on her own, but wanted to remind her she had his support.

She hoped she could get in, but if not, there was always community college. Either way, she *was* going to get an education.

That got her thinking about Dylan's future, his dreams and ambitions. She'd asked him a couple of times if he was happy with his life and where he was going, and each time he'd ducked out of answering. Once by saying he'd never been happier because he'd become involved with her. That had made her heart race. The other time, he'd grown quiet and introspective, murmuring something about her not knowing everything about his past.

Made her wonder if he was a corporate dropout or something. He certainly had the brains and drive to be a successful professional. Plus, he wouldn't be the first person who decided he really wanted to be a rock star instead of a lawyer or accountant and threw it all away to pursue his dreams. She wanted to know more, but Spence had seemed uncomfortable talking about it, so Cat hadn't pushed.

One thing she *did* finally work up the nerve to do was ask him to play for her.

Walking into her bedroom after her shower Wednesday morning, she found him sitting on her bed, strumming his guitar and singing very softly under his breath. He looked amazing, reclining against her pillows, wearing nothing but a pair of jeans. From his wet, fresh-from-his-own-shower hair, over his broad chest still glistening and damp, down to his bare feet, he was the picture of luscious male. And she instantly got hungry and warm, wanting to dive on him and get him all dirty and sweaty again so they'd each have to take another shower. Together.

"There's that song again," she murmured as she leaned against the doorjamb, watching him.

"Sorry," he said, lowering the guitar.

"No! Please, don't stop. I'd…I'd like to hear you. I haven't heard you play anything but your bass."

"I play a little of everything," he said as he brought the guitar back up into position and began to play it again.

The way his fingers moved over the instrument, stroking and flicking and plucking, made her shake a little, remembering the times he'd played her body in exactly that same way. Sighing, she closed her eyes and listened for a moment. "Sing that song for me, would you?" she asked, unable to resist.

There was silence for a moment, and when Cat opened her eyes, it was to find Spence watching her intently.

"You know which one I mean," she said.

He nodded once. Saying nothing, he began to pick out the melody, already familiar to her, then started to sing the lyrics. Somehow, without the backup of the band and the wild, partying audience, the song seemed more intense. Much more personal. Much more sensual. And when he reached the chorus, repeating the line, "the girl with the fire in her eyes," she nearly melted right there on the spot.

He must have been crazy for that woman. Crazy with emotion and with want, because both were so clear in every word, in every note.

Which hurt. She *hated* that he'd written that soul-surrendering piece of music for someone else. That he'd loved someone else that much.

She was jealous. Jealous of someone he said he'd never really been involved with, someone who was gone from his life. It wasn't his possible involvement with the woman that hurt. Cat was no angel, and she sure didn't expect Spence to have been a monk. Sex with people in the past she could deal with.

Complete, intoxicating love? Well, that was just a bit harder to swallow. So much so that when he was done, she gave him a grateful smile that hid her true thoughts, then grabbed her clothes and darted back into the bathroom to dress.

"Cat?" he called. "Did I hurt your eardrums or something?"

"No, no, it was great. I just…I just have things to do."

She held her breath, wondering if he'd follow her. After several long moments of silence, she heard him moving around, then heard the door to her apartment opening—and closing.

Staring into the mirror, she stood there for several minutes, wondering why the thought of Spence loving someone else, even before he'd met her, was so painful.

She had some suspicions. But she was nowhere ready to admit them, even to herself.

After drying her hair and pulling on her clothes, she left the apartment to look for him. The man deserved a thank-you…and an explanation. Not an *honest* one, but she had to tell him *something*, so she scoured Temptation. Not having any luck, she finally decided to check out back. That was where she found him.

She'd gotten used to Spence taking care of all the little things that needed to be taken care of around here, but this really surprised her. He was in the garden, squatting by the Cupid statue, going at it with a scrub brush and a bottle of bleach. Beside him was the newly scrubbed birdbath, which looked cleaner than it had in years. "What are you doing with those?"

"Cleaning them up," he replied.

"You really think they're worth salvaging?"

He looked up, meeting her gaze. "Absolutely."

Cat smiled a little, knowing why he was going to this trouble. It had everything to do with the magical hours they'd spent in the garden Sunday night. As if he wanted to hold on to a tangible reminder so the memory of it wouldn't fade.

She didn't think her memories of that night were *ever* going to fade. Among all the incredible moments she'd shared with Spence since she'd met him, their garden interlude would likely remain the strongest in her mind.

One thing was for sure—she'd never be able to drink a Slippery Nipple again, and she wasn't sure she'd ever be able to serve one. Because for the rest of her life, she suspected even the smell of it would probably make her have an orgasm on the spot.

"Spence? Thank you for playing for me. I'm sorry if I acted as though I didn't like it."

He said nothing, just watching her curiously, as if knowing she had more to say.

Taking a deep breath, she admitted the truth. "This is going to sound really stupid."

"Try me."

She stepped closer to the birdbath, running her fingers over the bright, clean edge of the bowl, not meeting his gaze. "Well, I just had this insane moment of jealousy. Silly, huh? But for a second there, I would cheerfully have scratched the fire right out of the eyes of that girl you wrote the song for."

To give him credit, he looked completely stunned. As if he'd expected her to say anything else. "You're… you're serious?"

She nodded, feeling a flush of embarrassment in her cheeks. "I'm sometimes, uh, not very ladylike, and can be, uh…a little ungracious in my thoughts. Particularly when I think of some other woman you wanted as much as you obviously wanted her."

Dropping the scrub brush, he slowly rose to his feet, brushing off the front of his jeans, which were splashed with water and algae. "Cat, you don't understand. That girl…that song…"

Cat put her hand up, stopping him. "Spare me the gory details, please."

Stepping closer, he said, "It was *years* ago."

Knowing he was about her age, she found that difficult to believe. Her skepticism obviously showed.

"Honest to God, I wrote that song when I was fifteen."

Her jaw dropped. Fifteen? He'd had that much talent—not to mention that much mature emotion— and *desire*—at the age of fifteen? "Wow."

"Exactly. And like I told you before, it was definitely a case of unrequited interest. I've never felt that strongly about a *woman* during any of my adult relationships." Something flickered in his eyes and his voice dropped. "Only you."

Somehow, the already sunny morning seemed to get a little sunnier and Cat couldn't contain a big, wide smile. "Whew!"

He laughed, apparently amused by her very visible

relief. Taking her hand, he said, "So you ready to take a break? I want to take you out to lunch."

"You won't let me pay you a penny even though you're working like a dog," she said with a scowl, "and you think I'm going to let you take me out to lunch?"

He grinned. "Okay, *you* take *me* out. I'm getting a little sick of Zeke's burgers."

Unable to resist his good humor, she nodded. "Let me make sure Dinah's okay covering the ghost-tavern, and then give me a half hour to get changed."

Though she didn't tell Spence, she also remembered she had some calls to make. Over the last couple of days, between the college paperwork and the incredible lovemaking, Cat had let the issue of Spence's salary slip her mind.

She completely understood his reluctance to take money from her, considering they were lovers. Since she would have felt exactly the same way, she couldn't blame him. But she wasn't going to let him do all of this for nothing but some mind-blowing sex.

Definitely mind-blowing.

Reminded now of his situation, she was more determined than ever to sneak his keys away, then get someone to work on his bike. When he was finished here, Spence deserved to ride away on a working machine.

Ride away. Lord, she didn't want to think about that, didn't want to even consider it. After next Thursday, when she closed the door to Temptation behind her for the very last time, there would be no more reason for Spence to stay around.

Which had been exactly what she'd wanted, right? Exactly the right thing to happen, given her new commitment to school and settling down to work toward her more responsible future.

So why did it feel so horribly wrong?

"You're an absolute fool, Cat Sheehan," she whispered as she walked back into the bar.

Because she'd gone and done the unthinkable. She'd fallen for him—totally, completely and irrevocably.

How on earth she ever could have imagined it would be safe to have a wild fling with Spence, she didn't know. This was in no way a wild fling. Fling didn't come close to describing the importance of this relationship.

It killed her to even whisper it in her own brain, but she very seriously suspected she was in love for the first time in her life with a guy who would soon be roaring out of it.

CHAPTER NINE

ON THURSDAY MORNING, CAT noticed that the shipment she'd ordered from her liquor supplier hadn't shown up. It wasn't too surprising that she hadn't figured it out earlier since she'd been so busy. Aside from the bar, she'd begun packing up her apartment, as well as finding a new one—which hadn't been too big a deal since she'd lived in Kendall all her life. She already had a good idea where she wanted to live and a single visit to a local apartment complex had settled that issue.

But between the packing and the planning and the phone calls, she hadn't even noticed the delivery man hadn't made it on Monday to restock Temptation after the weekend. The guy had been as regular as clockwork for three years, so it hadn't sunk into her brain that she hadn't seen him, not until last night. A decent-size crowd had come in—for the third night in a row—and the shortages had become obvious.

Cat figured the crowd was a result of this weekend's closing. Word had apparently spread, and old customers were drifting in each night to say goodbye. She saw many faces she hadn't seen since the road project began.

But because of those thirsty patrons, she was now totally tapped out of two of her house beers, and was dangerously low on her house brands of liquor.

She was about to reach for the phone to call and raise some hell about it when it rang on its own.

"Temptation," she said.

"I did something wild."

It took her a second to identify the voice as her sister's, because *Laine* and *wild* just didn't normally go together in a sentence. "Uh, wild? You?"

"I got engaged."

Cat's jaw dropped, and so did the receiver. She fumbled around with it for a second, then yanked it back toward her ear. "To who?" she asked, still reeling at the unexpected news.

"That guy I dated years ago, when I lived with Aunt Jen for the summer. His name is Steve. Wanna come to a wedding on Saturday?"

Saturday? Cripes, not only was her sister getting married, she was practically eloping! This was so not Laine. Then again, *her* life had been a little unusual in the past couple of weeks, too. Who knew she'd have fallen ass over elbows in love with a homeless musician?

Realizing Laine was awaiting an answer to her invitation, Cat cleared her throat. "I—sure I'll be there. Where else you gonna get a maid of honor?"

"No kidding?"

"No kidding. Maybe I'll even have a date to bring with me. Someone special."

This time, Laine was the one who sounded surprised. "Really?"

"Yeah," she admitted softly. But she didn't elaborate. This phone call was about Laine's upcoming wedding, not Cat's, uh...*wild and crazy fling. Just a wild and crazy fling.*

Maybe if she told herself that often enough, she'd actually start to believe it.

But probably not.

After her sister had filled her in on the details, Cat realized she had some quick plans to make. Flying to Georgia for one night wasn't going to be easy…particularly not during Temptation's final weekend in business! That her sister would even schedule her impromptu wedding for this weekend told her how completely out of her mind in love Laine must be.

Not wanting to bring her down, Cat didn't mention the bar or the fact that this would be the last Saturday night they'd ever be open. It was definitely a hardship. But there was no place else she'd rather be than at Laine's side on her wedding day.

"I still can't believe you're doing this," she said with a shocked laugh. "Does Mom know?"

"Yes, and she's coming." Laine went on to give her more details.

"Okay, I got it," she said, scratching down the information on a crumpled napkin. "Saturday the twenty-fifth, you can count on me."

Even as she made mental plans, she acknowledged that her relationship with her sister was changing, likely forever. She wanted that relationship to be a positive one. An open, honest one, particularly if Laine was gonna end up living in another state. "Maybe we can find a few minutes to talk," she said, holding tightly to the phone cord for courage. "A lot's been going on with me, too. I'm thinking about going back to college. I even have all the paperwork filled out."

"Wow." Laine paused for a second, then added, "Then the bonus money I earned for the cover of *Century* is going to come in handy."

Her sister's dreams really were coming true. Cat

knew how much this meant for Laine's career. "You got the cover? Really?"

"Yep. And it's definitely enough for tuition."

Cat immediately refused. "You keep the money... start a college fund for your first baby." Then something occurred to her, "Oh, God, you're not pregnant, are you?"

Laine laughed. "Definitely not."

"Okay, because one bit of wild, impulsive Laine news per day is my quota," Cat said. Knowing her sister, she stressed, "As for the money, I mean it, I'll be fine. I think the two of us are going to come out a little better than we expected on the furniture and fixture sales."

Her voice soft, Laine said, "You've been amazing the last couple of weeks, you know? I felt so overwhelmed when I left, as if everyone was relying on me to fix everything."

That hurt a little, since Cat had wanted so much from her sister—*except* fixing. "If you'd wanted out, all you had to do was say so."

"No, I couldn't. Temptation meant too much to you and Mom."

Yeah, it had. Whether she'd ever realized it before or not, she had to admit that her sister had made some sacrifices to help Cat keep the business up and running.

Laine added, "And don't worry about the closing. I'll be back to help with that."

"Seriously, you don't need to. I've got everything under control." Well, that was something of a whopper considering her personal life was about as out of control as it had ever been, but she meant it about the business. There was nothing Laine could do here and she didn't need to be brought down by dealing with it.

"Really? You're not just saying that?"

"No. I'm not. But is there any chance you can make a pit stop here before you guys go on your honeymoon? I'd love for you to be here for the party on Monday, after we officially close. I think Mom's even considering hopping a flight and coming...which means you gotta be here to referee."

"I wouldn't miss that for the world," Laine replied with a laugh. Then, after the slightest hesitation, she murmured, "And Cat, just in case you change your mind, remember, I'm always here if you need me."

Hearing the verbal olive branch, Cat reached out and grabbed it. "I know you are. You always have been." Then, smiling a little, she added, "I'll see you Saturday."

WHEN DYLAN ARRIVED back at Temptation Thursday afternoon, he found Cat involved in a flurry of activity. She was barking something over her shoulder at Zeke, who stood in the doorway to the kitchen, a laconic look on his grizzled face.

Cat's friend Vicki—who'd waited tables a few weekends ago—was back. She stood beside Dinah, nodding as Cat pointed at some signs and flyers strewn across the bar. Beside Cat was an older man, stoop-shouldered and white-bearded. He was paying careful attention to every word she said. Actually, judging by where most of the old geezer's attention was focused, he was paying much more careful attention to Vicki's legs, revealed by her skimpy jean shorts.

Dylan rolled his eyes, smothering a laugh. Then he realized what Cat was telling the old man: she was teaching him how to make a drink. When she reached for the familiar bottle of Irish Cream, Dylan coughed into his fist, wondering if she was telling him how to make the concoction Dylan had consumed off Cat's body the other night.

"You're back!" she said, her entire face lighting up with her smile.

God, that smile. He could live on that and nothing else and never want for anything. "I'm back," he said, ambling across the room. He reached into his pocket and dug out a bank envelope, then slapped it onto the bar. "That antique dealer went nuts over those two old pinball machines you said have been here since Prohibition. And he loved the old carousel horse, too."

Cat's eyes lit up. "Really?" When she reached for the envelope and started counting cash, shock washed over her face. "*This* nuts?"

Well, maybe not *that* nuts. Maybe Dylan had kicked in a little extra, but still, the antiques had commanded a good price. "There's a small fortune in the *junk* that broker so graciously offered to *take off your hands* for next to nothing."

"No kidding." She came out from around the bar and threw her arms around his neck, giving him a big loud kiss right in front of the others. "One more reason to be very thankful you came walking through my door two weeks ago, Dylan Spence."

"It's Spencer," he murmured, suddenly realizing he'd never clarified his full name for her.

"I should have figured," she said. Then she kissed him again and tried to step away. "Thanks again, Dylan Spencer."

Wrapping his arms around her waist, he held her close, not letting her pull away. "I'm glad I could be here to help. And I'll be right here until the last chair is paid for and the last light fixture carefully packed."

Her clear green eyes shifted away, as if his words had bothered her instead of reassuring her. "Cat?"

"You two gonna make out all day or finish teaching me how to make these girlie drinks?" the old-timer at the bar said, sounding as amused as he did surly.

"Sorry, Uncle Ralph," she said as she stepped out of Dylan's arms, then made the introductions. "Dylan, this is my uncle Ralph, who used to run the bar with my mom. He retired without ever learning the finer points of, uh…froufrou drinks."

Lowering his voice, he asked, "Hmm, does he know how to make a Slippery Nipple?"

"What was that?" her uncle Ralph asked. "Did he say what I thought he said?"

Dinah and Vicki were both grinning, neither of them stepping up to explain.

"No, he didn't," Cat said. Leaning up on tiptoe to kiss Dylan's cheek, she whispered, "He hears better than my mother did when I tried to sneak in after my curfew."

He laughed, as she'd intended him to, but after the way she'd said his full name for the very first time a moment ago, the image of Cat as a teenager made him edgy. If she started putting two and two together…she might come up with a rat.

Namely him.

This was getting crazy. He had to come clean. Every day that went by brought them closer to the end of her life here at Temptation, and closer to her future. A future he very much wanted to share.

So why haven't you told her?

There were a number of reasons, really. There was still work to do. Plus, he suspected Cat would need him emotionally after she locked the door for the last time after the last customer.

Oh, and there was the fact that he was a chickenshit.

He didn't want to lose her. Didn't want to see her face tighten with dismay—or, even worse, indifference—when she realized there was about as much chance of him riding out of here on that Harley as there was of old Uncle Ralph there ever learning how to make froufrou drinks.

"So why the hands-on training?" he asked, watching Cat walk back around the bar to rejoin her uncle.

"Uncle Ralph's going to cover for me Saturday night."

Sliding up onto one of the stools, Dylan gave her a curious look. "What's Saturday night?"

"I have to go out of town."

His jaw almost hit the bar. Cat was leaving town—leaving *him*—the day after tomorrow? Right in the middle of her last weekend in business? "You gotta be kidding me."

Cat shrugged. "No choice. Family comes first."

Oh, no, someone in her family was hurt. Sick. That was the only possible explanation. He felt like a first-class heel for his flash of dismay, which had been so selfish when Cat was in the midst of a family crisis. "I'm so sorry. Is it bad?"

"It's totally insane."

Very bad. "I'll help cover the bar. Anything you need."

Cat blinked, looking surprised. Then a hint of color rose in her cheeks. "I'd kind of hoped you might come with me."

He didn't hesitate, glad she'd want him by her side during a family tragedy. Because that's exactly where he most wanted to be. "Of course. Anywhere."

"Great. Do you…I hate to ask this, but do you have a suit?"

A *suit*? A dark suit? God, someone had died. "Who…"

"It's Laine."

Laine. Her sister. The photographer chasing wildfires in California. Dylan jumped off his stool and pulled her toward him, tugging her across the bar and into his arms. "God, Cat, honey, I'm so sorry."

Cat wriggled a bit, pulling back so she could look him in the eye. She half lay on the bar, supporting herself on her fists, and gave him a look as if he were totally nuts. "Spence, my sister is getting *married*."

Dylan closed his eyes and counted to ten, to savor his relief and hide his embarrassment at having jumped to a very wrong conclusion. When he opened them, he saw everyone in the room staring at him. "Good God, Cat, I thought you were telling me we were going to a funeral!"

Cat's eyes widened into twin circles, then she nibbled her lip. "Sorry, I guess I'm a little scatterbrained. It's been kinda crazy ever since she called and told me she's getting married Saturday, in Georgia."

"Georgia? Your sister is getting married *this* weekend, in another state?"

Cat probably heard the indignation in his voice. Judging by the frowns on the faces of the others in the room, they'd all been wondering the same thing…how could her sister have forgotten—or ignored—what this weekend meant to Cat?

"She's crazy in love," Cat explained with a helpless shrug. "And you know what? More power to her." She looked around the room, at the bare walls, the space where the pinball machines had stood, then back at him.

"If I'd stayed here, I would have been moping and sad and worried. This way, I have something wonderful and bright and beautiful to do on Saturday instead of crying in my beer about something I simply cannot change."

There was genuine honesty in her expression, and that excited smile still tugged at her beautiful lips. She obviously meant it. Which made him believe that, at last, Cat really was preparing to let go of the bar for good. That she was already looking forward to the future. Laine's…and possibly her own.

"Okay," he said. "I can manage a suit. When do we leave?"

"I plan to look into airfares right after I reach the liquor supplier, who I've been trying to call all morning." She put a hand up, stopping him before he could say a word. "And I *will* be paying for your ticket. You're doing me a favor by coming as my date, and since you're not letting me pay you, this'll make me feel better. Even though the amount I'll spend would be slave wages in comparison to the hours you've worked, especially since I've earned so much more than I would have if you hadn't been around."

He wasn't going to have this argument again, not in front of the others, especially. But soon—once he'd come clean to her about his real situation, including his finances—he'd make sure she let him pay her back. "You're on. So we'll be back here by Sunday for the official closing day?"

She nodded, rattling off the details. "I figured we'd fly out Saturday morning and back Sunday morning. Dinah, Vicki, Zeke and Uncle Ralph can cover Saturday night. We'll be here for one final day with the customers Sunday afternoon and evening. And then we'll have our big final private party on Monday."

She had everything figured out. Typical Cat…got knocked by some completely unexpected surprise and just rolled right with it. As always, she amazed him. "Sounds like a plan."

Vicki cleared her throat. "Uh, Cat, what liquor supplier do you use?"

"Texas Todd's," she murmured, already reaching for the phone. "Though, if they're going to be this unreliable, I might have to rethink that, which could be tough since they're the only supplier within sixty miles of here."

"Uh-oh," Vicki said softly. "Have you been watching the news or reading the paper at all this week?"

"No. I've been kind of busy. Why? What is it?" Cat asked as she slowly returned the telephone receiver to its cradle and gave her friend her full attention.

Seeing tiny, tense lines appear around Cat's mouth, he knew she was preparing to be hit by yet another crisis. Hit hard. Dylan stiffened. What, exactly, was about to land on Cat's shoulders now?

"I hate to tell you this," Vicki said, her reluctance evident in her tone, "but something happened at the Texas Todd's warehouse here in Kendall Sunday night. They said on the news that a bad wire sparked a fire that turned into an enormous blaze. The whole place went up in smoke. It was completely destroyed."

They were all silent for a moment, looking at the nearly drained bottles on the half-empty shelves. Dylan breathed deeply as the truth slowly sank in. Even if Cat could find another supplier in Texas close enough to stock her up in time for this weekend, what company would want to deliver to a bar that was closing the next day? He knew enough about the law to know there was a lot of paperwork and a ton of regulations governing businesses that sold liquor, and she'd have to jump through a lot of hoops with a brand-new company. That would take time. Time Cat simply didn't have.

Judging by the shock and dismay on everyone's faces, they'd all come to pretty much the same conclusion. But nobody spoke, not until her Uncle Ralph cleared his throat. "Well," he said, sounding philosophical, "Guess that means I don't have to learn how to make any frou-frou drinks after all."

Cat didn't say a word. She simply turned on her heel and stalked out of the bar.

SITTING IN A CHAIR by the window overlooking the back garden, Cat stared outside, deep in thought. She still couldn't quite believe it. She'd been all ready to close down after this weekend, somehow making herself believe she was totally okay.

But now…now the end had come and she hadn't even prepared herself for it. If they didn't run out of booze tonight, they would by tomorrow night. Meaning no matter what, Temptation was officially out of business in a little over twenty-four hours.

She didn't cry. Her eyes didn't even well up. Instead, she sat at the window, looking down at the greenery her grandmother had planted and tended two decades before. At the limestone wall she used to climb as a kid, when her parents were inside working and her older sister was off studying…being the angel.

Cat had spent most of her childhood here, with a family who worked 24/7 on their business. She'd knocked out her first tooth when she'd fallen off a stool by the bar. She'd come here after school every day growing up, doing her homework in the kitchen while her grandmother made the Irish stew Sheehan's Pub used to be famous for.

Her first date had picked her up downstairs, under the watchful eye of her parents and Uncle Ralph. Here's where she'd had her first job…her only job. And here's where they'd held the Irish wake for her dad, which had drawn more than three hundred people and had gone on all night.

Lots of memories. Lots of ghosts.

Still dry-eyed, Cat finally began to realize something. It wasn't the bar—or the *building* she was going to miss. It wasn't the customers or the smell or the sounds or the excitement. It wasn't the freedom or the fun or the music.

It was the past. She'd held on so tightly to this place because it linked her to the past and to the people who'd meant so much to her, who'd all drifted away. As if she could somehow keep them close by holding on to the place where they'd last been together.

Where she'd last seen their faces.

"You don't love working this bar," she whispered, knowing it was true. She just hadn't known any other way to live. And she'd thought that by staying here, she was keeping the whole family alive. But now, knowing she'd soon be leaving here for the last time, she began to accept that all those memories and moments she'd been so afraid of losing were going to be leaving with her.

"Cat?" she heard from behind her.

Spence. He'd entered so quietly she hadn't even known he'd followed her up to her apartment.

"Hey."

"You okay?"

She nodded. "Yeah. I am." Forcing a laugh, she

added, "At least now, I won't have to worry about missing work Saturday. I don't suppose we'll have anything to serve by last call tonight."

He squatted beside her chair, looking so worried, so concerned. The warmth in his brown eyes and the tenderness in his stare got to her. Really got to her, way down deep.

She in no way wanted to let this man get away. Because she loved him. Truly loved him, no matter what she'd been trying to tell herself. Cat would sooner strike a match and fling it at the bottles of liquor downstairs than let this man walk out of her life. "I'm so glad you're here," she finally said. "You've made this bearable, you know?"

"Is there anything else I can do?"

Reaching toward his long, silky hair, she ran her fingers through it, then offered him a shaky smile. "Help me make some Drink Till We're Dry signs?"

He laughed softly. Turning his head until his face curved against her hand, he gently kissed her palm.

"Will you do something else for me, Spence?"

"Anything."

Thinking about tonight, about Temptation going out in style, she asked, "Will you play tonight? Just you, with your guitar, play like Temptation's the *Titanic* and you're the orchestra?"

He didn't even hesitate. "Absolutely."

Smiling, she gave him a grateful nod.

"Will you do something for me, too?" he asked. "Tomorrow, when this is all over, will you come somewhere with me? I have something I want to show you… something I want to talk to you about. I think we should get some things out in the open."

Cat was, of course, curious, but her mind was already

caught up in how to get the word out about tonight. She had calls to make, signs to print up. The word would spread quickly, she knew, she just needed to get it started.

Yeah, there was definitely a lot to do…but a big part of her wanted to just stay here for a little while longer. With him.

"Cat? What do you say? Can we talk tomorrow?"

She nodded. "Sure. But for right now…"

"Yes?"

Sliding out of her chair, she knelt in front of him on the carpet, then wrapped her arms around his neck. "Right now, I want you to make love to me." Pressing her lips to his, she kissed him, mentally telling him all the things she'd realized but hadn't yet figured out how to put into words.

In silence, Spence rose, drawing her with him. Cat didn't even try to protest when he bent and lifted her into his arms, carrying her the short distance back to her bedroom. When he gently laid her on the bed, she drew him down with her, feeling weak and hungry, empty and fulfilled, all at the same time.

As always, Spence seemed to know exactly what she needed and how she needed it. In recent days, they'd made love in a lot of ways, a lot of moods. Crazy and wild and hot and intense.

But this time, it was incredibly sweet.

Kissing her deeply, he slowly drew her clothes off her body, stroking and caressing every inch as it was revealed. He focused all of his attention on pleasuring her. His every touch was delightful, every kiss intoxicating. All her nerve endings sparked and sizzled, until she could barely breathe because of the sensations washing over her.

"You're gonna be okay, Cat," he whispered as he pulled away long enough to take off his own clothes.

"I know."

Cupping her face in his hand, he stared into her eyes, then slowly entered her. Cat curved up, welcoming him, meeting his slow, deliberate thrusts, wondering how she'd ever thought she'd known anything about lovemaking before she met this man.

Sliding in and out of her with sweet hunger and passion, Dylan kissed her forehead, her temple, her eyelids. The beauty of it moved her, called to her and eventually overwhelmed her. For the first time in months, Cat gave in to the emotion, to the feelings battering her from all directions, knowing she was in the arms of a man who adored her and would keep her safe.

And finally, she let go. Let go of everything. Including her long-unshed tears.

DYLAN HADN'T PERFORMED *alone* in front of an audience in a long, long time. But somehow, Thursday night, it seemed easy. Maybe because, in spite of the crowd who'd gathered to say goodbye to Temptation, he always kept his focus on Cat.

She looked beautiful. Deciding to live up to the name of her establishment, she'd dressed all in vivid, hot, tempting red. Every guy in the place was drooling, but Cat's body language made it clear she was taken. By him.

He hoped she'd still feel that way tomorrow because he was going to come clean with her. Everything had to be out in the open *before* he went with her to her sister's wedding.

He simply couldn't put it off, couldn't go mingle with her family and stand by her side when he'd been lying to her for weeks. So he planned to take her out to his house and get everything out in the open. And then ask her to live in it with him. As his wife.

He definitely wasn't lying tonight. As he went through his repertoire of torchy rock songs on the stage, he really sang only to Cat. The rest of the crowd faded to insignificance, just background chatter. He was giving her what she'd asked for, entertaining her customers, but every heated word of every hot song was directed entirely at the woman tending bar. Particularly when he dug all the ones he'd written for her out of his brain.

Including one he'd been working on for the past several days. Called "In The Garden," it was something he'd been playing around with in private. He'd never had any intention of performing it, certainly not this soon after writing it. But just in case the bottom dropped out of his world tomorrow, and she decided she liked the biker, not the software engineer, he wanted to make sure she knew how he felt.

As soon as he sang the first few words, he knew he had her attention. Cat's head jerked, and she stared at him from across the room. Slowly lowering the bottle she'd been pouring from, she froze, standing in utter stillness, listening to the words.

He only hoped she remembered them tomorrow.

After it was done, she gave him an intimate smile that told him she understood—and appreciated—every word.

After he'd sung his third set, late in the night, he lowered his guitar, needing a drink and a break. It was nearly closing time, and, as Cat had predicted, they'd run out of most of their drinks earlier in the evening. But people were sticking around, wanting the friendship and the camaraderie to last a bit longer.

Making his way across the room, he accepted the thanks from the audience, saying his goodbyes to the regulars he'd come to know in recent weeks. But he never took his eyes off his target, who was watching his progress out of the corner of her eye.

"That was amazing," Cat said as soon as he slid up onto the only vacant stool at the bar. "The garden song... wow." He didn't know if it was the reddish glow from the lights, or a reflection off her devil-red blouse, but he'd swear her cheeks held a hint of a blush. "Did you... write that recently?"

Accepting a bottle of water from her, he nodded, then gave her an intimate smile. "Yeah. Very recently."

The color in her face grew deeper. Dylan couldn't contain a small chuckle. "I don't think I've ever seen you blush before."

"Yeah, well, don't get used to it. I only like red from the neck down."

He sat there with her for another half hour, as the crowd finally started to drift away. It was a work night, after all. Cat accepted tons of hugs and her tip jar looked ready to explode. Soon there were just a handful of people left, including Vicki, Dinah, Ralph and Zeke, all of whom were sitting at the bar, nursing their own bottles of beer, which Zeke had kept stashed in the kitchen fridge.

"This was great, Cat. Man, I'm really gonna miss this place," he heard someone say.

That comment had come from a guy behind him. Glancing over his shoulder, he saw a stranger, a young man, who gave Cat a friendly smile. "Girl, it's a damn good thing you called me to come work on that bike this afternoon, or I wouldn't known about tonight's closing-down party."

Casting a quick glance at Cat, he saw her eyes grow wide. "Uh, glad you could make it," she mumbled.

Dylan tensed, a sense of foreboding putting him on edge.

"But, you know, it's not like I could do anything," the stranger said, keeping his voice loud to be heard over the last of the crowd lingering nearby. Shouldering his way closer, until he stood directly beside Dylan, he added, "There's not a thing I could do with that Harley. She's a beauty, well-maintained, and purrs like a kitten. Don't know why you thought there was something wrong with her." Then he tossed a familiar-looking set of keys onto the bar, which he hadn't seen since he put them in the grungy duffel bag he'd gotten from Banks.

Damn. This guy was talking about Jeremy's motorcycle. No doubt about it. "Cat…"

"What do you mean it's running?" she asked sharply, looking back and forth between the stranger and Dylan. Her eyes narrowed. "You told me it was broken-down."

"You called a mechanic?" was all he could manage to sputter, instantly put on the defensive.

"Because you wouldn't let me pay you."

"Because I don't accept money from women I'm sleeping with," he shot back.

The stranger whistled. "Okay, I'm outta here."

Everyone else within earshot seemed much less considerate. The conversation at the bar seemed to drop to a dull drone.

Cat seemed to realize they'd drawn a lot of attention, too. Looking around frantically, she gestured toward her uncle Ralph. The old man nodded at her signal and came around to relieve her, though, with closing time just five minutes away, he wouldn't have much to do.

Focusing on Dylan, she muttered, "Let's go."

Trying to figure out how to explain, he followed her out of the bar and up the stairs to her apartment. Things were coming to a head a little sooner than he'd planned, and definitely not in the *way* he'd planned. Cat was already tense and upset. He just hoped he wasn't about to make things much, much worse.

"You lied to me about the motorcycle not running," she said as soon as they entered her apartment.

Kicking the door shut behind him, he nodded. "Yeah."

She crossed her arms. "Why?"

He thought it over, wondered what to say, then finally realized nothing would do but the truth. The whole, entire, lame-ass truth.

So that's exactly what he told her.

CHAPTER TEN

HE WASN'T A HOMELESS MUSICIAN. He wasn't a starving songwriter. He didn't ride a Harley and he didn't usually wear scruffy jeans and hard-rock-band T-shirts. He didn't live a carefree life and he didn't like to travel the world, being tied down to nothing and answerable to no one.

If she were just meeting him, Spence would be the man of her mature, grown-up Catherine Sheehan dreams. But she hadn't just met him. And she was still just Cat.

"You lying son of a bitch."

Spence's eyes widened slightly, but he didn't speak up in his own defense.

"You mean to tell me you have a car parked down the block? And you own a house in Tremont?"

"Yes."

"You…you're a software engineer of all things?"

He shoved his hands into his jean pockets. Through the thin, worn fabric, she could see them curling into fists. "Yes."

Still not quite believing it, Cat just shook her head, then slowly lowered herself onto her sofa, pulling her legs up in front of her. Wrapping her arms around them, she stared at him, trying to make sense of it all.

He'd faked being some broke, starving musician, living here and working like a dog for weeks. All the while, he'd had a house in what Cat knew was one of the priciest areas around. "Were you just playing a twisted game with me?"

"No game. You needed help. And I wanted to give it to you."

"That's ridiculous. You let me think you were some kind of unemployed laborer looking for work."

"I don't mind real labor, Cat." Pulling his hands out of his pockets, he stepped closer and sat down in a chair opposite her. He dropped his elbows onto his knees and leaned closer. "You needed help. I knew, deep down, that you wouldn't take my help if you didn't think I needed the job. Was I wrong?"

Still glaring, she stuck out her chin and refused to answer.

"That Sunday night…the night we danced on the bar…"

"Don't even go there," she snapped.

He ignored her. "That night, Banks made up that bullshit story about me needing a place to crash and not having a ride."

"Yeah, he did. I suppose he thought it was terribly funny."

"In his own, twisted way, he was trying to help me. Trying to give me a chance with you. I guess we'd both figured that once the Four G's finished playing that weekend, I wouldn't have any excuse to see you again."

She would have found a reason, but she didn't say that. "But *after* he made up all those lies, you went along with them."

"I was about to tell you the truth, but when I opened my mouth to, you started talking about how much you really *did* need help. I thought if you knew the truth you'd politely thank me for the offer, push me out, then try to do everything by yourself."

Yeah, she probably would have. Rubbing a weary hand over her eyes, she admitted it. "You might be right."

"I didn't want to lie to you. But I didn't want to leave, either. And if making you think I needed *you* as much as you needed *me* gave me a chance to see what could happen between us, that was more reason to go for it."

The truth continued to swirl around in her brain, so darned convoluted and yet so simple. When she thought about it, it was funny in an awful, twisted way.

She'd originally decided to steer clear of Spence because she'd thought he was a reckless, broke musician.

Then she'd plunged into an affair with him *because* she'd thought he was a reckless, broke musician.

Now that she knew he wasn't, she had absolutely no idea what she was going to do.

"You know, I'd told myself before you walked into Temptation that first night that I wasn't going to get involved with any more dangerous guys. You seemed a walking, living, breathing example of the kind of man I needed to steer clear of."

"But you changed your mind."

"Yeah. When Banks spun his story about you being the free-spirited drifter I'd imagined you were, I decided I'd have a wild fling with you before you rode away forever. Then I'd settle down and find someone serious and responsible to build a future with."

His jaw tightened. "A wild fling. That's what you wanted?"

She nodded. "That Sunday night when you offered to stay, I'd made the decision to seduce you."

"Because you thought I'd be good for a fling. No strings, no future, nobody you could ever really fall for."

That wasn't quite the way she'd been thinking. At least, she hoped not. Because it sounded awfully hard when spoken out loud like that.

"And now that you know I'm not, you still gonna shove me out of your life and go on to someone mature, responsible and serious?" He rose to his feet, thrusting a frustrated hand through his hair. "This is too damned confusing. You want me for one thing, then for something completely different. How the hell am I supposed to know what you really want? Do *you* even know?"

She leapt to her feet, too. "Well, how am I supposed to know who you really *are* when you haven't been honest with me since the minute you walked through my door?"

Tension snapped between them, as sharp and wicked as a live wire. Cat sucked in a deep breath, trying to remain calm, when she really wanted to smack him for not being who she'd thought he was. And for being exactly who she'd once thought she wanted.

Her head hurt.

"You want to know who I am?" he finally said, his voice thick and ragged. "I'll tell you."

He stepped closer, grabbing her shoulders and holding her steady. "I'm Dylan Spencer. The geeky little teenager you saved from annihilation in a school cafeteria more than nine years ago. The guy who fell a little in love with you right then and there. The one who went completely nuts over you one night when you stared into the flickering light of a bonfire."

Cat froze, having a hard time taking his words in.

Was she really hearing what she *thought* she was hearing? She'd *known* him? He'd been a classmate? "You're saying we went to school together?" she asked, completely dumbfounded.

"For one year. I was a senior and you were in tenth grade. You barely noticed me…I didn't exist for you. Too boring, too nondescript, too *normal*." His fingers tightening, he added, "But you definitely existed for me."

Shocked, Cat remained completely speechless. She had no idea what to say. She hadn't recognized him. Lord, she *still* didn't recognize him.

"It's okay, I know you don't remember me. There's no real reason you would. Ours paths almost never crossed, we never officially met." With a small laugh devoid of humor, he added, "And I've changed a whole lot more than you have."

As if realizing he'd been squeezing her hard, he released his grasp on her shoulders and stepped back. Shaking his head, he mumbled something under his breath, then turned on his heel, walking away from her.

"Wait, Spence, you…I don't understand this."

He paused. "Look," he said, not turning around to face her. "You want to know the real reason, the *main* reason I lied to you about who I really am?"

"Yes. I do."

His body straightened, his shoulders squaring, but still he didn't turn around. Cat's breath caught in her throat as she waited for something—some explanation that would make sense of all this.

In a low voice that she almost didn't recognize, he spoke again. "It's because I didn't want to see your eyes glaze over with boredom when you realized I wasn't the kind of guy who'd ever interest you." He paused, then spoke again. "I didn't want to be invisible to you again."

Cat's pulse raced and a roaring sound began to echo in her brain. Good Lord, this man thought he could ever be *invisible* to her? "Spence…"

"It's Dylan," he bit out. "Josh and Banks are the only ones who call me Spence." Striding to the front door, he put his hand on the knob. Before turning it, he finally glanced at her, his expression somber, his eyes hooded. "I'm sorry I lied to you, Cat. I'm truly sorry."

Opening the door, he began to step through it. But before walking out completely, he said one more thing. Something that made time stand completely still.

"And Cat? It was you. The girl with the flames turning her hair to gold and the fire in her eyes? It was you. It's *always* been you."

Then he walked out.

As if it wasn't bad enough that his relationship with Cat had just been blown all to hell, Dylan arrived home Thursday night to find his house trashed. Jeremy had apparently had his party. And considering the teen and two of his buddies were sprawled in lawn chairs by Dylan's pool, it hadn't ended yet.

Staring in disbelief at the stains on his carpets, the hole in the family-room wall and the broken lamp, he bellowed, "Jeremy Garrity, what the hell did you do to my house?"

The three guys launched out of their chairs and raced inside. Jeremy's face paled when he saw the fury in Dylan's. "You're home early."

"No shit, Sherlock." Glaring at the other two guys, he snapped, "Get to work or get out."

The two of them raced for the door, leaving so fast, Dylan barely had time to make a mental note of their faces.

"I'm sorry, man, I guess it got kinda out of hand. I cleaned almost everything up, just had this little bit left to do," Jeremy said weakly.

Almost everything? Shaking his head in disbelief, Dylan simply stared at the young man. Somehow, though, he couldn't muster up much righteous anger. It had simply dissipated. Because what the hell did a couple of stains and broken things matter in comparison to the mess he'd made of his life?

He'd lost her. He'd lost Cat for good. Not only because he wasn't the man she wanted, but because he'd lied to her.

Rat-brained moron.

But even as a part of him mentally kicked himself, another part of Dylan couldn't stop thinking about Cat's own confession. She'd considered him good enough for a wild fling—and nothing else.

That rankled. So maybe it was just as well she hadn't forgiven him for his deceptions and asked him to stay in her life. Because, at this point, he couldn't be entirely sure whether she wanted *him*, Dylan Spencer, or the phantom responsible, grown-up man she'd told herself she had to find.

"A buddy of mine has a brother who does drywall work," Jeremy said. He was bending down to pick up a few pieces of trash, as well as some of his clothes, which were strewn over the furniture. "He's coming out to fix the hole tomorrow."

"Forget it," Dylan said, rubbing a weary hand over his eyes.

Jeremy straightened and met Dylan's stare unflinchingly. "No, it was my responsibility. I'll pay to get it fixed."

Judging by the young man's earnest expression, he meant what he said. Dylan agreed and gave one short nod. "Your motorcycle's still parked where you left it. Cat has the keys."

The young man grinned. "So did it work? Is she all yours?"

Unable to contain a bitter laugh, he merely walked away.

Eventually, after cleaning up everything he could, Jeremy packed up his stuff and took off. Dylan barely noticed. He'd been locked in the spare room, where he stored his musical equipment.

Music always calmed him, evened him out. The harder the tune, the cooler he got. So by late Thursday night, he was rocking the walls off his house. And he kept rocking them, throughout most of the night, wondering if his neighbors were gonna call the cops, but not really caring.

Taking a break on Friday, he kept his mind off Cat for a while by checking his mail, paying his bills and getting in touch with a company he was supposed to do some programming for. But by that night, he was back in the studio, playing his guitar, his Fender or his keyboard, trying to work through his emotions the way he'd *always* worked through them.

By Saturday, he finally began to feel back in control. Somewhat sane, at least. He'd done a lot of thinking—

about the deceptions and the misunderstandings. Her words, and his own.

One thing was clear: they couldn't end things like this.

He loved Cat. He wasn't about to let her go without one more shot at making her believe that. Equally important, he truly believed she loved him. Or, at least, she loved the Spence she'd spent the past two weeks with.

So if he had to become that man to get her back, then by God, that's exactly what he'd do.

CAT THOUGHT SHE'D DONE a darn fine job of hiding her unhappiness during her whirlwind trip to Georgia. She'd smiled and talked and teared up during Laine's wedding to her beaming groom, Steve. She hadn't fought with her mother and had enjoyed getting to know Steve's family.

And she'd somehow managed not to break down and cry one single time. At least, not while anyone was around.

In private, she'd cried a lot.

But something happened Saturday night while she stood in the shadows, watching Laine dance with her husband, beaming up at him with happiness so bright it blinded. She realized she had been looking at Dylan the same way all week. Finding out that he'd been less than honest about his real life hadn't diminished her feelings. It had angered her, but it hadn't made her miserable.

No. What had made her miserable was the thought that she'd lost him. Really truly lost him. Exactly at the moment she'd started to realize just how long she'd *had* him.

He'd fallen for her years ago when she'd been a

flighty, silly high-school girl who hadn't even realized he existed. Maybe it had been a mere teenage infatuation, though, given the intensity of the beautiful song—the song he'd unbelievably written for *her*—she suspected it was something more. It didn't really matter. Because he'd most definitely fallen in love with her during the weeks they'd just spent together. Just as surely as she'd fallen in love with him.

So what the hell was she doing in Georgia, when he was back in Texas, probably wondering if she was ever going to talk to him again? "I need to go home," she whispered to no one in particular. "Now. Right now."

Which is what she did. Despite the fact that the reception was still going strong, Cat slipped away and headed straight for the airport.

Her flight home wasn't until early Sunday morning, but she managed to get a late Saturday night one instead. Before taking off, she'd made a quick cell phone call to Vicki, who did some quick research for her on the Internet. So she now had the home address of a certain Dylan Spencer of Tremont, Texas.

The plane was on the ground in Austin by 3 a.m. and by five, she was back at Temptation, trying to decide whether to go straight to his place now, or go upstairs and catch a couple of hours of sleep first. Knowing she wouldn't be able to sleep until she'd seen his face and made sure she could salvage their relationship, she opted to skip the nap.

The drive to Tremont wasn't a long one, and she was at the front door of Dylan's big two-story house by the time the sun started spreading its yellow-orange rays above the low-hanging clouds on the horizon. "Now or never," she told herself as she reached for the doorbell.

Jabbing it with her finger, she paused, then jabbed again. He'd probably need to be woken up.

Suddenly, the door was yanked open and Dylan stood there, rubbing at his eyes, all scruffy and sleepy, wearing only a pair of tight jeans that he hadn't even bothered to button.

Yum.

"Dammit, the party's over, you're a week late," he snarled.

"I am?"

His head jerked up. "Cat?"

"Yeah. Can I come in?"

He stepped back out of the way, allowing her to enter.

"I like your house."

"I can't believe you're here. The wedding..."

"Was lovely."

"You went?"

"Of course I did. Took a redeye home."

Their chatter was light and pointless and served only to let them both adjust to the reality of the moment.

She was here. This was their last chance. And they couldn't blow it.

Taking a deep breath to work up her nerve, Cat started at the beginning. "Dylan...about high school. I'm so sorry."

"Don't be," he said. "If I'd had any guts at all, I would have actually approached you and introduced myself. You just scared the hell out of me." Shaking his head, he admitted, "Sometimes, you still do."

She smiled a little. "You should have. You were *very* cute." Seeing his look of surprise, she explained. "I dug out my tenth grade yearbook. You were adorable." In her own defense, she added, "But you're right, you looked *nothing* like you do now."

"Late bloomer," he replied. He stepped closer, close enough so she could feel the brush of his bare arm on hers, not to mention the warmth of his body. "What are you doing here, Cat?"

Tilting her head back, she stared into his dark brown eyes. "I came to thank you for the song. It called to me from the very first time I heard it."

As if not even aware he was doing it, he lifted his hand to her arm and began to stroke up and down, putting all her senses on red alert. "You're welcome. Is that the only reason you came?"

Slowly shaking her head, she admitted, "I also came to tell you I forgive you. I don't like being lied to, but I think I can understand why you did it. You planned to tell me Friday, didn't you? That's the big 'talk' you wanted to have? And I suppose this house is what you wanted to show me?"

He nodded. "All of the above."

Yeah. She'd surmised as much. Which made things a little better, anyway.

As they both fell silent, Cat tried to figure out what to say next. Should she just blurt out her feelings? Try to be subtle? Jump on the man and be done with it?

"I forgive you, too," he finally said, still touching her so lightly, so delicately, she thought she'd melt. "For thinking I was only good enough for a fling. Hell, nine years ago, that would have sent me right out of my hormone-flooded mind."

Laughing, as he'd intended her to, she stepped closer, until the tips of her shoes nearly touched his bare toes. Their bodies were close together—so close she could see the way the wiry hairs on his chest moved with every breath she exhaled. Dying to tangle her fingers there, she forced herself to refrain, knowing there was more to be said.

He spoke first. "Yesterday, I decided…"

"Yes?"

Clearing his throat, he continued. "I decided that if it was a fling you wanted, I'd become the man you wanted to have one with. I planned to be at your door when you got home today."

Not sure what he meant, she watched as he reached up and tugged at the small earring decorating his earlobe. It didn't come off. "Oh, my God, you got it pierced."

"Uh-huh."

"You hate needles."

"No kidding. Which meant *this* was a real bitch." He pointed to his upper arm, tilting a little so she could see the splash of color on his skin.

She couldn't help gawking at the small Texas star just below his shoulder. "A tattoo? You really went out and got a tattoo?"

"I was just getting warmed up."

"Tell me you didn't pierce anything else on your body. Stick out your tongue!"

He visibly cringed at the possibility. "No more piercings. But there's something parked in my garage that you probably oughtta see."

What he meant dawned on her almost immediately. "You did *not* buy a motorcycle."

"Not exactly," he said with a small, apologetic shrug. "Cat, I'd intended to, but I just couldn't do it. Because I knew damn well you'd want to ride it and I'd be crazy worried every second. But don't you think it's just as dangerous, just as on the edge, to buy one of those Segway people mover things?"

It took a second for her to figure out what he meant. Then she couldn't help giggling out loud. "Considering you could finance the budget of a small country for what those things cost, I'd say, yeah, buying one is definitely living on the edge."

Laughing with her, he slid his arms around her shoulders and pulled her close to him. Cat burrowed against his chest, inhaling deeply, her body reacting to his familiar scent and his warmth. It had been a lonely two-and-a-half days and she never wanted to be out of his arms that long again.

Dylan touched her hair, running his fingers through it. He kissed the top of her head, then her temple. Finally, his lips brushed her earlobe as he whispered, "I love you, Cat."

Tilting her head back so she could look into his eyes, she gave the words right back to him. "I love you too, *Dylan*."

Rising on tiptoe, she pressed her lips to his, kissing him with all the emotion that had been building in her for weeks, silently telling him how much she loved him with every delicate brush of their lips and every lazy stroke of their tongues.

When the kiss ended, Dylan didn't release her from his embrace. "You know, the college is only a twenty-minute drive from here. Much closer than from the apartment you planned to move into next week."

"Oh, yeah?"

He nodded. "It'd save you lots of time. And would be much more economical…think of the money you'd save on gas."

Dylan was stroking her back, his fingertips trailing

a lazy circle just above her bottom, and Cat had a hard time focusing on anything he said. She just wanted him to pick her up and carry her to his bedroom. "Uh hmm."

"You agree?"

To anything. She'd agree to anything as long as he didn't stop those tender touches and the sweet kisses he'd begun pressing on her cheek and the corners of her lips. "Sure."

"Good. We'll just bring your stuff right here."

Blinking, she finally gave him her full attention. "My stuff? Wait, you're asking me to move in with you?"

"Yeah. I am. I know we should wait until you finish school, and I don't plan to interfere with that in any way." Lifting his hand to her chin, he gently tilted her head back so he could meet her eyes. "But I've waited a long time to have you in my life, Cat Sheehan. I don't want to wait any more. I want you in my house every day and in my bed every night. And whenever you're ready, I want my ring on your finger and my baby in your belly."

Her head began spinning as the visions of everything he'd just suggested spun in her mind. All of them perfect and so very, very possible. With a deep, contented sigh and pure happiness in her heart, she said, "Yes."

"To moving in?"

"Yes to everything."

AFTER SPENDING ALL DAY Sunday either in his bed or in his kitchen eating to regain their strength, Dylan finally convinced Cat she didn't have to cancel tomorrow's private closing-down party at Temptation. "You've been looking forward to that more than anything else for the last two weeks. You've gotta do it."

"And what am I going to serve?" she asked, her tone as disgruntled as her expression.

He scooped another spoonful of ice cream out of the container they were sharing on top of his kitchen table. "You could serve cocktail wienies and nobody would care. The point is to be together, not what everyone eats."

She shot him a look of impatience. "I mean to drink. What am I supposed to serve to drink? We're completely dry, remember?"

Holding the spoon up to her lips, he watched her lick off every drop of Chunky Monkey. The wicked things she did with her tongue made him wish they'd brought the ice cream to his bedroom.

He cleared his throat. "I suppose you can be forgiven since you haven't started college yet. But haven't you ever heard of those four wonderful little letters, BYOB?"

Frowning, she said, "I can't invite people to a party and then ask them to bring their own refreshments."

"Yeah. You can. A lot of people will be disappointed if you don't go through with it, including your sister and your mother, both of whom are flying in for this thing tomorrow, right?"

She nodded, growing quiet as she began to think about it. Nibbling her lip, with her brow knitted in concentration, Cat looked utterly adorable. He couldn't help smiling.

"What?" she asked when she noticed his expression.

"You're gonna be a lot of fun as a college student. I think I'm really going to like watching you study every night."

"Ugh. Remind me of the whole studying/test thing

again and you might just end up wearing this ice cream."

"Sounds cold…but definitely has possibilities," he said, wagging his eyebrows suggestively.

Laughing, she helped herself to another spoonful, then slowly said, "You really think people won't mind?"

"I'm sure of it, Cat. It's you they want to see and say goodbye to. You and the bar."

Finally, she nodded in agreement, then began making calls. And twenty-four hours later, as they stood amid the crowd of happy people at Temptation and he was proved right, he even managed to *not* say, "I told you so."

"I don't think we had this many people in here the entire last six months we were in business," she said, raising her voice to be heard over the chattering partygoers. "Some of these people are from my grandparents' generation."

Following her stare, he looked around the room, which was packed wall to wall. So many new faces, so many new names. Dylan was having a hell of a time keeping them all straight.

At least he knew a few people. Some, like Earl, had been customers he'd met while working here. Uncle Ralph showed up, of course, with his wife, Jill. Vicki was here. And Zeke and Dinah stood near the old jukebox, their arms around each other's waists. Judging by their intimate smiles, he figured his advice to Dinah to make the first move had worked out rather well.

His own friends had even heard about the party and come by. Banks, Josh and Jeremy were milling through the crowd, always up for a party, even if it was with a bunch of people they hardly knew. But they all liked

Cat and, per Banks, had decided to come armed with their instruments to make sure Dylan didn't try to do any more performing on his own.

The three of them had been particularly interested in Cat's friends. Josh had appeared dejected when he'd heard Gracie, the bookstore owner from next door, was involved with someone.

Most of the others in the crowd, however, were strangers to him. He assumed they were people who'd frequented the place when it was Sheehan's Pub, people who'd known Cat's father and grandparents. They told lots of stories and raised their glasses in a lot of toasts. Hearing them reminisce about the old days, he got a real glimpse into Cat's childhood and began to understand a bit more about why she'd become the woman she was. And why she could sometimes seem so alone, even in a crowd.

She'd almost *had* to become adept at that since her entire childhood had been filled with people—family and strangers alike. She'd found a way to disappear inside herself when she needed to…perhaps by shutting out the world with a book.

Or by gazing into the crackling flames of a bonfire.

Cat's family was easy to remember—her attractive sister wore a just-married smile that shone like a beacon. Plus, she had her doting firefighter husband glued to her side. They were so obviously newlyweds, there was no mistaking them for anyone else.

"I hear you're going to be living in sin with my daughter."

Ouch. That was the mother. No mistaking her, either. Brenda was direct, outspoken and a little bossy. But she had that same sparkle in her green eyes—so much like her daughter's—and she'd been a big help from the minute she'd arrived.

"Yes, but only until she'll let me make an honest woman out of her," he replied, meeting her stare evenly.

Brenda crossed her arms. "Are you going to tell me what magic spell you wove to get her to decide to go to college?"

"No magic. Cat did that all on her own. She always had the dream…she just needed the opportunity."

Gazing around the room, looking wistful, Brenda murmured, "Now she has her chance. Nothing tying her down here anymore."

Hearing the regret in the woman's voice, he gave her shoulder a squeeze. "She's always going to have this place in her heart. As well as everyone who ever walked through that door."

Brenda covered his hand with her own and nodded. "That's all that really matters, isn't it? The memories we take with us. Not the place where they were made."

Cat, who had walked up from behind just in time to hear her mother's comment, gave them both a warm smile. "Yes. That's all that really matters."

Cat's sister, Laine, also joined them. "Hear, hear."

Without saying a single word, the three Sheehan women exchanged a long, knowing look. Then, almost in unison, they each lifted their glasses—and their gazes—upward, making a silent toast to something above them. Something long gone but never to be forgotten. By the time they sipped their drinks, he'd swear there were tears in all of their eyes.

Before any of them had a chance to speak, Cat's friend, Tess—who'd arrived in an RV with a guy named Ethan—interrupted the chaos in the room. She had gone up onto the stage and was now speaking into the microphone attached to the karaoke machine. "Can I have your attention, please?"

"Oh, heavens, please tell me she's not going to sing," someone murmured. Looking, he realized it was Gracie—who did, indeed, have some of the prettiest eyes he'd ever seen…next to Cat's. She was giving Cat and Laine a worried look.

"I think this party needs a little music," Tess announced.

Cat groaned. "Oh, cripes, she *is* going to sing."

"Maybe love has improved her voice," Laine said doubtfully.

Once Tess launched into the song, appropriately called "The Party's Over," Cat winced and muttered, "Nope. It hasn't."

Cat, Gracie and Laine all started to smile, then to laugh, as all around them the crowd dutifully listened to Tess sing. Badly. Since they were the first to break into huge, loud applause when she was done, he supposed Tess's singing abilities had been a long-standing joke between them.

"Hey, we have a musical act right here who could play," Laine said, eyeing Dylan speculatively. "Why don't we see exactly what it is about you that made my sister go completely mental."

"Takes one to know one," Cat replied with a knowing stare toward Laine's bridegroom.

"Did I hear a request?" asked Banks, who'd been close enough to overhear. "Just been waiting to be asked." He beckoned for Josh and Jeremy. "You guys up for bringing down the house?"

As they nodded, Dylan looked to Cat for approval. She gave him a wide smile. "If it gets Tess away from the microphone, I'll personally hug every member of the Four G's." Then, tilting her head to one side, she asked, "What does that stand for, anyway?"

Banks and Josh both shot him a warning look, but Dylan was never going to keep anything from Cat again. "The Four Geeks."

Cat's jaw dropped, Tess—who'd just stepped off the stage—snickered. And a few others began to mumble softly.

"Uh, guys?" Jeremy said, looking a little shell-shocked. "Are you serious? Is that what it stands for?"

"Never mind. Let's go get our gear," Dylan said. Then he turned toward the door, leading the others.

"Uh, seriously, guys?"

"Shut up, Jeremy," Banks and Josh said in unison.

Jeremy didn't shut up, of course. He continued to gripe about the name as they set up onstage. Dylan finally told him if he didn't leave it alone, he was going to tell his mother about the wild party Jeremy'd had last weekend. That quieted him down.

Picking up his guitar and stepping to the front of the stage, he turned to the others and mumbled the name of an old Sinatra song. Not their usual stuff, but appropriate, he thought.

Cat was watching from the bar, surrounded by her loved ones. Her mother, her sister, her two best friends. So many others. All of them happy and laughing, building lots more memories to take with them when they walked out the door that final time.

"This one's for all of you," he said into the mike. "For everyone who's loved it here."

Then he slowly began the song, "One For My Baby (And One More For The Road)," never taking his eyes off the woman he loved.

As he reached the chorus, he saw her lips begin to move. Soon, he heard voices, and realized nearly everyone in the room had joined in. Everyone, it seemed, was feeling the magic of this place and giving it a proper farewell.

Which was, after all, no more than Temptation deserved.

After the song, there was a long moment of silence, followed by applause, hugs and tears. Though the party would continue, the goodbyes had been said.

Today had been an especially good way for Cat to say goodbye. Now she was ready to stride into her new life. With him.

The possibilities before them were limitless. He had Cat in his life at last, and together…well, together they were perfect. Magical.

As good as rock and roll.

EPILOGUE

One Week Later

Last Monday, during Temptation's last big blowout party, Cat had found time to whisper a request of Laine, Tess and Gracie. Which was why the three of them were here, late in the evening on the Fourth of July, watching her climb over the limestone wall into the back garden behind the building she'd lived in until last week.

"Is it open?" Tess whispered.

Cat tested the window, the one she'd purposely left unlocked when she'd left here for what was supposed to be the final time.

"It is. I'll meet you in a sec."

Climbing through the window, she quickly made her way through the deserted building. She moved easily through the shadows to the front door, not worrying about the near darkness. There was nothing to trip over. Not one piece of furniture, not one chair. Only the built-in mahogany bar sitting upon the bare, scarred wood floor. Everything else had been stripped out by the end of the day on Thursday, when Cat had had to turn over her keys to the city official who'd come to make sure she was out.

She'd counted on them not doing anything with the building until after the holiday weekend, and she'd been right. Nobody'd even been in to ensure the windows were locked. Lucky for her.

"Come in, quick," she said as she opened the front door to her friends. Like thieves in the night, Laine, Tess and Gracie stealthily crept in to join her, all of them dressed in dark clothing, all of them grinning like fools.

"What if we get caught?" Laine asked as she pulled the door closed behind them, peeking out to see if anyone was nearby.

Gracie nibbled her lip. "Will we get arrested?"

"We won't be here long enough for that," Cat said as she began unpacking items from the backpack she'd brought with her and placing them on the bar. A candle, which she lit. Plus a pitcher and some glasses.

It was time for one last Cosmo, for just the four of them.

"Do you realize it's been a month since we got together and did this?" Gracie asked. "It used to be we never missed a week."

Laine shook her head. "I know. But we're here now, that's what counts." Happy and tanned from her Mexican honeymoon, her sister wasn't seeing the negative side of anything.

For that matter, neither was Cat. "Can you believe the last time we did this, all four of us were single with zero in the way of prospects? Now, we're all either married or shacking up."

"I can't say I'm surprised that you and I are shacking up," Tess said. Jerking her thumb toward Gracie, she added, "But can you believe *this* one is?"

Gracie chuckled. "Gotta walk on the wild side now and then."

"By the way," Cat said as she poured their drinks, "I really like Evan, Ethan and Steve."

"Spence is great, too," Laine said. Then, lowering her voice, she added, "We're all going to be very happy, aren't we?"

That summed things up, really, and all four of them slowly nodded. They *were* going to be happy, though their lives had gone in completely unexpected directions. Laine was moving to Georgia, Tess was traveling the country in an RV. Gracie was going to law school and Cat planning for college.

And they were all in love with amazing men who adored them.

"Life doesn't get much better," Cat murmured.

Even as she said it, she was looking around the empty room that had held so much meaning for her, surprised to realize the sadness was already lessening. Thanks to her friends. Her family. Most of all, thanks to Dylan.

"So no more happy hours for the four of us here at Temptation," Laine said wistfully. "I can't believe the Cosmo Quartet is splitting up. Shall we drink a toast to ourselves?"

Raising a doubtful brow, Tess said, "Yes, on the toast. But Cosmo Quartet? If we're going to give ourselves a cutesy name, we can do better than that."

"Much better," Gracie said as she brought her drink to her lips. "Maybe we could name ourselves after that fifties band, the Temptation Four?"

Snickering, Tess said, "They were two groups. The Temptations, and the Four Tops. And it's still not right."

Cat cleared her throat, already lifting her own drink. "How about…to the Temptresses?"

The others immediately nodded at the perfect

description. Softly echoing, "To the Temptresses," they all raised their glasses in a tribute to good friends, good times and true love.

Within a few minutes, after they'd shed a few tears and said their goodbyes, they walked to the exit. Cat carried the candle to light their way and watched the others slip out into the dark night, one by one, until she stood alone in the doorway.

Turning one more time to face the room filled with twenty-one years of happy times, she pressed the picture into the memory album in her mind.

And blew out the candle.

* * * * *

SHOW & TELL

Rhonda Nelson

Once upon a time there was a towheaded,
chubby-cheeked, demonic little prankster
who grew into one of the best-looking,
most hardworking, kindhearted and admirable men
I have ever known—my brother, Greg Moore.
Being smarter than 98 percent of the population
called for a great dedication, eh, Bubba?

CHAPTER ONE

KNOX WEBBER ABSENTLY swirled the liquor around his glass as he watched the naked couple displayed on his television screen gyrate in sexual ecstasy. They sat in a pool of fuzzy golden light, face to face, palm to palm, the woman's hips anchored around the man's waist. Her long blond hair shimmered over her bare shoulders. She threw her head back and her mouth formed a perfect O of orgasmic wonder. The video's hypnotic narrator droned from the hi-fi speakers placed strategically around Knox's plush glass-and-chrome apartment.

"Let the tantric energy flow. You'll feel the power wash over you, through you and around you as your male and female energies merge. This wave of utter bliss will transport you and your partner to a new plane in sexual rapture, a new plane of enlightenment and awareness, where you'll flow in harmony with your lover and the rest of the world. Synchronized, controlled breathing is essential…"

Sheesh.

Knox snorted and hit the stop button on his remote control. He'd seen enough. He'd watched the how-to video on one of the best home-theater systems money could buy—a fifty-five-inch digitally mastered screen with superior resolution, picture in picture, and quality sound—and he still thought the entire concept of tantric sex was a load of crap.

Regrettably, it was becoming an increasingly popular load of crap and it just might be the one story he'd been looking for, the one pivotal article that would give him an edge over his competitors. Knox currently enjoyed a top spot in the Chicago scene of investigative journalism, but it wasn't enough. He wanted more. He wanted a Pulitzer. A wry smile twisted his lips. Granted, this story most likely wouldn't win him the coveted award, but it could put him that much closer to his goal. The thought sent a shot of adrenaline coursing through his blood.

Call it journalistic intuition, all he knew was each time Knox caught the scent of a good story, he'd get a curious feeling in his gut, an insistent nudge behind his navel that, so far, had never steered him wrong. This sixth sense had propelled him into his current comfortable position with the *Chicago Phoenix,* had earned him a reputation for staying on the cutting edge of journalism and keeping his finger on the fickle pulse of American society.

The nudge was there now, more insistent than ever, prodding him into action. But for the first time in his life, for reasons that escaped him, he found himself resisting the urge to pick up the scent and track down the story.

Knox chalked up his misgivings to inconvenience. Naturally, in the course of his work, he'd been mightily inconvenienced and had never minded the hassle. It was all part and parcel of his chosen career path, the one he'd taken despite howling protests from his more professionally minded parents. His mother and father considered Knox's career choice beneath him and were still clinging to the hope that he'd eventually come to his senses and use his Ivy League education for a more distinguished career.

They'd have a long wait.

Knox was determined to make his mark in the competitive world of investigative journalism, no matter the inconveniences. This wasn't just a career; it was his identity, who he was. He was a show-and-tell journalist—he unearthed facts, then he showed them to the American public, told them in his own outspoken way and encouraged them to draw their own conclusions.

He'd hidden in small dark places and he'd assumed countless disguises, some of which were completely emasculating, Knox thought, shuddering as he recalled the transvestite debacle. He'd made it a point to befriend a scope of unwitting informants, from assistants to top city officials to the occasional pimp and small-time thug, and all species in between, creating a network of eyes much like the Argus of Greek mythology.

The idea of being inconvenienced didn't disturb Knox—it was the form of inconvenience he was concerned about. Knox preferred to work solo, but for this particular story, that simply wasn't an option.

He'd have to have a partner, and a female partner at that. A wry smile turned his lips. After all, he couldn't very well attend a tantric sex workshop with a man.

Knox studied the glossy tantric sex pamphlet once more. This clinic—Total Tantra Edification—in particular was his target. While some workshops were probably on the up-and-up, something about this one didn't feel quite right. Hadn't from the beginning when this idea had first taken hold. The little brochure was chock-full of glowing testimonials from happy couples who had sworn that the workshop had saved their marriages, had brought their flat-lined sex lives from the brink of death via the energized, intimate therapy. Women, in particular, seemed to be thrilled with the results, citing multiple orgasms and even female ejaculation.

And why not? Knox wondered with a crooked grin. The whole technique seemed geared toward female gratification—a new twist in and of itself. According to his research, men avoided physical ejaculation completely, thereby prolonging their erections, and instead strove for full-body inner orgasms. The blast without the shower, so to speak, Knox thought.

Expensive tantric weekend workshops were becoming almost as common on the West Coast as surfers at the beach. While they hadn't gained as much popularity on the East Coast, interest in the subject was nonetheless increasing. A popular cable music program recently polled eighteen- to twenty-four-year-olds, and when asked what sexual subject they'd most like to learn about, tantric sex topped the list.

No doubt about it, it was a timely story. The nudge tingled behind his navel once more.

In this case, it was also a load of New Age baloney taught by aging hippies in unbleached hemp togas bent on feathering their retirement nests. Knox was sure of it. He glanced at the so-called instructors featured on the inside page. Drs. Edgar and Rupali Shea smiled back at him, the picture of glowing serenity and marital bliss.

Knox didn't buy it for a moment.

Honestly? What self-respecting man would purposely deprive himself of an orgasm during sex and claim inner enlightenment was better? Knox snorted, knocked back the dregs of his Scotch. Not a real man. Not a man's man, anyway. Sex with no orgasm? It was like a hot-fudge sundae minus the hot fudge. Hell, what would be the point?

Certainly, without ejaculation a man could keep an erection longer. But as long as one didn't detonate upon entry, what difference did it make? As long as you didn't leave your partner in the lurch—unforgivably lazy in his opinion—what was the problem with racing toward release? With grabbing the brass ring?

Absolutely nothing. While the concept of tantric sex had originated in India around 3000 B.C. and might have been genuinely used with a noble goal in mind, in today's time the technique had simply become a new twist on an old game designed to milk desperate couples out of their hard-earned money. Greedy, marketing-savvy businessmen had taken the concept and bastardized it into a hedonistic, spiritual fix-all.

Knox firmly intended to prove it and he couldn't do it alone. He'd have to have a partner.

Several possible candidates came to mind, but he systematically ruled them out. He didn't have a single female acquaintance who wouldn't expect his undivided attention, and this would be a business trip, not a weekend tryst celebrated with fine food and recreational sex. Complete focus would be mandatory in order to preserve the integrity of the story.

Knox liked sex as much as the next guy—he was a man, after all. It was his nature. And while the entire workshop would be centered around the technique of tantric sex, Knox knew better than to think he'd be able to do his job with any objectivity and be testing the theories at the same time. He'd have to have complete focus. So he'd have to take along a female who could appreciate the job he'd come there to do, and he could not—*absolutely could not*—be attracted to her.

Three beats passed before he knew the perfect woman for the job, and when the name surfaced, he involuntarily winced with dread—Savannah Reeves, his archenemy at the *Phoenix.*

The idea of having to share his byline with the infuriating know-it-all—honestly, the woman could strip bark off a tree with that tongue of hers—was almost enough to make Knox abandon the whole scenario, but he knew he couldn't.

He had to do this story.

This story would change his life. He could feel it. Couldn't explain it, but intuitively knew it all the same.

And if that meant spending a weekend with a woman whose seemingly sole goal in life was to annoy him, then so be it. Knox could handle it. All modesty aside, he could handle just about any woman. A quick smile, a clever compliment and—voilà!—she was his.

But not Savannah. Never Savannah.

She seemed charm-proof. Knox frowned, studied the empty cut-glass tumbler he held loosely in his hand. The one and only time he'd attempted the old routine on Savannah, she'd given him a blast of sleet with those icy blue eyes of hers and laughed in his face. His cheeks burned with remembered humiliation. He'd never repeated the mistake. It had been a lesson well learned and, while he didn't outright avoid her—he wouldn't give her the satisfaction—he'd made a conscious effort to steer clear of her path. She…unnerved him.

Nevertheless, he seriously doubted that she'd let her personal dislike of him keep her from jumping at the chance of a great story. Since she'd joined the staff a little over a year ago, she'd made it a point to usurp prime articles from him, to try to keep one step ahead of him. He'd never had any real competition at the *Phoenix* until her arrival. Though she irritated the hell out of him with her knowing little smiles and acid comments, the rivalry nonetheless kept him sharp, kept him on his toes.

Knox thoughtfully tapped the brochure against his thigh and once more reflected on his options…and realized he really only had one—Savannah. She was the only woman who fit the bill. Though he thoroughly dreaded it, he'd have to ask her to accompany him on the trip to California, to play the part of his devoted sex partner. A bark of dry laughter erupted from his throat. Oh, she'd love that, he thought with a grim smile.

Generally speaking, Knox was attracted to just about every woman of the right age with a halfway decent rack. Shallow, yes, but, again, his nature. He couldn't help himself. He didn't always act on the attraction—in fact, he was quite selective with his lovers—but it was always there, hovering just beneath the surface.

Regardless of his hyperlibido, Knox didn't doubt for one minute that one icy look, one chilly smile from the admittedly gorgeous Savannah Reeves would wilt even his staunchest erection. Savannah was petite and curvy with short jet-black hair that always looked delightfully rumpled. Like she'd just rolled out of bed. She wore little makeup, but with a smooth, creamy complexion and that pair of ice-blue eyes heavily fringed with long curling lashes, she hardly needed the artifice. No doubt about it, she was definitely gorgeous, Knox admitted as he forced away her distracting image.

But looks weren't everything.

Regrettably, Savannah Reeves had the personality of a constipated toad and never missed her daily ration of Bitch Flakes. Knox suppressed a shudder.

He definitely wouldn't have to worry about being attracted to her. He simply wouldn't allow it. And she certainly wasn't attracted to him—she'd gone out of her way to make that abundantly clear. Also she'd likely appreciate being in on the job.

In short, she'd be his perfect partner for this assignment. And she was too glory hungry to let a little thing like personal dislike get in the way of a fantastic byline. If he really wanted to, Knox thought consideringly, he could make her wriggle like a worm on a hook.

The idea held immense appeal.

"Not no, but hell no," Savannah Reeves said flatly as she wound her way through the busy newsroom to her little cubicle.

Knox, damn him, dogged her every step.

"But why not? It's a plum assignment, a great story and a wonderful opportunity. What possible reason could you have for saying no?"

Because I don't like you, Savannah thought uncharitably. She drew up short beside her desk and paused to look at him. She fought the immediate impulse to categorize his finer physical features, but, as usual, failed miserably.

Knox Webber had wavy rich brown hair cut in a negligent style that implied little maintenance but undoubtedly took several time-consuming steps to achieve. His eyes were a dark, verdant green, heavy-lidded, and twinkled with mischief and the promise of wicked pleasures. His lips, which seemed perpetually curled into an inviting come-hither grin, were surprisingly full for a man, but masculine enough to make a woman fantasize about their talent.

Even her, dammit, though she should know better.

If that weren't enough, he had the absolute best ass she'd ever seen—tight and curved just so and... Savannah resisted the urge to shiver. In addition to that amazing ass, he was tall, athletically built and carried himself with a mesmerizing long-limbed, loose-hipped gait that drew the eye and screamed confidence. He'd been born into a family of wealth and privilege and the very essence of that breeding hovered like an aura about him.

Though she knew it was unreasonable, Savannah immediately felt her defenses go up. She'd been orphaned at six when her parents had been killed in a car accident. With no other family, she'd spent her childhood in the foster-care system, passed from family to family like a yard-sale castoff. Did Knox know how lucky he'd been? Did he have any idea at all? She didn't think so. From what she'd observed, he seemed content to play the black sheep of the family—to *play* at being a journalist—until his father turned the screws and capped his sizable trust fund. And the hell of it was, Knox made it all look so damned easy. He was a talented bastard, she'd give him that. It was enough to make her retch.

"Come on, Vannah," Knox cajoled, using the nickname that never failed to set her teeth on edge. He was the only person at the *Phoenix* who dared call her that and the implied intimacy of the nickname drove her mad. "This is going to be a helluva story."

She didn't doubt that for one minute. Knox Webber didn't waste his time on anything that didn't promise a front page. And he had to be desperate to ask her for help, because she knew he'd rather slide buck naked down a razor blade into a pool of alcohol than ask her for a favor.

Still, there was no way in hell she wanted any part of a story with him, phenomenal byline or no. She didn't have to possess any psychic ability to know that the outcome could be nothing short of disastrous. An extended weekend at a sex workshop with Knox? The one and only man she didn't have a prayer of resisting? The one she continually fantasized about? A vision of her and Knox naked and sweaty loomed instantly in her mind's eye, making her tummy quiver with perpetually repressed longing.

No way.

Savannah firmed her chin and repeated her last thought for his benefit. "Forget it, Knox. Ask someone else." She gave him her back once more and slid into the chair behind her desk.

"I don't want to ask anyone else. I've asked you." Knox frowned at her and the expression was so uncharacteristic that it momentarily startled her. Savannah blinked, then gathered her wits about her.

"I can't believe you won't even consider it," the object of her irritation repeated stubbornly. "I thought you'd jump at the chance to have a go at this story."

Savannah tsked. "I warned you about that. Thinking upsets the delicate balance of your constitution. Best to avoid the process at all costs, Webber."

He muttered something that sounded suspiciously like "smart-ass," but Savannah couldn't be sure.

Still he was right. Had any other male co-worker asked her, she wouldn't have hesitated. In fact, it was almost frightening how much their minds thought alike. She'd been toying with the idea of a tantric sex article for a couple of weeks now and had been waiting for the concept to gel. She'd simply let him get the jump on her this time—a rare feat, because she'd made a game out of thwarting him.

"You don't know what it is, do you?" Wearing an infuriating little grin Savannah itched to slap off his face, Knox leaned his incredible ass against her desk.

"Know what *what* is?" Her eyes rounded. *"Sex?"*

With an indelicate snort, Savannah booted up her laptop and did her best to appear unaware of him. "Granted, I might not have as much experience as you—I'm sure you'd give the hookers in the red-light district a run for their money in the experience department—but I'm not completely ignorant, for pity's sake," Savannah huffed. She cast him an annoyed glance. "I know what sex is."

Though it had been so long since she'd had any, her memory was getting a little fuzzy about the particulars. If she didn't get laid soon, she'd undoubtedly be declared a virgin again simply by default. Or out of pity. Twelve- to fourteen-hour workdays didn't leave much time for romance. Besides, after Gibson Lyles III, Savannah didn't put much stock in romance, or in men, for that matter. She sighed. Men were too much work, for too little reward.

"Not just sex," Knox said. "*Tantric sex.* Do you know what it is?"

Savannah loaded her web browser, busying herself with the task at hand. "Sure. It's a complex marriage of yoga, ritual, meditation and intercourse."

Alternately, he looked surprised then impressed. "Very good. See? You're perfect."

"Be that as it may, I'm not going. I have work to do. Go away." Savannah smoothed her hair behind her ears and continued to pretend he wasn't there. No small feat when every single part of her tingled as a result of his nearness. Which sucked, particularly since, for the most part, she couldn't stand him. *"Go away,"* she repeated.

Knox continued to study her and another maddening twinkle lit his gaze. "I see. You're scared."

Savannah resisted the urge to grind her teeth. "Scared of what?"

"Of me, obviously." Knox picked an imaginary fleck of lint from the cuff of his expensive shirt. "Why else would you refuse such a great opportunity when it's painfully obvious that you've been considering the topic as well?" Something shifted in his gaze. "That… or you're into it."

"Ooh, you've found me out. Good job, Columbo. And don't flatter yourself. I am *not* afraid of you." Savannah chuckled. "I've got your number, Slick. Nothing about you frightens me." Savannah figured providence would promptly issue a bolt of lightning and turn her into a Roman candle for that whopper, but thankfully she remained spark free.

The silence lengthened until Knox finally blew out an impatient breath. "Won't you even consider it?"

"No."

His typically amiable expression vanished. "This is a great opportunity. Don't make me play hardball."

Exasperated, Savannah leveled a hard look at him. "Play whatever kind of ball you want, Knox. But you won't make me play with you. I'm not one of your newsroom groupies. Now get out of my cubby—you're crowding me."

Wearing a look of supreme frustration, Knox finally stalked off, presumably to ask another female to do his bidding. Good riddance, Savannah thought, though she did hate the missed opportunity.

But even had she been inclined to accept the offer, she really wouldn't have had the time to pursue the assignment—groveling to Chapman, her diabolical boss, and covering all of the demeaning little stories he gleefully threw her way were taking up entirely too much of her time.

Savannah and Chapman were presently embroiled in

the proverbial Mexican standoff, neither of them willing to budge. The problem revolved around a libel suit that had been filed against the *Chicago Phoenix* as a result of one of her stories. To Chapman's extreme irritation and despite various threats, Savannah stood by her story and refused to compromise her journalistic integrity by revealing her source. Chapman had bullied and blustered, wailed and threatened everything from being demoted to being fired, but Savannah simply would not relent. Her credibility would be ruined. To give up this source would ultimately wreck her career.

Besides, it was just wrong. She'd given her word and she wouldn't compromise her integrity simply for the sake of the paper. That's why they employed high-powered attorneys. Let them sort it out. She'd only been doing her job, and she'd done it to the absolute best of her ability. She refused to admit any wrongdoing, and she'd be damned before she'd claim any responsibility.

Savannah had been educated in the school of hard knocks, had been on her own since she'd turned eighteen and was no longer a ward of the state. She'd put herself through college by working three grueling jobs. Sure, covering the opening of a new strip mall was degrading, but if Hugh Chapman thought he could get the better of her by giving her crappy assignments, then he had another think coming. She stiffened her spine. Savannah was certain she was tough enough to take anything her mean-spirited boss could dish out.

Don't make me play hardball.

A premonition of dread surfaced as Knox's parting comment tripped unexpectedly through her mind.

She was wrong, Savannah decided. She was tough enough to take anything *but* a weekend sex workshop with Knox Webber.

CHAPTER TWO

"...So you see, this story has incredible potential. I have it on good authority that the *Tribune* is considering the angle as well."

Predictably, Hugh Chapman, editor in chief of the *Chicago Phoenix* bristled when taunted with the prospect of their rival paper possibly getting a scoop.

"You don't say," the older man grunted thoughtfully. As tall as he was wide, with large fishlike eyes, thick lips, a bulbous nose and pasty complexion, Chapman bore an unfortunate resemblance to an obese albino guppy. But Hugh Chapman was no harmless fish. He'd been in the publishing business for years and Knox didn't think he'd ever met a man more shrewd or calculating. Vindictive even, if the rumors were true.

Playing him was risky, but Knox desperately needed to do this story and he'd already tried the ethical route. It hadn't worked, so he'd been forced to employ a different tactic. His conscience twinged, but Knox ignored it. He'd given Savannah a chance to make the trip to California of her own accord. She'd refused. If Knox played his cards right, in just a few minutes she'd wish she hadn't.

Knox heaved a dramatic sigh. "Yeah, I'm afraid so. I'd really like to get the jump on them. Pity Savannah didn't go for the idea," Knox said regretfully. "And I can't do it without her. Oh, well. You win some, you lose some. I'm sure we'll beat them to the punch on something else." Knox smacked his hands on his thighs, seemingly resigned, and started to stand.

"Call her in here," Chapman said abruptly.

With an innocent look, Knox paused. "Sorry?"

"I said call her in here. You need her to go—I'll make her go." His beefy brow folded in consternation. "Presently, Ms. Reeves is in no position to refuse me. She's skating on thin ice as it is."

"Oh, sir, I don't know," Knox protested. "I didn't—"

"Webber, do what I told you to do," Chapman barked.

"Right, sir." Knox's step was considerably lighter as he crossed the room and pulled the glass door open. "Savannah Reeves, Mr. Chapman would like to see you."

Savannah's head appeared from behind her cubby. Knox's triumphant expression combined with the boss's summons seemed to register portents of doom because, within seconds, her pale blue eyes narrowed to angry slits and her lips flattened into a tense line. She stood and made her way across the room. Tension vibrated off her slight form.

"I told you not to make me play hardball," Knox murmured silkily as she drew near.

"If you've done what I think you've done," she returned with a brittle smile, obviously for the benefit of onlookers, since she clearly longed to strangle him, "you will be *so* very sorry. I will permanently extinguish your 'wand of light.'"

Knox choked on a laugh as she swept past into the inner sanctum of Chapman's office. In traditional tantra, the Sanskrit word for penis was *lingam,* which translated into "wand of light." She certainly knew her stuff,

Knox thought, surprised and impressed once more with her knowledge of the subject. He'd been right in forcing her hand. Annoying though she may be—the bane of his professional existence—Savannah Reeves was a crackerjack journalist. Very thorough.

"You wanted to see me, sir," Savannah said.

Knox moved to stand beside Savannah, who seemed determined to pretend he didn't exist. She kept her gaze focused on Chapman and refused to acknowledge Knox at all. His conscience issued another screech for having her called on the carpet, but he determinedly ignored the howl. If she had simply used her head and agreed, this could have all been avoided. It was her own fault.

Chapman gave her a long, unyielding stare, so hard that Knox himself was hard-pressed not to flinch. His scalp suddenly prickled with unease. What was it Chapman had said? She was on thin ice? Why? Knox wondered instantly. Why was she on thin ice?

"I understand Knox has asked you to accompany him on an extended weekend assignment and you have refused," Chapman said.

She nodded. "Yes, sir. That's correct."

Chapman steepled his fingers so that they looked like little pork sausages. "I'm not going to ask you why you refused, because that would imply that I care and I don't—that you have a choice, and you don't. You will go. Understood?"

She stiffened. "But, sir—"

Chapman's forehead formed a unibrowed scowl. "No buts." He looked meaningfully at Knox. "Surely it's not going to be necessary for me to remind you of why it would behoove you not to argue with me about this."

Though she clearly longed to do just that, Savannah's shoulders rounded with uncharacteristic defeat. She sighed. "No, sir. Of course not."

Knox frowned. What in hell was going on? How had she managed to land her name on the top of Chapman's shit-list? What had she done? he wondered again.

"That's what I thought. Knox," Chapman said, "see Rowena and have her tend to the necessary arrangements." He nodded at Savannah. "The two of you should get together and make your plans."

Knox smiled. "Right, sir. Thank you."

Savannah didn't say a word, just turned and marched rigidly out of the office. Knox had to double-time it to catch up with her. "What was that all ab—"

"That," Savannah said meaningfully, "is none of your business, but that's probably never stopped you before. Honestly, I can't believe that you did that—that you went to Chapman." She shook her head. "I knew you were a spoiled little tight-ass and a first-rate jerk, but it honestly never occurred to me that you'd sink so damned low."

Knox scowled at the tight-ass remark but refused to let her goad him, and followed her into her cubicle once more. "In case you haven't noticed," Knox pointed out sarcastically, "it's our job to make *everything* our business. That's what journalists do. Besides, I gave you the opportunity to do the right thing."

She blasted him with a frosty glare. "Wrong. You gave me the opportunity to do what *you* wanted me to do." Savannah shoved a hand through her hair impatiently, mussing it up even more. She took a deep breath, clearly trying to calm herself but failing miserably. She opened her mouth. Shut it. Opened it again. Finally she said, "Did it ever occur to you that I might have plans for this weekend? That it might not be convenient for me to jaunt off to California with you?"

Prepared to argue with whatever insult she hurled next, that question caught him completely off guard and Knox felt his expression blank.

"I thought so." She collapsed into her chair. "You pampered prep-school boys are all the same. Contrary to popular belief, Mr. Webber, the world does not revolve around you and your every whim." She laughed, but the sound lacked humor. "We peasants have lives to."

Peasants? Knox scrubbed a hand over his face and felt a flush creep up his neck. She was right. He hadn't considered that she'd have any plans. He'd just assumed that, like him, work didn't leave time for anything else. "Look, I'm sorry for wrecking your plans. That was never my intention. I just—"

"You didn't wreck my plans, because I didn't have any," she said tartly. She turned back to her computer, doing her best to ignore him out of existence.

Knox blinked. Felt his fingers curl into his palms. "If you didn't have any plans, then what the hell is the problem?" he asked tightly.

"I *could* have had plans. It's just a lucky coincidence that I don't."

Knox blew out a breath. "Whatever. When would you like to get together and see to the details of this trip?"

She snorted. "Never."

"Vannah…" Knox warned, feeling his patience wear thin.

"Savannah," she corrected, and he could have sworn he heard one of her teeth crack. "You can brief me on the plane. Until then, get away from me and leave me alone."

"But—"

She glanced up from her computer. "You might have won the battle, but you certainly haven't won the war. You've forced my hand, but that's all I'm going to allow. Do not speak to me again until we're on our way to California or, Chapman's edict or no, you'll be making the journey solo."

A hot oath sizzled on Knox's tongue, but he bit back the urge. He'd never met a woman who infuriated him more, and the desire to call her bluff was almost overpowering.

But he didn't.

He couldn't afford the risk. This story meant too much. He knew it and he needed to keep the bigger picture in focus.

Instead, though it galled him to no end, Knox nodded succinctly and wordlessly left her cubicle.

SAVANNAH HAD SILENTLY PRAYED that Knox would screw up and talk to her so that she could make good on her threat, but he didn't. Per her instruction, he hadn't said a single word to her until they boarded the plane. Since then he'd seemed determined to treat this assignment like any other, and even more determined to ignore the fact that she'd been an unwilling participant.

A typical man, Savannah thought. If he couldn't buy it off, knock it down or bully it aside, then he ignored it.

They'd flown out of O'Hare at the ungodly hour of five in the morning and would arrive in sunny Sacramento, California, by nine-thirty. At the airport, they would rent a car to finish the journey. The Shea compound was located in the small community of Riverdale, about fifty miles northwest of Sacramento. Barring any unforeseen complications, they should arrive in plenty of time to get settled and attend the Welcome Brunch. Classes officially started at two.

A volcano of dread erupted in her belly at the thought, but rather than allow it to consume her, Savannah channeled her misgivings into a more productive emotion—anger.

She still saw red every time she thought about Chapman's hand in her humiliation. Quite honestly, she'd been surprised that he hadn't taken every opportunity to belittle her in front of her co-workers—to make an example of her—and could only assume he acted on the advice of the paper's attorneys. Chapman seemed the type to feed off others' misfortune, and, frankly, she'd never liked him. She wasn't the least bit surprised that Chapman had sided with Knox. Knox was the golden boy, after all.

But the *Phoenix* had an unparalleled reputation, and she would have been insane not to accept employment at one of the most prestigious papers in the States. She had her career plan, after all, and wouldn't let a little thing like despising her boss get in the way. Though she assumed he'd never give her a glowing recommendation, her writing would speak for itself.

As for Knox's role in this…she was still extremely perturbed at him for not taking no for an answer. Without a family or mentor to speak of, Savannah relied solely on gut instinct. She had to. She didn't have a choice. In the absence of one perception, others became heightened, supersensitized. Just as the blind had a keener sense of smell, she'd developed a keener sense of perception, of self-preservation. When Knox had walked up and asked her to share this story with him, her knee-jerk gut reaction had been swift and telling—she'd almost tossed her cookies.

Going on this trip with him was the height of stupidity. Savannah could be brutally honest with herself when the need arose and she knew beyond a shadow of a doubt that this attraction to Knox was a battle she could not win. If Knox so much as touched her, she'd melt, and then he'd know her mortifying secret—that she'd been lusting after him for over a year.

Savannah bit back a wail of frustration, resisted the childish urge to beat her head against the small oval window. She didn't need to be here with him—she needed to be back in Chicago. Investigating the missing maintenance hole cover Chapman would have undoubtedly assigned her next. Watering her plants. Straightening her stereo wires, her canned goods.

Anything but being here with Knox.

Though she'd been making a concerted effort to imagine him away from the seat next to hers, Savannah was still hammeringly aware of him. She could feel the heat from his body, could smell the mixture of fine cologne and his particular essence. The fine hairs on her arms continually prickled, seemed magnetically drawn to him. Savannah surreptitiously studied him, traced the angular curve of his jaw with her gaze, the smooth curve of his lips. A familiar riptide of longing washed through her and sensual fantasies rolled languidly through the private cinema of her mind. She suppressed a sigh. No doubt about it, he was a handsome devil.

And due to some hideous character flaw on her own part—or just plain ignorance, she couldn't be sure—she was in lust with him. The panting, salivating, wanna-rip-your-clothes-off-and-do-it-in-the-elevator, trisexual—meaning "try *anything*"—type. Had been from the very first moment she'd laid eyes on him the day she joined the staff at the *Phoenix*.

Of course, he'd screwed it all up by opening his mouth.

Thanks to Gibson Lyles III, Savannah recognized the cool, modulated tones of those born to wealth. There'd been other signs as well, but initially she'd been so bowled over by her physical reaction to him that she hadn't properly taken them into consideration. The wardrobe, the posture, the polish. It had all been there once she'd really looked. And one look had been all it had taken for her to delegate him to her *hell-no* list. Since then she'd looked for flaws, probably exaggerated a few, and had not permitted herself to so much as like him.

Savannah knew what happened when rich boys took poor orphans home to meet the parents. Her lips twisted into a derisive smile. The rich boy got an all-expenses-paid tour of Europe…and the poor orphan got back-handed by reality.

Thanks, but no thanks.

Frustration peaked once more. Why had he demanded that she come? Why her, dammit? There were other female journalists employed at the *Phoenix,* other women just as qualified. What had been so special about her that none of the others would do?

When Savannah contemplated what this extended weekend would entail, all the talk of sex, having to share a room with him, for pity's sake, it all but overwhelmed her. How on earth would she keep her appalling attraction for him secret during a hands-on sex workshop? What, pray tell, would prevent her from becoming a single, pulsing, throbbing nerve of need? How would she resist him?

She wouldn't, she knew. If he so much as crooked

a little finger in invitation, she'd be hopelessly, utterly and completely lost.

Savannah knew a few basic truths about the art of tantric sex, knew the male and female roles. Knew that the art of intimate massage, of prolonged foreplay and ritual were particularly stressed themes throughout the process. But that was only the tip of the iceberg. There were other, more intimidating—and intimate—themes prevalent as well.

Tantrists believed that humans possessed six chakras—or sources of energy—and that during life, these energy sources got blocked due to the traumas humans suffered. But once these chakras were unblocked, and energy was free to move as it should, then when the male and female bodies merged, these energies merged as well, creating a oneness with a partner that transcended the physical and, thus, turned sex into a spiritual experience.

But how could a person take it seriously? Take some of the lingo for instance. His penis was a "wand of light." The Sanskrit word for vagina was *yoni,* which translated to "sacred space."

Please.

Who could say this stuff to their partner with a straight face? Sorry. She just couldn't see herself looking deeply into the eyes of her lover and saying, *Welcome to my sacred space. Illuminate me, baby, with your wand of light!*

Frankly Savannah didn't know what tact Knox wanted to take with this story, but she thought the whole idea was ludicrous. She liked her sex hot, frantic and sweaty and she didn't want to learn an ancient language to do the business either. Honestly, whatever happened to the good old-fashioned quickie?

She supposed she should give the premise the benefit of the doubt—that was her job, after all—but she seriously doubted that a massage and a few chants thrown in amid the usual twenty-minute flesh session would result in a spiritual experience for her. She liked the rub, lick and tickle approach, thank you very much. But to each his own, she supposed.

Knox elbowed her. "Hey, would you like anything to drink?"

Savannah started, then turned to see that the stewardess had arrived with the refreshment cart. "Uh…sure. A soda would be nice."

"Ditto," Knox said. He upped the charm voltage with a sexy little smile. "And an extra pack of peanuts, too, if you've got any to spare."

The flight attendant blushed and obligingly handed over the requested snack. Savannah rolled her eyes. And women were accused of using feminine wiles? What about men? What about masculine wiles? Knox, for example, had just dazzled that woman with nothing more than a little eye contact and a well-turned smile.

"Want some peanuts?" Knox asked, offering the open pack to her.

"No, thank you."

Knox paused to look at her and sighed. "What have I done now?"

Savannah inserted the straw into her drink. "I don't know what you're talking about."

"Sure you do. The temperature around your seat has dropped to an arctic level, when, just moments ago, I was enjoying the chilly-but-above-freezing climes of your sunny disposition." He smiled, the wretch. "Clearly, I've offended you once again. Don't be shy. Go ahead. Tell me what odious man-thing I'm guilty of now."

Savannah felt her lips twitch but managed to suppress a grin. "You're breathing."

Knox chuckled, a low rumbling sound that made his arm brush against hers and sent a shower of sensation fizzing up her arm. Savannah closed her eyes and pulled in a slow breath.

"I'm afraid I'm not going to attempt to remedy that offense," he told her. "I like breathing. Breathing is best for my continued good health."

"So is leaving me alone."

"Come on, Savannah. How long are you going to keep this up?"

"Dunno." She pulled a thoughtful face. "Depends on how long I'm going to have to work with you."

"Can't you even admit that this is going to be one helluva story? A coup for both of us?"

He was right. She'd grown increasingly weary of covering the mundane, was ready for a real assignment. Still...

"I don't have a problem with admitting that at all. I just don't like your methods. It was high-handed and sneaky, and I don't appreciate being made a pawn in the game of your career."

Knox shifted in his seat, then emptied the rest of the peanuts down his throat and finished the last of his drink before he responded. "Sorry," he mumbled.

Savannah blinked and turned to face him. "Come again?"

"I said I was sorry," Knox repeated in a little bit stronger voice.

Savannah widened her eyes in mock astonishment, cupped her hand around her ear and made an exaggerated show of not hearing him correctly. "Sorry, didn't catch that? What did you say again?"

"I said I was sorry!" Knox hissed impatiently. He plowed a hand through his carefully gelled hair, clearly out of his comfort zone when issuing an apology. "I shouldn't have gone to Chapman. But you didn't leave me any choice. I have to do *this* story and I needed *you* to go with me."

"Why me?" Savannah demanded quietly, finally getting to the heart of the matter. "Why not Claire or Whitney? Why did it have to be me?"

"Because I..." Knox swallowed, strangely reluctant to finish the thought.

"Because you what?" Savannah persisted.

He finally blew out a breath. "Because I couldn't take anyone with me who might be attracted to me. Or that I might be attracted to."

Slack-jawed, for a moment Savannah was too stunned to be insulted. She managed a smirk, even as dismay mushroomed inside her belly. "That irresistible, are you?"

"No, not to you," he huffed impatiently. His cheeks reddened. "You don't have any trouble at all resisting me. Hell, you've made a point of ensuring that I know just how resistible to you I am. *You* were the only logical choice. We have to stay focused, to remain objective. If I had asked any other woman at the *Phoenix* to make this trip with me, then you know as well as I do that they would have considered it a come-on. An invitation for seduction." He smiled without humor. "Did that occur to *you?*"

Savannah had readied her mouth for a cool put-down, but found herself curiously unable to come up with one. He was right. The idea of him wanting to seduce her had never crossed her mind—she'd been too worried about how hard it would be not to seduce him.

She'd known that he'd never been romantically interested in her—she'd purposely cultivated a hate-hate relationship with him to avoid that very scenario. Savannah knew she should be pleased with how well her plan had worked, but she found herself perversely unable to work up any enthusiasm for her success. He'd chosen her because she'd led him to believe that she wasn't attracted to him and because he, by his own admission, wasn't attracted to her.

All of that effort for this…this nightmare.

Irony could be a class-A bitch, Savannah thought wearily.

"Are we going to be able to get past this and work together?" he asked.

Savannah heaved a put-upon sigh. "Yeah…so long as you don't pull a show-and-tell session with your 'wand of light.'" She inwardly harrumphed. Didn't look like that would be a problem. And she was happy about it, dammit. This was a good thing. Really. She didn't want him to be attracted to her, any more than she wanted to be attracted to him.

Knox grinned, one of those baby-the-things-I-could-do-to-you smiles that made a woman's brain completely lose reason—including hers. "Let's make a deal. I won't show you mine unless you show me yours."

Savannah smirked, even as she suppressed a shiver. "Well, that'll be simple enough—*I* don't have a 'wand of light.'" She nodded succinctly. "Deal."

A sexy chuckle rumbled from his chest. "Deal."

CHAPTER THREE

"ARE YOU READY to discuss our cover?" Knox asked, when he'd finally navigated the rental car out onto the busy freeway.

He would have liked to cover everything while in the air where she couldn't have done him any bodily injury, but after his bungled apology, she'd feigned sleep for the rest of the flight. Knox didn't feel quite as safe in the car and he grimly suspected she wasn't going to care for the cover story he'd devised for the two of them. He'd made the mistake of filling out the application and accompanying questionnaire while still angry with her. Knox winced as he recalled the uncharitable things he'd had to say about his "wife's" shortcomings in bed.

She'd undoubtedly kill him.

Savannah fished her sunglasses from her purse and slid them into place. She'd dressed for travel in a sleeve-less sky-blue linen pantsuit that perfectly matched the startling shade of her eyes and showed her small, curvy form to advantage. She wore simple diamond studs in her ears and her short black locks were delightfully mussed. Her lipstick had worn off hours ago, but refresh-ingly unlike most females, she didn't seem to mind.

Knox was still trying to decide how much to tell her about their cover story when she said, "Sure, go ahead and fill me in."

He swallowed and strove for a nonchalant tone.

"We're registered as Mr. and Mrs. Knox Weston. Your first name is Barbie. We've been having a little—"

"Barbie?"

Knox winced at her shrill exclamation. "That's right."

With a withering smirk, she crossed her arms over her chest and turned to face him. "And why is my first name Barbie?"

Knox cast about his paralyzed mind for some sort of plausible lie, but couldn't come up with anything halfway believable and settled for the truth. "Because I was pissed and knew you would hate it." He threw her a sidelong glance and was pleased that he'd been able to—it meant that he still had his eyes and she hadn't scratched them out yet. "It was a petty thrill. I regret it now, of course," he quickly imparted at her venomous look. "But what's done is done and I can't very well tell them that I've made a mistake, that I didn't know my own wife's name." He forced a chuckle. "That would look pretty odd."

Looking thoroughly put out, Savannah studied him until Knox was hard-pressed not to squirm. "A petty thrill, eh?" She humphed. "Is there anything else—besides my name—that you might have falsely reported about me? Anything else I should know about?"

He shifted uncomfortably. "Er—"

"Knox…" Savannah said threateningly.

Knox considered taking the next exit. If she went ballistic and attacked him, he didn't want any innocent bystanders to be hurt. "Well, just for the sake of our cover, you understand, they, uh…might think that you're frigid and unable to reach climax."

Knox heard her outraged gasp and tensed, readied himself for a blow.

"Well, that can be easily explained," she said frostily,

"when I tell them that you're a semi-impotent premature ejaculator."

Knox quailed and resisted the natural urge to adjust himself, to assure himself that everything was in working order. "Well, I—I can hardly see where that will b-be necessary," he croaked. "One of us had to have a problem or we wouldn't have needed the workshop in the first place." A good, rational argument, Knox thought, congratulating himself.

She laughed. "Oh, I see. And *I* just had to be the one with the problem? Why couldn't *you* have been the one with the problem?"

"Because I—"

She chuckled. "Because you're such a stud that the idea of your equipment not passing muster—even fictitiously—was too much for your poor primitive male mind to comprehend. How pathetically juvenile." She smiled. "Do continue. We'll be there soon and I want to make sure that I'm completely in character."

Knox frowned at the words "pathetically juvenile," but under the circumstances, he let it pass. He cleared his throat and did his best to maintain his train of thought. "We've been married for two years and have never been completely satisfied with our, er, sex life. We're looking for something more and long for a closer relationship with one another. Our marriage is on the rocks as a result of our failure to communicate in the bedroom."

She snorted. "Because I'm frigid."

"Er…right."

"And you're impotent."

"Ri— Wrong!" Sheesh. A bead of sweat broke out on his upper lip. "That's, uh, not what our profile says."

"Because you filled it out. Look, Knox, if you think for one minute that I'm taking the total blame for our sorry sex life and our failing marriage during this farce, you'd better think again. You wanted this story, so you'd better damn well be ready to play your part. If I'm frigid, then, by God, you're going to be impotent."

Knox felt his balls shrivel up with dread. He set his jaw so hard he feared it would crack. She had to be the most competitive, argumentative female he'd ever encountered. The bigger picture, he reminded himself. Think of the bigger picture. "If you insist," he said tightly.

"I do."

"Fine." He blew out a breath. "There are still a few more things we need to go over. As for our occupations, I'm a veterinarian and you're my assistant."

She quirked a brow. "That's a bit of a stretch."

Smiling, Knox shrugged. "I got carried away."

Savannah's lips curled into a genuine smile, not the cynical smirk she usually wore, and the difference between the two was simply breathtaking. It was a sweet grin, devoid of any sentiment but real humor. To Knox's disquiet, he felt a buzz of heat hum along his spine.

"Be that as it may, I hope we're not called upon to handle a pet emergency," she said wryly. "I don't know the first thing about animals."

"What? No Spot or Fluffy in your past?"

A shadow passed over her face. "No, I'm afraid not."

Knox waited a beat to see if she would elaborate, and when she didn't, he filed that information away for future consideration and moved to fill the sudden silence. "Look in the front pocket of my laptop case, would you?"

Savannah turned and hefted the case from the back floorboard. She unzipped the front pouch. "What am I looking for? Your Viagra?"

"No." He smiled. "Just something to authenticate our marriage. Our rings are in there."

A line emerged between her brows and she paused to look at him. "Rings?"

Knox reached over, pilfered through the pocket and withdrew a couple of small velvet boxes. "Yeah, rings. Married people wear them. Fourth finger, left hand, closest to the heart."

"Ooh, I'm impressed. How does an impotent bachelor like you know all that sentimental swill?"

"I'm not impotent," Knox growled. "And I know because, having been best man at three different weddings in the past year, it's my business to know."

Savannah nodded. "Hmm."

"Hmm, what?" Knox asked suspiciously, casting her a sidelong glance.

She lifted one shoulder in a negligent shrug. "I'm surprised, that's all."

"Surprised that I've been a best man?"

"No, surprised that you had three male friends. I've never seen you with anyone but the opposite sex."

Knox shivered dramatically. "Oh, that's cold."

"Well, what do you expect? Us frigid unable-to-climax types are like that."

Smothering a smile, he tossed the smallest box to her. "Just put on your ring, Barbie."

Savannah lifted the lid and calmly withdrew the plain gold band. Anxiety knotted his gut. Though it had been completely unreasonable, Knox had found himself poring over tray after tray, trying to find the perfect band for her finger. He'd finally gotten disgusted with himself—they weren't really getting married, for Pete's sake—and had selected the simple unadorned band. Savannah didn't seem the type for flash and sparkle.

She seemed curiously reluctant to put it on, but finally slipped the ring over her knuckle and fitted it into place. She turned her hand this way and that. "It's lovely. And it fits perfectly. Good job, Knox. It had never occurred to me that we'd need rings. Where did you get these?"

With an inaudible sigh, Knox opened his own box, snagged his equally simple band and easily pushed it into place. "My jeweler, of course."

She winced. "Would have been cheaper to have gone to the pawnshop."

"Call me superstitious, but I didn't want to jinx this marriage—even a fake one—with unlucky bands."

"Unlucky bands?" she repeated dubiously.

"Yes. Unlucky. Think about it—if they'd been lucky they'd still be on their owners' fingers, not in a cheap fake-velvet tray in a pawnshop." He tsked. "Bad karma."

She chuckled, gazing at him with a curious expression not easily read. "You're right. You are superstitious."

"We're here," Knox announced needlessly. He whistled low as he wheeled the rented sedan into a parking space in front of the impressive compound—*compound* meaning *mansion*. The nudge behind his navel gave another powerful jab as Knox gazed at the cool, elegant facade of the Shea's so-called compound. When Knox thought of a compound, rows of cheap low-slung utilitarian buildings came to mind. This was easily a million-dollar spread and there was nothing low-slung or utilitarian about the impressive residence before him.

The house, a bright, almost blindingly white stucco, was a two-story Spanish dream, with a red tiled roof and a cool, inviting porch that ran the length of the house. The front doors were a work of art in and of themselves, arched double mahogany wonders with an inlaid sunburst design in heavy leaded glass. Huge urns filled with bright flowering plants were scattered about the porch, along with several plush chaise longues and comfortable chairs.

Knox would have expected a place like this to have been professionally landscaped, but there was a whimsical, unplanned feel to the various shrubs and flora, as though the gardener had simply planted at will with no particular interest in traditional landscaping. There were no borders, no pavers, and no mulch to speak of, just clumps of flowers, greenery and the occasional odd shrub and ornamental tree. Julio, his parents' gardener, who was prone to a symmetrical design, would undoubtedly have an apoplectic fit if he saw this charmingly chaotic approach to landscaping.

"Quite a layout, huh?" Savannah murmured.

Knox nodded grimly. "Quite."

Savannah unbuckled her seat belt. "Before we go in, just what exactly is your opinion of tantric sex?"

Knox surveyed his surroundings once more. "In this case, I think it's a lucrative load of crap."

"For once we're in agreement."

A miracle, Knox thought, wondering how long the phenomenon would last. "Get your purse, Barbie. It's show time."

SAVANNAH ABSENTLY FIDGETED with the ring on her finger. It wasn't uncomfortable, just unfamiliar, and it fit perfectly. She covertly peeked at it again and a peculiar ache swelled in her chest. The smooth, cool band was beautiful in its simplicity and made her wonder if she'd ever meet anyone who would long to truly place a ring on her finger and be all to her that the gesture implied.

She doubted it.

Knox had unwittingly tapped her one weakness with the ring he'd bought her as a prop—her desire to be wanted.

Other than those few woefully short years with her parents, Savannah had never been truly wanted. While she'd certainly stayed with a few good families during her stint in the foster-care system, most families had taken her in either for the compensation or to add an indentured servant to their household. Sometimes both. A live-in maid, a built-in baby-sitter. But no one had ever truly wanted her.

Savannah had made the mistake of letting that weakness impair her judgment once with Gib, but she'd never do it again. Rejection simply hurt too much and wasn't worth the risk. She'd learned to become self-reliant, to trust her instincts, and never to depend on another person for her happiness.

"Wow," Knox murmured as they were led down a wide hall and finally shown into their room.

Wow, indeed, Savannah thought as she gazed at the plush surroundings. The natural hardwood floors and thick white plaster walls were a continued theme throughout the house, creating a light and airy atmosphere. Heavy wooden beams decorated the high white ceilings, tying the wood and white decor together seamlessly.

A huge canopied bed draped with yards and yards of rich brocade hangings occupied a place of honor in the middle of one long wall. Coordinating pieces—a chest of drawers, dresser and a couple of nightstands—balanced the room perfectly. A dinette sat in one corner and a small arched fireplace accented with rich Mexican tile added another splash of color and warmth. Multicolored braided rugs were scattered about the room, adding more depth to the large space. Light streamed in through two enormous arched windows. It was a great room, very conducive to romance, Savannah thought.

A ribbon of unease threaded through her belly as she once again considered why she was here—and what she'd have to resist. Savannah glanced at the bed and, to her consternation, imagined Knox and her vibrating the impressive four-poster across the room, her hands shaped to Knox's perfectly formed ass as he plunged in and out of her. She imagined candlelight and rose petals and hot, frantic bodies tangled amid the scented sheets. Savannah drew in a shuddering breath as dread and need coalesced into a fireball in her belly.

Knox cased the room, checked out the closet and adjoining bath. He whistled. "Hey, come check out the tub."

Given her wayward imagination, Savannah didn't think that would be wise. Visions of Knox wet and naked and needy weren't particularly helpful to her cause.

"So," Knox said as he returned from admiring the bath. "Which side of the bed do you want?"

Savannah blinked, forced a wry smile. "I think the question is which part of the floor do you want?"

Knox glanced at the gleaming hardwood and absently scratched his temple. He wore an endearing smile. "Do I have a prayer of winning this argument?"

"No." Savannah hated to be such a prude, but having to sleep next to him would be sheer and utter torture. Simply being in the same room with him would be agonizing enough. Savannah grimly suspected that were they to share that bed, she'd inexplicably gravitate toward him. Toward his marvelous ass. Considering he didn't reciprocate this unholy attraction, she wasn't about to risk embarrassing herself and him.

He sighed. "As the lady wishes. I suppose we should head to the common room for the Welcome Brunch."

Savannah nodded. Without further comment, the two of them exited the room and, with Knox's hand at her elbow, they made their way down a long wide hall back to the foyer and then into what had been dubbed the common room. A long table piled with food sat off to the side of the enormous room and little sofas and armchairs were grouped together to encourage idle chitchat. Savannah's stomach issued a hungry growl, propelling her toward the food.

"Hungry, are you?" Knox queried.

"Ravenous."

"I offered to share my peanuts with you," he reminded teasingly.

Savannah grunted. "I wasn't about to partake of your ill-gotten gains."

Knox chuckled, a deep silky baritone that made her very insides quiver. Jeez, the man had cornered the market when it came to sex appeal. It was the same sort of intimate laugh she assumed he'd share with a lover. Something warm and quivery snaked through her at the thought.

"I simply flirted a little, Savannah. It's not like I raped and pillaged. Honestly, have you not ever batted your lashes and tried to get out of a speeding ticket?"

"No," she lied as she selected a wedge of cheese and a few crackers.

He chuckled again. "Liar."

"That's different," she said simply for the sake of disagreeing with him, which she did a lot. "And it's Barbie, you idiot. Do you want to blow our cover from the get-go?"

"Whatever." He paused. "Oh, look, our host and hostess have arrived."

Savannah turned and her gaze landed on an older

couple—early to middle fifties, she guessed. Bare feet peeked from beneath the hems of their long white robes. The woman wore her completely silver hair in a long flowing style that slithered over her shoulders and stopped at the small of her back. Silver charms glittered from her wrists and a large, smooth lavender stone lay suspended between her breasts via a worn leather cord. This woman seemed to embody everything their glossy pamphlet proclaimed. Serenity, harmony and all those other adverbs that had been touted in the trendy brochure.

As for the man, a calm strength seemed to hover about him as well. He appeared relaxed yet confident, as though he was the only stud for his mare. A niggle of doubt surfaced as Savannah studied the two. Could the art of tantric sex really be all this couple claimed it was? Quite honestly, it seemed impossible to Savannah, but for the first time since she'd accepted that she'd be working on this story with Knox, Savannah wondered if she'd been too hasty in forming her opinions.

The man smiled. "Welcome. I'm Dr. Edgar Shea and this is my lovely wife and life partner, Dr. Rupali Shea. We're so glad that you're here." He paused. "Some of you are here as a result of frustration, some of you are here as a result of your partner's prodding, and some of you are here because you're simply curious." His grin made an encore appearance. "Regardless of why you are here, we're exceedingly glad and are looking forward to teaching you everything we've learned about the art of tantric lovemaking. What we will teach you, what we'll freely share and will graphically demonstrate for your benefit, will change your lives…if you are open to the possibilities."

"At the beginning of each session," Rupali began,

"we like to do a little preliminary test, to see for ourselves just how much ground we need to cover, to see which couples will require one-on-one instruction." She paused and smiled to the room at large. "Now don't look frightened. It's a simple test. But first we'll introduce ourselves and share our inadequacies. No embarrassment, no boundaries," she said. "Only truth healing."

Savannah and Knox shared a look of dread. She almost felt sorry for him, but quickly squelched the sentiment. This was a hell of his own making. He could burn with humiliation for all she cared. The couples around them looked as miserable as she and Knox and that made Savannah feel marginally better. As she listened, one man admitted chronic masturbation as his problem. There were a couple of other women delegated to the frigid-and-couldn't-reach-climax list, and even more men who embarrassingly mumbled impotency as their major handicap.

Rupali beamed at them when they were finished. "Now, for the test." She paused again, garnering everyone's attention with the heavy silence. She steepled her fingers beneath her chin. "Do any of you know what the most intimate act between lovers is?" she asked. "I'm sure that all of you are thinking about intercourse, or possibly oral sex…but you'd be wrong. It's kissing. Kissing requires more intimacy than any other facet of lovemaking. And that will be your test. You will embrace your partner and kiss, and Edgar and I will observe." She beamed at them. "See, that's easy enough."

Savannah heard several audible sighs resonate around the room, but hers and Knox's weren't among them. Kissing? Kiss Knox? In front of all these people? Right now? Knox seemed to be equally astounded, as he wore a frozen smile on his face. Panic ping-ponged through her abdomen, the blood rushed to her ears and every bit of moisture evaporated from Savannah's mouth.

Knox drew her to him, anchored his powerful arms about her back and waist. Longing ignited a fire of need in her belly. "Quit looking like she's just issued a death sentence," he hissed through a brittle smile. "We're supposed to be married, remember?"

Savannah made the mistake of looking up into his dark green eyes and felt need balloon below her belly button. An involuntary shiver danced up her spine and camped at her nape. Oh, hell. She was doomed. "Right," she said breathlessly.

"It's just a kiss," he said unsteadily. "We can handle it."

"On my count," Rupali trilled. "Three, two, one… kiss!"

With equal parts anticipation and anxiety, Savannah's eyes fluttered shut as Knox's warm lips descended to hers. The exquisite feel of his lips slanting over hers instantly overwhelmed her and she swallowed a deep sigh of satisfaction as his taste exploded on her tongue. He tasted like soda and peanuts and the faint flavor of salt clung to his lips. *And oh, mercy, could he kiss.* Savannah whimpered.

His kiss was firm yet soft and he suckled and fed at her mouth until Savannah's legs would scarcely support her. Oh, how many times had she dreamed of this? How many times had she imagined his mouth hungrily feeding at hers, his built-like-a-brick-wall body wrapped around hers? With a groan of pure delight, she pressed herself even more firmly against him and felt her nipples tingle and pearl. A similar experience commenced between her thighs as her feminine muscles dewed and tightened. Their tongues played a game of seek and retreat, and for every parlay, Savannah grew even more agitated, more needy. Knox tightened his hold around her, and she felt his hand slide from the small of her back and cup her bottom. Another blast of desire detonated, sending a bright flash of warmth zinging through her blood.

From the dimmest recesses of her mind, Savannah realized that the room had grown ominously quiet. She reluctantly dragged her lips away from Knox's and laid her head against his rapidly rising chest.

Edgar and Rupali Shea grinned broadly at them. Their eyes twinkled knowingly. "Clearly Knox and Barbie have passed our little test with glowing marks and no one-on-one instruction will be required."

A titter of amusement resonated around the room.

Savannah's cheeked blazed and it took every ounce of willpower not to melt out of Knox's embrace. She extricated herself with as much dignity as she could muster, considering she'd all but lashed her legs about his waist and begged him to pump her amid a room of confessed sexually challenged spectators.

She was pathetic. Utterly and completely pathetic. How on earth would she keep her attraction for him secret now? How? she mentally wailed.

Deciding the best defense was a better offense, Savannah leaned forward and whispered in his ear, "How about a little less tongue next time, Slick? I don't know what you were looking for back there, but I had my tonsils removed years ago." She patted his arm and calmly moved to pick up her plate.

Knox's dumbfounded expression was unequivocally priceless, igniting a glow of another sort.

CHAPTER FOUR

A LITTLE LESS TONGUE? Knox wondered angrily. To his near slack-jawed astonishment, he'd never enjoyed kissing another woman more. He'd been so caught up in the melding of their mouths that all he could think about was how amazingly great she tasted, how wonderful her lips felt against his, and how much he longed to have her naked and flat on her back...

It was too much to contemplate. This was Savannah. *Savannah.*

Admittedly, he'd always thought her gorgeous. The first time he'd met her, he'd felt the familiar tug of attraction. But then she'd blasted him with a frigid blue stare and she'd opened her sarcastic mouth, and he'd never entertained another amorous thought about her. That's why he'd chosen her for this trip, dammit, and yet the moment his lips had met hers he'd gone into a molecular meltdown. He'd wanted to show her how hot she made him, tell her how much he wanted her and...

And seconds after that mind-blowing kiss, Savannah had calmly offered criticism and then just as calmly returned to her lunch.

Knox was unequivocally stunned.

He'd been too bowled over by the impact of that kiss to even regulate his breathing, much less pretend that he hadn't been affected...and she'd not only been un-affected, but apparently had been so unmoved by the experience that she'd been able to remain detached and offer advice.

Heat spreading up his neck, Knox loaded his own plate from the buffet and inwardly fumed. He'd always considered himself an attentive lover, had always prided himself on learning what techniques turned a woman on, what would give her pleasure. He liked a vocal partner, one who didn't expect him to be a mind reader. He liked hearing what made a woman hot and enjoyed doing it for her even more. Throughout his career in the bedroom, he'd heard countless breathy pleas—*harder, faster, there* and *there,* and *almost* and *oh, God, there! Touch, suck, lick* and *nibble,* even *spank,* he'd heard it all.

But never—*never*—had he ever had a woman criticize his kiss.

His kiss had always been above reproach, with no room for improvement. Though most men considered kissing as a simple means to an end—Knox included, most of the time—he'd nonetheless made it a point to excel at that particular form of foreplay.

Ask any man and he'd tell you that, given the choice of having his tongue in a woman's mouth, or his hand in her panties, the panties would win hands down every time. That was the ultimate goal, after all, and men were linear thinkers. Point A to point B in the most economical fashion.

Sure they might get distracted by a creamy breast and pouty nipple, might even linger around a delightful belly button for a few seconds, but settling oneself firmly between a woman's thighs was always, without question, the ultimate goal.

While kissing Savannah a few moments ago— though the kiss couldn't have lasted more than thirty seconds—Knox's thoughts had immediately leaped ahead to the grand finale. He'd already imagined plunging dick first into the tight, wet heat of her body. Had been anticipating her own phenomenally cataclysmic release as well as his.

While she'd been critiquing his kiss.

Knox had never anticipated being attracted to her and had known that she wasn't attracted to him, had chosen her for that particular reason. But having the knowledge confirmed in such a humiliating fashion wasn't an easy pill to swallow. Particularly since he'd all but devoured her and had made such a horny ass out of himself. Jesus. After that lusty display, there couldn't be one shred of doubt in her mind about how he'd reacted to her. How hot he'd been for her.

All due to a simple kiss she hadn't even enjoyed.

Simmering with indignation once more, Knox cast a sidelong glance at the object of his present irritation. Savannah's cheeks were a little pink—obviously embarrassed by his zealous response to their "test"—but aside from that, she appeared completely composed. She absently nibbled a cracker, her perceptive gaze roaming around the room people-watching, presumably looking for fodder for their story.

Which was exactly what he should be doing, Knox realized with an angry start. He mentally snorted. Undoubtedly she was already forming an angle, had already thought of an intro to their piece. Well, he'd have the most input, thank you very much. This story had been his brainchild, and if there had been any way he could have done it without her, he would have. And he wished he could have. They'd scarcely begun this damned workshop and already he'd become too distracted by the supposedly *undistracting* female he'd brought with him.

How screwed up was that?

"I hope you don't plan to pout the entire afternoon," Savannah said with a sardonic smile. "Honestly, Knox, it was only a small criticism. Surely that enormous ego of yours can take one minor unflattering assessment."

Ignoring a surge of irritation, Knox mentally counted to three, then arranged his face into its typically amiable expression. "Pout?"

Her eyes narrowed, clearly seeing through his innocent look. "Yes, pout. You've been glowering at the room at large for the past five minutes. Jeez, I didn't mean to hurt your feelings." She neatly bit the end off a stalk of celery. Her lips twitched. "Frankly, I wasn't aware that you had any."

Ah…back to familiar ground. Knox forced a smile, affected a negligent shrug, though he longed to wrap his hands around her throat and throttle her. He'd learned to appreciate her acidic sarcasm, but right now he wasn't in the proper humor to applaud her clever witticisms. He ignored her last comment and decided a change of subject was in order.

"So, what's your initial impression of the Sheas?" Knox asked.

Savannah winced, wiped a bit of salad dressing from the corner of her luscious lips. "They're what I expected…but then again they're not." She paused consideringly. "I don't know. It'll take more than a welcome speech for me to make an accurate assessment."

"I didn't ask for an accurate assessment. I asked for an initial impression."

"There's a difference?"

He nodded. "Of course."

"What is it?"

She had to be the most infuriating female he'd ever met. "Stop being difficult and answer the question."

Seemingly resigned, Savannah blew out a breath. "They were impressive, Knox," she admitted reluctantly. "If I was like these people, desperately looking for a way to better my relationship with a significant other, my husband, or simply needing a little show-and-tell to jump-start my sex life, I'd like them. They seemed genuine."

Secretly he agreed. Hokey togas aside, the Sheas seemed to share some secret something. Something the rest of the room lacked, or wasn't privy to. Still… "'Seemed' is the key word."

"I know." Savannah discarded her empty plate and dusted her hands. "So what's next on the agenda?"

Knox stacked his empty plate on top of hers. "We pick up our registration packets."

She nodded. "Then let's do it. I want a chance to go over everything before our first class starts."

Still feeling a little put out, Knox followed Savannah from the large common room and into the hall where the registration table had been set up. Several couples had been equally eager to start and Knox recognized the one in front of them with a little wince of dread—the masturbator and his wife.

Savannah's steps slowed. "Is that who I think—"

"Yes, it is," Knox hissed through a false smile as the couple in question turned with bright grins to greet them.

"Hi," the wife enthused. "Knox and Barbie, right? We're the Cummings. I'm Marge and this is my husband, Chuck." With a roll of her eyes, she jabbed her husband in the side. "Jeez, Chuck, where are your manners? Shake Knox's hand."

Knox felt his frozen smile falter and his gaze dropped to Chuck's outstretched hand with a paralyzing dread.

Beside him, Savannah covered her mouth with her hand and quickly morphed a chuckle into a convincing cough. He'd kill her when this was over with, Knox decided. He'd simply wring her neck.

The silence lengthened past the comfortable and Knox was resignedly readying his hand for the shake when Marge chirped "Gotcha!" amid a stream of high-pitched staccato laughter. The laugh went on and on and had the effect of fingernails on a chalkboard.

Chuck, too, was caught up in a fit of hilarity. His beefy face turned beet-red and, wheezing laughter, he pointed at Knox. "Man, if you could have seen your face! Oh, Marge, that was priceless. Utterly priceless. The best one yet."

Marge's laughter tittered out and she wiped her streaming eyes. "It's a little joke we like to pull," she confided, as though this whole scene was perfectly normal. "Everyone knows Chuck's a chronic masturbator—hell, I had to pry his hand away from his groin during your kiss a little while ago—so no one ever wants to shake his hand. *Ever*," she added meaningfully. "I mean, who would, knowing where it's been, right?" She and Chuck shared a secret smile. "So we like to pull a little prank with it. We've gotten a variety of reactions, but yours was by far the best we've seen in a long time. You looked like he'd whipped out his poor overworked penis and asked you to shake it."

Marge and Chuck dissolved into fits of whooping laughter once more.

Savannah, of course, was observing the whole

scenario as he would expect—tickled to death at his expense. Her pale blue eyes glittered with barely restrained laughter. Knox could tell she was on the verge of pulling a Marge and he cast her one long, pointed look to dissuade her. Hadn't she ever heard of loyalty? She was supposed to be his wife, dammit, and should be outraged on his behalf. Not quivering with amusement over his immense discomfort.

Knox decided this was the point where he was supposed to laugh and managed to push a weak little ha-ha from his throat. It was exceedingly difficult, considering he longed to plant his fist through a wall. Or possibly Chuck's face.

"FYI, he's left-handed," Marge shared with another maddening little smile. "You could have shaken it without a thing to worry about."

Knox forced his lips into a smile. Thankfully, Marge and Chuck's turn at the registration table came, sparing him a reply.

"Well," Savannah whispered through her curling lips, "that was certainly interesting."

Knox felt a muscle jump in his jaw. "You think?"

"Funny, too."

"I'm glad you were amused," Knox ground out.

"Marge was right," she went on to his supreme annoyance. She rocked back on her heels. "The look on your face *was* priceless. I wish I'd had a camera."

Knox smirked. "You're really enjoying this, aren't you, Savannah?"

She aimed a smugly beautiful smile in his direction, clasped her hands behind her back and batted her lashes shamelessly. "Yes. Yes, I am." She sighed. "After what you pulled with Chapman, can you really blame me?"

Knox exhaled wearily. He supposed not, and reluctantly admitted as much. "Still," he told her. "Gloating does not become you. Enough already, Savannah. We've got a job to do," he reminded her pointedly, as much for his own benefit as hers. Focus, Knox told himself. The big picture. He needed to push the kiss and the masturbator encounter out of his mind and keep the ultimate goal in sight—the story.

"I know that," she snapped, clearly perturbed at the reminder. "Believe me, that's the only reason I'm here—for the story. Let's just register and go back to our room. I want to prepare for this class." She chuckled darkly. "And let's pray there aren't any more surprise tests."

Damn right, Knox thought. At the moment, he wasn't up for another failing grade from "Barbie."

As soon as they returned to their room, Savannah made a beeline for the bathroom. She needed a few moments alone—just a few precious seconds away from Knox's distracting company to regroup and pull herself together. Once behind the closed door, she blew out a pent-up breath, then ran the tap and splashed cold water on her face. It felt cool and refreshing and helped alleviate some of the tension tightening her neck and shoulders.

Her muscles had atrophied with stress after The Kiss.

Sure, she'd managed to put on a good enough show, had forced herself to appear cool and unaffected when the truth of the matter had been that Knox's kiss had all but melted her bones. When his talented mouth had touched hers...

Mercy.

Remembered heat sent a coil of longing swirling

through the pit of her belly. Her nipples tightened and a familiar but woefully missed warmth weighted her core.

She'd known—hadn't she?—that he would be utterly amazing. Her every instinct had told her so, just as every instinct had warned her against him. She'd managed to undermine his self-confidence this time, managed to miraculously pull off a grand performance, but he'd undoubtedly see through her if anything like that happened between them again.

Though she hadn't yet had a chance to go through the curriculum, Savannah nonetheless knew that the kiss was just the beginning of what the workshop would entail. She and Knox would be called upon to do much more than kiss. The success of the Sheas' workshop depended upon it.

She wished that she and Knox could keep up the ruse without having to participate physically in class, and the wishing, she knew, was an act of futility. They would have to participate to some extent in class, otherwise they'd call attention to themselves, or, worse still, would lead the Sheas to believe they needed more intensive therapy.

Savannah shuddered. Neither scenario inspired confidence.

Irritation rose. Savannah ground her teeth and resisted the urge to beat her head against the door. This was precisely why she didn't want to be here, she inwardly fumed. Savannah knew her limits, knew her shortcomings and knew what sort of effect Knox Webber had on her libido. Attending a sex workshop with him was like waving a joint in front of a pothead.

Knox would be addictive to her and the addiction could only lead to heartache—hers.

She simply wouldn't allow it.

Chapman had forced her hand by making her attend. Despite her misgivings, Savannah would do her job and write a great story—and she'd do all that the task entailed, including being an objective participant in this godforsaken workshop—she was a professional, after all. But she would not let it become personal.

She wouldn't.

Seeing as sex was about as personal as it got, Savannah wasn't exactly sure what her heartfelt affirmation meant, but it made her feel better and she'd use any means available to shore up her waning confidence.

A tentative knock sounded at the door, startling her.

"Savannah...you all right in there?"

"Y-yes, of course." Savannah flushed the commode for appearance's sake, drew in a deep bolstering breath and smoothed her hair behind her ears.

"I, uh, wouldn't bother you, but I need to change and, frankly, I've gotta go."

Frowning, Savannah opened the door. "Change?" she asked. "Change for what?"

Knox had tossed a long white garment over his shoulder. It looked suspiciously like the same sort of costume the Sheas wore.

"For class," he told her. "We have to wear a *kurta*. I'm going to feel like a complete moron," he confided with an endearing, self-conscious smile, "but they're mandatory. I laid yours on the bed."

Good grief, Savannah thought, wondering what other little surprises would be in store for this weekend. She sighed heavily and massaged the bridge of her nose. "A *what?*"

"A *kurta*. It's an Indian gown."

Savannah eyed the getup warily. She crossed her arms over her chest. "You've got to be kidding."

"Nope...and it gets worse."

The hesitation in Knox's voice alerted her more than the actual words he'd said. "Worse?"

He winced regretfully. "Yeah—no undergarments. And no shoes."

Savannah blinked, flabbergasted. She was supposed to walk around naked under a toga? "No undergarments?" she repeated blankly, certain that she'd misunderstood him.

He tunneled his fingers through his hair, mussing up the wavy brown locks. "Yeah, I'm afraid so. It's to promote chakra healing, and, of course, the symbolic message of no boundaries."

And easy access, Savannah thought, for those graphic hands-on demonstrations. Her mouth parched and dread ballooned in her chest.

"Uh, if you're finished in there..." Knox reminded her.

Belatedly Savannah realized she still stood in the threshold of the bathroom. "Oh, sure. Sorry," she mumbled, hastily moving out of his way.

"I've had a quick look through the itinerary for the weekend," Knox called through the door. "After you get dressed, you might want to flip through it."

"I plan to," Savannah murmured absently as she picked up the long, white gown. The cool, soft cotton material smelled of fresh air. It had probably been line-dried, Savannah decided, not tossed into an industrial-sized appliance. Still, knowing that she'd be walking around buck naked underneath the almost see-through fabric quickly dispelled any pleasant musings.

Oh, hell. Knox would be out of the bathroom soon,

so unless she wanted to do a little striptease for him, she'd best change before he came out. Savannah hurriedly removed her shoes, pantsuit, bra and undies, then picked up the gown and pulled it over her head. The fabric settled on her shoulders lightly, whispered over her body and came to rest just above her ankles. It felt surprisingly…good. Wicked even, if she were honest. Something about the way the garment caressed her body made her feel beautiful, free and sexy. She particularly liked the way the material felt against her bare breasts and rump.

"Are you dressed yet?" Knox called.

Savannah scrambled up onto the bed, put her back against the headboard and settled a pillow over her lap. She grabbed the handbook and made herself look studious and calm. It took a tremendous amount of effort.

"Uh…yeah," she finally managed.

Knox exited the bathroom. He'd obviously brushed his hair, as the brown waves were once more smoothed back into place. His lips were curled into an almost bashful, self-deprecating grin and those incredibly lean cheeks were washed in an uncharacteristic pink. He'd folded his clothes and had tucked them up under his arm. A curious emotion swelled in Savannah's chest.

Knox gestured to the *kurta*. "I don't think that I've ever felt more emasculated in my life. If I'd known that wearing a damned dress with no drawers on underneath would be a mandatory part of this workshop, I simply would have said to hell with the story and found something else to write about."

Well, Savannah thought, as every drop of moisture evaporated from her mouth, he might feel emasculated, but he definitely didn't *look* emasculated.

In fact, if he looked any less emasculated, he'd be

X-rated. She could clearly see through the fabric, and the impressive bulge beneath indicated that Knox Webber was, without question, the most unemasculated man she'd ever seen—and he wasn't even hard. Fascinated, she swallowed. That was just…him. Just…there. All him.

Sweet heaven.

Every cell in her body was hammeringly aware that less than five feet from where she sat stood the most incredibly sexy, most generously endowed man she'd ever seen in her life. She instantly imagined him out of the *kurta* and sprawled on the bed next to her. Her blood thickened and desire sparked other fantasies, so she took her wicked illusion to the next level and imagined herself sinking slowly onto the hot, hard length of him. Sweet mother of heaven…

Savannah bit her lip, fully engrossed in the picture her wayward imagination had conjured. Up until now she'd always been preoccupied with his ass—he had an amazing ass, after all—but Savannah grimly suspected that fixation had just been replaced with another. Honestly, how did he make all of that fit in—

"What about you? Do you feel ridiculous?" Knox asked.

Savannah blinked drunkenly and then, feeling stupid and ashamed, recovered the next instant. "Er, yes. Yes, I do."

Knox paused to look at her. A line emerged between his brows. "You're acting weird. Are you sure you're all right?"

"Yeah, I'm fine." She manufactured a smile and thumped the booklet that lay in her lap. "Just thinking about some of the names for these classes."

Seemingly satisfied, Knox smiled knowingly. "You mean like *Love His Lingam, Rejuvenate His Root?*"

Savannah laughed. "Yeah. And *Sacred Goddess Stimulation.*"

Thank God those classes would come later, Savannah thought. They got to learn all about their chakras first with *Beginning Tantra, Energetic Healing.*

"So, what do you say?" Knox asked. "Ready to go get your chakras aligned?"

Savannah heaved a put-upon sigh. "Honestly, Knox. This isn't like the front end of your car. You're not getting anything aligned. Haven't you done your homework? You're getting unblocked." Savannah slid from the bed and gathered her things.

"Getting what unblocked?"

A sly smile curled her lips. "Well, for starters, your ass."

CHAPTER FIVE

FOLLOWING SAVANNAH out the door, Knox involuntarily tightened the orifice in question. *"What?"*

"For someone who was so determined to do this story—*had* to do this particular story," she emphasized sarcastically, "it would seem that you would have put a little more research into the project."

"I did my research," Knox insisted with a sardonic smile. "But I didn't come across anything that suggested tantra partners began foreplay with an enema."

Savannah chuckled darkly. "Who said anything about an enema?"

"Well, how else—" Knox drew up short as realization dawned. His ass instantly clenched in horror.

Oh, hell.

Catching his appalled expression, Savannah's pale blue eyes sparkled with amusement. That sinfully beautiful mouth of hers curved ever so slightly with mockery. "Aha. Light dawns on marble head."

Knox swallowed and continued to follow her down the hall. He'd rather be eviscerated with a rusty blade than even think about anal sex, much less discuss the loathsome subject with Savannah. He didn't need to get unblocked, thank you very much, and after a moment told her so. Forcibly.

She winced, clearly enjoying his discomfort. "Don't worry, Knox, I was kidding about the visit to the back door. But I have to say, you have one glaring characteristic of a man who needs to have his root chakra unblocked."

A muscle worked in his jaw. Knox knew better than to ask, but found himself forming the question anyway. "Really? And what characteristic would that be?"

"You're a tight-ass. I think I've pointed that out to you before."

Knox smirked. "Cute."

He held open the heavy front door and allowed her to pass. Their first class was on the south lawn in the outdoor classroom. Butterflies and bumblebees flitted from flower to flower through the Sheas' eclectic garden, Knox noticed as he and Savannah made their way across the lush lawn. Grass pushed between his toes, bringing a reluctant grin to his lips. It had been a long time since he'd been barefoot in the grass.

A peek at Savannah confirmed that she was enjoying the sensation as well. A small smiled tilted her lips and she'd turned her face toward the kiss of the sun. A light breeze ruffled her black bed-head locks and that same breeze molded the white, all-but-see-through *kurta* to her small, womanly form.

It was at this point that Knox became hopelessly distracted.

Naturally, over the course of Savannah's career at the *Phoenix,* Knox had observed her body and noted its perfection. He was a man, after all, and men—being men—tended to notice such details.

But noticing and really appreciating were two completely different things.

Knox's gaze roamed leisurely over her body and, much to his helpless chagrin, his visual perusal ignited a spark of heat in his loins.

The delicate fabric lay plastered against the unbound globes of her breasts, and the rosy hue of her nipples shadowed through the clinging material. Knox could easily discern the flat belly, the sweetly curving swell of her hips and the black triangle of curls nestled at the apex of her thighs.

She was beautiful. Utterly and completely beautiful and…

And feeling his dick begin to swell for sport, Knox mentally swore and made a determined effort to direct his lust-ridden brain toward a more productive line of thought—like his story. With that idea in mind, he studied his surroundings.

Picnic tables, some already occupied with couples, were arranged in a large circle beneath a huge white-washed octagon canopy. Crystals of various sizes and shapes dripped like icicles from the perimeter of the canopy, sending rainbows of colorful reflected light dancing through the air. The tinkling tones of wind chimes sounded, adding another element to the mystical environment. A white silk chaise sat upon a raised dais in the center of the outdoor room. Who knew what sort of depraved acts had been committed upon that little bench, Knox thought with a grim smile.

"Where should we sit?" Savannah asked as she surveyed the circle of tables.

"Somewhere in the middle," Knox told her. "If we sit in front, we'll look eager and too easy to snag for demonstrations. If we sit in the back, they'll think we're bashful and will want to draw us in and make us participate." He guided her toward an appropriate table.

Savannah grinned. "Why do I feel like this is the voice of experience and not a fabricated load of BS?"

"Because it is. I honed the skill in grade school."

With a roll of her eyes, Savannah sat down. "Sounds like you were trying to figure out a way to do the least amount of work possible."

Knox returned her grin and attempted to sit down next to her. He wasn't used to navigating in a dress and almost toppled chin first into the picnic table when the hem of the *kurta* caught the seat. He scowled, smoothing the damned gown back into place. "That was one of the perks," he finally said. "Be sure and take good notes. I always copied someone else's."

She gave him a droll glare. "I'm sure you did."

Actually, he hadn't. He'd only been trying to needle her. What did she think? That he'd been able to sail through an Ivy League school on nothing but his parents' money and his charming personality? And she had the nerve to think him a snob?

She'd never said it, of course. Just like none of his other co-workers had ever said it. But Knox knew they were laboring under the mistaken assumption that his wealthy background had afforded him his present career and, moreover, that his being talented could have nothing to do with it.

Knox smothered a bitter laugh. Let them think what they would. Screw 'em. He didn't care. In fact, he purposely invested a great deal of time making sure that no one—least of all any of those co-workers at the paper—knew just how much he longed to be respected for his work, rather than simply tolerated with virulent envy.

Between his condescending co-workers and equally condescending parents, Knox was doubly determined to succeed.

For reasons that escaped him, Savannah's opinion, in particular, annoyed the hell out of him. But what did he expect? That after spending one day with him, she'd see him any differently than she always had? That his character would have suddenly jumped up a notch in her esteemed estimation? Not likely. And he didn't care, dammit. He *did not* care. When he made it, when he proved himself, she'd be just like everyone else—eating crow.

Curiously, the thought didn't inspire the smug satisfaction Knox anticipated and, instead left him feeling small and petty. He shrugged the sensation aside and focused instead on the Sheas as they finally moved onto the dais.

"Welcome to your first class," Edgar began. "The title of this lesson is *Beginning Tantra/Energetic Healing.* We have much ground to cover over the course of this weekend and everything we teach you will be built upon these basic tantric principles, so please have your pad and pencil poised and be ready to learn."

"Before we begin," Rupali said to the class at large, "there are a few things we must cover." She steepled her fingers beneath her chin, the picture of glowing serenity. "I'm sure you are all wondering why you've been asked to wear the *kurta* and remove your shoes. Let me address the *kurta* first. The *kurta* denotes purity, helps promote chakra healing and enables us all to remove psychological boundaries. At times, our clothes can be our armor against our sensual selves." Her keen gaze landed pointedly on a few people. Savannah, too, Knox noticed with mild surprise. "We'll have no armor here. Only truth and healing." She paused. "As for not wearing shoes, we need to be grounded to Mother Earth, to let her energy flow up through our feet and connect us once more with the force of all that's natural, that's pure. Curl your toes in the grass—let it massage your feet," she instructed. "Isn't it nice? Can you feel Mother

Earth's power?" she asked, smiling. "If not, you will by the end of this clinic, I promise you. All of you will leave here with a new sense of energy, of purpose, of happiness."

"That's a mighty big promise," Savannah whispered from the side of her mouth.

Knox nodded. "Yeah, but it's what she didn't promise that's wise. She didn't promise impotent men erections, and she didn't promise you frigid-unable-to-climax types an orgasm."

"You're right," she quietly agreed. "It's inferred, but not stated. Smart move. Very crafty."

"Are there any questions so far?" Rupali wanted to know. "If not, then we'll move on to the next item on the agenda before we officially begin class. In order to insure that you fully understand and appreciate what sort of sexual gratification tantra can add to your sex lives, you need to understand what was lacking in the first place, and you need to be able to instantly discern the vast difference between the lovers you officially are today and the new lovers you will become. What I'm about to ask of you will be exceedingly difficult, but it's simply crucial to the success of your experience—you must abstain from physical intercourse until the end of the workshop."

A chorus of shocked gasps and giggles echoed under the pavilion.

"It's crucial," she repeated firmly. "Men, through tantra we're going to teach you the most effective way to bring your lover pleasure. We're going to teach you to worship your goddess. The techniques you will learn will enable you to prolong your own inner release as well as hers."

"Likewise ladies," she continued, "we will teach you

the most effective way to worship your man, to massage and heal, and bring pleasure beyond anything he's ever experienced before. We want you to make love, want to encourage you to grow spiritually as well as sexually with your partners. But there are lessons to be learned first." She laughed. "Lessons that will have you writhing with pleasure and begging for the most carnal form of release. But you can't have it…yet. Consummation will occur on Sunday night and not a moment before. Does everyone agree to this rule?"

After a few reluctant nods and one gentle but firm admonishment to Chuck, who'd been busy throughout her speech, Rupali finally concluded, and Edgar stood once more.

He clapped his hands together. "Okay, let's begin," he said.

While Edgar began a brief summary of each of the chakras, Knox's thoughts still lingered over Rupali's revelation—no consummation until Sunday. He couldn't begin to imagine why this was relevant to him as he and Savannah weren't going to be consummating anything. Still…

Just knowing that they were going to have to participate in everything—learn all of the supposed pleasure-enhancing techniques—up until that point and then miss the grand finale was heartily depressing. Unreasonable, he knew. The whole point of bringing Savannah along was to remain asexual about the entire concept, to remain focused on the story. The nudge was still there, powerful as ever.

Jeez. He was pathetic. Obviously, he was so preoccupied with his pecker that being denied even mythological sex irritated him. Knox cast a sidelong glance at his companion and felt his lips twitch with wry humor.

If she had any inkling of the direction of his thoughts right now, she'd undoubtedly pull a Lorena Bobbitt and permanently extinguish his "wand of light" like she'd so lethally threatened before.

So, he could either keep this one-sided attraction to himself—which unquestionably would be the sanest and most healthy thing he could do—or he could work on her until it was no longer one-sided.

With luck, the weekend would be over before he came to a clear decision.

"DOES ANYONE KNOW what the word *tantra* means?" Edgar asked. "It means to weave, or extend."

Right, Savannah thought. She'd known the answer, but couldn't make her sluggish brain form the required definition—she was too busy mourning the loss of the great spiritual sex she'd never intended to have in the first place.

And not just any sex.

Sex with Knox.

Savannah knew she shouldn't feel like wailing with frustration. Shouldn't feel like whimpering with regret. But she did. He'd been sitting beside her for the past hour, and her palm had literally itched to reach over to shape her hand to the oh-so-clearly defined length of him. She wanted to stroke him, to feel him grow in her hand, grow inside her. Which was ludicrous. Knox had admitted that the sole reason he'd asked her to attend this sex workshop was because she happened to be the only woman he could bring along that he *wouldn't* want to sleep with. He'd admitted that he didn't find her the least bit attractive.

And that was a good thing, dammit. She didn't want him to be attracted to her. It would be nothing short of ruinous. She'd already dated a pretty prep-school play-boy and he'd given her the old heave-ho the minute his parents had squawked their disapproval. As far as the Lyleses had been concerned, Savannah had been foster-care trash, not worthy of their precious pedigreed son.

There were a gazillion reasons why she shouldn't have hot, sweaty phenomenal sex with Knox. Savannah's insides grew warm and muddled at the mere implication of the act. Still, he was like Gib, he had a love-'em-and-leave-'em reputation, he was a co-worker... The list went on and on.

Yet none of them—or the combined total—could hold a candle to the ferocity of the attraction.

Every part of him that was male drew every part of her that was female. She yearned for him. Longed to have those big beautiful hands of his shaped around her breasts. That talented mouth tasting every mole, every freckle, everywhere that was white and everywhere that was pink.

And she wanted to touch him as well, wanted to slide her fingers over each and every perfectly formed sinew. Wanted to feel that powerful body unleashed with pas-sion and, ultimately, sated with release. She sighed.

She just wanted.

Savannah swallowed another frustrated wail. She'd kept her distance, hadn't she? She'd even made herself dislike him, all in an effort to avoid this very predica-ment. All of that hard work for this beautiful mess.

Even if the talk of sex finally sparked some latent interest in him, he'd never be so pathetically unprofes-sional as to act upon it. For reasons Savannah didn't un-derstand, this particular story was incredibly important to him. He'd coerced her into coming, after all. He'd never jeopardize the story, regardless of how much he might like to overthrow his traditional tastes and take her for a quick tumble between the sheets.

So she needed to put the whole idea out of her mind. She'd forget that damned kiss and pray they wouldn't have to participate in that madness again. She'd ignore the enormous penis draped across his thigh beneath that *kurta* and her own beaded nipples and moist sex and…

And, Savannah realized with mounting frustration, she'd undoubtedly end up masturbating the entire weekend, just like poor oversexed Chuck.

"Hey," Knox said as he gently nudged her in the side. "I thought I told you to take notes. You stopped at the genital chakra."

That seemed appropriate, Savannah thought. "Sorry," she mumbled.

"Don't worry about it. We've got to go over all of it and work on unblocking as many chakras as we can tonight for homework. At the end of this lesson we move on to building trust between partners and the art of erotic massage." Knox waggled his brows suggestively. "They have scented massage oil in the gift shop."

Six and a half feet of gloriously oiled, aroused male loomed in her mind's eye. "Great," she managed to deadpan. "You can rub it all over yourself."

Shaking his head, Knox tsked under his breath. "Now what could we possibly learn from that? How can we do this story justice without at least trying some of the techniques?"

She couldn't fault his reasoning, though that was her first impulse. Still, if they tried one, she'd want to try them all. Which meant it would be best to forgo the whole lot. "I suppose you should have thought of that before you hauled me to a sex workshop."

"Who said anything about having sex? It's just a massage. Are you planning on giving this story anything but your best objective opinion?"

Savannah bristled. "Of course not."

"Then it's a no-brainer," he said with a negligent shrug. "Tell you what, I'll go you one better and do you first. How does that sound?"

Like torture, Savannah thought. Delicious torture, but torture all the same. "Whatever." She gestured toward the Sheas. "They're about to conclude the lesson. Shut up and pay attention."

"In a few moments we'll take a short break, and then we'll move on to part one of our erotic massage lesson," Edgar said. "Before we stop, however, let's take a moment to quietly reflect and connect with our lovers."

Oh, hell, Savannah thought with a premonition of dread. That didn't sound good.

"Everyone please stand," Rupali instructed. "For some, this is a very difficult exercise, but Edgar and I didn't promise that this weekend would be easy. The level of intimacy we want our students to achieve requires that fears and inadequacies be set aside, that the true self be revealed."

Savannah resisted the urge to squirm. It was sounding worse.

"One of the simplest ways to do that is to maintain eye contact, to search your partner's eyes and reveal past hurts, regrets, happiness and love." Rupali paused and gauged the room's reaction to her words. "In time, you will be able to look into your partner's eyes and see your *Imago,* or mirror image, reflected back at you. While you might be uncomfortable now, the longer you practice tantra, the more you strive for a more spiritual union, you will eventually learn to prize this very special connection."

Edgar set the timer on his watch. "Men, pull your women to you, so that their heart beats against your chest. So that you can feel the steady rhythm of her life force thumping against you."

Knox, damn him, didn't appear the least bit annoyed or uncomfortable by this new test as, smiling, he did as Edgar instructed and pulled her firmly up against the hard wall of his magnificent chest.

With a decidedly sick smile, Savannah's own heart threatened to pound right through her ribcage. In addition to feeling Knox's heartbeat, she felt the telltale ridge of his "wand of light" against her belly button and, to her eternal chagrin, her "sacred space" swiftly grew warm and wet. If he'd branded her with the damned thing, she couldn't have felt it more.

"Now, women, wrap your arms about your man's waist. Wrap him in your love. Let him see it." Edgar chuckled. "It's true men are visual creatures. They have to see to believe. Make him *believe*."

"For the next ninety seconds," Rupali said, "we're going to stand together and gaze into each other's eyes. Blink if you must, but try to maintain eye contact. Don't look away and do not speak. Say it with your eyes, use your brow chakra to learn your lover's secrets. You may begin…now."

Feeling utterly and completely ridiculous, not to mention incredibly uncomfortable, Savannah did as Rupali said and looked up into Knox's twinkling green eyes. Commiserating laughter lurked in that verdant gaze, Savannah noticed to her marginal relief. She quelled the desire to squirm. Her breasts had already tightened into hard little buds and if she moved as she wished to, she might not be able to stop. Pathetic, but true.

Knox's eyes were heavy lidded, with long, curling lashes. The green was pure, just flecked with lighter and darker hues, but no shades of brown commonly found in a color as dark as his. Some of the humor faded from his gaze and another indiscernible emotion took its place. Something heavy and intense and altogether sexy. Savannah pulled in an unsteady breath. She thought she saw a reciprocating heat, but knew that couldn't be the case. Simply wishful thinking on her part.

Still, the longer the stare went on—Jesus, who would have thought that a minute and a half would seem like a lifetime?—the more aroused she became. Her limbs had grown heavy and she'd transferred some of the weight by leaning more closely into him. She had the almost overpowering urge to lower her gaze to his lips, then let her own mouth follow that path.

If she lived to be one hundred, she didn't think she'd ever want to kiss a man more.

The desire was completely out of the realm of her limited experience. The pressing need built and built until the longing and weight of that heady stare seemed almost unbearable. Savannah felt herself sagging closer and closer to him and, though she knew better, she simply didn't possess the strength to stop it. If this didn't end soon, she'd—

"Time's up," Edgar called, and the group underneath the pavilion heaved a collective sigh. "Now kiss your lover, then we'll adjourn for a break."

A relief of another sort gripped Savannah and she eagerly met Knox's mouth as it descended hungrily to hers. The unmistakable—enormous—length of him nudged her navel and, rather than be alarmed, which would have been the intelligent reaction, Savannah merely smiled against his mouth and thought, *Oh, thank God, I'm not the only one, after all.*

Knox Webber could claim he wasn't attracted to her, but she'd just been presented with some hard evidence that proved otherwise.

Granted, men awoke with a hard-on, and could typically get it up for just about any woman. His reaction was likely due to part of the intense lesson and all the talk of genital chakras, but for this moment—*just this one*—she would pretend otherwise. Savannah generally avoided lying to herself at all costs, but surely this one little fib couldn't hurt. Right?

It's not like she'd ever be so cork-brained as to delude herself into thinking that he felt anything but mild disdain toward her. She may have been able to turn on his "wand of light," but when it came to generating any real interest, the lights were off and no one was home.

CHAPTER SIX

KNOX STARED DOWN into Savannah's ice-blue gaze and the effect of that cool stare left him anything but chilly. The first fifteen to twenty seconds of their so-called exercise she'd been adorably shy, utterly miserable and obviously so far out of her comfort zone he'd found himself smiling to reassure her.

Knox was a man who always questioned everything—that insatiable curiosity had prompted his career choice. Savannah's reaction to this particular test raised many questions, the most pressing of which was, who or what had happened to her to make her so damned distrustful? Because something definitely had.

At some point in her life, or perhaps repeatedly, she'd been deeply hurt. Betrayed. The knowledge made his mind momentarily go black with rage and the unreasonable urge to right old wrongs for her, heal old hurts.

How could he have been so blind? He could see the truth now, hovering beneath the bravado, beneath the sarcasm, and he wondered again how he'd ever missed it in the first place. Knox mentally snorted. Hell, he knew how. She'd never let him close enough. Never let anyone close enough, for that matter.

To be honest, Knox hadn't been thrilled with the prospect of another test, but when Edgar had instructed them to wrap their arms about their woman, Knox had grown decidedly more enthusiastic about the lesson.

He'd watched her emotions flash like neon signs through her eyes and the one that finally managed to completely undo him was passion.

Those cool blue eyes had rapidly warmed until they glowed like a blue flame. A resulting heat swept him from the top of his head to the tips of his bare toes. His heart had begun to pound, sending the blood that much faster to his throbbing groin. The hairs on his arms prickled and the nudge he normally associated with work began an insistent jab.

As the seconds ticked by, Savannah gravitated closer and closer to him until he could feel her budded nipples against his chest. Could feel the rhythmic beating of her heart as the Sheas had instructed. Feeling that rapid, steady beat did have a curious effect on him, Knox conceded. He'd never thought much about his heart, other than being aware that it pumped his blood, but something about feeling hers made him want to pull an Alfalfa, cancel his membership in the He-Man-Woman-Hater's Club and beat his chest and roar. He'd made her heart pound. Him. What a turn-on.

Knowing that she was naked underneath that gown, that nothing more than a thin wisp of cotton separated his skin from hers tortured him, made his hands itch to feel her through the fabric. Knox pulled in a shaky breath and quelled the almost overwhelming urge to back her onto the picnic table, hike up that *kurta* and bury himself into the slick velvet heat of her body. Piston in and out of her until their simultaneous cries of release rent the air and he spilled his seed deep into the tight glove of her body.

Clearly he'd lost his mind, to be having such thoughts about Savannah. They were here to do a job, nothing more, and yet he'd give everything he owned right now just to kiss her. Just to taste her. Just one small—

"Time's up," Edgar called. "Now kiss your lover and we'll adjourn for a break."

Kiss your lover...

Knox groaned with giddy relief and quickly lowered his mouth to hers. To his immense delight, Savannah met him halfway and her mouth clung to his, fed greedily until nothing existed but the feel of her against him, the exquisite taste of her on his tongue.

What the kiss lacked in finesse it more than made up for with passion. She lashed her arms about his neck and all but crawled up his body to get closer, ran her hands all over him, cupped his ass and growled her approval right into his mouth. She eagerly explored his mouth, slid her tongue around his, tasted the fleshy part of his lips. She nibbled and sucked, and it occurred to Knox that, at some point in the near future, he'd like to have her do the same thing to his rod. She wriggled and writhed, alternately sighed and purred with pleasure and each little note of praise caused *both* of his heads to swell, particularly the one below his waist. It jutted impatiently against her.

He might as well have jabbed her with a hot poker, for the way she abruptly tore her mouth from his and stepped back. With a frustrated huff, she looked up and glared at him. "Good grief, Knox," she hissed. "You're supposed to be impotent. Could you at least try to stay in character?"

Knox blinked, astounded. In character? She'd been acting? Again?

Savannah looked down at the front of his tented *kurta*. Her lips curled into that oh-so-familiar mocking smile. "Well, at least the premature ejaculator part looks real. You've got a huge wet spot on the front of your dress."

Mortified, Knox felt a blush creep up his neck. "It's not a dress," he ground out.

Luckily the rest of the class had moved toward the refreshment table, which had been set up on the lawn. Only the Sheas lagged behind. To his further humiliation, the two of them noticed the evidence of his mortification and smiled knowingly.

"I see you've made progress already," Edgar said. "Embrace your healing, Knox," Edgar encouraged with a fatherly clap on the shoulder. "There's no shame in flaunting your seed. There is power in procreation."

Rupali gestured toward Savannah's pearled nipples. "Likewise, Barbie," she said mistily. "You should be proud of your puckered breasts. They await your lover's kiss with tight invitation. Someday the milk of life will pour from those twin orbs. Flaunt them, as Edgar said." She smiled serenely, cupped her own breasts reverently. "Embrace your femininity. Be proud of being a woman."

Having blushed to the roots of her hair, Savannah managed a strained smile and nodded mutely. The Sheas threaded their fingers together and walked away, presumably to offer more little bits of tantric wisdom to other students.

Enjoying her discomfort, Knox smiled. "I see I'm not the only one who had a hard time staying in character."

Savannah closed her notebook and clipped her pen to the front. She gave him a blank look. "I'm sorry, what?"

"Staying in character," he repeated. "I'm not the only one who got hard." He stared pointedly at her breasts.

She gave him a frosty glare and her lips formed a withering smirk. "I was cold, you moron. What's your excuse?"

His eyes narrowed. "Your tongue was in my mouth."

"And less of yours was in mine this time. Well done, Knox. It's nice to know I'm not going to be choking on yours the entire weekend."

No one could deliver a backhanded compliment quite like Savannah. Knox ignored the gibe and refused to let her change the subject. "You were not cold. You were hot, *damn hot,* and I could feel you."

"How could you not feel me?" she asked, her voice climbing. "Edgar made us practically crawl into each other's *kurta*s. Basic physiological fact, Knox. The human body's normal temperature is ninety-eight-point-six degrees. That's hot and that's what you felt. End of story."

The hell it was, Knox thought, but whatever. He didn't know what sort of insanity was eating at his brain to make him want to force her into admitting that something had happened between them. She was right to play it down. Keep it professional. He'd play it her way.

Or maybe not.

Knox shoved a hand through his hair and sighed heavily. "You're right. It is a little chilly out here today." Another lie. It was a pleasant seventy, at least.

Her gaze flew to his. "I'm right?" she asked, then nodded emphatically. "Right. Of course, I am."

Knox suppressed a triumphant smile. So it was okay for her to lie about the attraction and make him feel like a class-A jackass, but apparently she didn't like wearing the shoe on the other foot.

Women, Knox thought. Had the Lord ever made a more fickle creature? This was a prime example of why he'd never decided to keep one around on a permanent basis. They said yes when they meant no, and no when they meant yes. Who needed the grief? The confusion? Knox kept in touch with a select few women who knew him and knew the drill. Great date, great conversation, great sex. No strings. Everybody went home happy.

He would reluctantly admit that at times he longed for a deeper relationship, something more like his parents had. But so far he hadn't found anybody he'd want to spend a solid week with, much less the rest of his life. He was too preoccupied with the present to contemplate the future, at any rate.

Savannah could lie to him—and probably herself— all she wanted, but Knox knew the truth. Cold, hell. She'd been hot for him. If that kiss had been any hotter, the two of them would have surely gone up in flames. He'd never been so turned on from a mere kiss. Savannah Reeves had one talented mouth and it made Knox wonder just what other hidden abilities she possessed, and made him all the more determined to find out.

Without question, this unplanned, unwanted attraction posed many problems. For instance, how were they supposed to get through the rest of the weekend without going insane with lust? If he and Savannah detonated with heat over a couple of kisses, what would happen when they moved on to erotic massage, to *Love His Lingam,* and *Sacred Goddess Stimulation?* What would happen on Sunday night, when the rest of the class was putting all their new know-how into practice? Furthermore, and more important, how on earth would he be able to maintain the focus needed to pull together an objective story if all he could think about was how much he wanted to plant himself between her thighs?

The two of them locked in various depraved positions

flitted rapid fire through Knox's mind—his own personal little porn show where he and Savannah starred in hedonistic orgasmic splendor. He'd read the *Kama Sutra*. In his mind's eye Knox had her all but standing on her head when Savannah abruptly tapped him on the arm.

"Pay attention," she whispered. "They're about to resume the lecture."

Knox started, then moved to sit back down at their table. Savannah took her place beside him and, thankfully, began to take notes while Edgar and Rupali lectured on the importance of trust and announced that they would be doing a couple more little exercises before the lesson concluded for the day. They would have a great deal of "homework" this first night and would be provided ample time to get it all done.

In addition, all evening meals would be served in their rooms, with special instructions on how to enjoy them. Rupali and Edgar shared a secret smile that inspired equal parts curiosity and apprehension.

Great, Knox thought, as a wave of trepidation and anticipation washed over him. As if he didn't have enough to worry about.

SAVANNAH DIDN'T KNOW what was worse—attending the nerve-racking classes, or being alone with Knox. By the time they'd finished that last trust exercise, which she'd failed miserably at and which had consequently been added to their considerable homework, Savannah's raw nerves had been ready to snap. She'd tried to play off that second kiss with Knox, but it hadn't worked. Not by any stretch of the imagination.

He'd known, damn him.

She could see it in the cocky tilt of his head and the even cockier curve of his splendid lips. As if that gigantic ego of his needed another reason to swell, Savannah thought derisively. Even if he hadn't known then, he would have by the end of that lesson. Edgar and Rupali were firm believers in the oral chakra and the powers of kissing. According to Edgar and Rupali, the act taught patience to the men and promoted sexual harmony for the women. They'd had them necking at the end of each additional test, as well as the conclusion of the lecture. To her helpless joy and consternation, she and Knox had practically stayed in a perpetual lip-lock the rest of the afternoon.

If that hadn't been enough to shake her generally stalwart fortitude, there had been the *homework*.

When they'd returned to their room this afternoon, they'd found several things awaiting them. Fresh *kurta*s, a new booklet that gave detailed information on how to unblock each of the chakras—and there was a lot more to it than even Savannah had realized—as well as instructions which had to be followed to the letter for the rest of the evening.

They were supposed to begin their evening with a shared bath.

Knox, damn him, had raised a hopeful eyebrow at this news, but Savannah had quickly disabused him of that notion.

The shared bath had also come with a few handy tips on how to enhance intimacy, like soaping your lover's body, washing each other's hair and light genital massage, along with the stern reminder that intercourse was forbidden.

Savannah had to admit that it sounded absolutely wonderful. That huge sunken marble tub might as well have had *Do It Here* written on little sticky notes scattered all over it—on the recessed steps, the back, the front and the side. It was a veritable Garden of Eden.

Furthermore, the idea of Knox's hands, slick with soap and hot water sliding all over her body was enough to send her heart rate into warp speed. Her palms actually tingled when she thought about giving him the same treatment, smoothing her own hands over the intriguing masculine landscape of his magnificent form. Over that incredible ass she'd finally gotten her greedy little hands on this afternoon. Honestly, she'd almost climaxed from the thrill of it.

She'd said no to the bath when she'd wanted to say yes, but to do anything different would have been a complete overthrow of her principles.

One of them had to remain focused and, though he'd claimed he'd brought her here because he didn't find her attractive, apparently Knox's primitive base instincts had overridden her general lack of appeal because, since that second kiss, he'd made absolutely no attempt to hold back.

In fact, Savannah grimly suspected he was goading her on purpose, arousing her for the pure sport of it. Because he knew he could, the bastard.

She had no idea how she should combat such an attack, but had finally decided that if he didn't back off soon, she'd launch an offensive of her own. If he continued to play with her and use her own reckless desire against her, Savannah would begin a similar assault upon his weakened libido and she'd have him begging for mercy.

While she'd lacked confidence in just about every other aspect of her life, there were two areas in which she knew she excelled. She was a damn fine journalist and, when she was with someone she trusted without question, a sadly rare occurrence, she was one hell of a lover.

Savannah might not have had as many partners as Knox, but it wasn't so much the quantity as the quality, and she'd never failed to satisfy a man in the bedroom. Savannah enjoyed sex, was very uninhibited, and those qualities came through in her performance. In fact, she'd never had bad sex. If her partner didn't do it for her, she'd simply roll him over and take care of matters herself. Savannah grinned. What man didn't like that?

There was something so elemental, so raw and intense when it came to sex. Any pent-up emotion could be vented, exorcised, and the simple act made her feel more human, more connected, than any other.

And it had been too long, Savannah thought with a despondent sigh. She imagined the combined factors of sexual deprivation and Knox were the reason she was so rabidly horny now. She hadn't made love since Gib.

Initially she'd been too hurt to even consider building a relationship with another man. Then once she'd gotten past that point, her career had begun to take off and there simply hadn't been time.

Savannah didn't do casual sex. In addition to it not being safe, there was nothing casual about sharing your body with another person. At least, not for her. Her character had not been formed for that increasingly popular pastime and she'd just as soon go without.

Until now.

Now she'd become the proverbial bitch in heat. She wanted Knox—had always wanted Knox—but had managed to keep the attraction under control by avoiding him as much as possible and by generally striving to be the most unpleasant person on the face of the planet anytime he was around.

But she couldn't do that now. They were here, sharing a room, and while he might sound like Gib, and occasionally act like Gib, Savannah knew her desire to dislike Knox had been more of a defense mechanism than anything else. Just a way to prevent herself from liking him because she didn't want to make the same mistake twice.

Knox chose that particular moment to open the bathroom door. Scented steam billowed from behind him as he strolled in all his almost-naked glory to the bed to retrieve his clean *kurta*. He'd anchored a bath sheet loosely about his waist and a few small droplets of water skidded down the bumpy planes of his ridged abdomen. An inverted triangle of dark brown hair dusted his chest and arrowed into a slim line that bisected that washboard abdomen and disappeared beneath the line of his towel.

His muscular legs and arms were covered in the same smattering of hair, and had it continued around to his back like a pelt, Savannah might have stood a prayer of not melting into a puddle of panting female at the mere sight of his practically naked body.

But it didn't.

He was perfect, damn him, and she hungered for him as if she hadn't eaten in weeks and he were a decadent slab of prime rib.

She swallowed and did her best to rid her expression of any lingering lust. "You've been in there forever. I-is there any hot water left?" She strove for a put-out tone, but the sound was more breathless than irritated.

"Yeah," he said distractedly. His brow puckered and he lifted the *kurta* from the bed, tossed it aside and glanced at the floor. He bent over and checked beneath the bed skirt, and then paused, seemingly at a loss. He settled his hands at his hips, causing every well-formed muscle to ripple invitingly. Particularly his pecs. Savannah had always been a sucker for a gorgeous set of pecs.

"Have you lost something?" Savannah asked.

"Yeah. My underwear. Have you seen them?"

He knew perfectly well that they weren't allowed to wear any underwear. He was simply trying to annoy her, to remind her that he wouldn't be wearing any. Savannah glanced to the prominent bulge beneath his towel and sighed. As if she'd need reminding.

"No, sorry. I haven't." She smiled sweetly. "I seem to have lost mine as well. While you're looking for yours, why don't you be a dear and look for mine, too?"

Surprised, his patently perplexed expression vanished and he slowly looked up. A playful gleam suddenly lit his gaze. "Sure. I'd be happy to. Er…wanna tell me what they look like?"

Uh-oh. This wasn't exactly the scenario she'd hoped for. For some reason, she'd thought he'd feign sudden inspiration and laughingly remember the no-undergarment rule. She should have known better. He rarely resisted a challenge.

Still Knox needed to know whom he was dealing with, and this seemed to be as good a way as any to teach him, Savannah decided, warming to her tact.

"They're black silk. There's not much to them, barely a scrap of fabric. You might have a hard time finding them."

Knox's eyes darkened and she watched the muscles in his throat work as he swallowed. Feeling decidedly triumphant, Savannah stood and started toward the bathroom.

"Black silk, eh?" Knox said, his voice somewhat rusty. "Are there, uh, any distinguishing features? Anything that would make them more recognizable?"

Savannah paused with her hand on the doorknob and turned around. Her amused you're-playing-with-fire gaze met his and held it. "Yeah. They're thong underwear. Black lace with little black pearls."

Silence thundered between them at this glib description, then, his eyes never leaving hers, Knox casually dropped his towel. The sheer power—utter perfection and beauty—of his nude body rooted Savannah to the floor.

Seeing an outline of his penis hadn't prepared her for the actual article. He was only semiaroused, yet huge and proud—as he most certainly had every right to be—and every cell in her body responded to the blatantly virile part of him. She couldn't have looked away if she'd wanted to.

Knox picked up the *kurta* and, with a sexy grin, said, "Pity we can't wear underwear this weekend. I'd love to get a peek at that particular pair of panties. If you find them, why don't you show them to me?" He paused and his voice lowered to a more intimate level, sending a chorus of shivers down her spine. "I'll bet you look great in them."

Savannah determinedly ignored her initial impulse, which was to walk across the room, drop to her knees and suck him dry. Another talent of hers, if she did say so herself.

However, she would not let him win this little scene.

She'd been prepared for a battle royal and the smug

devil thought he'd gotten the better of her with this little display. He'd best think again. She'd seen a dick before. Granted not one as splendidly formed as his, but she was familiar enough with the male anatomy not to look like the shocked little virgin he apparently expected.

Savannah shot him a confident grin. "Not nearly as good as I look *out* of them."

With an exaggerated swing of her hips, she sauntered into the bathroom and shut the door.

Then she ran her bath, settled into the hot fragrant water, and imagined a naked Knox on the other side of the door…imagined everything she'd ever wanted to do with him and to him and everything she'd ever wanted him to do to her….

With a frustrated groan of the hopelessly, futilely aroused, she spread her thighs, parted her curls and, with a whimper of satisfaction…pulled a Chuck.

CHAPTER SEVEN

SAVANNAH APPEARED considerably less tense after her bath, Knox noted. Her movements were languid, leisurely and there was something altogether relaxed about her. She'd towel-dried her hair and the blue-black locks curled madly around her face, sprouting up in chaotic disarray all over her head like little question marks. She looked charmingly unkempt as always. He grinned. Even wet, she looked messy. She'd removed her makeup and her pale skin glowed with health and vitality. Her cheeks held a rosy hue and that plump bottom lip looked a little swollen, as though she'd been chewing on it.

Knox felt his eyes narrow and suspiciously considered her once more.

Relaxed, rosy and a swollen bottom lip. She'd obviously had more than a bath, Knox realized, astonished. He knew perfectly well what a woman looked like after release and clearly, by the sated look of her, she'd had a damn good one. He didn't know whether to be irritated or pleased. Irritated because he would have gladly taken care of her—would have loved to have brought her to climax—or pleased because she'd been so hot for him she'd had to take care of herself.

He decided to be pleased and covertly considered her once more. It was a rare woman who felt comfortable enough with her body to tend to her own needs. In his experience, women loved to be touched but didn't necessarily enjoy touching themselves. Clearly Savannah didn't suffer from any such inhibition. A snake of heat writhed through his belly at the thought. But that's the kind of woman she was. She would never rely solely on a man to get what she wanted, Knox thought with reluctant admiration. She had to be the most self-reliant woman he'd ever known.

Once again Knox wondered about her past. Just who exactly was Savannah Reeves? What had made her so independent, so determined to be an island unto herself? What had made her into this distrustful, autonomic loner? He knew absolutely nothing about her, he realized. Where she'd grown up, whether or not she had any brothers and sisters—nothing.

What was *her* story? he wondered, and felt a familiar nudge. Knox didn't know, but he firmly intended to find out before this weekend was up. Right now, however, they had other issues to deal with.

Like dinner.

A wonderful spread complete with all the romantic trimmings had arrived just moments before she'd walked out of the bathroom and distracted him. Knox had had a moment to peruse the instructions and he strongly suspected that Savannah would not enjoy their next assignment.

Which meant he wouldn't either because he would starve.

"Did you enjoy your bath?" Knox asked lightly.

Savannah pilfered through her toiletries until she located a bottle of moisturizer, uncapped the lid and poured a little into the palm of her hand, then began to massage the cream onto her face and neck. "Immensely," she all but sighed. "That's a great tub."

"Yeah, it is," he agreed, imagining her naked in it,

her little fingers nestled in her curls and her head thrown back in orgasmic wonder.

Savannah's gaze lit upon the dining cart and a smile bloomed on her slightly swollen lips. "Oh, good. The food's here. I'm *starving*."

Knox smiled knowingly. He'd just bet she was. Having a bone-melting climax typically did that to a person. Still, he had a feeling she was about to lose her appetite.

Savannah made her way across the room and inspected their meal. She took a deep breath, savoring the hickory scent of grilled steak tips with sautéed mushrooms, au gratin potatoes and steamed asparagus. "Oh, this looks heavenly," she groaned with pleasure.

Wondering how long it would take her to figure out what was wrong with the *heavenly* meal, Knox started to count. *One...*

She moved things around on the tray. "I love steak. And this looks wonderful."

Two...

"And I haven't had it in a long time. What a treat." Her brow wrinkled. "Hey, where's the—"

Three.

"—silverware?"

"There isn't any."

Her head jerked up and her delighted expression vanished. "What?"

"There isn't any," Knox repeated. He rattled the instructions for their meal in his hand meaningfully. "Here're our instructions. Would you like to read them yourself or would you rather I summarize them for you?"

Predictably, Savannah marched across the room and

snatched the sheet from his hand. "I'll read them myself, thank you."

Three beats passed before she'd gotten past the mystical mumbo jumbo and found out why they didn't have any utensils. Her outraged gasp sounded, and then she glared at Knox as though it were *his* fault. As though this were his idea. Hell, he hadn't made the rules.

"Feed each other?" she growled with a lethally icy look. "It's not enough that you've hauled me across the country to this godforsaken workshop, that I've had your tongue down my throat all blessed day, and now—*now*—if I want to have anything to eat it has to come from your fingers?" she asked incredulously. Those chilly blue eyes blasted him with another arctic look. She crossed her arms over her chest and, with a grim disbelieving look, she shook her head. "This is insane and is *so* not going to happen."

Knox shrugged. "I thought it sounded fun."

She snorted. "You would."

"And I'm hungry."

She hugged her arms closer around her middle and gazed longingly at the tray. "I was."

Knox paused, then said, "I agree that the shared bath was an unreasonable expectation, one I would have done had you been willing. But surely we could at least make an effort with this exercise." He lifted a shoulder. "Like you said, we've been kissing all day. How could me feeding you be any more personal? We've got to participate in as many of these exercises as we comfortably can to lend credibility to our story, to do our best work. What's the big deal?"

Indecision flashed in her eyes. She fidgeted and glanced back at the dining cart with another woebegone look. He knew he had her when her stomach rumbled. Knox suppressed a triumphant grin.

"Oh, all right," she finally relented. "But no funny stuff, Knox. I'm hungry. I want to eat, unblock a few chakras and go to bed."

Savannah pivoted, stalked back to the dining cart and swiftly began to move the plates and glasses onto the table. She didn't bother with the fresh-cut flowers and bent over and extinguished the candle with a determined breath.

Knox waited until she'd finished arranging things to her satisfaction and then joined her at the table. "What would you like to start with?"

"Oh, no," she said with a calculating grin. "I'll feed you a bite first, that way you'll understand exactly how I want you to feed me."

Knox knew he was going to enjoy this too much not to be at least a little accommodating. He nodded. "Fine."

Her cheeks puffed as she exhaled mightily. "So, what do you want to start with?"

"Steak."

Savannah picked up a steak tip. "Okay. Open up."

Knox did. Her fingers stopped just shy of his lips and she tossed it into his mouth so hard it bounced off the back of his throat and almost back out of his mouth. Knox managed to hang on to it and, smiling at her ingenuity, chewed the tasty morsel. This was not going as he'd planned. Next she'd be catapulting potatoes into his mouth and throwing asparagus at him like javelins.

And she looked so damned pleased with herself, Knox thought. Those clear blue orbs sparkled with unrepentant laughter.

Knox finally swallowed, cleared his throat and gave

her a droll look. "I'll need to see you balance a ball on your nose before I feed you like a seal."

Tongue in cheek, her lips twitched. "I didn't mean to throw it quite s-so hard."

"Right." It was his turn. He selected a steak tip and held it up for her inspection. "Ready?"

She nodded and hesitantly opened her mouth. Knox fed her the bite without incident and was careful not to let his fingers linger. He wanted her at ease, not guarded. This, too, was another trust builder and Savannah so desperately needed to learn to trust someone.

Knox had decided that person should be him.

He didn't know when he'd come to the decision or, for that matter, even why. But he wanted to be worthy of her trust. Wanted to be the person who brought her out of her isolated existence. He supposed he'd fully realized the extent of her distrustful nature this afternoon when they'd been practicing another faith-building exercise. It should have been simple. All Savannah had to do was stand in front of him, fall backward and allow Knox to catch her.

She couldn't do it.

Just as she'd start to fall backward, she'd abruptly stop and right herself. They practiced over and over again. But for all that work, she still hadn't been able to trust him enough to catch her. As a result, they were supposed to practice that exercise tonight, too. An idea occurred to him.

"Why don't we look at that chakra homework while we're eating dinner?" he asked.

Savannah nodded. "That's a good idea. Don't touch anything. I'll get the book."

She double-timed it back and opened the volume to

the appropriate page. "Give me another bite of steak, would you?" she said as she perused the page.

She absently opened her mouth for three more bites before Knox finally laughed and said, "Hey, what about me?"

Distracted, Savannah picked up a bite of steak and placed it on his tongue, then unwittingly licked her fingers.

His dick jerked beneath the *kurta*.

"Okay," she said. "We'll pass this book back and forth. I'll start with the first one, which is the perineum chakra or root chakra," she said. "Then you can take—"

"Er…why don't we skip that one?" Knox suggested. He knew all he needed to know about that particular chakra.

"Consider the story, tight-ass," she said with an infuriating little grin. "We'd hate to mislead our readers by not having all the facts."

"I'm not a tight-ass," Knox growled.

She grinned. "Hit a nerve, did I?"

"I'm driven. That doesn't make me a tight-ass—it makes me a professional."

She tsked under her breath. "A professional wouldn't balk at learning about his root chakra… unless he was a tight-ass."

Knox heaved a mighty sigh. "Fine. Gimme some potatoes, would you?"

Savannah tensed but loaded the requested side dish onto a couple of fingers and gave him a bite. Knox wrapped his lips around her fingers, sucked the potatoes off and sighed with satisfaction. "Mmm," he groaned. "Those are good. Want some?" he asked innocently.

Her shoulders rounded and she shot him a put-upon look. "Oh, hell. Why not? Yes," she sighed. "I do."

Knox curved a couple of fingers and scooped up a generous bite and ladled it into her mouth. Her eyes rounded with delighted wonder. "Oh," she said thickly. And then, "Ohh, these are great. More, more."

Laughing, Knox scooped up another helping and she wasn't so quick to avoid his fingers this time. She actually licked off a hunk of cheese that she'd missed on the first go around from his index finger. The slide of that tongue felt great and it didn't take much imagination to picture her lips wrapped around another prominent part of his anatomy. Still, she'd just begun to marginally relax, so Knox tried to appear unaffected.

He nodded to his plate. "How about letting me try that asparagus?"

"Sure." She picked up a spear and fed it to him. "What do you think? Is it good, or should we stick with the steak and potatoes?"

Swallowing, Knox nodded. "It's good, too. Hell, all of it's good." He inspected the table. "What did we get for dessert?"

Savannah peeked beneath a couple of smaller lids and her eyes all but rolled back in her head. A purr of delight emanated from her throat. "Strawberries and fresh cream. Forget the chakras. Let's eat. We can study later."

"Agreed."

Without further discussion, they promptly began to feed each other. Savannah loaded her fingers while sucking her bites from his and vice versa. Knox made sure that he got a suggestive lick in every third or fourth bite, but rather than giving him a frosty glare, Savannah eventually began to take it as a challenge. Sucking particularly hard one time, giving a clever flick of her facile tongue another. She was so damned competitive, she didn't intend for him ever to get the upper hand. Big surprise there, Knox thought. She took everything as a challenge and he seemed to be her favorite opponent.

Knox tolerated the main course with amazing restraint, but began to have a problem when they moved on to dessert. Watching Savannah's lips pucker around a strawberry, watching her lick the cream from his finger and around her mouth without having a screaming orgasm was proving to be damned difficult. To be honest, he didn't particularly like strawberries, but kept eating them anyway so that he could taste her fingers. He'd never imagined that feeding someone, or being fed, could be so damned erotic.

But it was.

And they'd get to repeat the whole process tomorrow night, and the next.

Savannah polished off the last strawberry with a deep sigh of satisfaction. Her tongue made a slow lap around her lips, making sure that she'd savored every bit of the arousing dessert. "That," she said meaningfully, "was excellent."

Without a doubt, Knox thought. He seriously doubted he'd ever eat again without thinking about this experience. Gave a whole new meaning to the term finger foods.

Savannah stood, placed her palms on the small of her back and stretched. *Newton's Third Law: For every action there is an equal and opposite reaction.* For reasons that escaped him, this was the thought that tripped through his head as Savannah's naked breasts were pushed up and against the thin fabric of her gown. He longed to taste her through the fabric, to draw the crown of that creamy breast into his mouth.

Savannah finally relaxed. "I'll wheel this dining cart

out into the hall, then we'll get started on our chakra lessons."

"Fine." Knox lay down at the foot of the bed.

Her step faltered on her return trip to the table. "What are you doing?"

He gestured to the bedside lamps. "Better lighting."

"Right." She smirked.

Oh, hell. One step forward, two steps back. She didn't drop her guard for anything. "You can lean against the headboard," Knox told her. "We'll be more comfortable."

"There is that. You'll need to be comfortable when we unblock your perineum chakra."

"My perineum chakra isn't blocked," Knox said through gritted teeth.

"We'll see," she said maddeningly.

Savannah retrieved the book, then did as Knox suggested and settled herself against the headboard of the bed. The bedside light cast part of her face in shadow and the other in stark relief. The pure white gown practically glowed, giving her an almost ethereal appearance. Knox swallowed as an unfamiliar emotion clogged his throat. If he'd ever seen a more beautiful woman, he couldn't recall.

"Okay," she sighed. "Let's get down to business." She read for a moment and then her laughing gaze tangled with his. "According to this, the root chakra deals with the desire to own and possess. People who have difficulty expressing themselves, who limit spontaneity, and are inflexible are generally tense in this chakra." She gave him a pointed look. "In short, they are tight-asses. Like you." She frowned innocently. "Do you have a problem with hemorrhoids, Knox?"

His lips twisted into a sardonic smile. "Right now, you're the only pain in my ass."

She laughed—actually laughed out load, a femininely melodious sound. He'd worked with her for over a year and had never heard her more than chuckle briefly. Another breakthrough, Knox decided, irrationally pleased with himself.

"In order to unblock this chakra, you're supposed to insert your finger into your lover's *rosebud* and—"

Knox felt his butt draw up again. "*What?* What's a rosebud?"

She grinned evilly. "It's tantric slang for asshole."

"Nobody is going to insert anything into my rosebud," Knox said flatly.

"It won't bloom," Savannah warned.

"Good."

Wearing a wicked smile, she shrugged. "Okay, for the sake of our respective rosebuds, let's just assume that neither one of us is blocked in the root chakra."

Knox felt his ass relax. "That'll work for me."

Savannah read on for a moment, then looked up. "Okay, we're supposed to align our chakras, express our love—"

Knox sat up. "Align? Did you say align?"

"Yes."

He smiled triumphantly. "And isn't that what I told you we were supposed to do in the first place?"

Savannah gazed at him. "You might have," she admitted hesitantly.

He collapsed onto the bed once more. "I knew it. I knew we were supposed to align something, by God."

She heaved an exasperated sigh. "You don't align your chakras until you unblock them. We've unblocked our root chakra. Now we align, express our love, and chant *lam*."

Savannah set the book aside, moved away from the headboard and lay down in front of Knox. "We're aligned. Now chant."

Knox frowned. "You call this aligned? Shouldn't you be closer?" He gestured to the thirty-six inches that yawned between them.

"This'll do."

Knox shook his head doubtfully, snaked an arm around her waist and tugged her toward him. He fitted her snugly up next to his body and growled low in his throat. "Now *this* is aligned."

She looked up at him and twin devils danced in her eyes. She batted her lashes. "Express your love, Knox."

Knox grinned. "I love your ass."

Another laugh bubbled up, making her shake against him. She smelled like strawberries and cream and apple lotion, and she felt utterly incredible in his arms. Lust licked at his veins, stirred in his loins.

"That'll do," she finally replied. "Let's chant. *Laaaammmmmm. Laaaammmmmm.*"

Knox made a halfhearted attempt but couldn't continue. The absolute absurdity of it hit him and he'd begun to laugh and couldn't stop. "Can you believe that right now, while we're lying here, people in this house are having their r-rosebuds digitally probed and are chanting this stuff?"

Savannah giggled. "And Chuck's probably whacking off."

Knox guffawed until his sides hurt, then rolled over onto his back and smoothed his hair off his forehead. He blew out a breath. "Because they think that this is going to cure them, that this tantric stuff is going to fix whatever is wrong with their lives."

Savannah's chuckled tittered out. "It's kind of sad, huh?"

"Yeah," Knox admitted solemnly. "It really is."

"If it doesn't work, we'll report it," she said at last. "That's what we do."

"I know."

"I'm looking forward to writing this story," she admitted, much to his surprise.

"*We're* writing," Knox felt compelled to point out. "*We're* writing this story."

"About that…" She winced. "Just exactly how are we supposed to do this story? I've always worked alone— I've never collaborated on an article before."

"Neither have I," Knox confessed. "I suppose we should just toss out ideas until the right one fits and go from there."

"What if we don't agree? What if you don't like my ideas and I don't like yours? Then what?"

He shot her a look. "Sounds like you've already made up your mind to hate my ideas."

She grinned. "Well, of course."

Another laugh rumbled from his chest. "Don't hold back, Savannah. Tell me how you really feel." Knox sighed. "I don't know. Let's just cross that bridge when we come to it. We're still a long way from putting pen to paper."

Savannah's breath left her in a small whoosh and she pulled away from him and sat up. "I don't know about you, but I'm tired and don't feel like having anything else unblocked and aligned tonight."

"Nah, me neither."

Knox sat up as well. He snagged a pillow from the

bed and found a spare blanket in the chest of drawers. Sleeping on the floor didn't appeal to him whatsoever, but he'd made a great deal of progress with Savannah tonight and he didn't want to jeopardize it by begging for a spot in the bed. He fixed his pallet on top of the floor pillows and gingerly lowered himself onto the lumpy makeshift bed.

"G'night, Knox," Savannah murmured.

He smiled and glanced up at her. "Night." *See,* he mentally telegraphed to her, *see how damned sweet I can be?* She turned off the light, plunging the room into darkness.

He heard Savannah settle in and sigh with satisfaction. Knox twisted and turned, fluffed and flattened pillows. Hell, he'd be better off sleeping in the damned bathtub, he decided, after several failed attempts to get comfortable. He groaned miserably and rolled over again, this time cracking his elbow painfully against the wall.

Savannah heaved a beleaguered breath. "Oh, for pity's sake, Knox, just get in the bed."

He stilled. "Really?"

"Yes," she huffed. "I suppose if I can kiss you all day and eat from your fingers, I can stand to have you sleep beside me. Just stay on your side and keep your hands to yourself."

Knox happily hoisted himself from the lumpy pillows, trotted over to the bed and slid under the covers. He thought he heard Savannah whimper when his weight shifted the mattress.

"Are you all right?" he asked.

He felt her move onto her back. "I'm fine." She paused. "Look, Knox, I'm used to sleeping alone, so I generally hog the whole bed. If I roll onto you, or crowd you, just shove me back onto my own side."

"Sure," he said, mildly perplexed. Was she a thrasher or something? he wondered. "I'm used to sleeping alone, too. You do the same for me."

"I will." Something ominous lurked in her tone.

Knox smiled. "G'night, Vannah."

She rolled onto her side once more, giving him her back. "It's *Savannah*," she growled. "Now shut up so that I can get come sleep."

There's my girl, Knox thought with a sleepy smile. His bitch was back. Funny, but she didn't sound so tough anymore. Knox heard the fear and vulnerability behind the surly attitude. What would it take, he wondered, to make her lose that edge? To strip away the destructive defenses and build her back up with a more productive emotion?

Knox didn't know, but he was grimly determined to find out.

CHAPTER EIGHT

Savannah awoke early in the exact position she'd feared she would—draped all over Knox.

Presently her cheek lay cuddled up to his sinewy shoulder, her arm was anchored around his lean waist and she'd slung a thigh over his delectable rear. Jeez, even in her sleep she couldn't resist him. Savannah knew that she should carefully extricate herself from him before he woke up and found her melted all over him, but she couldn't summon the necessary actions to move away just yet.

He felt…nice.

His big, warm body threw off a heat like a blast furnace, chasing away the early morning chill. She breathed in a hint of woodsy aftershave and male, and the particular essence that was simply Knox, and felt a twine of heat curl though her belly, lick her nipples and settle in her sex.

Savannah was accustomed to waking up hungry, but the appetite that plagued her this morning wouldn't be satisfied with a mere muffin and a cup of coffee. She wanted an order of Knox with hot, sweaty sex on the side.

On the side of the bed.

On the side of the tub.

Her side.

His side.

Inside or outside.

Any side.

She honestly didn't care. Savannah bit back a groan of frustration. She was starving here, starving for him and the hunger had all but gotten the best of her.

Savannah had set out on this confounded assignment against her will, wholly determined to resist Knox. She'd known that the story had immense potential, and she hadn't underestimated her attraction, but she had underestimated Knox.

He wasn't the shallow, thoughtless, lazy playboy she'd forced herself to believe he was.

Some innate sense of self-preservation had kicked in when she'd first met him, because her subconscious had recognized him as a potential threat to her heart. Savannah had looked at him and unfairly projected each and every one of Gib's character flaws upon Knox.

While the character flaws had been false, one glaring fact still remained—Knox still posed a threat to her heart. If she let down her guard one whit, Savannah knew Knox would burrow beneath her defenses, fasten himself onto that traitorous organ and, short of a transplant, she'd never get rid of him.

He wouldn't have a problem getting rid of her, though, Savannah thought with a bitter smile. No one ever did. That's why, regardless of how charming and witty, how adorable and sweet—how sexy—he turned out to be, she had to keep things in perspective. Keep her defenses in place.

They'd spent scarcely twenty-four hours together and, nerve-racking kisses and chronic masturbators aside, Savannah had had more fun in this single day with Knox than she'd had in years. He'd made her laugh, a rare feat. Sad, Savannah realized, but true. Given the opportunity, she wondered, what other rare feats could Knox facilitate? What other hidden talents did he have?

He stirred beside her and Savannah tensed and held her breath, silently praying that he wouldn't wake up and find her all but planting a flag in his groin. He didn't. But to Savannah's immense pleasure and frustration, he wrapped his hand around hers and, murmuring nonsensical sounds, tugged her even closer than she'd been before. Her breasts were now completely flattened against his muscular back and, of course, reacted accordingly. They grew heavy with want and her nipples hardened into tight, sensitive peaks. Her clit throbbed a steady mantra of *I'm ready!* One clever touch, Savannah knew, and she'd shatter.

Knox, damn him, was asleep, completely oblivious to her torture and exempt from his own.

Well, Savannah thought, she could either lie there and simmer in her sexually frustrated misery, or she could get up and try to put a more productive spin on the morning. Breakfast would be served in the common room at eight, and another lecture—more erotic massage—would begin promptly at nine. This lecture in particular was supposed to be one of those graphic, hands-on demonstrations the Sheas' brochures had promised and would segue into tomorrow's *Love His Lingam* and *Sacred Goddess Stimulation*. Savannah both dreaded and looked forward to those lessons. She'd be less than honest if she didn't admit to at least some morbid fascination.

Besides, she liked to excel at everything and if she gleaned even the slightest knowledge on how to please a future lover—or please herself—then she'd leave this damned workshop better than she arrived.

A careful look at the bedside clock told her that she

and Knox needed to get the lead out. They'd only unblocked one chakra and had totally skipped her building-
trust homework. Humiliation burned Savannah's cheeks.
Naturally she knew that she had certain trust issues—
she'd never been in a relationship in her life that hadn't
ended in some form of disappointment. But she hadn't
realized the true extent of her distrust until yesterday.
She'd been the only person in the entire class who'd
flunked the "blind trust" test. The symbolism hadn't
been lost on her or, more embarrassingly, him.

All she'd had to do was stand with her back to Knox,
fall backward and let him catch her. Most couples had
nailed it on the first try. She and Knox had attempted the
exercise until the end of class and she still hadn't gotten
it. Edgar and Rupali had shared an enigmatic look, then
instructed her and Knox to work on the exercise for
homework.

Quite frankly, Savannah didn't give a rip what the
Sheas or any of these other people here thought about
her. Beyond this weekend she'd never see them again.
But that wasn't the case with Knox. She'd see him on a
day-to-day basis and, during that idiotic test, she'd had
the uneasy privilege of watching his emotions leap from
teasing mockery to pity and, finally, to curiosity.

It wouldn't be enough that he knew she had trust
issues—he was a journalist and would have to know
why. If she wouldn't tell him when he covertly inter-
viewed her—and she had no doubt whatsoever that he
would—he'd dig around until he raked up every bit of
her unfortunate past. She inwardly shuddered with
dread.

She'd become a *story,* Savannah realized, an exposé,
and Knox, despite his laid-back attitude, was nothing
short of a bloodhound when he caught the scent of a

story. He'd use his particular brand of talent to unearth every unpleasant aspect of her past and he'd pull one of his legendary show-and-tell tactics on her. While she'd love to play a little show-and-tell with him, she didn't want it to have anything to do with her private life.

Despite her present predicament with Chapman, Savannah had a good reputation at the *Phoenix*. She'd worked hard to garner the respect of her peers, and if Knox used his trademark talent on her, she'd have to watch that respect become tempered with pity.

She would not be anyone's object of pity.

Savannah was wondering what tack she should take when Knox abruptly stirred once more. He stretched beside her, yawned, and she knew the exact instant when he awakened and the full realization of their position registered, because he grew completely still. Then he abruptly relaxed and she didn't have to see his face to know that he undoubtedly wore a cat-in-the-cream expression.

Feigning sleep, Savannah moaned softly and nonchalantly rolled away from him and onto her side. There, she thought. She'd escaped. She'd saved face and would—

To Savannah's slack-jawed astonishment, using the exact same tactic she'd just employed, Knox promptly spooned her. The force of his heat engulfed her as he bellied up to her back. He twined an arm around her middle and unerringly settled his palm upon her breast. Savannah hadn't recovered from that brazen move before he pushed his thigh between her legs and sighed with audible satisfaction right into her ear. The combined masculine weight, heat and scent of him caused a tornado of sensation to erupt below her navel.

She couldn't believe his gall. At least she'd molested him while she'd been asleep and unaware of her transgressions. Knox, the sneaky lout, was in full possession of his senses and had used the lucky opportunity to take advantage of the situation. Still, her conscience needled, she hadn't abruptly drawn away from him when she'd woken up. She'd lain there and savored the feel of him against her, just as she was doing now.

Which was madness, she thought with a spurt of self-loathing. Why didn't she just forgo all of the niceties and hand him her heart to break?

Savannah drove her elbow into his unsuspecting stomach. "Get...off...me."

Knox's breath left him in a quick, surprised whoosh and he promptly released her throbbing breast and rolled away. "Wh-what?" he asked with enough sleepy perplexity to look genuine. But she knew better.

Savannah glared at him. "I thought I told you to stay on your side of the bed."

Knox sat up in bed and rubbed a hand over the back of his neck. His mink-brown hair was mussed and the flush of sleep still clung to his cheeks. Those heavy-lidded eyes were weighted even more with the dregs of slumber. He looked almost boyish, yet the term didn't quite fit, because there was absolutely nothing boyish about the way her body reacted to his.

"Huh?" he managed.

Savannah blew out a breath. "I thought I told you to stay on your side of the bed," she repeated.

"Didn't I?" he asked foggily.

He knew damn well he hadn't, the wretch. "No," she said tightly. "You did not."

He frowned. "Oh, sorry. Hope I didn't crowd you."

"I woke up with your hand wrapped around my breast."

A smile quivered on his lips. Knox threw the covers

off and planted his feet on the floor, but didn't readily stand. He leveled a droll look at her. "Funny. I woke up with your hand inches above my dick and your thigh on my ass, but you don't hear me complaining."

Savannah flushed. She could win this argument, but not without admitting fault on her own part, so she didn't bother. "Just get ready," she huffed. "We've got less than an hour before breakfast."

THEY WERE TEN MINUTES LATE for breakfast. Knox had been wrong. Savannah did take great pains with her hair—it just didn't do any good.

She'd spent the better part of thirty minutes this morning trying to force the unruly locks into some semblance of a true style and when she'd finally exited the bathroom, she'd looked exactly as she had when she'd gone in. "I don't know why I bother," she said when she walked out.

Knox had bitten his tongue to keep from saying, "Me, neither."

He kept his mouth shut, of course. He'd already pissed her off this morning with the sleepy-hand-upon-her-breast bit and didn't dare risk her further displeasure by agreeing with her dead-on assessment about her hair. Besides, her hair had character. Knox thought it was adorable.

Having her draped all over him this morning had been a pleasant surprise. She'd smelled curiously like apples, a scent he'd associated with her before, and the feminine weight of her body nuzzled against his had been incredible. He'd felt the press of those delectable nipples against his back and that sweet hand snugged against his abdomen. If she hadn't moved when she did, his randy pecker would have nudged under her palm like an eager puppy begging for a stroke.

He'd known he shouldn't have rolled over with her, but for some perverse reason, he hadn't been able to help himself. His palms literally itched to touch her.

The one woman he'd imagined he wouldn't be hot for had unaccountably turned into the one woman he simply had to have.

Knox had never in his life longed to root himself between a woman's thighs more. He wanted her legs hooked over his shoulders, her arms lashed around his waist and her tongue in his mouth, and not necessarily in that order.

A moment after they entered, the Sheas moved to stand side by side in front of the room and garnered everyone's attention. "Greetings and good morning to you," Rupali said. Knox noticed that when Rupali moved forward to speak, Edgar instinctively moved slightly back and behind her. Support, Knox realized with a jolt of surprise and admiration. "We hope that you all passed a pleasant night and adhered to the rules set out for this retreat." She paused. "Did everyone adhere to the rules?"

A chorus of assents passed through the room, though Knox spotted at least two guilty faces. One was Chuck's, of course.

"What about homework?" Edgar asked. This time, it was Rupali that moved behind him. So the respect and support was reciprocated, not just one-sided.

Despite all of the questions and doubts surrounding this workshop and tantric sex in general, Knox had to admit that their relationship seemed genuine. They obviously cared very deeply for each other.

What would it be like to be on the receiving end of

such unwavering love and support? Knox wondered as a curious void suddenly shifted in his chest. What would it be like to have someone who believed in you so much that they instinctively knew to get behind you when you needed it, or perhaps even when you didn't? He'd had that sort of support from his family until he'd majored in journalism, but after that he'd lost their encouragement. It had hurt, but the desire to succeed had been a balm to his disappointment.

"Let's have a status report on our chakras," Edgar said. "We'll start and go around the room. Tell what sort of breakthroughs you experienced, as well as how many chakras you believe you unblocked. Who would like to go first?"

Several hands shot into the air at this question. Needless to say, his and Savannah's weren't among them. Chuck and Marge began and proudly reported that they'd unblocked their perineum, genital and belly chakras. Several other couples continued in this vein sharing their experiences, reporting multiple chakra breakthroughs. Knox began to get a little nervous. He hadn't realized just how little he and Savannah had gotten done last night. They'd have to take their break this afternoon and play some catch-up; otherwise they were going to be lagging behind the rest of the class. That was simply unacceptable. Knox didn't lag behind anyone.

Apparently, the realization had hit Savannah as well. Her lips had flattened into an adorably mulish expression. Knox felt his lips twitch. He knew that look—heaven knows he'd seen it often enough—and it meant watch your back.

"Is there anyone who hasn't reported?" Rupali asked.

"Knox and Barbie haven't," Marge replied helpfully. Knox gritted his teeth and smiled at her.

"Well, Knox and Barbie," Rupali said. "How did it go?"

Knox looked to Savannah, hoping in her ire, she'd step up and answer the question. For all appearances she smiled encouragingly, but Knox saw the evil humor dancing in that ice-blue gaze. Her look clearly said, "You made your bed, now lie in it."

"We, uh, worked on the trust exercise so much that we only got the r-root chakra unblocked," Knox reported. From the corner of his eye, he saw Savannah's eyes narrow fractionally. Obviously, she didn't appreciate taking the blame for their poor performance.

"Don't be so modest, baby," Savannah said sweetly. "Tell the rest."

The rest? Knox wondered as his breakfast curdled in his stomach. His smile froze. "That's private, pumpkin," he all but growled through gritted teeth. He had absolutely no idea what she was talking about, but instinctively knew she intended to humiliate him. Royally.

"Nothing is private here, Knox," Rupali reminded with a smile. "Truth and healing, remember? You obviously have something to be proud of. Barbie is proud. Please share," she encouraged gently.

"I—"

"Oh, very well," Savannah said, with a humbly mysterious look about the room. "I'll tell them." She paused dramatically. "After we unblocked Knox's root chakra—which took a great deal of time because of his tight-ass tendencies—he got an *erection!*"

This theatrical announcement was met with a mass of delighted oohs and aahs and a spattering of applause.

Savannah clasped her hands together excitedly and

looked meaningfully around at everyone. "It lasted for almost *two whole minutes!*"

She was evil, Knox thought as he felt his face flame with embarrassment. Evil. And he would make her pay. With a grand show of delighted support, Savannah grabbed hold of his arm and pressed close to him. "I'm so very proud of you, baby."

Edgar and Rupali beamed at him. "That's indeed something to be proud of, Knox. Congratulations on your erection."

Knox had been congratulated for many things over the years, but he could truthfully say that having a man congratulate him on an erection was a wholly new experience. A couple of the truly impotent men glared enviously at him.

"Er, thank you," he muttered self-consciously.

Beside him, Savannah sighed with sublime satisfaction, the faux picture of wifely adoration.

Rupali threaded her fingers through her husband's. "This is precisely why we have opened our home and hearts, why we decided to start this clinic. So that impotent men like Knox can come and reclaim their masculinity. With harmony and truth healing and the art of tantric ritual, perhaps he will be able to surpass even this breakthrough and lead his lover to climax." She gave Savannah an enigmatic look. "I don't think your problem lies in the lower chakras, Barbie. You will learn what I mean, and I would appreciate your telling me when it happens."

Looking somewhat startled, Savannah merely nodded. Now what did Rupali mean by that? Knox wondered. After a moment, he leaned over and asked Savannah.

She shook her head, clearly bewildered. "I have no idea."

"Well, tell me when it happens. I want to know, too."

"Oh, hell, Knox, you know as well as I do that nothing is going to happen."

"Now how would I know that?" he replied sardonically. "Just think about me and my whopping two-minute erection."

She had the nerve to laugh. "Save your indignation. After this morning, you deserved it."

"I wasn't the only one copping a feel," Knox replied, somewhat miffed. "And I wasn't the one who was so horny I had to masturbate during my bath to get some relief."

Her head jerked around and her stunned gaze found his.

"Yeah, that's right," he said with a crafty grin. "I know."

He had to give her credit—she recovered well. She blew out a disbelieving breath. "Don't be ridiculous. Honestly, Knox, the size of your ego never ceases to amaze me. I—"

"It wasn't the size of my ego that sent you into the bathroom and had you slipping your finger into—"

"Shut up," she said, squeezing her eyes tightly closed.

Knox tapped his finger thoughtfully against the chin. "Come to think of it, I think that was a violation of the rules. Perhaps I should report *your* climax—seeing as you're frigid and that would be a breakthrough," Knox threatened. "Then the whole room could applaud you and celebrate your orgasm."

"I'm sorry," she hissed.

"What?"

"I'm sorry, dammit."

He eyed her, his gaze lingering on her guarded

expression. "Just what exactly is the problem?" Knox wanted to know, serious now. "What have I done—besides making you do this story—that has you alternately assaulting my character and my ego?" *Why don't you like me?* he demanded silently. *Why can't I charm you? For the love of God, why do I even care?*

She swallowed. "Nothing. It's my problem, not yours."

Oh, no. That was the closest thing to a personal admission she'd ever made and he had no intention of letting her get away with not finishing the thought. *"What is it?"* he pressed.

"We don't have time to go into this right now," Savannah hedged. She tucked her hair behind her ears. "Trust me, it's nothing. You're right. I've been unfair."

"If it was nothing, you wouldn't want to go for my throat every time the opportunity presented itself. Spill it, Savannah. I've got a right to know."

"Y-you remind me of someone, that's all."

"I remind you of someone," Knox repeated. "Who?"

Seemingly embarrassed, she huffed a breath and refused to look at him.

"A guy?" Knox guessed, annoyed beyond reason.

"Yes," she finally relented. "A guy. Are you happy now?"

No, he wasn't. He was anything but happy. "If I remind you of a guy and it's not a good thing, then one could logically deduce that this particular guy was a bastard who broke your heart. Am I right?"

"He did not break my heart," Savannah insisted icily. "I hadn't given him my heart to break."

No, only her trust, Knox realized, which any moron should have realized was almost as precious as her heart. "Do I look like him?"

"No."

"Do I act like him?"

Her shoulders slumped with an invisible weight. "I'd made myself believe that you did. But you don't."

Knox scowled, hopelessly confused. "If you no longer believe I act like him, then what's the problem?"

She emitted a low, frustrated growl. "Being here with you, this whole workshop…" She gestured wildly. "How am I supposed to stay out of the bathroom," she said meaningfully, "and not do what I—"

"Masturbate?"

"—did, when I'm here with *you* and we're surrounded by sex, sex and more sex?" Her voice climbed. "How am I supposed to think about anything else with all this talk of orgasms and erections and—"

Understanding suddenly dawned and Knox felt a self-satisfied grin spread across his lips. "You want me."

She shot him a dark look. "I didn't say that."

Something warm and tingly moved through his rapidly swelling chest. *"You want me."*

She paused. "Don't look so proud of yourself. I'd want just about anybody under the circumstances."

"Yeah…but you're not here with *anybody*. You're here with *me*."

"Brilliant deduction, Einstein."

"Would it make you feel any better if you knew I was having the same problem?"

She snorted. "Don't lie. You've already told me that the reason you brought me here was because you *weren't* attracted to me."

"Things have changed."

"Yes, I'm sure they have. You're a man and you've decided to make do with whomever is available. Which happens to be me. Meanwhile, neither one of us has any business being attracted to the other because we're here to do a job. And we can't truly do that job correctly unless we have sex, so it really is a screwed-up conundrum, isn't it, Knox?"

Another thought surfaced and suddenly everything became clear. "Ahh," Knox said with a knowing twinkle. "You wanted me *before* we left Chicago. That's why you didn't want to come. That's why you were so determined not to attend this workshop with me."

"Keep this up, you cocksure moron. You're quickly losing your appeal."

Savannah promptly stood and followed the rest of the group to the classroom, leaving Knox to glow with her revelation.

Savannah Reeves wanted him…and apparently always had. What to do with this new information? Knox wondered. Just exactly what the hell was he supposed to do? She'd told him for a reason—she hadn't just dropped this little bomb without some inkling of the consequences.

Did she expect him to be a hero and abstain, or was she simply putting the ball into his court? Did she want him to take the sexual lead, so that any blame could be laid squarely on him when this weekend was over?

Knox didn't know, but he knew he'd better figure it out. Otherwise, he feared he might single-handedly be responsible for Savannah never trusting a man again.

CHAPTER NINE

SAVANNAH COULDN'T BEGIN to imagine what had possessed her to all but admit that she'd been lusting after him for a year, but once the burn of humiliation cooled, she knew she'd undoubtedly feel better. It would be a relief not to have to pretend that she didn't want him. Since he'd deduced what had occurred during her bath last night, Savannah thought with a rueful grin, she hadn't been doing such a great job of pretending otherwise anyway.

He'd seen right through her.

The only reason she'd been able to hide the truth as long as she had was because she'd made a point of avoiding him.

But she couldn't avoid him here.

He was everywhere.

In her mind, in her mouth, beneath her hands, in her room, even in her bed.

Everywhere.

She couldn't escape him and was rapidly losing her resolve to try. The attraction had simply become bigger than she could handle, more than she could conceivably take on. She'd been doomed from the moment Chapman, the vengeful bastard, had forced her to come on this ill-conceived trip. No, Savannah thought with a dry chuckle, she'd been doomed from the moment she'd met Knox. It had all been simply a matter of time before she'd fall victim to his lethal appeal and her equally lethal attraction.

Knox sat down on the padded mat next to her. The hairs on her arms prickled at his nearness, seemingly drawn like a lodestone to him. For reasons she didn't dare dwell on, all of the chairs had been removed from the room and had been ominously replaced with big cushy mats.

"Have they started yet?" Knox whispered low.

God, she even loved the sound of his voice. It was deep and smooth and moved over her like an old blues tune. Could she get any more pathetic? "Not yet," Savannah finally managed.

Confusion cluttered his brow. "What are the mats for?"

"Dunno." *And don't care to speculate,* Savannah thought.

Knox glanced idly around the room. "Well, at least we know they aren't going to ask us to do it yet. That doesn't happen until tomorrow."

Tomorrow. The word hung between them and conjured a combined sense of anticipation and doom. Savannah didn't dare let herself think about what would happen tomorrow afternoon after they'd completed their so-called tantric-lovemaking training, and were sent to their room armed with that knowledge and a long night ahead of them. She supposed they should work on the story that they'd come here to get, but without actually having tried tantric sex to see if it truly worked, she didn't know how exactly they were supposed to do that.

When they'd first arrived, doing a fair article without participating in tantric sex seemed plausible. Now it didn't, and she could no longer tell if that idea was a product of journalistic integrity or sheer unadulterated lust. Probably a combination of both, Savannah decided.

With a sexy curl of his lips, Knox shifted on his mat and leaned closer to her. "I know this is going to sound strange," he confided, "but I'm starting to like this *kurta*. It's extremely comfortable. Feels good. I like being… unrestricted."

Savannah felt her lips twitch and tried not to think of which part of him was so friggin' unrestricted. Clearly he'd decided to torture her with his new information. His effort was redundant—she couldn't possibly want him any more. "It's a progressive-thinking man who can admit that he likes wearing a dress."

"It's not a dress," Knox corrected amiably. "It's a *kurta*, and if they have them in the gift shop, you can bet your sweet ass I'm buying one and taking it home."

Savannah chuckled drolly. "If you wear it anywhere but at home, I would strongly advise you to put on some underwear." She looked pointedly—*longingly*—at his crotch. "Your entire package is plainly visible through the fabric."

"So is yours," he murmured suggestively. "Tell me, is that little star-shaped thingy on your right butt cheek a mole or a birthmark?"

He'd studied her ass that closely, eh? Swallowing her surprise, Savannah said, "It's a birthmark."

He nodded thoughtfully. "I thought as much."

Before Savannah could ponder that enigmatic comment any longer, the Sheas stood before the class and called order to the room.

"This morning we're going to teach some of the finer points of erotic massage," Edgar said. "Now, so that you understand the difference, erotic massage and genital massage aren't the same thing. We will cover those genital areas that bring such pleasure tomorrow, in *Love His*

Lingam and *Sacred Goddess Stimulation.* I'm sure you are all looking forward to that," Edgar said with a small smile.

"What we're going to show you today, however," he continued, "will be how to heighten full-body awareness to bring ultimate pleasure. There are other areas of our bodies that enjoy touch. Our faces, for instance. Which is where we'll begin. We'll take our time about this, so that both partners can enjoy the exercise. To get the full enjoyment of this lesson, the receiver should be nude; however, we will leave that option up to each of you." He smiled encouragingly. "Men, you shall be givers first."

Nude? Savannah thought frantically as the couples around them swiftly began to disrobe, including the Sheas. Savannah watched in fascinated horror as Edgar and Rupali casually slipped out of their *kurtas.*

"Givers sit crossed-legged and cradle your receiver's head in your lap," Edgar said.

Knox shrugged loosely, heaved a resigned breath and moved to draw his *kurta* over his head. He wore the slightest, sexiest grin, and those slumberous dark green eyes glinted with wicked humor and hidden sin.

"What the hell are you doing?" Savannah hissed, her heart beating wildly in her chest. "You don't have to get undressed. Clothing is optional."

"And I'm opting to come out of it." His lips tipped into a slow, unrepentant grin. "When I'm the receiver, I don't want anything between your hands and my skin."

His words sent gooseflesh skittering across her own skin. Nevertheless, unreasonable though it may be, she only wanted him naked with her. Not with a roomful of observers. A wee bit possessive, but she couldn't help herself. Her eyes narrowed. If even one of these sexually repressed sluts so much as looked at him, she'd break their fingers.

"Then you can be nude in our bedroom," she said icily. "But not here."

He paused, something shifted in his gaze and he smiled knowingly. "Ah, so you want me nude all to yourself?"

Did he have to be so arrogantly perceptive? Savannah thought with a stab of irritation. Was she that transparent? "What I want is for you to leave your clothes on," she told him, struggling to keep her patience.

"Knox? Barbie? Is there a problem?" Rupali asked.

To Savannah's continued mortification, the whole nude room turned to stare at them. "Uh, no. We're fine, thanks."

"There is no shame in flaunting our nude bodies," Rupali said with that misty tone. "We were created to delight in their perfect design. The human form is art in motion. You will find no judging eyes here." With a melancholy smile, she gestured to herself. "My own body is growing old and wrinkled. My breasts aren't as firm as they used to be, nor my stomach as flat." She straightened. "But I am proud, because this is the body I live in, and I am beautiful to myself."

Savannah envied the woman's confidence. In an age where the words *thin* and *youthful* defined beauty, Rupali could look at herself and feel imperfect but proud. How often had Savannah looked into the mirror and thought, *If only my breasts were larger? If only my thighs were thinner?*

Be that as it may, she was still just modest enough not to want to get naked in front of a roomful of strangers. Savannah summoned a wobbly smile. "I-I'd prefer to stay dressed."

Rupali nodded. "As you wish."

Everyone settled into the required position at Edgar's instruction. "Let's begin with a scalp massage," Edgar told them. "Be sure and ask your receiver what feels good to her. What she likes. Learn what makes your lover feel good and commit it to memory. Trust me," Edgar laughed. "You will reap the benefits of your effort tenfold."

Knox slid his fingers into her hair and began to knead her scalp with strong little circling movements. Savannah couldn't help herself, the audible moan of pleasure slipped past her smiling lips before she could stem it.

"Like that, do you?" Knox asked. She'd closed her eyes, but could hear the humor in his voice.

"Indeed, I do," she sighed softly.

Savannah had always enjoyed having her hair washed at her hairdresser's, had always found it relaxing, but she couldn't begin to compare that crude rubdown to the sensation of having Knox's warm, blunt-tipped fingers manipulating her tense scalp. The light scratch of fingernails, the strong press of his fingertips swirling over her head, lulled her. He caressed every inch from her hairline at her forehead, to the very nape of her neck, where tension had the tendency to gather. She hadn't anticipated this to be such an erotic experience, but a warm sluggish heat had begun to wind through her seemingly boneless body, proving her wrong.

"Let's move on, class," Edgar said, to Savannah's supreme disappointment. "Givers, move your attention to your receiver's face. So much emotion, so much feeling is transmitted through the muscles of our face. Consider the smile and the frown. These muscles, too, need attention. Caress your lover's face, and, remember, be sure to ask her what she likes," Edgar reminded. "Watch for what makes her feel good."

Savannah smothered a sigh of satisfaction when she felt Knox's big warm hands cradle her face, felt them slide over her cheeks as he mapped the contours of her face. He smoothed his fingers over her closed lids, slid a thumb over the curve of her eyebrow, down her nose. *Heavenly,* she thought as another smile inched across her lips.

Knox brushed the back of his hand down the slope of her cheek. That move was more tender, more reverent, and somehow more personal than the others. Savannah longed to open her eyes, to look into his, and see if she could discover any inkling of his present thoughts, but the idea was no sooner born than abandoned, because Knox suddenly slid his thumb over her bottom lip.

Savannah had the almost irresistible urge to arch her neck, open her mouth and suck that thumb. She so desperately wanted to taste him that any part would do, and this particular part was most readily available. She settled for licking her lips after his finger had moved on, searching for even the smallest lingering hint of him.

To her immense gratification, she heard the breath stutter out of Knox's lungs, felt a slight tension creep into his touch. He shaped her face once more with his hands, slid them down her arched throat and back up and around again. His touch grew slower yet more deliberately sensual. Savannah struggled to keep her breathing at a normal respiration, but it was getting considerably more difficult with each passing second.

Desire weighted her limbs and something hot and needy unfurled low in her belly, arrowed toward her wet and pulsing sex. She pressed her legs together and bit back the urge to roll over, scale his magnificent body and impale herself on the hard throbbing length of him.

If he could turn her into a quivering lump of lust with a scalp and face massage, just exactly how would she manage to control herself when he moved on to other erogenous zones? She wouldn't be able to bear it, Savannah decided. She simply—

"Before we continue," Edgar said, interrupting Savannah's turbulent thoughts, "let's change positions. Both the men and women need to find out how it feels to touch and be touched."

"Couples tend to get carried away as this lesson progresses," Rupali chimed in with a dry chuckle. "Please go ahead and change positions."

A reprieve, Savannah thought, profoundly relieved. As she sat up, she glanced at Knox and her gaze tangled with his. His eyes were dark and slumberous and a knowing, self-satisfied twinkle danced in those wickedly arousing orbs. The wretch knew exactly what he'd been doing to her, knew that he'd lit a fire in her loins that only a blast from his particular *hose* would put out.

Savannah narrowed her eyes into a look that promised retribution and more. Nobody set her on fire, then failed to get burned.

He would pay. With pleasure.

KNOX HAD SEEN that look in Savannah's eye before and knew it boded ill, undoubtedly for him. A flush of arousal tinged her creamy skin and her eyes were as hot as a blue flame. He'd known what he'd been doing to her during that massage, known that he'd lit her up.

Who would have ever thought that something as simple as a scalp and face massage could ignite such a blazing fuse of sexual energy? He'd listened to her little purrs of pleasure, felt her alternately go limp with relaxation and then vibrate with tension.

It had been the most singularly erotic sensation Knox had ever had.

Knox had been sexually active since his early teens. His sexual experiences had run the gamut of the highly romantic, to the down and dirty, and all species in between. He'd been drizzled in chocolate and licked clean, had eaten grapes from the pale pink folds of a woman's sex, had done it in a cab, in an elevator, and once in the bathroom of his dentist's office.

Yet, for all of his vast experience, nothing had prepared him for the complete and total, all-consuming need he felt for Savannah. With each touch he'd become more aroused, more hungry for her. Feeling the delicate planes of her face beneath his hands, the soft swell of those lush lips, the sweet curve and soft skin of her cheek beneath his knuckles...

Something had happened to him in that instant, something so terrifying that Knox didn't dare name it, much less contemplate it. He'd looked at that beautiful, serene face of hers, that mess of bed-head curls, and a curious emotion had swelled in his chest, pushed into his throat and had forced him to swallow. His hands had actually trembled.

The picture she'd made in that instant was indelibly imprinted in his mind. No matter how much she blared and blustered, no matter how much blue sleet she slung in his direction, Knox would always remember the way she'd looked right then. She didn't know it yet, but she'd never be able to freeze him out again.

"Okay," Rupali said. "Let's begin."

Savannah leaned over him and smiled. "Let me know if I hurt you."

Oh, hell.

She slid her small fingers into his hair and rolled his

scalp in little circles, front to back and side to side, alternating pressure with light touches and firmer kneads until Knox heard a long, decidedly happy growl of approval and realized it had come from the back of his own throat. She skimmed her fingers over the sensitive skin behind his ears, tunneled them into the thick hair at his nape. She scratched and massaged, kneaded and rubbed. Unexpected pleasure eddied through him and, though he imagined Edgar and Rupali would think that he'd totally missed the point of this exercise, it didn't take long for Knox to decide that those talented little fingers could be put to better use south of his navel.

He was a man, after all. He wouldn't be satisfied until her hand was wrapped around his throbbing rod, pumping him until he exploded with the force of his climax.

Still, Knox thought, as Savannah's fingertips slid through his hair once more, this was nice. Perhaps Edgar was onto something with all this erotic massage stuff. Every muscle was languid and relaxed, save for his dick—hell, he could do a no-hands push-up, he was so friggin' hard right now.

"Are you planning on hosting a party down there?" Savannah leaned down and asked him.

Knox slowly opened his eyes. "What?"

She was smiling one of those secret little smiles that made Knox feel as if he'd been caught with his fly down. "Are you planning on having a party down there?" She glanced pointedly at his groin. "You've erected quite a tent."

"Not a party," Knox told her silkily. "An intimate dinner for one. You hungry?"

Her eyes narrowed and then she licked her lips suggestively. *"Starving."*

If he hadn't been exercising tremendous control, Savannah would have turned him into the premature ejaculator she'd claimed he was with that little dramatic display.

"Givers," Rupali said, "move on to your receiver's face. Remember to note what pleases your lover."

"Would you like to know what pleases your lover, Savannah?" Knox murmured. "Would you like me to tell you?"

She swallowed and he felt her fingers tremble against his cheek. "I don't have a lover."

"That can be easily remedied."

She laughed softly, swept her fingers over his brow, down his cheek and along his jaw. "You wouldn't say these things if there was any blood left in your head."

Knox laughed. "If I'm not mistaken, *all* of it's in my head."

"Not the one that is responsible for logical thinking." She pressed a couple of fingers against his lips. "Shut up, Knox. People are starting to stare."

"Let 'em. I'm like Rupali. I'm proud. Besides, I've got something to prove." He grinned. "I'm going to break my two-minute erection record."

She tsked regretfully and massaged his temples. "Sorry, can't let that happen. Someone must protect our cover."

"Baby, you can't stop me."

"Wanna bet?"

Knox stilled and looked up at her. Clearly she hadn't gotten it yet, and wasn't going to until he spelled it out for her. "Savannah, my head is in your lap, inches away from the part of you that I want more than my next breath, and your hands might be on my face—which feels lovely, by the way—but in my mind, your hands are wrapped—along with your lips—around my rod and I'm seconds away from coming harder than I ever have in my life." He paused and let that sink in, watching her expression waver between determination and desire. His gaze held hers. "There is absolutely nothing you can say that's going to make me lose this erection."

A long, pregnant pause followed his blunt soliloquy. She blinked drunkenly for a second, then recovered and said four words that were guaranteed to make any hetero male lose even his most valiant erection.

"Chuck's whacking off again."

"Aw, Savannah," Knox woefully lamented. With a wince of regret, he squeezed his eyes shut but couldn't force the image away. The ick factor of Chuck and his happy hand swiftly deflated Knox's prized hard-on.

"And the big top comes down," Savannah whispered dramatically.

Knox opened his eyes and glared at her with amused accusation. "You are evil."

She smiled with faux modesty. "I try."

Knox felt a silent laugh rumble deep in his chest. "I'm sure you do."

A comfortable silence ensued, broken only by the soft sighs of pleasure that ebbed through the room. Savannah continued her sweet assault upon his face, gently massaging him. He'd let his lids flutter closed, but could feel the kiss of her gaze examining his every feature, measuring the muscle and bone against her hands. He heard a poignant, almost resigned sigh slip past her lips and wondered just what heavy realization she had come to. What he'd give to have even a glimpse into those thoughts.

Just as Knox was truly beginning to relax, Rupali interrupted the sensual play with more instructions. The givers and receivers were once again directed to change positions.

"We will massage backs and bellies, rumps and thighs, calves, insteps and even the smallest toe," Rupali told them. "No part of our bodies—aside from our genitals—shall be overlooked."

"You will know your lover's body better than your own by the end of this day," Edgar chimed in. "You will know what he or she likes, and you will discover neglected areas of your own body that bring pleasure when touched. Think of your lover's body like a musical instrument. Her sighs, her moans of pleasure, are your music, her quivers your applause."

"Women, the same holds true for you," Rupali shared. "Every indrawn breath, every expression of pleasure, every guttural growl from your man is his own primal music. While learning how to play your man, and while you, in turn, are played, your inner harmony begins to take form. The voice of your one-being will become clearer." She paused. "Seek that place, class. *Kundalini*," she emphasized. "Combined life force and sexual energy. Once you have experienced it, nothing else will ever suffice."

Knox whistled low, and he and Savannah shared a look. Her beauty, the absolute perfection of her face, struck him once more and the desire to reach out to slide his fingertips over those smooth features almost overpowered him.

Once you have experienced it, nothing else will ever suffice.

Knox grimly suspected those words held a double meaning for him. After Savannah…no one else would ever do.

CHAPTER TEN

THOUGH IT TOOK a monumental amount of restraint, Savannah limited her bath to just that—a bath. She and Knox had managed to make it from class back to their room after the all-day erotic massage session and, though her limbs had quaked and were limp as noodles, and her loins had been locked in a pit of permanently aroused despair, she'd managed to survive without begging him to plunge into her and put her out of her sexually frustrated misery.

Her only consolation was that Knox had been mired in that pit as well and, quite honestly, had not fared as well as she. Savannah's lips quivered. Her nipples didn't quite cause the stir his prominent erection did. When Knox was aroused, everyone knew it, could hardly fail to notice. She hated to dwell on it so, but Savannah couldn't seem to conquer her fascination with his enormous... article.

Neither could anyone else, for that matter, a fact that both annoyed and delighted her. For all intents and purposes of this workshop, that colossal penis was *hers* and hers alone. Both men and women alike gazed at them with envy, the men at Knox because they longed to be equally blessed, and the women, like her, were most likely astounded at the sheer size of him. Savannah enjoyed the being envied part—it was their greedy gazes lingering on her borrowed penis that pissed her off.

She'd heard a couple of the women talking about the phenomenon on the way out. "Pity he can't keep it up longer than two minutes though," one had said regretfully and to Knox's extreme embarrassment. During that session, his problem had seemed genuine to all. Every time that sucker had stood at attention longer than it should, Savannah had whispered the magic words, and *poof!* it would disappear. The magic words being, "Chuck's whacking off again." Cruel, she knew, but not any more cruel than what she'd suffered.

If she possessed even a shred of sanity by the time this workshop was over, Savannah would consider herself extremely lucky.

The evening ahead would undoubtedly be as trying as this day had been. As soon as she'd mentioned taking a bath, Knox had proclaimed it an excellent idea, and had once again tried to come out of that damned *kurta*. Truthfully, Savannah would have liked nothing better than to have taken him up on the idea, would have liked nothing better than to have had his hot, hard wet body wrapped around and pulsing inside hers. The tub had been designed for sin and so had his body and she wanted it more desperately with each passing second.

Quite honestly, Savannah didn't have a clue what they were supposed to do now. She'd laid all her cards on the table, and she supposed Knox had, too. He'd admitted that he wanted her now, and it was the *now* that kept messing with her head, the *now* that she was having trouble getting past.

A part of her wanted to say, *Consequences be damned, you've wanted him forever, here's your opportunity, just go for it already!*

But another part hated knowing that he *hadn't* wanted her to begin with, that it had taken a sex workshop for

him to consider her attractive, and she seriously suspected her newfound appeal had more to do with con-
venience than actual interest. If she gave in to her baser
needs and rode him until his eyes rolled back in his head
as she so very much wanted to do, would she regret it
later? Or would she regret it more if she didn't?

Savannah didn't know and, luckily, wouldn't have to
decide until tomorrow…provided she didn't expire from
longing first.

Knox rapped on the bathroom door, startling her.
"The food's here. Come feed me."

A wry grin curled her lips as she opened the bathroom door. "I should let you starve," she told him.

"Why?"

"Just for the hell of it."

He shivered dramatically. "Chilly, chilly." That verdant green gaze was shrewd and glinted with humor.
"You must not have had as much fun in the tub this
evening. Don't worry, I can cure what ails you." His
voice was low, practically a purr, and it sent a flurry of
sensation buzzing through her.

She'd just bet he could, Savannah thought with a
mental ooh-la-la. Did she have a prayer of resisting him?
she wondered with furious despair.

After everything else they'd been through over the
past twenty-four hours, feeding each other seemed
downright tame. They spoke little during the meal, just
systematically fed each other the tender strips of Hawai-
ian chicken, green beans, and macaroni and cheese,
the latter being particular messy and involving a lot of
cleanup.

Which meant a great deal of licking and sucking, and
tongue in general.

Presently, a couple of Savannah's fingers were

knuckle deep in Knox's hot mouth, and he'd decided to make a grand spectacle of getting her clean. He slid his tongue along her finger and alternately nibbled and sucked. Soft then hard, slow and steady, and, all the while, his heavy-lidded gaze held her enthralled.

Initially Savannah had managed a mocking smile, but she gloomily suspected it had lost its irreverent edge and had been replaced by a stupidly besotted grin. Her pulse tripped wildly in her veins and the desire that had never fully receded came swirling through like a riptide, washing away reason and rationale and anything that closely resembled common sense.

Knox finally commenced his cleaning and released her tingling fingers. "Savannah…can I ask you something?"

She blinked, still wandering in a sensual fog. "Sure."

"Where are you from?" he asked lightly. "Where did you grow up?"

The fog abruptly fled. Savannah suppressed a sigh and took a couple of seconds to shore up her defenses and decide how she should respond. She'd known that he'd ask—she'd watched the very questions form in his mind. Perhaps if she told him enough to satisfy his curiosity, he'd leave well enough alone. One could hope, at any rate.

Savannah pushed her plate away. "I grew up in lots of different places."

"Military?"

She blew out a breath. "No…foster care. My parents died when I was six."

Knox winced. "Oh. Sorry." He looked away. "Damn, I—"

Savannah hated this part. It was the same scenario

every time. As soon as she told someone about her parents, they always apologized and then lapsed into an uncomfortable silence. She'd secretly hoped Knox would be different, but—

"That sucks, Savannah," Knox finally said. He plowed a hand through his hair, clearly out of his comfort zone, and his concerned gaze found hers. "I know that sounds so lame, but damn…that just really sucks."

No points for eloquence, Savannah thought as her heart unexpectedly swelled with some unnamed emotion, but he definitely scored a few points for the blunt, wholly accurate summation. "Thank you. You're absolutely right." She smiled, blew out a stuttering breath. "It did suck."

He arched a brow, leaned down and casually rested his elbows on his knees and let his hands dangle between his spread thighs. "No family you could have gone to live with?"

"No," Savannah replied with a shake of her head, shoving the old familiar hurt back into the dark corner of her heart where she kept it. "There was no one. We were a family of three and they died…and then there was me."

"No brothers or sisters?"

"Nope." Time for her part of the interview to be over, Savannah decided, drawing in a shaky breath. She smacked her thighs. "No more questions, Knox…unless you want to answer a few of mine."

He smiled and lifted one heavily muscled shoulder in an offhanded shrug. "Go ahead. Shoot. My life is an open book."

We'd just see about that, wouldn't we? Savannah thought. "Why do you work so hard at looking like you don't work hard?"

His affable mask slipped for half a second, and if she hadn't been watching closely, she would have missed it altogether. "What?"

Savannah leveled him with a serious look. "I've watched you. I used to think that everything just came so easily to you…but I was wrong. You work very hard at your job, yet you make it a point to look like you don't." She paused. "Why is that, Knox?"

He looked away. "I don't know what you're talking about."

"The hell you don't. Be honest."

Knox swallowed. "Do you want the truth?"

"No," she deadpanned. "Tell me a lie. Of course, I want the truth!"

He smiled at that, then looked away once more. "It's simple, really. Everyone expects me to fail, and I don't want anyone to know just how much I want to succeed." He laughed self-consciously. "There you have it. My big dark secret."

He was right. It was simple, and yet more meaning and explanation lurked in that one telling sentence than she could have hoped for. Another thought surfaced.

"What do you mean *everyone?*" she asked.

Another dry humorless laugh rumbled from his chest. "Just what I said—everyone. Parents, co-workers, they all expect it." He passed a hand wearily over his face. "My parents keep waiting for me to come and work with my father, and so does everyone at the *Phoenix*. No one realizes that I'm not going anywhere, that I've chosen my career." His determined, intent gaze tangled with hers. "I'm a journalist. This is who I am, what I do. Does that make sense?"

Regret twisted her insides. Suddenly lots of things were beginning to make sense, Savannah thought, including the fact that she'd been no better than anyone else, if not worse. She'd taken one look at Knox, panicked, and had not gone to the trouble to look beyond her first impression, beneath the surface of his irreverent attitude. She'd formed the one uncharitable opinion and held fast to it, because she'd been too terrified to face the alternative.

Savannah swallowed. "It, uh, makes perfect sense. And Knox, for what it's worth, I think you're one helluva journalist."

His guarded expression brightened and dimmed all in the same instant. He looked away. "You're just saying that."

Savannah grinned at him. "Have you ever known me just to toss out a compliment?"

Those sexy lips tipped into an endearing smile. "No."

"Then the proper response is thank you."

He nodded. "Thank you."

The mood had become altogether too serious, Savannah decided. "We should get started on those chakras," she told him.

Knox winced, rubbed the back of his neck. "You're right. Do you mind if I grab a quick shower first?"

Savannah shook her head. "I need to organize my notes. We have a story to write, after all."

And she had some thinking to do…and a decision to make.

"I SWEAR I'LL CATCH YOU."

"I know that," Savannah said, exasperated.

"Then what's the problem?"

She speared her fingers through her hair and glared at him despairingly. "I can't let myself fall. I—I just can't do it. It's not a question of you being able to catch me—it's the whole idea of letting you. Don't you get it?"

Regrettably, he did, Knox thought. They'd been at this blind-trust test for the better part of thirty minutes and she still hadn't been able to let him catch her. Her reticence made perfect sense, now that she'd shared a little of her history.

Though Savannah had been very glib about the loss of her parents and her childhood, Knox had nonetheless glimpsed the little girl who'd felt abandoned beneath the woman who had learned to cope. Hell, no wonder she had trust issues. She'd had to learn to trust herself and no one else. She was completely alone. That wholly depressing thought had fully hit him while he'd been in the shower.

Savannah Reeves didn't have anyone.

Not a single living soul in this world to share her life with. Granted, his parents hadn't always supported him the way he would have liked…but at least they were there. Had provided the necessities and more to see him raised.

Savannah had gone through the foster-care system and apparently had come through the experience without so much as a mentor. If there had been anybody—anybody at all who'd made a difference in her life—she would have shared that. What she'd said had revealed a lot, but what she hadn't said revealed more.

In all truth, Knox could have waited to take his shower in the morning, but after listening to her resignedly tell him about her parents, Knox had suddenly been filled with self-loathing and disgust. He'd turned into the whiny little rich boy he'd always sworn he'd never become. So what if his parents didn't like his job? They'd get over it. So what if his co-workers at the *Phoenix* didn't respect him? He'd do his job to the best of his ability, and he'd *make* them, by God. He wouldn't leave them a choice.

When compared with the trials of Savannah's life, Knox's little letdowns had seemed petty, selfish and small. *He'd* felt small, and Knox had decided that the only way he could redeem himself was to become someone she respected…and someone she trusted.

Thus, he'd come out of his shower prepared to conquer her trust issues. Knox frowned. So far, it wasn't working.

"Okay," Knox finally said. "Let's try something different. Face me and fall forward."

Savannah heaved an impatient sigh. "This is pointless. I'm not—"

"Do it."

"Oh, all right." She moved to stand in front of him. "Now look at me and fall."

She chewed anxiously on her bottom lip, fastened her worried gaze onto his and fell…right into his outstretched arms.

Knox grinned, unaccountably pleased. His mood lightened considerably. "Now that's more like it."

She smiled hesitantly. "It is, isn't it? Thanks, Knox. That was a good idea."

His chest swelled, amazed that he'd been able to impress her. "Okay, now let's try this. Stand with your side to me and fall."

She did, from both sides, and both times fell right into his arms.

"And now for the final test," Knox teased. "Let's try the blind-trust test again."

Savannah's hopeful smile warmed him from the

inside out. She swallowed and nervously gave him her back. For half a second, Knox thought she would go for it, would take the proverbial plunge, but just short of letting gravity have its way, Savannah drew up short with a frustrated wail of misery.

"Why?" she railed with a whimper. "Why can't I do this?" Defeat rounded her shoulders and the breath left her lungs in a long, dejected whoosh.

Knox, too, felt the drag of disappointment. "You'll get it," he encouraged. "You've definitely made some improvement."

"I know, and thank you." She shot him a sheepish look. "I don't mean to sound ungrateful. I just— I just *hate* to fail."

Knox summoned a droll smile. "I don't think anyone particularly cares for it."

Some of the tension left her petite frame and her lips twitched adorably. "I suppose not."

"Why don't we move on to the chakras? We're behind, you know." Knox strolled across the room and sprawled across the foot of the bed as he'd done the night before. He heaved a disgusted breath. "Marge and Chuck are beating us."

Savannah cast him a sidelong glance. "Humph. Mostly Chuck just beats himself."

Knox felt his eyes widen and a shocked laugh burst from his throat. He looked over at Savannah, pushing down his smile. "So, what's the next chakra we're supposed to unblock?" Knox asked innocently. He knew, of course. He simply enjoyed messing with her.

Her gaze twinkled with perceptive humor. "It's the genital chakra, which you well know," she added pointedly. She settled herself against the headboard, placed the book in her lap and opened it to the appropriate page. He watched her lips form the words as she read silently. After a moment, she looked up. "Well, now this is interesting. According to the book, this chakra can be one of the most difficult to deal with."

"That being the case, should I get naked?"

"I think not."

"Damn," Knox said with chagrin. "Funny, but I distinctly remember you saying that I could be naked in our room."

Though she refused to look at him, Knox discerned a slight quiver at the corners of her lips. "I lied. Now shut up and listen." She paused and read some more. "I—I don't think either one of us is blocked in this chakra."

That figured. This was the only one he'd looked forward to working on. Knox scowled. "Are you sure? I'm feeling a little blocked. I think that you should unblock me. Does it say how you're supposed to do that?"

Savannah poked her tongue in her cheek. "Yes, as a matter of fact, it does."

Anticipation rose. Knox turned over onto his back and laced his hands behind his head. "Then do it."

"Are you sure?" she asked gravely.

Oh, was he ever. "Yes, I'm sure."

"Well, if you're sure." Knox felt the bed shift as she moved into a better position. "You'll need to roll over."

Something in her too innocent tones alerted Knox to the fact that all was not as it seemed. Obviously he wasn't going to get the hand job he'd been dreaming of. With a premonition of dread, he opened his closed eyes and glanced at her. Just as he suspected, mischief danced in that cool blue gaze. "Roll over?" he asked slowly. He dreaded asking, but knew he must. "Why?" he asked ominously.

"Because, according to my handy booklet, I'm supposed to unblock your root chakra while I'm unblocking your genital chakra." She smiled. "So why don't you—just try to relax and I'll—"

Realization dawned, and the semiarousal he'd enjoyed instantly vanished. His ass shrank in horrified revulsion. Knox slung an arm over his eyes. "Forget it," he growled.

"—make this as painless as possible." She paused. "What?" she asked innocently.

"Forget it."

"Are you sure? I'd be happy—"

"Savannah…" Knox warned. What was with the preoccupation with a person's ass? Knox wondered.

She laughed, not the least bit repentant. "I tried to tell you that we weren't blocked. Let's just chant the couples blessing and move on."

"What's that?" Knox asked, still perturbed.

Savannah aligned her body with his and Knox felt marginally better. She pillowed her head on the crook of her arm and held the book aloft with her other hand. Amusement glittered in her eyes and her lips were twitching with barely suppressed humor. "Okay, I'm supposed to say, 'I love you at your lingam and bless your wand of light.'" She promptly dissolved into a fit of giggles.

Knox laughed as well. "And what am I supposed to say?"

"You're supposed to say, 'I love you at your yoni and bless your sacred space.'"

How could people say this stuff with a straight face? Knox wondered. "Consider yourself loved and blessed," he said dryly. "Let's move on. What's next?"

Savannah sat up and wiped her eyes. "The belly chakra."

"Does my ass have anything to do with this one?" Knox asked suspiciously.

"Er...I don't think so."

He nodded. "Then continue."

"Okay, now this one is actually pretty interesting," Savannah said. "Our bellies are the feeling centers. Our emotions are energy in motion and tend to grow out of our bellies and take whatever path is appropriate for their expression."

Knox nodded thoughtfully. That did make a sort of strange sense. He considered his nudge. It definitely came from his belly. "That one seems almost plausible," Knox admitted.

Savannah's brow furrowed thoughtfully. "It does, doesn't it? Just think of butterflies in your belly, and nausea, and that sinking sensation when something isn't quite right. Gut reaction, gut feelings." She hummed under her breath, read a little more. "I can actually relate to this one. We're supposed to chant *ram* now."

"Ram," Knox deadpanned. "I'm unblocked, what about you?"

"Ram, it's a miracle, so am I."

Knox grinned. "Amazing, isn't it?"

She grinned adorably. "Without a doubt."

"What's next?"

Savannah flipped the page. Her eyes widened. "Ooh, the heart chakra. The center of love, courage and intimacy." Her brow wrinkled in perplexity. "A broken heart is most often the cause of a block in this chakra. We're supposed to share our hurts with each other to promote healing. It also says that a woman generally has to feel love in this chakra before she can experience sexual intimacy and that, likewise, a man must have sexual intimacy with a woman first in order to build trust." She snorted. "Hell, no wonder we're all screwed up. Men and women are completely opposite."

A bark of dry laughter bubbled up Knox's throat. "Was there ever a doubt?"

Savannah thwacked him with the book. "Pay attention. You're supposed to be telling me about all of your old heartaches."

"Sorry, I can't."

"Why not?"

"Because I don't have any."

Savannah raised a skeptical brow. "You've got to be kidding. You've never had your heart broken?"

"No," he sighed, "can't say that I have."

She paused. Swallowed. "Well, I don't know whether to congratulate you, or offer my sympathies."

The confident smile Knox had been wearing slipped a fraction. "What do you mean *offer your sympathies?*"

The twinkling humor had died from her eyes and had been replaced with something mortifyingly like pity. "Well...that's just sad, Knox."

Knox blinked, astounded. "You think it's sad that I've never had my heart broken?" Was she cracked or what? he wondered, feeling a curious tension build in his chest.

Savannah sighed, seemingly at a loss to explain herself. Finally she said, "Not that you haven't had your heart broken, but that you've never been close enough to another person for it to have happened. Everybody needs their heart broken at least once."

He scowled. "I think I'll pass."

That soft sympathetic gaze moved over him. "You

don't get it. It's what you're missing up until you get your heart broken that makes it all worthwhile."

"Is that the voice of experience talking?" Knox asked, mildly annoyed.

He didn't know why her words bothered him so much, but they did. His skin suddenly felt too tight and his palms had begun to sweat. What? Did she think him incapable of love? Did she think him too shallow for such a deep emotion? If he ever found the right person, he could love her, dammit. He was capable of loving someone. He'd simply not found anyone he wanted to invest that much emotion in, that's all. But it didn't mean he couldn't do it.

Savannah's gaze grew shuttered and she tucked her hair behind her ear, an endearingly nervous gesture. "Yes, it's the voice of experience. I've…almost had my heart broken."

"Almost?" Knox questioned skeptically.

"I'm still in denial."

"Oh. Well, I still wouldn't think it would be a pleasant ordeal," Knox replied drolly.

She smirked. "No, it wasn't."

"You should probably share this with me," Knox told her magnanimously, "seeing as we're supposed to heal old hurts to unblock this chakra."

She pinned him with a shrewd glare. "You have absolutely no interest in unblocking my heart chakra, you great fraud—you're simply curious."

Smiling, he shrugged. "There is that."

Savannah picked at a loose thread on her *kurta,* but finally relented with a sigh. "There was someone once," she admitted. "His, uh, parents didn't approve of me, though, so he broke up with me and went to Europe."

Knox abruptly sat up. *"What?"*

She laughed without humor. "It's true, I swear."

"What kind of a pansy-ass were you dating?" Knox asked incredulously.

She lifted her shoulders in a halfhearted shrug. "A spineless one with no class, as it turned out."

That summed it up nicely, Knox thought. What sort of ignorant prick let his parents pick his girlfriend? he wondered angrily, much less ditched Savannah for Europe? Hell, no wonder she didn't trust anybody. No wonder she couldn't pass that blind-trust test. When had anyone ever given her a reason to trust them? When had anyone been worthy of it?

"I've had enough heart chakra healing," Savannah told him. "Let's move on. We're almost finished."

It took a considerable amount of effort, but Knox finally forced his violent thoughts away and managed to concentrate on the task at hand. "Sure. What's next?"

"The throat chakra, the source of authentic expression." She chewed the corner of her lip and read some more. "Okay, we're supposed to hear and heed our inner voices, express our most dangerous emotions, even rage. But we have to learn to do this in gentle tones with our lovers and save our loud voices for when we're alone."

Knox nodded. "That's simple enough. We're not supposed to scream at one another."

"Right. We're supposed to tell our truths and sing our true songs, sanctify sex and choose words that glorify our sexual organs, such as *sacred space, wand of light,* etc...."

"Got it. What else?"

Her brow furrowed. "This is another one that sort of makes sense. Communication flows through this chakra. Think of some of the things that happen physically to you when you get upset."

"Like what?" Knox asked, not following.

"A lump in your throat, for instance. Or being too overcome to speak."

He nodded. "Makes sense. Anything else?"

Savannah glanced at the book. "Uh…we're supposed to place our hand over each other's throats and tell each other to sing our true songs, then chant *ham*."

Knox leaned forward and placed his hand over Savannah's slim throat. He grinned. "Sing your true song, baby. *Ham*."

Savannah reciprocated the gesture. "Ditto."

"How many more of these chakras do we have?" Knox asked as he rolled back onto his side.

"Just two."

"Okay."

"Why? Do you want to quit for tonight?"

"No. We're going to need lots of time tomorrow night to work on *Love His Lingam* and *Sacred Goddess Stimulation*." And he couldn't wait.

Savannah pulled in a slow breath. "Right," she all but croaked. "Okay, the next one is the brow chakra, logic and intuition, the third eye and all that. Think of people with psychic ability, or with a keen mind. Dreams and such. All of those things are a product of the brow chakra."

Another one that was almost plausible, Knox thought, as possible angles for their story spun through his mind. His grandmother had been psychic, so he knew such powers existed. "Are you blocked in that chakra?"

"No," Savannah said. "Are you?"

"No."

Another smile quivered on her lips. "Then we're supposed to join brows, stare at each other until our eyes seem to merge and say, 'I r-rejoice in how you comprehend and intuit.' Then we chant *ooo*."

Smiling, Knox rubbed the back of his neck. "You've got to be kidding."

"Nope," she said, tongue in cheek.

"Okay." Knox rolled himself into the center of the bed, then sat up on his knees. Savannah set the book aside and, mischief lighting her eyes, assumed the position as well. Gazes locked in mutual amusement, they leaned forward and their brows met.

"I feel utterly ridiculous," Savannah said, her sweet breath fanning against his lips. "What about you?"

"Most definitely."

The words were no sooner out of his mouth than an altogether different sensation took hold. Several sensations, in fact. The simultaneous registration of her sweet scent, the press of her body and the proximity of her lips hit him all at once. His heart thundered in his chest, pumping his blood that much faster to his groin. Fire licked through his veins, and he burned with the need to possess her, to lay her down, spread her thighs and bury himself so deeply into her that there would be no beginning and no end, just *them*.

Savannah's eyes darkened with desire, the heat burning away any vestiges of lingering humor. He could feel the quickened puff of her breath against his lips, heard her swallow.

Knox's blood roared in his ears, drowning out any would-be protests. He'd kissed her repeatedly since the beginning of this damned workshop, but it had always been at Edgar's or Rupali's prompting. He hadn't taken the plunge and made the conscious decision to kiss her, taste her of his own accord. But he was making that decision now—he couldn't help himself—and he wanted her to know the difference and, more important, to feel it.

Knox gently cupped her face, held her gaze until his lips brushed lightly over hers. He hovered on a precipice, he knew, yet he didn't possess the power to keep from plunging headlong over it. Then his eyelids fluttered closed under the exquisite weight of some unnamed emotion…and he sighed…and eagerly embraced the fall.

CHAPTER ELEVEN

SAVANNAH HAD KNOWN the moment that her brow touched his that she'd made a tactical error—she'd touched him. She knew, didn't she, that she couldn't touch Knox without melting like a Popsicle on the Fourth of July? She knew, and yet it hadn't made one iota of difference because she simply could not resist him. She had been inexplicably drawn to him from the moment she'd first seen him, had been lusting after him in secret torment every day since.

Just seconds ago, she'd watched the humor fade from his gaze, chased away by the power of a darker, more primal emotion. His entire body had grown taut, and then, as though he'd made some momentous decision, she'd discerned a shift in his posture. Then those amazing hands she'd imagined roaming all over her body in all sorts of wicked acts of depravity had cupped her face in a gesture so truly sweet she'd almost wept with the tenderness of it.

In the half second before his lips touched hers, Savannah realized the import of that soft touch, and her heart, along with the rest of her wayward body, had all but melted.

Knox Webber wanted her. *At long last.*

With a sigh of utter satisfaction, Savannah eagerly met his mouth, threaded her fingers through his hair and kissed him the way she'd always dreamed of kissing him. She poured every single ounce of belated desire into the melding of their mouths and was rewarded when Knox responded with a hungry growl of pleasure. The masculine sound reverberated in her own mouth, making her smile against his lips. His tongue slid over hers, plundered and plumbed, a game of seek and retreat that soon had Savannah's insides hot, muddled and quivering with want.

Knox molded her to him, slid those talented hands down her back and over her rump, and back up again. His hands burned a heated trail of sensation everywhere they touched and she longed to have them plumping her swollen breasts, sliding over her belly and lower, then lower still until his fingers worked their magic on the part of her that needed release most of all.

As though he'd read her mind, Knox smoothed his hand up her rib cage and cupped one pouting breast. She sagged under the torment of the sensation and, with a groan of satisfaction, Knox followed her down upon the bed. His warmth wrapped around her and the long, hot length of him nudged her hip.

She sucked in a harsh breath between their joined mouths and then sent her hands on their own little exploration of his body. The smooth, hard muscles of his shoulders, down the slim indention of his spine and back over the tautened sinews of his magnificently formed back.

Having mapped that terrain, she moved onto the sleek slope of his chest, the bumpy ridges of his abdomen, and over one impossibly lean hip. He was magnificent, the most perfectly put-together man she'd ever laid her greedy little hands upon. She claimed each perfection as her own. *Mine,* Savannah thought as she grasped his shoulders once more. *Mine,* she thought again as she slid her hand down his side. *Mine, mine, mine,* with each new part.

All mine.

Savannah winced as the *kurta* bunched annoyingly beneath her hungry hands. Knox had thrown one heavily muscled thigh across her leg and Savannah had the hem in her hand and had begun to swiftly tug it up his body before the significance of what she was doing surfaced in her lust-ridden brain.

Swallowing a cry of regret, she tore her mouth from his and pried his hand off her breast. "We can't…do this," she breathed brokenly.

Knox's lips curled in invitation and he nuzzled the side of her neck. "Oh, but we can," he told her. He tugged at the neckline of her *kurta,* attempted to bare her breast. "Come on, I'll show you mine if you show me yours."

Savannah dragged his head away from her neck and ignored the fizzle of warmth his wicked lips had created. Ignored his invitation to play a sexy game of show-and-tell. "Knox," she said desperately. "*Think.* We can't—"

"Thinking is overrated. In fact, you've told me repeatedly that I should try not to think. Remember? Something about it upsetting the delicate balance of my constitution." He bent his head and sucked her aching nipple into his mouth through the soft cotton fabric. The shock of pure sensation arched her off the bed and rent a silent gasp from her throat.

Sweet heaven.

Though it nearly killed her, Savannah wrenched his head from her breast. "Stop. We have to talk. We can't—"

"Talk?" Knox tsked and thumbed her nipple distractingly. "You know we can't talk for more than two minutes without arguing. This is a much more agreeable way to pass the time and you know it." He slid his fingers up her thigh and brushed her feminine curls.

Savannah bit her bottom lip and whimpered, resisted the urge to press herself against those teasing fingers. Knox took her hesitation as permission, and gently stroked her through the fabric.

She squirmed with need and her clit throbbed and her womb grew even heavier with want, but Savannah managed to stay his hand with a will born of stubborn desperation. "*Listen,* please," she insisted breathlessly. "We can't do this *now.*"

She watched Knox's sinfully sculpted lips ready a protest, but the *now* registered a second before he could push the sound from his lips. He arched a sulky brow. "What do you mean *now?*"

"The rule," Savannah reminded impatiently. "No sex until tomorrow night."

For better or for worse, she'd just told Knox Webber that she'd sleep with him tomorrow night, Savannah realized. She refused to consider anything beyond Sunday, anything that might remotely resemble second thoughts or regrets. She'd wanted Knox…forever. There was simply no other way for this weekend to end. She'd known the outcome, had known this would happen, the moment Chapman had commanded that she come to this workshop.

And, though it sounded like a lame excuse, at least they would know for sure if there was any real merit to the tantric way. They would be able to lend true credibility to their story.

That should please Knox, anyway, Savannah thought

with a prick of regret. After all, that's what had brought them here.

"Are you saying what I think that you're saying?" Knox asked carefully. Desire tempered with caution glinted in that sexy green gaze.

Savannah swallowed tightly. "Yes, I am." She managed a shaky grin. "It's inevitable, right? And then there's the story to consider."

A shadow shifted over his face and he grew unnaturally still. "The story?"

"Right." Savannah shrugged out from under him and stood. "I mean, how can we really tell our readers if there is any truth to the whole concept of tantric sex if we don't try it?"

Knox stared at her for several seconds with a curiously unreadable look, then he abruptly smiled, but it lacked his typical humor. "You're right. We need to do it, we need to sacrifice ourselves, for the sake of the integrity of our story."

There was subtle sarcastic tone to Knox's voice that needled Savannah. Honestly, she didn't think it would be that big a damned sacrifice. Clearly she'd said something that had pissed him off, but she didn't have a clue what that something could be. *Sacrifice?* she wondered again, even more perturbed. If she hadn't stopped him just a few minutes ago, they'd undoubtedly be enjoying the aftermath of an earth-shattering orgasm, and yet now—because he'd have to wait until tomorrow—he was sacrificing himself? Well, to hell with him, Savannah thought.

"I'm going for a walk," she said tightly, and headed for the door. She was embarrassingly close to tears.

"Savannah, wait," Knox said. He muttered a hot

oath and pushed a hand through his hair. "I'm bungling this."

She paused and turned around. "Bungling what?"

His tortured gaze met hers and held it. "If we make love here tomorrow night, it's not going to have anything to do with a damned story," he said heatedly. "At least, not for me. I want you, dammit—I want you more than anything—but it doesn't have anything to do with getting a story. And I certainly don't expect you, nor want you, to sleep with me for the sake of one. Do you understand?"

Something light and warm moved into her chest and swelled. She blinked, swallowed. "I think I'm getting it."

"Good."

"I'm still going for a walk."

He nodded.

Savannah opened the door, then paused. "Just so you know," she said haltingly, "it wouldn't have been about the story for me, either." Her wobbly smile made an encore appearance. "It was only a face-saver, you know, in case you regretted things later."

His steady green gaze rooted her to the floor with its intensity. "I won't regret it."

"Neither will I," Savannah murmured, and prayed fervently that statement proved to be true.

"DON'T WE NEED TO GET that last chakra out of the way before we go to breakfast?" Knox asked. He didn't want anything besides *Love His Lingam* and *Sacred Goddess Stimulation* between him and Savannah after they wound up classes today.

"Yes, we do," she called from the bathroom. "Just let me finish my hair and we'll go over it."

Her hair, Knox thought with part chuckle, part snort. Well, he had several minutes then and he would use them to think about everything that had happened between him and Savannah last night. She'd cut her walk short—after catching Chuck and his hand making love on the front porch—and when she'd returned, they'd lain in the dark and talked and laughed until the wee hours of the morning.

They'd talked about everything from favorite soft drinks, to work, and a multitude of subjects in between. Had even managed to agree—after *much* discussion—on what angle to use for this story. Knox had picked up on a great deal of hostility between her and Chapman, but when he'd asked, naturally she'd clammed up and quickly changed the subject. Knox didn't know what had happened to create such animosity, but as soon as he returned to Chicago, he was determined to find out. If not from Savannah, then from a different source.

Journalists didn't come any finer, more professional, than Savannah Reeves. If there was a problem, undoubtedly it was on Chapman's end, not hers. And if that were the case, and Chapman had been treating her unfairly, he would soon be held accountable. Knox's hands involuntarily balled into fists. Boss or no, Chapman would pay.

Savannah finally emerged from the bathroom wrapped in a towel Knox mentally willed to fall off but, to his regret, didn't. Other than a hint of makeup and the fresh look of her, Knox could discern no significant difference. Her hair still looked as if it had been hit with a weed-whacker, then combed with a garden rake. He grinned. Adorably messy, as always.

Catching his smile, Savannah's steps faltered as she

went to put her things into her overnight bag. "What are you smiling about?" she asked cautiously.

Knox rested his chin on his thumb and index finger. "Your hair," he replied honestly.

She rolled her eyes. "This is as good as it gets. If you're ashamed to be seen with me, I suggest you get over it."

"Who said anything about being ashamed? I like it."

She shot him a look. "Right."

"I do," Knox insisted. "It looks all messy, like you just rolled out of bed."

She heaved a resigned sigh. "Wow, Romeo. Is that supposed to be a compliment? Gonna write me an Ode to Bed Head?"

"Of course it's a compliment. Your normally quick wit seems a little sluggish this morning. Didn't you hear the part about the bed?"

"Yes, and I fail to see the relevance."

"Of course, you don't. You're not a man."

Savannah's lips curled. "Another brilliant observation. The power of your deductive reasoning astounds me."

"Aw, hell. Think for a minute, Savannah. If I look at you and think that you just look like you rolled out of bed, then what other things am I likely to think about?"

"Bad breath, drool, pillow creases—"

Knox chuckled. "You're thinking like a woman. Think—"

Her eyes widened in mock astonishment. "Imagine that."

"Come on. Think like a man," Knox told her.

Savannah shrugged. "I don't know. I—"

"Then I'll tell you. I'm thinking about what you were

wearing in that bed. Do you sleep in the nude, in a
T-shirt or a silk teddy? What have you been doing in
that bed? Better yet, what could you do with me—or—to
me in that bed? What would I do to you if I had you in
bed? What would—"

"I've got it," Savannah interrupted, her face flushed.
"You look at my hair and think about sex."

"Right."

"Knox, when do you look at a woman and *not* think
about sex?"

"I've just paid you a compliment, right?"

"I suppose."

"Then the proper response is thank you," he said,
reminding her of the proper compliment etiquette she'd
been so quick to share with him.

A slow grin trembled into place. "Thank you."

"You're welcome." He smiled contentedly. "Now
what about that crown chakra?"

Savannah pulled her *kurta* on over her head, tugged
it into place and then shimmied out of the towel. What
a dirty trick, Knox thought. He'd been nice enough to
drop his towel for her and she couldn't show a little
consideration and reciprocate the gesture? "I'll get the
book," she said drolly. "You just sit there."

Knox frowned innocently. "What? What did I do
now?"

"Couldn't you have gotten this book and gone over
it yourself while I was getting ready?"

"No."

She looked taken aback at his simple, honest reply.
"Why the hell not?"

"Because I've been thinking about having sex with
you."

A shocked laugh burst from her throat and she flushed

to the roots of her hair. She swallowed and seemed incapable of forming a reply. Speechless *and* blushing, Knox thought. Damn, he was good.

"The crown chakra," Knox prodded.

"Right." The tip of her tongue peeked from between her lips as she turned to the end of the booklet. "Okay," she began. "The crown chakra is the center of spiritual connectivity. Now that all of our chakras have been unblocked, we're supposed to imagine white light and lotus blossoms flowing from the tops of our heads." Savannah's twinkling gaze met his astounded one.

"What?"

"Lotus blossoms and light flowing from our heads." She twinkled her fingers above her head. "We're supposed to merge and inhale one another and feel in unity with the universe. We chant *mmm*."

"Should we merge now or later?"

Her lips twitched. "Later. Come on, we're going to be late for breakfast."

Knox heaved an exaggerated sigh and reluctantly stood. "I'd rather inhale and merge with you."

"Later," she laughed.

He would take that as a promise.

"WELCOME TO THE long-awaited *Sacred Goddess Stimulation* class," Rupali said with a secret smile. "I know you have all looked forward to this, but, before we begin, I would like to take a moment to caution you about what you are about to see and hear in this particular class." She paused. "This is a very dramatic lesson, very graphic. There is simply no way to adequately show you how to perform these services for your lover without demonstrating them. You are welcome to practice on your lover during class, but your time would be best spent observing and learning from Edgar and me. If you are in any way going to be uncomfortable with what I have just explained, then you shouldn't be here."

Well, that ruled her out, Savannah thought. That huge map of a vagina sitting on the easel next to Rupali had, quite frankly, shocked the crap out of her. "Knox, I—"

"No."

Well, all righty then. Savannah settled back into her seat, and did her dead-level best to ignore the huge vaginal chart.

"Is there anyone who would like to leave this class?" Rupali asked.

Several headshakes and soft-spoken no's filtered through the room, assuring Savannah that they were all a bunch of perverts, herself included. She didn't know exactly what all *Secret Goddess Stimulation* entailed, but she strongly suspected that it would have been something better learned in the privacy of their room with a handy how-to video.

"Okay, then. Let's begin." Rupali looked to her husband and he stepped forward.

"Men, this class is about learning how to properly please your woman, what makes her feel good, what will bring her pleasure." His gaze lingered on the class at large for a moment, then he continued. "First, we're going to cover the basic anatomy of the female sex."

To Savannah's growing discomfort, Edgar pointed out all of the necessary female parts, lingering particularly on the clitoris, which he described as the pearl of sensation.

Edgar held up a glass jar—his *yoni* puppet—and demonstrated the proper way to find a woman's G-spot. He curled his ring finger and wiggled it back and forth.

"Can everyone see? It's not the depth, the length, or the size which stimulates this concentration of sensitive cells, it's the positioning. Once you get it right, you'll be able to bring her to climax—possibly even ejaculation—every time you make love." He smiled. "And, yes, I said ejaculation. Though it's known to be a rare occurrence in traditional intercourse, women can and do typically ejaculate during tantric sex. Ah, I see a few skeptical faces in the crowd. In just a few moments I will provide the proof of that statement."

Rupali laughed. "I think it is *I* who will be the one providing the proof, darling."

Savannah had to confess a degree of morbid fascination. She'd read about female ejaculation before, but had never imagined she'd get to witness the phenomenon.

"Jesus," Knox breathed next to her.

"What's the matter?"

"I don't know if I can watch this," he said.

"What?" She swiveled to look at him. "I thought this was the class that you'd been waiting for?"

A muscle worked in his tense jaw. "Yeah, but I was wrong. I don't want to look at this woman's yoni—I want to look at yours. This is too weird, too cracked. It's like watching my parents."

"Well, it's too late now," Savannah hissed. "We're stuck here. Just avert your eyes."

"Can't," Knox said. "It's like looking at a highway accident. You dread it, but you can't look away."

"Well, try. It'll be over soon."

Knox startled her by sliding his hand in hers, sending a flush of delight and warmth straight to her rapidly beating heart.

It wasn't over soon—it lasted forever. Rupali and Edgar were seasoned tantrics and believed in letting the class get their money's worth because, much to Knox and Savannah's horror, Edgar showed how to pleasure Rupali repeatedly. With his hand, his penis and a few battery-operated gadgets that Savannah had never seen. Several members of the class had decided to test their newfound knowledge during the session as well. So, not only did they get to see Rupali and Edgar's "sacred spaces" and "wands of light," they got to see several others, too.

In addition to those orgylike images, Rupali and Edgar made good on their promise—Rupali ejaculated. Knox had become increasingly miserable throughout the lesson, but seemed particularly disturbed by watching Rupali's *amrita*—or "sweet nectar"—arc through the air like a clear rainbow.

Soon after Edgar and Rupali announced a brief intermission for refreshments between classes. *Love His Lingam* would start momentarily.

"I want to go to the room," Knox whispered tightly.

"You don't want to participate in *Love His Lingam?*"

"No."

"Knox, I hesitate to bring this up, but you're the one who planned this trip and you're the one who wanted to do this story. I'm not remotely interested in going in here and learning how to blow you or give you a hand job—I can do that without any instruction and guarantee that you won't have any complaints. But if we're going to do this story the way we should, then you know we need to just suck it up and go."

Knox grinned. "Suck it up, eh?"

She jabbed him. "You know what I mean," she said impatiently.

"Oh, all right," Knox finally relented. "But I am not going to like it," he growled.

"I didn't say you had to like it, I just said you had to suck it up."

"Only if you will, baby," Knox muttered. "Only if you will."

Savannah conjured a sexy grin, leaned forward and, to Knox's complete astonishment, stroked him through the *kurta* the way she'd been wanting to for the past forty-eight hours. "You can bet your sweet ass."

CHAPTER TWELVE

BY THE TIME Rupali had finished *Loving Edgar's Lingam,* Knox was in a shell-shocked, near-catatonic state. Sure he'd gleaned a few little tidbits of knowledge about his equipment that he hadn't known, such as where his supposed G-spot was located. That, Knox remembered with ballooning horror, explained the acute fascination with the *rosebud.*

His G-spot would remain a virgin, thank you very much.

Edgar had also lectured on attaining the inner orgasm, and had preached against the "squirt," which was reputed to waste a man's sexual energy and rob a woman of her potential multiple orgasms.

In order to avoid the outer orgasm, men were encouraged to practice deep, controlled breathing and to tighten their pubococcygeal and anal sphincter muscles—Knox inwardly shuddered—and to draw the force of their inner ejaculation up through their unblocked chakras, then out of their crown chakra.

Kind of like a volcanic orgasm, Knox had decided after watching Edgar shimmy and shake and look all but ready to blow. Knox winced. Quite frankly, the process looked—and sounded—painful. It had also been very noisy.

Honestly, he hadn't heard so much groaning, moaning and grunting since he'd visited the pig barn at the county fair as a child. Apparently, though, noisy sex promoted tantric energy and so the class was encouraged to sing with their true voices and get as loud as they wished tonight.

Tonight.

Undoubtedly the whole damn villa would come crumbling down around them, brought on by the racket and vibrations of noisy sex.

Edgar and Rupali stood arm and arm in front of the class their cheeks flushed from an exertion Knox would just as soon forget. "This concludes our teachings," Edgar said, smiling. "We hope that what you have learned will promote sexual health and healing, and will deepen your sexual and spiritual connection with your lover."

"Tonight, you will go to your rooms and put all of the lessons we have taught you into practice," Rupali interjected airily. "Open yourselves up and connect with each other as you never have before. Embrace your lover, let your true songs be sung, and seek the harmony of the *kundalini.*" She smiled. "There are no additional instructions for tonight. Build upon the intimacies of the shared bath and dinner. Enhance them to fit your purposes, your pleasures. Go…and enjoy. We will meet in the common room and share our experiences and bid our farewells in the morning." The class began to disperse eagerly.

Savannah turned to Knox and a tentative, endearing smile curved her lips. "Well," she said nervously.

Anticipation and some other curious emotion not readily identified mushroomed inside him. With effort, he swallowed and threaded his fingers through hers and tugged her toward their room. He grinned. "Come on, Barbie."

The walk back to their room seemed to take forever and in those few interminable minutes, a fist of anxiety tightened in Knox's chest, momentarily dousing the perpetual fire he'd carried in his loins.

He'd made love to women countless times, had committed carnal acts so depraved and hedonistic they would make even the unflappable Dr. Ruth blush. Knox was no stranger to sex and was confident in his ability to pleasure a woman.

But Savannah Reeves wasn't just any woman and the importance of that fact had hit him just seconds ago when she'd turned to him with eyes that were equally lit with desire and trepidation. Knox inexplicably knew that this woman—this time with this woman—was going to be different...and it scared the living hell out of him.

He could feel the tension vibrating off her slim frame as well, and wondered if she had suddenly had second thoughts. Knox opened the door and let her pass. Her anxious expression made him feel like a class-A bastard. He'd pushed her into this, he knew. He hadn't left well enough alone and now—

Savannah whirled around as soon as the door closed behind them, grabbed on to the front of his *kurta* and launched herself at his mouth.

Knox staggered back against the wall as the force of her desire blindsided him. Savannah's tongue plunged hungrily in and out of his mouth, suckled him, and burned through any doubts as to why she'd been anxious.

She wanted him.

She was here in his arms, feeding at his mouth, her hands roaming greedily over him, as though she couldn't—wouldn't—ever get enough of him.

Knox sucked in a harsh breath and a strange quiver

rippled through his belly. The nudge commenced with an insistent jab. Lust detonated low in his loins, made him want to roar with desire, haul her to the bed and plow into that hot, wet valley between her thighs.

With a growl of pleasure, Knox molded her slim, supple body more closely to his, felt her squirm against him in an unspoken plea for release. Her pebbled breasts raked across his chest, igniting a trail of indescribably perfect sensation.

Savannah drew back. Blue flames danced in her somnolent gaze. "Do you know how I got through that last class?" she asked huskily.

Knox shook his head.

"I kept thinking about getting to do all those things to you. My hands on your body, you in my mouth…" She pulled in a breath. "I have a very keen imagination and for the past several hours, I've been imagining this night," she said, her foggy tones almost hypnotic. "Imagining everything that I want to do to you—and with you—and everything I want you to do to me." She cocked her head invitingly toward the bathroom. "Now I want to show you. Whaddya say we start with a bath?"

Savannah stepped back and, in a gesture so inherently sexy it stole his breath, she pulled the *kurta* up over her head and let it drop to the floor. Then, with a saucy wink, she turned and walked to the bathroom.

She'd undoubtedly be the death of him, Knox thought, if indeed a man could expire from sexual stimulation. But, oh, what a way to go…

SAVANNAH POURED a bottle of scented oil that had magically appeared in their bathroom today into the steaming tub and felt a feline smile of satisfaction curl her lips.

She'd been waiting for this day forever, had been waiting for this time with him forever, and now—at long last—she would have him.

Repeatedly, she hoped.

Something, warm, hot and languid snaked through her body at the thought, sending a pulse of sensation straight to her quivering womb. Her breasts grew heavy and her nipples tightened and tingled hungrily in anticipation of Knox's hot mouth.

The object of her lusty thoughts chose that moment to stroll naked into the bathroom. Savannah let her gaze roam over his magnificent body slowly, committing to memory each perfect inch of his impressive form. His eyes were dark and slumberous, and burned with a heat she recognized because it sizzled in her as well.

Her gaze skimmed the broad, muscled shoulders, washboard abdomen, lean waist and then settled drunkenly on his fully erect—*enormous*—penis, the one she simply couldn't wait to take into her mouth and, later, feel throbbing deeply inside her. His thighs were powerfully muscled, yet lean and athletic. And, oh, that ass… There was absolutely nothing about him physically that could be improved upon. Even his feet were perfect.

Savannah pulled in a shuddering breath as every cell in her body became hammeringly aware of him, clamoring for him and the cataclysmic release she knew she would find in his arms.

While she'd been openly appraising him, she in turn had been undergoing a similarly intense study. Knox's hot gaze had raked down her body in a leisurely fashion that felt more like a caress than a mere look, and the heat that presently funneled in her womb as a result of that narrow scrutiny was rapidly whipping her insides into a froth of insatiable need.

His lips quirked into a slow sexy grin. "You've told me what you've been thinking about today. Why don't you get in that tub and I'll *show* you what I've been thinking about."

Oh, sweet heaven. Savannah's bones all but melted. She stepped into the warm, scented water and sank down until only the tips of her breasts peeked above the foggy surface.

Knox slid in behind her so that she sat in the open vee of his thighs. Savannah's eyes fluttered shut and a sound of pure contentment puffed past her smiling lips as he snaked an arm around her waist and tugged her back against him. His warmth engulfed her, the hot, hard length of him pressed against the small of her back. Knox reached around her, filled his cupped hands with water and then palmed her breasts, kneaded them, rolled her beaded nipples between his thumb and forefinger. Savannah gasped, curled her toes and pressed her back more firmly against him.

He nuzzled her neck. "This was one of the things I've been thinking about," Knox murmured huskily. "Feeling your plump breasts in my hands, thumbing your pouty nipples. Do you have any idea how perfect you are? How absolutely beautiful?" His hands mimicked his words and played languidly at her sensitized breasts, forcing another gasp of pleasure from her lips.

Savannah didn't bother to answer, but raised an arm, cupped the back of his head and turned to find his lips. She kissed him long and hard, soft and deep, slow yet purposefully, and all the while, Knox continued a magnificent assault on her aching breasts. Then he moved lower, over her trembling belly, until finally he parted her curls and swept a finger over her throbbing, woefully neglected clit. Savannah jerked as sensation bolted through her, and she whimpered against his plundering mouth.

Knox drew back and slid his fingers into the hot, wet folds of her sex. "I've been wanting to do that as well," he said, rhythmically stroking her. "Feel the slick heat of your body, swallow your gasps, taste your groans."

Savannah's feminine muscles clenched beneath the exquisite pressure of his fingers. A long, slow drag, a swirl over her nub, and back again, over and over with his tender, mind-numbing assault. Her breath came in rapid, helpless puffs. Savannah felt her womb quicken, recognized the sharp tug of the beginning of a climax. She bit her bottom lip, a pathetic attempt to stem the steady flow of longing hurtling through her. He rocked gently behind her, mimicking the steady thought-shattering pressure. It built and built, like the tightening of a screw until something inside her finally—blessedly—snapped. Her body bowed from the shock, the explosion of sensation, and wept with the pulsing torrent and sweet rain of release.

Knox continued to gently rub her, light delicate strokes that made the orgasm seem to go on forever, more than she could bear.

She twisted away from those wicked fingers and turned around, straddled him and kissed him deeply once more. She sucked his tongue, nipped at his lips. The feel of his wet, hard body, slickened with the vaguest hint of oil, felt excessively hedonistic beneath her questing palms. Savannah pulled in a shaky breath as she felt the incredibly long length of him slide along her nether lips. She pressed her aching breasts to his chest and quivered with delight as his masculine hair abraded her sensitive nipples. She slid her hands down the smooth planes of his chest, ran her nails over the hardened nubs of his nipples and was rewarded when Knox hissed with pleasure.

"Damn," he groaned.

Savannah smiled evilly. "Oh, no baby, that's not a damn. *This* merits a damn." She reached down between their practically joined bodies and took him in her hand.

Knox drew in a sharp breath and jerked against her palm. "Y-you're right," he stuttered. "That is most definitely a damn."

Savannah ran her hand up and down the length of him, palmed the sensitive head of his penis and marveled once again over the sheer size of him. He was extraordinarily large, marvelously huge…and for the time being, all hers. Every splendid inch of him.

She worked the length of him, up and down, long steady strokes, feathery touches, but soon touching him simply wasn't enough.

She wanted to taste him.

She gestured toward the steps and gently moved his body in that direction, and eventually managed to put him exactly where she wanted him—in her mouth.

Knox's swiftly indrawn breath was music to her ears. Sing your true songs, indeed, Savannah thought with a smile as she licked the swollen head of his penis. She alternated nibbles and sucks down the sides of him, ran her lips up and down his long length, and cuddled his testicles. Emboldened, she touched her tongue to those, too, and pulled one into her mouth and rolled it around her tongue.

Knox jerked and hissed another tortured breath. "Damn."

Savannah paused her ministrations. "Yeah, that

should qualify as a damn." She smiled against him. "And so should this."

With that enigmatic comment, Savannah wrapped her lips around him, took him fully into her mouth and sucked hard. She curled her tongue around him, licked and suckled, over and over, and dragged him deeper and deeper into her mouth. She worked his base, gently massaged his testicles, and slid him in and out of her mouth. Knox's breath grew ragged and his thighs tensed, heralding the arrival of his impending climax.

When the first taste of his salty essence hit her tongue, Savannah drew back, took him in her hand and pumped him hard. She felt the rush of his orgasm shoot through the length of him like a bullet down the barrel of a gun, then felt him jerk and shudder as the hot blast burst from his loins. She milked him, drawing every last ounce of pleasure from him that she could.

Knox halted her ministrations with the touch of his trembling hand. "Enough," he growled. He stood and drew her up with him. "Let's go to bed."

She'd thought he'd never ask, Savannah thought. Knox snagged a towel from the bar and gently swabbed down her body, then hastily ran it over himself as well. Within seconds, they were rolling around the bed, a tangle of desperate arms and legs. The first orgasm had merely taken the edge off, but hadn't begun to dull the attraction. She still wanted him more than she wanted her next breath. Still couldn't wait to feel him plunging into her, couldn't wait to have his hot hands anchored at her waist while she sank down upon him.

Breathing hard, Knox pinned her down and his gaze tangled with hers. "You've tasted me—now I want you to lie still and take it while I taste you."

What? Savannah thought. Did he expect her to argue? She giggled. "Go ahead," she told him. "Eat me."

His eyes widened, then narrowed and his slow, sexy grin melted into one of the most sensual smiles she'd ever seen. "Oh, you are evil."

Savannah raked her nails over his chest. "Yeah…but you like it."

Those dark green eyes twinkled. "Yeah, I do." He bent down and drew her budded nipple into his mouth, pulling the air from her lungs in the process. "And I like this, too."

"Mmm," Savannah sighed. "So do I."

Knox thumbed one tingling nipple while he tortured the other with his mouth. He swiveled his tongue around the sensitive peak, then sucked it deeply into his mouth. Savannah pressed her legs together as the one sensation sparked another deep in her womb. Her clit pulsed and her feminine muscles contracted, begging—crying—for release. Seemingly reading her mind, Knox slid his hand down her shuddering belly and slipped his fingers into her drenched curls.

Savannah whimpered and pressed herself shamelessly against him, willing him to put her out of her sexually frustrated misery. She was on fire, burning up from the inside out, and the only antidote to this mad fever was a shot of him planted deep inside of her.

Knox kissed his way down her belly, swirled his tongue around and inside her navel, and then continued a determined path down to her sex. He knelt between her legs, parted her nether lips, then fastened his mouth onto the small hardened nub of desire hidden in those quivering folds and sucked hard. He worked his tongue up and down her valley, thrust it inside her, then suckled her again. Savannah bowed off the sheet, bucking beneath the most intimate kiss. Lust licked at her veins, and a deep tremble shook her seemingly boneless body.

He slid a finger deep inside her and hooked it around, savoring the moment that she practically arched off the bed. A groan tore from her throat and her eyes all but rolled back into her head.

The ultrasensitive patch of cells could only be her G-spot. Up until this very minute, Savannah hadn't known that she had one.

"Did you…learn that…this weekend?" Savannah asked brokenly as her hands fisted in the sheets.

Knox massaged the tender spot, while lapping at her clit with his wicked tongue. "I improved my technique, yes."

If he improved it any more, she'd undoubtedly burst into flames, shatter and fly into a million little pieces. The thought had no sooner flitted through her mind than the climax caught her completely unaware and broke over her like a high tide, sweeping her under, drowning her in the undertow of sparkling release.

She'd barely caught her breath before Knox snagged a condom from the nightstand, ripped into the package with his teeth, withdrew the thin contraceptive and then swiftly rolled it into place. Seconds later, he'd positioned himself between her thighs and then, with a primal groan of satisfaction, plunged into her.

The room shrank, swelled and then righted itself in the same instant. It was all Savannah could do to keep from passing out, he filled her so very completely. She stilled, waiting for her almost virgin-again body to accommodate his massive size.

"Are you all right?" Knox asked. Concern lined his brow.

Savannah resumed breathing and then tentatively

rocked her hips against him, drawing him deeper into her body. "Yes, I am. I just—"

"I just nearly killed you because I plowed into you like a battering ram." He winced. "I'm sorry, I—"

"Knox," Savannah interrupted, "no one appreciates the fact that you have learned to apologize more than me…but we really need to work on your timing."

His face blanked. "My timing?"

"Yes, timing. For instance, now—while you're inside me, where I have wanted you to be for oh-so-long—is not the time to be apologizing. Now you need to be fu—"

The rest of her sentence died a quick death as Knox drew back and plunged into her once more. Savannah hiked her legs up and anchored them around Knox's waist, parlayed his every thrust. She rocked against him, clamped her feminine muscles around the hot, slippery length of him and shuddered with satisfaction as the friction between their joined bodies created a delicious draw and drag as he pumped frantically in and out of her.

Knox bent down and latched his mouth onto one of her nipples, sending another bolt of pleasure down into her quivering loins. Savannah ran her hands down his back, reveling in the taut muscles rippling beneath her palms, the slim hollow of his spine, and then she grabbed his magnificent ass and, with a tormented cry, urged him on. Knox understood her unspoken plea and upped the tempo, pumped harder and faster, pistoned in and out of her.

Harder, faster, and harder still.

She caught another bright flash of release and felt her body freeze with anticipation. Her heart threatened to beat right out of her chest and her breathing came in short, little jagged puffs. The tension escalated, steadily climbing like a Roman candle shot into the sky, then having gone as high as it could, exploded into a billion multicolored stars. Slowly, she drifted back to earth, spent but sated…and thoroughly pleasured.

With a guttural cry of satisfaction, Knox plunged into her one final time, his body bowed with the redeeming rapture of release. He shuddered violently, then his breath left him in one long whoosh and he sagged against her.

Knox rolled them quickly onto his side and fitted her more closely to him. He pressed a lingering kiss in her hair between rapid breaths. "Savannah, that was—I've never—"

Savannah felt a slow smile move across her lips and something warm and tingly bubbled through her chest. "A wordsmith, and yet you're speechless," Savannah teased.

"That," he said meaningfully, "was indescribable."

Savannah heaved a contented sigh. "It really was, wasn't it?"

Knox absently drew circles on her arm. "It was," he agreed.

She'd known it would be, Savannah thought. She'd never doubted it. She'd wanted Knox Webber since the very first moment she'd seen him. She'd yearned for him in secret silence and had nearly gone crazy as a result of the one-sided attraction. Her breathing had barely returned to normal and yet just feeling him next to her did something to her insides. She should be exhausted, she shouldn't be thinking about the delicious weight of his body pressed against hers, or the long, semiaroused length of him nuzzled against her hip.

Yet she was.

Were he to roll over and kiss her right now, she'd eagerly spread her legs and beg him to fill her up once again. The moment Knox had entered her, it was as though a wellspring of repressed emotion had been plumbed. Colors seemed brighter, scents stronger, her entire world had come into sharper focus. In that instant, Rupali's sage words had come back to her. *I don't think your problem lies in the lower chakras...*

And the older woman had been right. Knox had touched her heart. He'd fixed something this weekend that had been broken inside her. If nothing ever came of their time together, then at least she would have that.

Savannah had never felt anything like this before, had never had a lump in her throat after hours of mind-boggling, body-drenching, sweaty, wonderful sex.

But she did right now, and Savannah grimly suspected that were she to truly consider its origin, she would weep with regret.

So she wouldn't.

She'd simply tell herself that the reason she was so utterly moved by their lovemaking was the result of years of pent-up emotion and stress. She'd tell herself that the feelings that were currently taking root in her foolish heart were a product of a weekend of tremendous sexual stimulation, even possibly the result of the tantric rituals. She would tell herself these things...and pray that by the end of this weekend she'd believe them.

The alternative was unacceptable—she wouldn't permit herself to fall in love with Knox Webber...if it wasn't already too late.

CHAPTER THIRTEEN

WHEN KNOX AWOKE on Monday morning, the first few tendrils of pink were spreading across the horizon, chasing away the early gray of dawn. Savannah was spooned with her back to his belly and he'd cupped her breast and slung a thigh over her inert form sometime during the night.

Feeling her next to him, having that delectable body snuggled up against his, engendered a host of sensations, of feelings. Before he'd so much as opened his eyes a smile had unaccountably curled his lips and a light, warm emotion had filled his chest, then inexplicably crowded into his heart.

Knox knew his heart had absolutely no business getting involved in what had happened between him and Savannah—it was supposed to have been sex and nothing more—but he gloomily suspected this feeling currently lurking in his chest was more than he'd bargained for, and definitely more than she had.

Knox had thought that the nudge of the story had brought him here, but he knew better now. The insistent nudge that had propelled him to this place didn't have anything to do with a story...and never had, Knox realized belatedly.

It had been Savannah.

When he'd failed to act on his own, his nudge had

taken over and done the business for him, had made sure that he'd found her.

Knox recognized a good thing when he had it, and Savannah Reeves was a good thing. She was bright and witty and charming, and sexy as hell, and just being with her made him feel like a better man, made him *want* to be a better man. Knox didn't have a clue what the future might bring, but the idea of a future without her in it held absolutely no appeal.

He supposed he was in love with her, and he waited for the mental admission to jump-start a wave of panic, for the fist of anxiety to punch him in the gut, at the very least prod his insides with a finger of dread.

It didn't.

Instead, his chest swelled with the sweet, foreign emotion, forcing a contented grunt from his lips. He didn't have any idea how Savannah felt about him and wouldn't allow himself to think about it. If she hadn't fallen in love with him, he'd make her. It was as simple as that.

Given her history, Knox knew he'd have his work cut out for him—she'd have to trust him before she'd love him, he knew—but he hadn't gotten this far in life without patience and tenacity. He had the attraction working in his favor and would just build on that until she was ready for more. As far as a plan went, it might not be the best one, but it was the only one he had at present.

Failure was not an option. Come hell or high water, he'd make Savannah Reeves his.

A glimpse of white at the window snagged his attention. Rupali and Edgar were just scant feet outside their bedroom window. Edgar drew up short and parked a wheelbarrow filled with various shrubs and flowering plants. They were landscaping? Knox wondered. At this hour of the morning? The thought drew a reluctant smile. They were truly a bizarre pair, but this life they'd chosen seemed to fit them.

In fact, tantric sex seemed to fit them, too.

Knox was certain now that the Sheas believed and put into practice everything they taught. They weren't the crooks he'd originally thought them to be. True, some of the practices and beliefs were out of the realm of his comprehension, his scope of understanding, and he seriously doubted he'd ever become a true tantrist, but he no longer believed that it lay out of the realm of possibility—just his.

Knox watched as the Sheas joined hands, lifted their faces to the sky and chanted. An early morning breeze lifted Rupali's long white hair, billowed their *kurtas* out around them. After a moment, they stepped back and Knox watched Rupali draw something from her pocket—multicolored rocks, they seemed to be—and then toss them into the air. To Knox's astonishment, Edgar began to unload the wheelbarrow and place the plants and shrubs where the rocks had fallen.

That explained the whimsical feel to the landscaping he'd noticed when they'd first gotten here, Knox thought with soft, disbelieving amusement.

Savannah stirred beside him and he bent his head and pressed a kiss to her achingly smooth cheek. A lump of emotion formed in his throat, and for one terrifying instant, Knox's considerable confidence wavered and he wondered if he'd really be able to make her love him. Could he really do it?

A sleepy smile curled her lips and she stretched languidly beside him. "Good morning," she murmured groggily.

Knox's gaze caressed her face, lingered over each

and every line and curve. "So far," he said. "I'm here with you."

Savannah sighed with sleepy pleasure and rolled to burrow into his chest. She nuzzled his neck and snaked an arm around his waist. The hard-on he'd awoken with promptly jerked for sport. But that was hardly surprising, was it? He was a man and, were that not enough explanation, he was a man in bed with a naked woman.

"What time is it?" she asked.

"It's early. Pushing six, I'd say."

She smoothed her hand up his side, sending a wave of gooseflesh skittering across his skin. Smiling, Knox sucked in a trembling breath.

"Good," she murmured. "We've got time."

"Time for what?"

"Here, I'll show you."

Savannah rolled him onto his back and straddled him. Her wet sex rode the ridge of his erection and Knox watched her eyes flutter shut and her lips slip into one of the most sensual smiles he'd ever seen. With a growl of satisfaction, he anchored his hands on the sweet swell of her hips and rocked her against him.

The picture she made in that moment was utterly incredible. Those jet-black bed-head curls sprouted in sexy disarray all over her head and the rosy tint of sleep clung to her creamy cheeks. Her eyes were lit with the blue flame of desire, still slumberous and heavy-lidded, weighted with the vestiges of sleep. Pale pink nipples crowned the full globes of her breasts, and her belly was gently rounded and completely feminine. The thatch of silky curls at the apex of her thighs rocked against him and…

And the rest of that thought fragmented as Savannah took him in her hand, swiftly sheathed him with a condom, then slowly sank down onto him. Her wet, tight heat gloved him so thoroughly that it ripped the very breath from his lungs.

Savannah's eyes fluttered shut. She smiled with sublime satisfaction and bit her bottom lip. A purr emanated from her throat as she buried his dick as far into her heat as she possibly could.

She flexed her naughty muscles around him. "Do you have any idea how long I've been wanting to do this? How many times I've done it in my dreams?" she asked. She lifted her hips and settled onto him once more.

"N-no," Knox breathed raggedly. "Tell me."

Savannah winced with pleasure, slid up and down in a long, sinuous motion. He felt the greedy clench and release of her body as she moved above him, felt the exquisite friction of their joined parts.

"More times…than I…can conceivably count… this weekend." Her breath came in startled little puffs as she upped the tempo, rode him harder.

"I would have g-gladly accommodated you," Knox replied, thrusting into her, matching his rhythm to hers. Savannah's skin glistened, had flushed into a becoming rosy hue. She arched her neck and little nonsensical sounds—the sound of great sex—bubbled up from her throat.

The fire in his loins rapidly became an inferno that engulfed every inch of him. He felt her tense, watched her mouth open in a silent gasp. She pumped harder and harder on top of him, rode him frantically, clearly racing for the brass ring of release. Knox leaned up, latched his mouth around one nipple and sucked hard, flattening the crown of her breast deep into his mouth. He reached down between their joined bodies and massaged the nub hidden in the wet folds of her sex.

Savannah cried out, bit her lip and whimpered.

He felt her muscles contract, felt her entire body still in awe of the explosion of the coming climax. The gentle pulsing and rush of heat was all it took to send Knox past the point of endurance and he joined her there in the brilliant flash of release.

Savannah sagged against his chest, not pulling away, but keeping him inside her. Something about the gesture made him want to roar his approval, made him feel more elementally manly. Instead, he trailed his trembling fingers down her spine, then slid his hands back up and hugged her close.

Savannah leaned up and glanced at the top of his head. Her brow creased with perplexity.

Knox frowned. "What? Is something wrong with my hair, because if it is," he said, imitating her, "this is as good as it gets and—"

He felt her laugh against him. "No, it's not your hair. I was just looking for some lotus blossoms. I know this is going to come as a shock…but I can't find any."

Knox chuckled. "Come as a shock, eh? I didn't feel any lotus blossoms fly out of my skull, but I sure thought my head was going to blow off during that last go-around." He lowered his voice. "That was awesome."

She flushed adorably. "Thank you. I try."

"Ah, so I'm not the only one who has learned how to take a compliment."

Her twinkling gaze met his and she winced with regret. "I hate to, but we've got to get up."

"I know," Knox said reluctantly.

"Everyone will be giving their progress reports this morning. It'll be interesting to see what everyone will have to say."

He'd thought about that as well. He arched a brow and

lazily swirled circles on her back. "Given any thought as to what you're going to say?" he asked innocently.

Savannah gently raised herself off him and rolled back onto her side of the bed. He immediately missed her warmth. "Yes, as a matter of fact I have."

Knox waited. "Well?" he finally prompted.

She swiveled her head to look at him. "I'm going to say that my 'sacred space' has never been so magnificently illuminated, and that you have the biggest 'wand of light' I've ever seen."

His "wand of light" stirred at the compliment. "High praise, indeed."

"What about you? Surely you're going to correct my frigid-unable-to-climax legacy."

Knox grinned. "You can bet your sweet ass, baby. I'm going to report a multiple orgasm breakthrough and sing the praises of your 'sacred space.'"

She nodded, seemingly pleased. "Ugh," she groaned. "We've got to get up. They'll be starting soon, and we really need to hear everyone's input for the story." She paused. "When are we going to work on this story, by the way?"

"I thought we could work on it on the way back. Is that all right with you?"

Savannah inclined her head. "Sure, that'll be fine. Think we'll have time to finish it?"

"Yeah. I could be wrong, but I think this is going to be one of those stories that tells itself. If not, we can always finish it at my place…or yours."

She stilled and something in her gaze brightened and dimmed all in the same instant. What? Knox thought. Did she think that this had simply been a weekend fling? If so, he needed to swiftly disabuse her of that notion. She also needed to understand that he wasn't the bastard who'd broken her heart—he was someone she could trust.

"I'd, uh, planned on you spending quite a bit of time from here on out at my place, and hoped that I'd be invited to yours," Knox said, laying it all out on the line. He didn't want to frighten her, nor did he intend to mislead her.

It was a short story. He wanted her. The end.

When she didn't readily reply, Knox felt the first prickle of unease move through his belly. Savannah just stood there, looking at him with an unreadable expression that made his insides knot with anxiety. "Have I read too much into this?" he asked.

"No," she replied hesitantly, and his tension lessened slightly. "I, uh…" She shrugged helplessly. "To be honest, I hadn't let myself think beyond this weekend. I didn't want to get my ho— I just thought it would be best to hedge my bets."

"And now?" he prodded.

"And now my thoughts are along the same lines as yours."

"So we'll be spending a lot of time together, then?" he queried lightly, just to be sure they were on the same page.

He caught the feline smile that curved her lips a fraction of a second before she turned and headed toward the bathroom. "You can bet your sweet ass," she said, giving him a wonderful view of hers.

SAVANNAH DIDN'T KNOW what to make of Knox's morning-after behavior. Frankly, she'd expected him to be charming but withdrawn. She'd expected him to try and put a more professional spin on their relationship, to try to regain some lost ground. In short, she'd expected him to act like a typical man…but as she'd learned over the course of this weekend, Knox Webber wasn't a typical man.

He'd done the one and only thing Savannah *hadn't* expected—he'd expressed a wish to see her again and, though she was trying very hard not to let her heart get carried away, if she'd understood him correctly—and she thought she had—he wanted to see her *a lot*.

Considering she'd fallen head over heels in love with him this weekend, Savannah decided that was very promising.

There had been several times over the course of last night and this morning when she'd caught Knox giving her poignantly tender looks, but Savannah had convinced herself they'd been wishful thinking, the product of her imagination…anything but what they were. She'd been so careful of getting her hopes up that she'd ignored every sign of some deeper emotion—and there had been plenty, now that she thought about it. Belated delight bloomed in her chest.

She'd have to be careful, of course. Tread carefully—she'd been burned too many times not to be a little reticent. But the idea that she might have found someone who genuinely wanted her—after almost a lifetime of being alone—was so achingly sweet.

The back of her throat burned with emotion and her insides quivered with hesitant joy. She'd longed to be wanted, to be part of a family for what seemed like forever. Someone to spend Thanksgiving and Christmas with, to help celebrate her birthday. Little things that other people simply took for granted were things that Savannah had, for the most part, never had.

Savannah didn't know anything about the Webber family other than that they were wealthy and that they didn't approve of Knox's career. Did that mean they wouldn't approve of her either? Savannah wondered, remembering Gib's family with a shudder. More important, would it matter to Knox if they didn't? Savannah paused consideringly, mulling the question over. She honestly didn't think so. If he'd gone ahead and chosen to be a journalist despite their protests, then surely he'd use the same headstrong logic when choosing a wife.

Wife?

Jeez, where had that thought come from? Savannah shot a surreptitious glance at Knox to make sure that the absurd thought hadn't somehow been transmitted from her brow chakra to his via mental telepathy. Presently, Knox was working the room, subtly interrogating couples about their tantric experience. She should be doing the same thing, Savannah thought with a stab of self-disgust, instead of mooning over her new boyfriend.

Still her shoulders drooped with relief and her heart inexplicably swelled when his gaze caught hers. Those dark green orbs shone with humor and a hint of kindled lust, but thankfully no panic or fear, which she definitely would have detected should he have been privy to her *wife* thought.

So much for treading carefully, Savannah thought with a rueful smile. She absently twisted the thin gold band on her finger, and a prick of regret pierced her heart. She knew it was foolish, but she didn't want to give it back. She wanted to keep it and wear it and be everything to Knox that the token implied.

Knox sidled up next to her and nuzzled her ear. "Is it getting on your nerves?"

Savannah started guiltily. "What?"

"The ring. Is it getting on your nerves?"

She swallowed and forced a smile. "No, not at all. I

was just admiring it. Don't let me forget to give it back to you. Maybe you can take them back and your jeweler will give you a refund."

"And risk bad karma?" Knox asked playfully. He shook his head. "I think I'll keep them. You never know when you might need a set of bands."

With that enigmatic comment, Knox steered her toward the front of the room where the Sheas waited to bid their farewells. "Good morning, class." Edgar beamed. "Rupali and I have had the opportunity to speak with several of you this morning and, by all accounts, last night was a resounding success."

Rupali smiled serenely. "We are so very thrilled for each and every one of you. Our time together has come to an end, but please continue to use what you have learned here in your daily lives. Take the love and harmony you've found in our house home to yours. Remember truth and healing, sing your true songs, speak with your true voices and draw from the energy of Mother Earth. Cleanse your chakras, forbid blocks and continue to grow in spiritual and sexual health. Women, honor your man, never cease longing to please him. He will return your effort with pleasure tenfold."

"Likewise, men, honor your woman. Respect her, be worthy of her love, and strive to continually bring her more pleasure. For to do these things for another is to do them for yourself."

Edgar and Rupali joined hands. "We bid you well," they said in unison.

Knox threaded Savannah's fingers through hers and squeezed. "Well, that's that then. You ready?"

Savannah nodded. She supposed so. They'd donned their regular clothes this morning for the journey home, and already the bra and undies seemed to chafe her skin. She never thought she'd say it but, like Knox, she'd grown rather fond of the free feeling of the *kurta*.

Knox had gone out this morning and loaded the car, so everything had been packed. There was absolutely no reason to linger, and yet, for some reason, Savannah found herself curiously reluctant to leave.

"Barbie," Rupali called. "May I have a word before you go, please?"

Savannah nodded. Knox gave her a perplexed look, but left at her prodding when she promised to meet him at the car.

Savannah cleared her throat. "You wanted to speak with me?" she asked nervously. Something about this woman's perceptive gaze unnerved her.

Rupali laid a soft, bejeweled hand on her arm. "Did you experience any breakthroughs this weekend? Did your world shift and come back into brighter focus?"

Unbidden tears stung her eyes. A short laugh erupted from her throat and she nodded. "Yes," Savannah choked out. "It did."

Rupali nodded in understanding. "Good. I'd hoped you would. My third eye is my strongest chakra, and I had a feeling about you," she told her. "I know that you'll have cause to doubt, but you'll be all right now, you know."

"Thank you," Savannah said, inexplicably reassured by this woman's calm assessment.

To her surprise, Rupali leaned forward and hugged her in a motherly fashion, a gesture Savannah hadn't had in such a long, long time. She blinked back tears once more. "Go, child," Rupali told her. "He's waiting."

Savannah withdrew from Rupali's embrace and hurried out to the car. Knox took one look at her and his jaw went hard. "What happened?" he demanded. "What's wrong?"

"Nothing," Savannah said shakily, wiping the moisture from beneath her eyes. "Just women stuff. It's nothing. Really."

Knox didn't look convinced. "You're sure you're all right? You're sure there's nothing wrong?"

His concern touched her deeply, made her want to vault across the seat, plant herself in his lap, and rain kisses all over his outraged face. A champion, what a novel experience. Savannah's heart galloped in her chest and joy fizzed through her, until finally it bubbled right out of her mouth in a stream of delighted laughter.

Knox looked at her askance. Worry replaced the outrage. "Are you sure you're all right?"

"Yes," Savannah said emphatically. For the first time in her life *everything* felt all right.

CHAPTER FOURTEEN

ON ANY GIVEN DAY, Knox typically enjoyed walking into the offices of the *Chicago Phoenix*. His world. He loved the hustle and bustle, the murmur of conversation and the ceaseless ring of the telephones. This was the chaotic world of the newsroom, where breaking news mingled with the mundane, juicy gossip and the occasional super-hot exposé.

Their tantric sex piece wouldn't be considered any of those things, Knox knew, and yet it had turned out to be a great story that both he and Savannah were very proud of. The article had come together so seamlessly that it had, as predicted, practically written itself. He and Savannah had simply framed it up with words, ones that he hoped would do justice to their experience with the ancient technique. The piece had been informative, skeptical in a humorous way, yet left plenty of room for possibility. Ultimately it had let readers draw their own conclusions.

Knox had always worked alone, had always considered writing a solitary business. But, to his delight, he and Savannah had worked extremely well together. Their styles complemented each other and they intuitively played to each other's weaknesses. In short, they were great together. They wrote like they made love—splendidly.

Knox had left Savannah at her apartment eight hours

ago and, during that time, he hadn't stopped thinking about her.

He simply couldn't.

She consumed his every waking thought and had even invaded his dreams. And he wanted to know her every thought, her every dream, her every secret. He wanted to learn all of her little idiosyncrasies, to wake up with her in the morning and go to bed with her each night. He wanted to shower her with the affection she'd missed as a child, to make up for every heartache she'd ever experienced. He wanted her to trust him…and he wanted to be her hero.

Basically, he just *wanted* her.

Knox felt the perpetual smile he'd worn since yesterday morning when his whole world had changed. To his surprise, he found himself whistling as he strolled into work this morning.

It had been late when they'd arrived back in Chicago, so after dropping Savannah off at her apartment, Knox had brought the piece down here to leave for Chapman to proofread. His boss usually arrived a good hour before the rest of the staff, and Knox knew that Chapman would be eager to read the article. Knox was equally eager to hear what Chapman thought of it.

A look through the glass confirmed his boss was in. Knox rapped on the door and Chapman beckoned him inside.

"It's brilliant," Chapman said. "It's damn brilliant. I read it first thing this morning."

Knox slowly released the pent-up breath he'd been holding. "Thank you, sir. We're proud of it."

"And I have a surprise for you—it'll run with your byline only."

Something cold slithered through him. Knox blinked, certain he'd misunderstood. "Come again?"

"You're not sharing your byline. I never intended for you to. Ms. Reeves needed to be taught a lesson, Webber, and this is the way I've planned to do it."

Fury whipped through Knox. "Look, I don't know what's going on—"

"And you don't need to, as it doesn't concern you."

"Doesn't concern me?" Knox repeated hotly. "Like hell. I just spent the entire weekend working with her. *We*—not I—just wrote a great piece." Knox glared at him. "She did the work, she deserves the credit."

Chapman smiled infuriatingly. "Be that as it may, she's not going to get it."

Knox fisted his hands at his sides and silently willed himself to calm down. Beating the hell out of his boss, which was exceedingly tempting at the moment, wouldn't benefit anyone.

He'd heard stories about Chapman's legendary ruthlessness—hell, everyone in this city had—but had always thought they'd been exaggerated. While he'd never considered Chapman a friend, he'd nonetheless always respected the man and his opinion. Clearly, that was at an end, Knox thought, swallowing his bitter disappointment.

"I don't appreciate being dragged into this," Knox said, his jaw set so hard he feared it would crack. "Furthermore, I don't care for your methods."

"You don't have to." Chapman narrowed his eyes. "Have you forgotten who is the boss here, Webber, whose name is on that door? If so, let me refresh your memory—it's mine. I do things my way, and people who don't realize that—or choose to ignore it—pay accordingly or end up unemployed. Have I made myself clear?"

Knox smirked as a red rage settled over his brain. "Perfectly."

With that, Knox pivoted and stormed from Chapman's office. He knew any argument was pointless. Several co-workers called out greetings, but Knox wasn't in any frame of mind to play the amiable rich boy today. He needed to intercept Savannah before she came in this morning and prepare her for Chapman's little bomb.

More important, he needed to make sure she understood that he hadn't played any part in it.

Anxiety roiled in his gut and his heart stumbled in his chest as the implications of what had just transpired in Chapman's office fully surfaced in Knox's furious mind.

He could lose her because of this.

He could lose her.

He'd forced her hand, had gone to Chapman and had made her go on that assignment when she'd expressly and repeatedly insisted that she didn't want to go. She'd undoubtedly believe that he'd been in on it, that he and Chapman had plotted out her punishment together. Hell, even he had to admit that he looked guilty. What was it he'd told her? *Don't make me play hardball.* Knox snorted and shook his head. What a pompous idiot he'd been.

It wouldn't matter that they'd made love all weekend, that they'd shared the most mind-blowing, soul-shattering sex, that he'd all but told her he'd fallen head over heels in love with her. Granted, he hadn't said those words per se, but surely she'd understood the implication. He hadn't been able to keep his hands off her, for pity's sake.

But none of it would matter, Knox needlessly reminded himself. She didn't trust him with her heart yet and if she talked with Chapman before Knox had a chance to talk to her, he most likely would never get the opportunity.

Nausea curdled in his stomach.

Just what in the hell had she supposedly done that would make Chapman sink to such measures of retribution? Knox wondered angrily. What unforgivable offense had she committed? Knox hadn't heard the first rumor, so whatever it was had been kept quiet. Secrets didn't typically last in a newsroom, but obviously this one had.

Knox breathed relief when the elevator doors finally opened, hurried inside and impatiently stabbed the button for the lobby. In the end it didn't matter what she had or hadn't done.

The only thing that mattered was making sure that she understood that *he* hadn't had anything to do with this mess—that he hadn't betrayed her, and he would do whatever was necessary to make her believe it.

His insides twisted with dread and he broke out in a cold sweat. He wouldn't lose her, dammit. Knox slammed his fist into the elevator wall.

He couldn't.

SAVANNAH ROCKED back on her heels and waited patiently for the elevator to deliver her to the eleventh floor, home of the *Chicago Phoenix*. She'd awoken this morning with a lighthearted smile and the irrepressible urge to get to work. Savannah knew her anxiousness had less to do with the desire to do her job and more to do with the desire to see—and do, she thought wickedly—Knox.

It had been late by the time they'd gotten back to Chicago and, though he'd all but turned her into a quivering puddle of need with that marathon good-night kiss, Savannah hadn't asked Knox to spend the night. He'd been very proud of their piece—as had she—and Knox had wanted to swing by the *Phoenix* and leave the article on Chapman's desk so that he could read it first thing this morning.

Though she didn't particularly care for their boss, it was obvious that Knox valued the older man's opinion. Savannah supposed that in absence of his father's approval, Knox had attached special meaning to Chapman's. She had the old bastard's number, though, and knew Knox's trust had been misplaced. She dreaded when Knox would reach that conclusion as well. She'd swallowed more than her share of disappointment and knew that it left a bitter aftertaste.

As for her, Savannah had wanted to get here early this morning to hear Chapman's opinion of the story as well. She hoped that, having gone on this little trip at his bidding to serve penance for her so-called offenses, he would back off now and let her return to her job.

Savannah chuckled. Her punishment had backfired.

Big time.

Chapman had sent her on this trip with the notion of knuckling her under, of humbling her. Little did he know that she and Knox had found something indescribably perfect together, that they'd spent the weekend in hedonistic splendor, and that he'd unwittingly forced her to admit what her heart had known all along—Knox Webber was The One.

Rather than continuing to nurse her animosity toward Chapman, it occurred to Savannah that she should thank him instead.

Doing the tantric piece with Knox had been utterly

wonderful. They'd worked amazingly well together and the story had only served to whet her appetite for more. She was tired of covering the mundane, had grown weary of the half-assed assignments Chapman had foisted upon her since she'd pissed him off. With luck, when she walked into the office this morning, things would have finally changed for the better.

Savannah had no more than set foot out of the elevator when Chapman summoned her into his inner sanctum. Suppressing a secret smile, she squared her shoulders and strolled in.

"Good morning, sir," Savannah said.

"Good morning," he returned, his smile a wee bit too smug for Savannah's liking. A finger of trepidation slid down her spine. "I've had a chance to read the article you and Webber did." He inclined his head. "Great stuff."

Savannah's tension eased marginally and she smiled. "I'm glad you like it, sir. Knox and I are very proud of it."

He winced regretfully. "I've only got one minor revision, though."

"Certainly. What's that?"

"The byline," Chapman said, his fat lips curling into a malevolent smile. "I'm eliminating a name from it—yours."

For all intents and purposes, the ground shifted beneath Savannah's feet. Her ears rung, and nausea pushed into her throat. She blinked, astonished. "I'm sorry?"

"I'm sure you are."

"What?"

"I never intended to let you take credit for this story. You need to learn some respect, Ms. Reeves. You also need to learn to heed my wishes. From this day forward, you will do that. Do you understand?" he asked in softly ominous tones. "I am the boss here and you will answer my questions when I ask them, regardless of your so-called journalistic integrity…or else. Let this be a lesson to you, my dear. Don't screw with me. You'll lose."

"But I did the work," Savannah said angrily.

He leaned back in his seat and stacked his hands behind his head. "But you won't get credit for it, or any other article until you learn some respect."

The implication of everything she'd just heard hit Savannah like an unexpected blow to the belly. She swallowed her disappointment, her anger—ate it until she thought for sure she would vomit.

A horrible suspicion rose. "But Knox—"

"—has done and will always do exactly what I tell him to," Chapman said meaningfully. His eyes glittered with evil humor. "He's a model staffer."

Savannah crossed her arms over her chest and snorted with bitter regret. Her world dimmed back into its usual muted focus and the light heart she'd enjoyed only moments ago instantly turned to lead. "I see," she finally managed. She had to push the words from her seared throat.

"Good," Chapman said. "I thought that you would when you'd been shown the bigger picture."

Without further comment, Savannah turned and walked out of Chapman's office, through the busy newsroom, and eventually out of the building. She got into her car and, amazingly dry-eyed, drove across town to her small efficiency apartment.

For those long interminable minutes, she was utterly and completely numb. It had been like Chapman's words had cut off the circulation to her feelings, had prevented her from experiencing even the least amount of emotion.

But the second Savannah entered her apartment, that tourniquet was released and the pain ripped through her, wrenching an anguished, silent sob from her throat. It drove her to the floor, the weight of the torment so unbelievably unbearable.

Savannah knew this woeful routine, had been a player in this all too familiar scene. But she didn't understand now any more than she ever had, just exactly what she'd done to deserve this kind of heartache. What made her so unworthy of even a sliver of happiness? A lump formed in her tight throat. Hot tears slipped down her cheeks and splashed onto her shaking hands. She bit her lip to stem the flow, but it didn't work. The pain was an emotion that had to come out, and this was the body's natural way to cleanse itself of hurts.

He'd known, damn him. He'd had to have known, and Chapman, the vengeful jerk, had all but told her so.

Knox has done and will always do exactly what I tell him...

And obviously he had, Savannah thought miserably as another dagger of regret twisted in her chest. Knox had forced her to take that trip, hadn't he? Had gone to Chapman when she refused. Savannah didn't think that Knox had known why she was going to be punished—he'd seemed genuinely curious about that— but she didn't doubt for a minute that he'd known what was going to happen. He'd known that Chapman never planned to let her have that byline. Had known that all of her effort had been for naught.

And if that weren't a bad enough betrayal, he'd let her go and make a fool out of herself by admitting her damned attraction. Had let her give him her body—and her heart, though he didn't know it. Humiliation burned her cheeks and her heart drooped pitifully in her chest.

Savannah had fancifully imagined spending the rest of her life with him, had imagined them working together, celebrating accomplishments, holidays, all of life's major events. She'd imagined waking up with him and going to bed with him. Had imagined a happily-ever-after.

She pulled in a shaky breath as another tear scalded her cheek. Clearly it had all been just that—a figment of her lonely imagination.

The whole weekend had been about the story, after all.

KNOX HAD SPENT the entire day and the majority of the night trying to make Savannah listen to him. But she wouldn't. He'd repeatedly knocked on her door. He'd alternately called her cell and her home phone number, had even filled her answering machine tape with the whole sordid explanation. But none of it had done one whit of good, and as the day had progressed, he'd become increasingly panicked and afraid that nothing ever would.

The one and only time she'd answered the phone, it had not been with a customary hello, but a couple of succinct words that, frankly, he couldn't believe she'd said. He'd been so shocked she'd hung up on him before he'd had the time to frame a reply.

Knox was at a loss. He simply didn't know what else to do. He'd tried reasoning with Chapman once more, but to no avail. Chapman held fast to his position and wouldn't relent. The story would run with Knox's byline only, and Knox knew if that happened, he and Savannah would never be able to patch things up. Frankly, even without that in the scenario, he wasn't so confident that he could bridge the chasm between them.

Though he knew that he shouldn't be, a part of him was angry with her for thinking so little of him. How could she possibly believe that he'd known about this? After what they'd shared, what they'd done together, how could she continue to doubt him?

True, evidence certainly existed to the contrary, but he'd honestly thought that after he'd explained everything, his word would have been enough to exonerate him. Knox blew out a frustrated breath. It probably would have been with anyone *but* Savannah. She'd been hurt, disappointed too many times. She didn't trust anyone. He wondered—even if by some miracle they got past this—would she ever fully trust him? Or would she continue to paint him with the same brush of uncertainty she used on everyone else?

To his surprise, Knox found himself back at the office. Aside from the typesetters, only a few die-hard employees were there at this hour. Knox stilled as the beginnings of an idea stirred.

Only the typesetters...

When Knox had decided to pursue a career in journalism, he'd made a point of knowing the business from the ground up. He'd had a passion for the process and had wanted to experience it all—from the stories and articles that went into the papers, to layout and design, and finally...typesetting.

The idea gelled, sending a course of adrenaline rushing through his blood.

A slow smile curled his lips. Savannah Reeves would have her byline...and Knox would have her.

SAVANNAH'S HEAD FELT like it had been stuffed with cotton. Her eyes were swollen and her nose would undoubtedly require a skin graft to remove the red. But she was alive and healthy and, if for no other reason than her heart continued to beat, she'd live.

She'd heard of people dying due to grief or a broken heart, but Savannah told herself that she'd been made of sterner stuff, and surely she'd sustained more than this. If it felt like she hadn't, or if she sometimes wandered into a room and forgot what she'd been doing, then she simply told herself that it would pass.

Eventually.

But she would get over it.

Knox had called repeatedly, had knocked on her door, had left so many messages on her machine that after the fifth one, she'd hit the erase button. For one anguished second, she'd almost let herself believe him—he'd sounded so desperately sincere—but then reason had returned and she'd clung to her anger. He and Chapman had made a fool of her once—she'd be damned before she'd let them do it again.

Savannah had called in sick to work—something she'd never done before—and had decided to take this day and pull herself back together. She couldn't afford to quit, as she wasn't independently wealthy like Knox, so faxing her resignation wasn't a viable option—attractive, yes, but simply not prudent. She would, however, take a few minutes to update her résumé and put out a few feelers. As soon as she landed another job, she'd tell them both to kiss off. A reluctant grin curved Savannah's lips. She'd said worse to Knox last night.

The one and only time she'd finally given in to her frustration, she'd answered the phone and growled a couple of choice words she'd never said before right into his ear. She'd taken advantage of his stunned silence to hang up on him. Savannah had finally grown weary of hearing the phone ring and the answering machine messages, so she'd unplugged them. A brief reprieve, she knew, as she'd have to go back to work tomorrow and deal with the whole sordid business, but for the time being she simply wanted to be left alone.

Her heart squeezed painfully in her chest as she shuffled to the door to get her paper. Might as well take a look at the damned thing, Savannah thought. It had certainly cost her enough.

Coffee in hand, she trudged back to her sofa, sat down and, with trembling fingers, finally unfurled the paper. She found the article on page three under the heading Tantric Sex—Old New Fad Or Stranger Than Fiction? Not a bad title, Savannah thought and was in the middle of a shrug when the byline snagged her attention.

By Savannah Reeves and Knox Webber.

Savannah blinked, astounded. Her heart began to race. But how had that happened? What had changed Chapman's mind? It had been thoroughly set, Savannah knew. In one of the many messages left on her machine, Knox had promised to find a way to fix this, but she hadn't believed him. Had he done this? she wondered, hope sprouting in her traitorous breast. Had Knox somehow managed to change Chapman's mind?

Well, there was only one way to find out. Savannah tossed the paper aside, scrambled from the couch and plugged her phone back in. She hit speed-dial and Chapman answered on the first ring.

"Make it quick," her boss said by way of greeting.

"Sir, this is Savannah Re—"

"I know exactly who this is," he snapped. "What do you want?"

Savannah gritted her teeth and resisted the infantile urge to smash the receiver against the wall. "I wanted to thank you for going ahead and giving me my byline. I really—"

"Don't thank me, Ms. Reeves. I had no intention of giving you that byline. You can thank Webber. He came down here last night and distracted a typesetter and added your name to the article," Chapman said stiffly. "He's been terminated."

Savannah gasped. *"You fired him?"*

"Speedily," Chapman said. "One more misstep and you'll be down at the unemployment office applying for benefits right along with him." The dial tone rang in her ear.

Savannah sank onto the edge of her sofa and let the weight of that conversation sink in before trying to stand again. Knox had distracted a typesetter? He'd added her name? He'd gotten fired because of it? Savannah massaged her throbbing temples. It was simply too much to take in.

What on earth had possessed him to do such a reckless thing? True, Knox had always been Chapman's golden boy but, regardless of that status, Knox had surely realized Chapman would never tolerate such an overt act of defiance from one of his employees, golden boy or no. Knox had to have known that particular act of insubordination would put him out of a job. He'd had to know…and yet he'd done it.

For her? she wondered hesitantly.

Savannah stilled. She'd assumed many things on Knox's behalf over the past twenty-four hours. Sitting here and making assumptions based on word-of-mouth testimony didn't make good journalistic sense.

She'd need to go to the source.

Knox had begun his morning by getting fired and things had steadily proceeded to worsen from there. his mother had made her weekly you-should-come-to-work-for-your-father spiel and when she'd asked him about things at the paper, he'd made the monumental mistake of telling her he'd been fired. Since then his father had called, his sister, and his brother. Undoubtedly, his entire family—all of which was employed by Webber Investments—would be lobbying for him to join the family business.

It wasn't going to happen. Knox was a writer. He'd find another job in his field. He would not go to work for his father.

Besides, he'd known last night when he'd made the decision to add her name to the byline that he'd lose his job. Knox grunted. Hell, it had been a no-brainer. But when it had come right down to it, making sure that Savannah knew that he was in this for the long haul, that he hadn't betrayed her and that he was worthy of her trust had been more important.

If this sacrifice wasn't enough, then he'd just think of something else until he finally convinced her that she could depend on him. Where others had failed, he would not. It was as simple as that.

Provided he could ever get her to speak to him again, Knox thought. He'd tried to call her again last night, and then again this morning, to tell her to be sure and get her paper, but apparently she'd unplugged her phone and answering machine because her line had simply rung and rung. Patience and persistence, the bigger picture, Knox told himself as he heaved a hearty sigh and dialed her number once again.

He muttered a curse and disconnected when his doorbell rang. His mother, no doubt, Knox thought with a spurt of irritation as he strode angrily to the door. He didn't have time for this, dammit. He needed to get in touch with Savannah. Needed to try—

Knox drew up short as he swung open his door and found the author of his present heartache standing on his threshold. His greedy gaze roamed over her. Her hair looked as if it had never seen a brush and her pale blue eyes were puffy and swollen. Her nose was red and a mangled tissue poked from the pocket of her wrinkled denim shirt. She looked like hell, but a hell he'd gladly embrace.

Hope bloomed in his chest. "Savannah?"

"I needed to talk to you, and calling seemed too impersonal. Mind if I come in?"

Still stunned, Knox belatedly opened the door. "Uh, sure."

Knox guided her into his living room and gestured for her to sit down.

She gazed around his spacious apartment with an appraising eye. "Nice place."

Knox rubbed the back of his neck. "Thanks."

"I heard a rumor today and I wondered if you could confirm it."

"I'll try. What was it?"

"That you went down to the paper last night, distracted a typesetter and added my name to our story, and that you got fired because of it. Is that true?"

Knox blew out a breath. "Yeah, that about sums it up."

Savannah sprang from the couch and glared at him accusingly. "You idiot! What did you do that for? Didn't you know you'd get fired? Have you lost your mind?" she ranted, that blue gaze flashing fire.

Frankly, this was not how Knox had imagined this scene playing out. He was supposed to be a hero, dammit, not an idiot. She was supposed to be grateful, fall into his arms and profess her undying love.

"No, I haven't lost my mind," he said tightly. "I've lost something a great deal more important than that."

She frowned, looking thoroughly irritated. "What exactly is that?"

"My heart."

She stilled, and her frantic gaze finally rested to meet his. "Y-your heart?"

"That's right. You're here for the facts, aren't you? Well, the fact is this—I fell in love with you this weekend. I didn't know anything about Chapman's plans, and didn't know any other way to convince you of it." Knox shrugged. "So I added your byline…and the rest is history."

"But what about your job?" she asked breathlessly. "You loved your job."

Jeez, he'd just told her that he loved her, and she was still harping about the damned job. When was she going to get it?

"Savannah, I don't give a damn about the job if it means that I'm going to lose you. Your trust means more." Knox stood and traced a heart on her cheek. His gaze searched her tormented one. "*You* mean more. I can get another job, baby. But *you're* irreplaceable."

Knox watched her gaze soften and a smile tremble across her lips. He breathed an inaudible sigh of relief. "So are you," she said. Savannah pulled her cell phone from the pocket of her jeans and punched in a number. "Chapman, Savannah Reeves here. I quit." Then she casually ended the call and, with a cry of delight, launched herself into his arms.

"I'm s-so sorry," she cried brokenly. "I should have known better—I should have listened to you. But I was so afraid of getting hurt, I—I just couldn't." She drew back and looked up at him. Blue mist shimmered in her eyes. "Thank you so much for doing this for me. I just— I don't—"

The feeling of immense dread he'd been carrying around for the past day promptly fled and his chest swelled with sweet, giddy emotion. "I know," Knox said, and cut off her inarticulate attempts to describe the indescribable.

"I, uh, love you, too, you know," Savannah said shyly.

"Yeah, I know." He cupped her cheek in his hand. "But will you ever trust me?"

Something shifted in her gaze and Savannah stepped out of his arms and turned around. Knox panicked. He'd pushed her too far again. He'd asked for too much. Dammit.

"Savannah—"

She fell backward and right into his suddenly out-stretched arms. The blind-trust test. She'd done it! She'd let him catch her...which meant she trusted him. Knox felt a wobbly smile overtake him.

Savannah's laughing gaze met his. "Ask me that again."

"W-will you ever trust me?"

She arched up and kissed him hungrily. She might as well have hot-wired his groin, for the effect Knox felt. "Baby, you can bet your sweet ass."

* * * * *

REQUEST YOUR FREE BOOKS!
2 FREE NOVELS PLUS 2 FREE GIFTS!

❦ Harlequin® *Blaze*™

red-hot reads!

YES! Please send me 2 FREE Harlequin® Blaze® novels and my 2 FREE gifts (gifts are worth about $10). After receiving them, if I don't wish to receive any more books, I can return the shipping statement marked "cancel." If I don't cancel, I will receive 6 brand-new novels every month and be billed just $4.24 per book in the U.S. or $4.71 per book in Canada. That's a saving of at least 15% off the cover price. It's quite a bargain. Shipping and handling is just 50¢ per book in the U.S. and 75¢ per book in Canada.* I understand that accepting the 2 free books and gifts places me under no obligation to buy anything. I can always return a shipment and cancel at any time. Even if I never buy another book, the two free books and gifts are mine to keep forever.

151/351 HDN FC4T

Name	(PLEASE PRINT)	
Address		Apt. #
City	State/Prov.	Zip/Postal Code

Signature (if under 18, a parent or guardian must sign)

Mail to the **Reader Service:**
IN U.S.A.: P.O. Box 1867, Buffalo, NY 14240-1867
IN CANADA: P.O. Box 609, Fort Erie, Ontario L2A 5X3

Not valid for current subscribers to Harlequin Blaze books.

Want to try two free books from another line?
Call 1-800-873-8635 or visit www.ReaderService.com.

* Terms and prices subject to change without notice. Prices do not include applicable taxes. Sales tax applicable in N.Y. Canadian residents will be charged applicable taxes. Offer not valid in Quebec. This offer is limited to one order per household. All orders subject to credit approval. Credit or debit balances in a customer's account(s) may be offset by any other outstanding balance owed by or to the customer. Please allow 4 to 6 weeks for delivery. Offer available while quantities last.

Your Privacy—The Reader Service is committed to protecting your privacy. Our Privacy Policy is available online at www.ReaderService.com or upon request from the Reader Service.

We make a portion of our mailing list available to reputable third parties that offer products we believe may interest you. If you prefer that we not exchange your name with third parties, or if you wish to clarify or modify your communication preferences, please visit us at www.ReaderService.com/consumerschoice or write to us at Reader Service Preference Service, P.O. Box 9062, Buffalo, NY 14269. Include your complete name and address.

HBI1

red-hot reads

IF YOU ENJOYED THIS STORY FROM

Leslie Kelly

YOU'LL WANT TO READ HER SIZZLING NEW TITLE

TERMS OF SURRENDER

What woman can resist a man in uniform? Marissa Marshall doesn't have any trouble.

A former army brat, she wants nothing to do with the military. But she'd definitely like to do something to sexy Danny Wilkes. *Lots of things.* Too bad she has no idea that his friends call him *Commander....*

Available June 2011 wherever books are sold.

Exclusively from Harlequin® Blaze™.

*If you enjoyed this story from Leslie Kelly,
make sure to pick up her upcoming book…*

TERMS OF SURRENDER

Available June 2011 from Harlequin® Blaze™.

WHEN MARISSA MARSHALL meets the devastatingly handsome Danny Wilkes, the attraction between them is undeniable…

He was gorgeous.

The man, who wore faded mechanic's coveralls, approached Mari, wiping his hands on a towel.

Was he coming over to tell her he'd seen London and France when she'd done her front-seat striptease? How embarrassing! Though, not as bad as it would be if he told her he'd seen the Netherlands. Still, a girl couldn't have visible panty lines, could she?

She told herself to cool it. Maybe he just wanted to say hi. Or he could be coming over to tell her he'd heard that weird clunky sound coming from her car's engine. Given the way he was dressed, she'd pegged him for a mechanic.

Say anything except I know you're not wearing any panties.

Reaching her, the man studied her from behind his sunglasses, which were necessitated by the bright sunshine that painted the tips of his light brown hair gold. She couldn't help wondering what color his eyes were. Warm chocolate? Jade-green? Something dazzling, she imagined. Because only a perfect set of eyes belonged in that face, with its high cheekbones, strong jutting jaw and broad, sensual mouth.

Masculine. That was the only word to describe him.

"Afternoon," he said, pleasantly, as if they'd just been introduced at a social event rather than both of them standing here thinking about her being panty-less.

"Hello," she mumbled.

He pushed the sunglasses up onto the top of his head with the tip of his finger. *Oh, my.* Not brown, not gold… something in-between. Like fine, clear amber. Absolutely beautiful.

"Wow," she whispered.

He heard. Because now, those eyes were twinkling. Definitely twinkling. She'd heard the expression, but always figured it for an exaggeration. It wasn't. This guy had you-can-trust-me-I'm-adorable written on his very eyeballs.

His cheeks were slightly stubbly, a faint smear of grease visible beside his strong nose. His skin was bronzed, his hands calloused, his muscles, she would bet, coming from hard work, not from a fitness club. And the mouth. Oh, did the man have mouth—all soft, sensuous, smiling lips.

A shiver moved throughout her entire body, so delicate she almost didn't notice. It took her a second to realize that shiver had been a pure, feminine response to him: Attraction. Major attraction. She was no longer calculating how good-looking he was, her gears had shifted smoothly from *assess* to *covet.*

Stop it. She'd obviously been single far too long if a hot guy playing Peeping Tom was making her quake with need.

Only he didn't peeping Tom you…you Sharon Stone'd him!

*Things are about to get steamy
in this sexy book by Leslie Kelly!*

TERMS OF SURRENDER

Available June 2011 from Harlequin® Blaze™.